As the bloody hand ~~~~~ smiled the nastiest sm~~~~~ Swag had ever seen. It was all capped teeth and pink gums. A second later, he began to shake. That's when Swag smelled it, the scent came through the guy's wet breath, through the stench of the subway. It was the smell of almonds. Cyanide. Swag felt all the neck muscles tighten and spasm beneath his arm. He took a step back, and let the dead guy drop. . . .

"Swag is the most convincing, violent, nasty, brutish, and ugly future world since . . . uh . . . the one we live in. Wicked fun."
　　　—Jim Morris, author of *The Devil's Secret Name* and *War Story*

"First-rate from start to finish . . . Take a pinch of Bond, a dash of Bolan, and a generous helping of Eastwood and you have Swag, who can kick butt with the best of 'em."
　　　　　　—David Robbins, author of the *Endworld* series

"Gritty . . . a rollercoaster tale of High Tech and Low Greed."
　　　—Jim Adair, author of *WWIII: Behind the Lines* and the *Deepcore* series

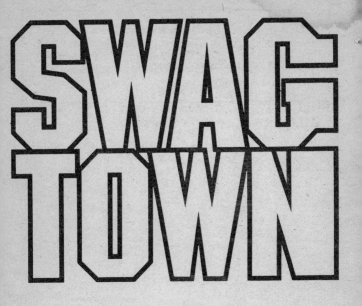

SWAG TOWN

L. S. RIKER

ST. MARTIN'S PAPERBACKS

SWAG TOWN

Copyright © 1992 by L. S. Riker.

Cover art by Steve Gardner.

ISBN: 0-312-92694-4

Printed in the United States of America

St. Martin's Paperbacks edition/May 1992

10 9 8 7 6 5 4 3 2 1

Dedicated
to
MELISSA SUZANNE
and to
My editors Ed Stackler and Mike Sagalyn. They both showed great patience and understanding. And to Frank T. for Thursday-night pizzas, antipasto, and conversation. And to anyone who has ever lived by their wits.

"What do I care about law? Hain't I got the power?"
—Cornelius Vanderbilt

preface

THIS IS THE WAY it happened. Eight hundred banks failed that year. The Japanese traded in their T-bills for francs and headed for Europe's Common Market. A loaf of white bread cost three dollars, and unemployment was over eighteen percent. A Republican was in the White House.

Then came the war . . .

There were only a thousand of them. Five hundred field operatives and another five hundred support personnel. Their passports identified them as businessmen, students, and diplomats. They flew from the Middle East to Paris, Germany, and Rome. Then they traveled coach on commercial airlines and suffered the food and unnaturally happy stewardesses to Kennedy, Dulles, LaGuardia, and LAX.

It took two years from when the first suitcase rolled off the carousel at Kennedy Airport to when the last member of the team was in place in Chino, California. They brought only the software. It was embedded on compact disks with clever labeling that read Mozart, Liszt, Motley Crüe, and Iron Maiden. The remainder of the equipment had been purchased on site through shell corporations and private citizens.

The first casualty was a GS-11 government official. They caught him on the second Saturday in May as he mowed the lawn of his Silver Spring, Maryland home. When the phone rang inside, two men and a woman followed him from the fictitious plumbing company van through the unlocked door and into the kitchen. One put a pistol to his head while another took the phone. He spoke three rapid code words into the receiver and hung up.

Then they hustled the GS-11 down to the rec room. They turned up the stereo, taped him to a chair from the breakfast nook, and began cutting off his fingers with a pair of Swiss pruning shears.

He was a tough one—a former Navy Seal. And he wouldn't give them the time of day. They went through his fingers one by one, making a neat row of the severed digits along a towel spread out across a glass-top coffee table. But the GS-11 just grunted and gritted his teeth, barely fighting against the silver duct tape as a small pool of blood formed around his Nike running shoes. It was the woman, a doctor, who treated him for shock.

They had clipped off seven of his fingers when the G-11's wife and seven-year-old daughter returned home from the shopping mall. They taped the wife down to a reclining lounger, then secured the girl to a miniature pink and white rocking chair.

Speaking softly and calmly, they gave the little girl a candy bar, and then the woman doctor injected her with a carefully measured dose of adrenaline. In a few seconds the little girl's eyes turned large and glassy. Then they began working on her with the shears.

The GS-11 gave up the three Federal Reserve computer access codes he knew after the second small finger joined the line on the bloodied towel. The codes were phoned in to a room at a Hilton just outside the Beltway. The woman doctor, who made the call, frowned slightly when she heard the muffled sound of MTV on the hotel room's television. She read the numbers twice, speaking slowly and looking intently past the family to her accomplices, who were passing the time by playing a home video game.

The GS-11 made frequent eye contact with his wife and child. From beneath the duct tape gag he reassured them that everything would be all right. But of course it wouldn't. When the confirmation came back an hour later, checked against another call, the woman nodded to the men and watched as they shot the GS-11, his wife, and daughter in the back of their heads.

There were others, of course; a dozen data processing executives from the largest banks; six security officers from the Fed and several banks' data backup facilities. And a scattering of telephone company employees. Most of them did not hold out as long as the GS-11. All were executed.

The actual attack began at dawn the next day and was launched from hotel rooms, airport pay phones, rented offices, and car phones. Fifty different programs sang out over the telephone lines into the heart of the nation's financial computer systems. The assault was double fail-safe. Each targeted system was attacked twice with different versions of the same software hybrid logic-bomb virus.

The viruses entered the systems undetected, attaching themselves to voluminous machine-language code of operating system languages and utilities. Primary and backup units wormed the invasion data through their tapes, chips, and disk drives. Each access, download, and communication between units worked the invading viruses deeper into the heart of the systems.

For twenty-four hours the viruses spread out over dedicated land lines, off satellites, over microwaves, to secreted backup facilities and into personal files, harmless and unnoticed. Nobody knew what activated them, but by the time technicians began shutting the systems down, it was already too late.

Across the country, phones and beepers sounded in the homes of dead men. The compact disks were long gone—burned, cracked, and discarded—lost forever.

The public violence didn't begin until Sunday evening. A sniper with a silenced Heckler & Koch rifle and night-vision scope put a bullet into the head of the Federal Reserve Board's chairman outside of a Georgetown restaurant. The gunman hesitated a moment, then in an unordered burst of initiative, fired on two of the Secret Service bodyguards and a parking attendant. While an injured guard crawled back to the car, the gunman shot himself in the head with a Chief's Special.

The next day the Republican chairman of the House Ways and Means Committee was shot on the sixteenth green by a caddie who took a Secret Service bodyguard and a member of the foursome along with him when the grenade exploded.

Then followed the Secretary of the Treasury, six members of the Office of Management and Budget, the chairman of the General Accounting Department, and the three members of the President's cabinet.

Four major bank presidents were shot, and another blown up in his limousine on the way to a charity lawn party in Wilton, Connecticut.

The chairman of the New York Stock Exchange was gunned down in Le Cirque, falling face first into his ninety-dollar veal entrée. The chairmen and families of NASDAQ, the Pacific Stock Exchange, and American Stock Exchange were killed in their homes, sparing them the knowledge that their computer systems had already been crippled.

Two dozen security guards died when cleaning crews blasted their way into storage areas and planted magnetic and plastique bombs in a major IRS data processing facility.

Then came the assassinations of seven governors of the Federal Reserve Board and five Reserve Bank presidents. When the *New York Times* reported that these killings effectively crippled the Federal Open Market Committee, few took notice, except on Wall Street, where the markets headed south with record velocity. Sell orders were phoned, faxed, telexed, and transmitted in before brokers had a chance to wash the morning newspaper ink from their fingers. The markets' backup systems, which had significantly been spared, lagged behind actual prices by two hours at eleven in the morning.

The war was over by Monday evening. There were less than two hundred casualties, and half of those died by their own hands. It would be seventy-two hours before the full impact would be known.

The dollars flooded back in a trillion-dollar tsunami of dead presidents. Eurodollars, petrodollars, Japanese trade-deficit dollars began pushing the value of American currency down at the opening of the Far Eastern markets and followed the sun around the globe. They washed over the government's defenses of promises, currency swaps, and steadily rising interest rates.

Pension and mutual fund managers, the movers of big money, sweated through their pinstripes as they took aggressive positions in European markets. Adding their dollars to the flood, they sold their country down the river.

Within weeks the shock waves that had first appeared as shifting numerals on computer terminals were felt from New York to Seattle. The machinery of commerce came to a thudding halt. Almost from the beginning the utter, sickening reality of it was apparent to all but the most dim-witted. The years of economic chaos, moral decline, and disparity between rich and poor that preceded the Big Takeover had made possible its success.. America, whose future had been its golden promise, was without hope. And somebody was going to pay. Old scores needed to be settled.

The few who were able fled to Europe and the shelter of Swiss, German, and Belgian bank accounts. They ran to the comfort of rented villas and luxury suites of four-star hotels, where they read the dispatches in the *International Herald Tribune*. In interviews they proclaimed their profound sadness, patriotism, and hopes for America's future. There was nothing they would not do for their country, except live there. Many who had been in positions of power hatched plots, expounded on theories, published their memoirs, and drank a great deal.

For those left behind, the big ones ate the little ones.

In smaller towns old debts were settled at night. Often it began with a growl of engines as a line of headlights illuminated sprawling suburban homes. Deer rifles and shotguns were pulled down from over the rear windows. Bankers, judges, and car dealers did not fare well.

In the cities wolf packs took to the streets, then swarmed up through the towers of glass and steel. They busted through the wrought-iron gates of century-old town houses into entranceways of Carrara marble. There they found luxury surpassing the glossy fictions of television. In well-appointed homes and offices, a painful and long-suspected truth was revealed: *The rich motherfuckers had taken everything for themselves.*

It was payback time, and everyone knew it.

There was no escape from the nightmare. The soothing voices of a thousand televised speeches could not quell the violence. Every word was assumed a lie, though what they really masked was a desperate fear. For those who struggled in positions of power, the world had gone mad. But on the street word was out that the world had just wised up.

When the human targets vanished in the bloodbath, the crowds turned to symbols of privilege and power. In Los Angeles, Chicago, Detroit, and New York, buildings burned, reducing the corporate vanity of old men to sooty clouds that billowed over skylines by day and cast an orange glow into the skies of the cities by night.

Occupants were pulled from luxury cars, beaten, then thrown back across leather seats before the gas tanks were ignited.

When at last the carrion of wealth and privilege had been consumed, peace was bought with bread and fear.

As the cities burned and food grew scarce, the political jackals leapt, snarling and lapping at the Bill of Rights. Laws were passed quickly and others repealed. The reign of the TelePrompTer had ended. There were no more promises to be made. The rule of force had begun.

The military was deployed and local provisional governments established. Martial law and curfews were enforced by order of the newly instituted Provost Marshals. This was a time of quiet trials and involuntary disappearances. The provosts were the law.

Military convoys rumbled across the interstates. Their cargo was food and troops—just enough food and more than enough men. In the cities lines began forming before midnight. Whole families stood dazed, waiting for dawn rations. Entire cities had been reduced to begging scraps.

And then the buyers arrived. They came from the Pacific Rim, from Europe, from the Middle East. In the center of the country they found rich farmland. In California they found a high-tech brain trust; in Chicago and Detroit, salvageable factories and cheap labor. It all went at bargain prices. What had taken ten generations to build was sold off in less than a year. The safety of the new owners had been assured by the highest U.S. officials.

After two years a tenuous and welcome peace was returned. This was the dawn of the New Order. The politicians labeled it a Partnership with the World. Across America people struggled to believe that somehow it would again be as it once was. Except in New York. In the city whose soul is commerce, you could sell anything but a cheap lie.

chapter one

THE SUN WAS LOW on the horizon. A big red sucker, it hung in the sky across the river, descending slowly toward the dark and distant outline of Jersey. Not a postcard sunset, Swag thought, but a nasty bastard that went down hot and ugly, bleeding across every canyoned street on the West Side. A New York summer sun.

From where he was standing on West 38th, Swag had a clear view of the sky, the docks, and more importantly, the street. He liked this place at dusk. Eighth and Ninth Avenues were nearly deserted—the buildings lined up solid, their doorways and street-level windows gated with gray steel, held secure by fist-sized locks.

The line of steel gates on each side of the street was broken by a dozen alleys, dark recessed entranceways to abandoned factories and empty parking lots bordered by chain link and topped with loose spirals of razor wire.

Once it had been the garment district. Black and Puerto Rican guys pushed racks with next season's fashions, and fat women from the Bronx worked twelve, sixteen hours a day on piecework behind industrial-sized Singers. Now the section had a reputation as the city's last wide-open piece of real estate, a place to do business in privacy.

Swag was smoking the last cigarette of the pack and watching a perfect sphere of a sun burn through Jersey's chemical haze. He knew that the odds were bad that Johnny G. would make the trip down from high on the East Side.

The story he'd told a guy two nights before was so lame that it couldn't stand up on crutches. But Swag also knew that greed and stupidity had a way of bringing in the long shots.

No sooner had he thought it than Johnny came around the Ninth Avenue corner. Even halfway down the block Swag couldn't miss him. He was dressed in the latest street fashion, a faded yellow Kevlar vest and black jeans. The vest was cut away at the waist and hung wide open in front, giving a full view of Johnny's overdeveloped chest. Shaved and shiv-scarred, the chest was a point of vanity with Johnny G.

Swag had heard that Johnny had done a pound in either Great Meadows, Coxsackie, or Attica. As the story went, he spent a total of three days in general population, then said the wrong thing, and six Colombians took him apart in the gym. After a year in the hospital ward, the Colombians were still making threats, so they moved Johnny up to the protective custody cellblock—punk city. He lasted two weeks in P.C., shouting insults out at the Colombian trustees in Spanish as they walked by his cell. Apparently, he only knew about six words of Spanish, but that was enough. Somebody bought the deputy warden a Florida bungalow, and Johnny went back into general pop. When he was paroled, it was out of the hospital ward.

Now, as he approached, Swag could see that maybe the prison doctors hadn't been able to put all the pieces back right. And maybe they hadn't tried all that hard. State institutions weren't going to put the German and Swiss clinics out of business. Everything about Johnny seemed a little off center—the rolling lopsided gait, the strange tilt of his head, even the way his clothes hung. Swag thought that probably nothing would ever fit him right, except maybe state issue. He was a walking ad for the Attica charm school.

Johnny had been a body builder once, and the thick arms swung loosely and slightly out from his sides. Swag guessed that there was a piece in the small of his back. It would be a stylish little automatic or shiny belly gun. Something to show the ladies and tourists. As much as he thought Johnny was a punk, Swag knew he couldn't waste time. He would take care of the arms first.

Then Johnny came closer, squinting into the shadows to check out whoever it was that was leaning in the doorway. When he was fifteen feet away, he called out, "Hey Swag," forcing a pair of misshapen and scarred lips into a grin that revealed a mouth full of perfect teeth. "Swag in his Hawaiian shirt and cowboy boots. Man, I clocked you half a block away. Those shirts, they like a fashion statement or something?"

Swag moved slowly, took the cigarette from his mouth, and dropped it as he stepped to the center of the sidewalk. "*Que pasa*, Johnny? I gotta talk to you," he said, trying to smile, and enjoying the way Johnny flinched slightly at the Spanish.

"No time, I'm on my way to some business. Got a full schedule," Johnny said, stopping anyway. He spoke without moving his lips, which could have been either practiced prison style or just the way guys who've spent a lot of time with their jaws wired shut speak. "Got a lady waiting uptown. Then a little video business, real sweet."

"German?" Swag asked, feigning interest.

"Dutch," came the reply. "Kinked as shit. Came in to load up on snuff tapes. Wet stuff, she's into knives."

"Moving up in the world, huh?" Swag replied, then searched his pockets for a cigarette. "A real freak?"

"You got no idea," Johnny said, laughing. "This video stuff, it's just a side business now. But hey, if you got a connect, *we* can do some business. They gotta be American made, no Flip or Mex product, and shrink-wrapped packages of new theatricals, half-hour trailers up front. She says customs is coming down hard, Class B felony now. No more fooling around on their end."

"I don't know, Johnny, maybe I know a guy," Swag answered loosely, trying to keep him interested. He was facing Johnny sideways, feet slightly apart and pointed downtown. "You got a cigarette?"

"Sure Swag," came the answer. And Johnny brought up a hand to one of two front pockets sewn into the vest.

But before his fingers touched the Velcro fastener, Swag had him by the wrist, bending the hand back toward the ground and hustling him over toward the brick wall. The arm and the hand were slick with sweat. Swag knew that if he lost his grip, this punk would kill him real quick.

"Hey, what's your beef, huh?" Johnny managed, feet shuffling away, then knees giving in to the pain. But even as he slowly bent to his knees, Johnny's left hand went for the back of the vest.

Swag didn't answer; in a final, grunting effort he got the arm up behind Johnny's back. Then he pulled Johnny's bulky form up again and pinned him face first to the brick wall. The kid's free hand was still reaching around, going for the piece. But Swag worked Johnny's wrist, forcing his hand far up, so it was nearly between his shoulder blades. Stepping in close, he leaned into the twisted arm as he dug out the small gun from where it was held by a Velcro hitch through the trigger guard. It was a shining five-shot Ruger with cherrywood grips, very stylish. Swag stuffed it into the front of his jeans.

"Hey man, what's your problem, huh? This some kinda roust or what?" Johnny managed, his cheek crushed against the rough brick. "You gone wacko or what?"

"I just want to talk to you," Swag said, bending down low and whispering right in Johnny's ear. "Just want to talk is all."

"Let go of my goddamned arm and we'll talk," Johnny managed. "You don't know who you're messing with."

"I wouldn't be talking to the guy who ripped off my two French."

"I don't know shit about any French," Johnny groaned. "And you're rousting the wrong guy."

Swag brought up the arm an inch or two higher and began bending the wrist back. "No roust, Johnny, this is payback."

"You're wacko, man," Johnny said. "You lose a frog client, and you start bustin' up people. You're wacko."

"Let me tell you something about those frogs," Swag said, turning genuinely mad at the memory of it. "They were a five thousand franc job. Their security was worth five K to me."

"I didn't know they were your frogs, màn," Johnny whined.

Swag increased the pressure a little more until he could feel Johnny's arm about to pull from the socket. "'Why didn't they pay you, Swag?'" Swag said, mimicking Johnny's high-pitched whine of a voice. "Well, Johnny," Swag continued in his own voice, "they didn't pay me cause some two-bit take-out artist shot one in the eye and kneecapped the other in a suite at the Carlyle while I was out fetching them an authentic New York Chinese dinner."

"I didn't know they were your frogs," Johnny whined. "It was a business thing. If I'd have known you were the security, I wouldn't have made no play."

"They were a five thousand franc job," Swag hissed. "Or didn't I mention that? Five thousand to keep them safe while they shopped."

"Sometimes you lose some," Johnny tried. "Everyone does. You shouldn't blame yourself. Shit happens, you know?"

"I don't blame myself, Johnny," Swag shot back. "I blame you, asshole." And that's when Swag dislocated Johnny's arm. He brought it up fast, hearing the sharp pop of the shoulder joint and Johnny G.'s groan at the same moment. As the arm came loose in his hand, Swag lowered in slightly, twisting against the muscles. Then he snapped Johnny's wrist back and twisted. It broke with a wet crack.

Johnny went to the ground in pain, his face riding the bricks all the way down. When his head hit the concrete, full upper and lower plates jumped from his mouth. The state-furnished teeth bounced once, and Swag crushed them under his boot heel.

"Aw man, not the teeth," Johnny lisped. "Why'd you have to bust my teeth?"

"Impulse," Swag replied, and ground his boot down on the upper plate.

"You're nuts," Johnny moaned in a lisp against the pain. "And you're playing a real low-yield game, scumbag. Someone's gonna take you out one day, real hard."

"That wouldn't be you, Johnny?" Swag asked, grinning now as he knelt down across Johnny's spine. "You're not threatening me, are you?"

"No, man," Johnny moaned. "I ain't threatening you."

"That's good, then," Swag said, as he stood partially back up, hunching slightly as he kept his grip on the dislocated arm with the ruined wrist, placing his boot heel where his knee had been.

"No, I ain't threatening anyone," came the answer.

"Because if you were threatening me, I'd be better off doing you with your slick little piece," Swag said, turning the arm slightly. Johnny's palm was twisted back at an impossible angle, each movement caused him to groan and squirm in pain. "I let you leave this spot, amigo, maybe you'll go out, find some new teeth, and maybe start getting ideas."

"Swag, man, don't do it," Johnny said. "It ain't good. It ain't good business, believe me. Please."

"What isn't good business, Johnny?" Swag answered. "Whacking you out right now? Sound business sense, if you ask me. Would help maintain my reputation as someone not to fuck with, isn't that right?"

Johnny was sweating heavily now, sensing that Swag might just do it. "Don't man, please," he pleaded. "I'm into a good thing now, real high-line. I'll make a phone call for you."

Swag increased the pressure on the arm a notch, brushing aside the thought of getting into the video business, and said, "Listen to me, Johnny. I'm not going to kill you."

"That's good, man," Johnny lisped. "That's real good thinking. Now let go of the arm."

"Don't you want to know why?"

Johnny squirmed a little, testing Swag's grip. When he discovered that he was still held tight, he answered. "'Cause you're a stand-up guy," Johnny said. "And you wouldn't flake someone over a couple of frogs."

"Wrong," Swag snapped back, twisting harder on the arm. "I'd kill you over a French poodle. But you're going to be my own personal advertisement. I can count on you to tell every take-out artist above Houston not to screw around with my clients, isn't that right?"

"Yeah, sure, man," Johnny said. "Anything. I'll fuckin' wear a sign. Now let go of the arm."

"Johnny," Swag said calmly. "As long as we're talking, real honest and up front, can I give you some advice?" Swag ended the sentence with another jerk of the arm that sent a jolt of new pain through Johnny.

"Sure man, anything," came the lisping answer, "but let go of the arm."

"Just some professional advice. Are you sure you don't mind?" Swag asked, twisting on the arm again. He could feel the muscles begin to rip away. "Some people, I've found, can't take advice. They're offended by it. The way you come on with this 'low-yield' crap, I'm not sure you take advice, Johnny."

"Sure man, sure," came the answer.

"Good, then here it is," Swag said, releasing the arm as he pulled his Browning Hi-Power automatic from its back holster. The arm fell limp across Johnny's back. "Stay away from the Plaza, the Pierre, the Carlyle, the Drake, and the Intercontinental."

"Sure man, anything," Johnny said. Swag was right in his face now, bending down low. The gun was pointed right in Johnny's left eye, so that he could see it.

"Because," Swag said in a whisper, "if I see you outside one of those hotels, at a service entrance, the main entrance, a bar entrance, anywhere near one, then I'll flake you. Do you *comprende*, Johnny?"

"I understand, man," he said, strength coming back into

his voice. "Now let me up so I can get to the emergency room."

"I'm not finished yet, amigo," Swag said, bringing his face closer, until it was almost as close as the gun. "What do you have to say about killing my frog client and crippling the other?"

"Man, I didn't know they were yours. I swear man," Johnny moaned. "It was a business deal."

"What do you say, Johnny?"

"I don't know, man, just let me up."

"You say, 'I'm sorry Swag for killing your frog client and crippling the other.' Say it Johnny."

"I'm sorry I did your fuckin' frog, okay? Now let me the fuck up!"

"Johnny," Swag said, his voice gentle and patient. "I enjoyed this Johnny. It relieved *beaucoup* stress on my part. But let me tell you something about yourself. You're just another street punk going solo. You inconvenience me again I'll slice you up and sell you off a piece at a time to the first low-rent bio-chop shop I find. I'll trade your kidneys and corneas in as a goodwill bonus. And that'll be your next piece of business, chief, laid out on a gurney in a Chinatown basement. You understand?"

"Fuck you, man," Johnny said, but his voice didn't have much conviction in it.

"Johnny, you must like it down there," Swag said. "What do you want, to stay here? I'll keep twisting on the arm and we can shout 'fuck you' at each other. That sound like fun to you, or what?"

"No, but you're doing some damage here," Johnny said. "Please, just let me up."

"That's better," Swag answered. "Better for both of us, because I have a meeting." Swag brought the gun away from Johnny's face, rose slightly, then backed off a step without turning away.

Johnny tried to roll over, flopping the bad arm across his side to the front. Just below Johnny's pant cuff Swag caught a glimpse of an ankle holster's nylon edge, then a flash of pearl handle.

Johnny's good hand was six inches from the holster when Swag shot out his knee. He fired so close that the entire leg kicked straight out, then twisted sideways, pulling the ankle holster out of reach as the sidewalk splattered red to the curb.

There was the sound of a car at the corner. Swag looked up slowly, reached around to slip the Browning back into its holster and began walking toward the car. The limo that was turning the corner had stopped; the driver seemed to hesitate, debating whether to continue on. Probably some tourist anxious to get an early start at the West Side sex clubs, Swag thought.

The car was one of those new Mercedes. Low and black, with no chrome. The tires were almost completely covered by panels, but no steel plating. This model featured aluminum oxide ceramic tiles. Top of the line.

The limo made the turn and slowly approached. The vague outline of a face appeared through the rear black-tinted window facing Swag. Then the window came down smoothly, revealing a man's head of gray, nearly white, hair, followed by a smooth forehead, then the palest and coldest pair of blue eyes Swag had ever seen. The limo's passenger could have been twenty-five or fifty-five. The eyes stared unblinking for a long moment, then vanished as the window came back up and the limo continued down the street.

Swag kept walking up the block toward Eighth, thinking. First, he thought that anyone with the kind of money to hire out those wheels was crazy for heading to a West Side club, then he thought about how much Johnny G. would be worth to a bio-chop shop.

"Hey, scumbag!" Johnny G. called when Swag was half-way down the block. "That shirt you got on, you look like a goddamned Jersey lowlife!"

chapter two

SWAG ARRIVED AT the Plaza Hotel twenty minutes after warning Johnny G. off his territory. That little piece of business had taken longer than expected, and he was ten minutes late for his assignment.

Swag found it marginally more pleasant to work midtown. The city's decay seemed to recede just a little near the Plaza. They say that the future isn't what it used to be, Swag thought. But strangely, he felt an ache, right down in his guts for that old-time future of his childhood. It was, he knew, some odd reflexive hope lingering from the past—like some tourist who's had his wallet lifted, but keeps reaching for it anyway.

As a kid, his parents had taken him to the '64 World's Fair. He could still remember the subway ride out to Queens, where smart promoters had built the fairgrounds on a valley of ashes back in the late thirties. Could still remember the gleaming science-fiction fantasies of the future set up in pavilions. Kitchens where wholesome gourmet meals magically appeared. Robots. Atomic energy. Buck Rogers spaceships. Aerodynamic cars with bubble tops. All bullshit. They were as wrong about the cars as anything else. He could remember it now and think it was more pitifully naive than quaint. Who would have guessed back then that the city would break down under the weight of unseen forces into crumbling concrete, rust, and fissured streets?

Six flags were flying out front: Swiss, German, French, Hungarian, Italian, and Austrian. They hung limp in the breezeless heat above the wrought-iron awning. These were about all anyone ever saw flying in front of any New York hotel. Once in a great while there was the Japanese flag, but that was a rare error of protocol. The Japanese were discreet, if not secretive, about their vices. They would rather see the Rising Sun outside a bordertown whorehouse, anything but a New York midtown hotel, though both amounted to much the same thing.

There were six white-gloved doormen on duty; two worked the line of limos that arrived, escorting guests into the hotel with military precision. The other four acted as backup, Mac-12's hidden from view under summer uniforms. All six looked sharp, their eyes quartering the landscape for any signs of trouble.

But Swag knew this was all theater, right down to the flesh-tone communication earpieces the doormen wore. Everyone was a soft target, even at the Plaza.

As Swag crossed the checkerboard-patterned sidewalk and walked up the red-carpeted stairs, two of the four backups stiffened, recognized him, and then nodded him through a brass revolving door. The air-conditioning hit him like an arctic blast. The temperature dropped from near ninety out on the baking concrete and softening tar of the street to a pretentious sixty-two in the deeply carpeted and gilt-trimmed lobby.

Swag turned left and wasn't halfway to the desk before the concierge produced a blue linen blazer. The blazer cost Swag six hundred American a month, up front, to store. Come fall he would replace it with the Harris tweed. The concierge, a little black-haired weasel, didn't so much as say a word to Swag. For six hundred you couldn't expect much. Twelve hundred would have had him scampering around the marble counter to help Swag put it on.

Glass cases were set into the walls of the corridor leading to the elevators. Jewelry in the smaller ones, clothing in the larger. Those nearest the elevator boasted firearms. Slowing his pace, Swag noticed that the management was pushing Glock 9's this month. The pistols were artfully arranged on scalloped lengths of red and gold satin. The gold cloth matched the double-P Plaza logo that was tastefully stamped into each polymer grip. The center case held a disassembled Glock frozen in Lucite and a selection of 9mm ammunition. Heavy loads and hollowpoints were in style this month. Next month the tourists would be buying Teflon.

Swag didn't notice the blond-haired man in the tan poplin suit and French running shoes as he moved past the handgun exhibit. He was an older guy who walked with a light-footed gait that hesitated only slightly as he caught sight of Swag. Coming down the corridor, he slowed, keeping back forty feet or more as a frown creased his tanned face and forehead.

Three of the Provost Marshal's lackeys lounged by the elevator bank. They wore tiger-striped nylon jumpsuits and were discussing wine. Fat guys from Jersey, Queens, and Staten Island. Weekend warriors who hit the career lottery when the shit came down. They'd gone four-star native with their first taste of the commandeered good life.

Colonel Bammer, who ran military ops in the city, heading a cooperative effort of the Justice Department in D.C. and the U.S. Army, took about six seconds to appropriate this, the choicest real estate. It fit his image of gentleman soldier just as neatly as the meticulously tailored and pressed uniforms he favored. Bammer had arrived at the Plaza with the first detachment of provosts, and never left.

For Bammer, the Plaza was class, and he insisted his elite platoon join him as guests of the management. Now guys who wouldn't have gotten through the front door four years ago were bivouacked in two-thousand-franc-a-day suites and talking Beaujolais over the barrels of their Steyr automatics.

The soldiers stopped their wine discussion just long enough to cut Swag a look of vague contempt as the elevator arrived. The three uniforms hustled in first and pushed the Close button before Swag was through the door. Catching the door with his hand, Swag squeezed through and positioned himself between the largest two, pressed the button for his floor and stared up at the indicator, listening to the piped-in harp music.

"We almost got the fucker under control," one of the uniforms whispered from deep in his gut. "It's the trash that keeps things shitty."

"Fuckin' punks everywhere now," another answered.

They were between two and three. Swag was going to five. The military suites were on twelve.

"Fuckin' street trash."

"I'd know how to deal with them. Only one way. Full-auto."

"Rock 'n' roll 'em under the West Side Highway."

"And what did you do in the war, Daddy," Swag said in a child's nasal plea that caused two of the uniforms to stiffen.

"Well, son," Swag answered himself in a deep growl with more than a hint of Jersey in it. "Me and da boys, we shot teenage looters in the back with automatic weapons up on Broadway, den boosted der boosted shit. Dat's why I don't live in Jersey no more."

One of the uniforms was eyeing him with barely concealed disdain, taking special note of the Hawaiian shirt under the blue blazer.

"Fuckin' asshole, punk," the heavy said to Swag's back as the door closed. "Don't let the sun set on ya in midtown."

The suite was down a long, carpeted hall. Swag already knew by the number that it would be on the north side, a park view, which meant a thousand francs a night minimum. With the recent devaluation in the dollar, the third in the last year, that meant fifteen thousand dollars a night.

When he knocked on the door, it was opened by a blond uniformed maid who showed Swag into the sitting room. Times had been good to the Plaza. This was partly true because of Bammer and his men. The gilt furniture, the carpets, every eggshell-thin tea cup, all survived. Management had reopened the carpentry shop on the top floor. Craftsmen toiled beneath the green verdigris copper and gray slate of the mansard roof to assure nothing would be lost to the slow, cruel slide of time or the accidents of careless guests.

Swag was halfway across the sitting room when he stopped dead in his tracks. There—perched like a sick vulture—at a small spindle-legged table across from his client, was Arturo, King of the Queens Miners. His sample cases were spread out across the table, the jewelry catching the last bit of sun from the window.

They can smell it, Swag thought to himself after the shock of seeing Arturo had sunk in. They can smell the money from the street. Smell it right through the air-conditioning and the closed doors of rooms filled with complimentary flowers and wine.

"Ah, Mr. Swag," the blond woman said, looking up from the glitter of the black felt-lined cases. "But I had nearly given up on you."

She spoke in the slightly accented English taught at the best of the Swiss boarding schools and spoken in the best European resorts. She might have been German, French, or Swiss. Even passports didn't tell the whole story with these people.

"Swag," Arturo said, clearly not happy at what he saw. "Is Ms. Lorette *your* client?"

Arturo's face was stone gray. The dry, flaking skin hung off his bones like a hastily stolen coat. Once Arturo had weighed two hundred pounds. Now, two of him could have fit into the ancient Armani suit he wore. There was also an inch or more between the withered neck and the unstarched collar of the Turnbull and Asser shirt that hung in folds under the suit. If he tipped the scale át one twenty, he was lucky. He was dying and he knew it. Swag put Arturo at thirty, thirty-five at most, but he looked seventy sitting there on the gilt chair.

"She booked my protection months in advance, Arturo," Swag said, forcing himself to cross the room.

"Ah, but you two know each other," the woman said, with some pleasure. "This is *fantastique*."

"We're old friends, Ms. Lorette," Arturo replied, then cast Swag a look that said don't blow the deal.

"Ms. Lorette, everyone knows Arturo, King of the Queens Miners," Swag replied, solicitous.

"Oh, how very interesting," the woman said. "But it is such a very small world, no? He has been kind enough to come and show me the most lovely things. Simply exquisite."

Swag took a step closer. Arturo's felt-lined cases glittered with platinum and gold jewelry. One case held loose diamonds, none smaller than two carats.

"Very nice," Swag said, picking up a platinum filigree pin inset with diamonds. "Heirloom quality, I'd say. Are these heirloom quality, Arturo?"

"Yeah, sure," came the answer; all pretense of sedate class had fallen away with the sickening certainty of Swag burning him, big-time.

"Ms. Lorette," Swag said. "Did Arturo tell you how he happened upon these pieces?"

"But of course," she replied. "Although he's been ever so discreet. As you may know, some prominent families are forced to sell. We live in such difficult times. It is *très terrible*, no? Arturo is only acting as, what is the word, broker. I would die to know the names of some of his clients."

"That's strictly confidential," Arturo said, seeing a dim hope that Swag wouldn't ruin it for him. "Mr. Swag is sometimes useful. At this moment, I believe I owe him a fifteen percent commission on a rather large item."

But Swag didn't rise to the bait. "Mr. Arturo is what's called a 'Queens Miner.' Have you heard that expression?"

The woman turned from the table toward Swag. Her hands rested very properly on her lap. "Why no, I cannot say that I have."

"Or was that twenty points?" Arturo tried desperately.

"Arturo, I've never worked with you," Swag answered.

"But what is this, 'Queens Miner'?" the woman asked.

"Arturo, do you care to tell Ms. Lorette or should I?"

"My sources are entirely confidential," Arturo repeated by way of an answer.

So Swag explained what a Queens Miner was to Ms. Lorette. He gave it to her in the short version; about how Arturo and his buddies drive a van out to Queens cemeteries at night with lengths of PVC tubing, three fifty-gallon drums of industrial corrosive, an auger, and a Briggs & Stratton pump. Then Arturo and his merry band dig two holes in choice graves, insert the tubing and pump corrosive down, around, up, and through the grave cavity in a continuous cycle. Jewelry is captured in the pump's filter.

And Arturo just happened to be a legend in the field. He was the first to bribe funeral home lackeys for the interment prep files detailing who was buried with what. Until he arrived on the scene, there were a lot of what became known in the trade as "dry holes." Knowledge of bronze- or steel-reinforced caskets also helped. Business boomed for two years. Passengers on flights coming into Kennedy and LaGuardia would look out their window seats and see cemeteries checkerboarded where the corrosives had turned the plots yellow.

Then Arturo got hit with an adult portion of irony. Smart thieves fear irony more than the law. The corrosives gave Arturo more cancers than a lab rat.

Swag grabbed the wig off Arturo's head to prove his point to Lorette, revealing a nearly bald and, ironically, skull-like noggin.

"Give it back," Arturo insisted, making a futile grab for the toupee that Swag dangled just out of reach. As he reached, the sleeve of his coat fell back to reveal a small rectangular watch. The case was old gold, but the band was new.

"Tell me, Arturo, that a Patek Phil you're wearing?"

Arturo ignored the question. "I'm gonna beat this thing cold, fucker," he spat. "I got a connect up in the Bronx for radiation, chemo, anything I want. I got four Rican ladies in Brooklyn killing chickens and lighting candles for me. I got a tub of nasty smelling shit from Haiti under my bed. There's two pounds of kick-ass psychic crystals sewn into this suit. I got a motherfuckin' herbalist down in China-town!"

For a second the room fell silent. The woman's gaze went from Arturo to Swag then back to the jewelry, neatly arranged in velvet drawers.

"But you are not well? Oh, you poor, poor man," the woman said at last. "That is simply horrid. *Très tragique*, no?"

Arturo didn't answer; rather, he took the opportunity to snatch his hair back and straighten down on his head. His head was held high in an odd sort of belligerent dignity.

"But these things, they are so lovely. I simply cannot decide which to choose," Ms. Lorette said at last.

chapter three

THERE WAS A FAMILIAR LOOK about her. Swag could see it in the diminishing light outside the hotel. In the summer twilight Swag looked again at Lorette and saw in her the soft corruption of old money and new vices. Her skin was smooth, tan, and tight. Maybe she was thirty-three or thirty-four, but the spas, with their ointments, exercise, and nimble-fingered surgeons, had rolled the calendar back a decade. Nothing about her was cheap, right down to the mixed scents or perfume and soap that Swag could smell over the exhaust fumes of Fifth Avenue.

Somewhere in Geneva or Basel there was a husband. He'd be twenty or twenty-five years older, and going to fat beneath his Savile Row suits. Maybe she was his second or third wife. A youthful prize to dress in Paris fashion and flawless gems. She was a picture on the desk for business associates to admire; a portrait in the hall of the summer home, done in the best style of the moment.

Swag had seen her kind before. She was, in fact, almost too perfect a specimen. She was the original from which only imperfect copies could follow. He took her arm at the elbow and led her across the street, his eyes scanning the traffic-clogged landscape. Uniformed drivers lounged by their cars, three or four of the men making a show of polishing black fenders with white cloths. Beyond the small park with its fountain was Fifth Avenue and a steady flow of traffic.

She wanted to go shopping. Appointments had been made at a half-dozen jewelers, and Swag knew, just by looking at her, that she had the kind of name and money that would keep the discreet second-floor and third-floor galleries along Fifth Avenue open well past their closing times. Even now, he imagined, somber men in somber suits were checking their watches, waiting for her arrival and planning their deferential strategies.

As they reached the curb Swag released her arm, and she offered a small appreciative smile. Where was the husband? Swag wondered. Probably in a paneled office, clicking away at a terminal, checking the markets and talking on the phone. Swag steered her forward, toward Fifth Avenue, and they crossed along the slate path of what used to be called the Grand Army Plaza and was now just the Plaza with its cascading fountain topped by a Pomona—a fine-looking woman, looking cool, even in the heat. A few vendors had set up their wares along the walkway on blankets. Mostly tourist trinkets, Swag noted. Handicrafts from Jersey and Brooklyn, they were something to purchase on impulse for a not-very-close or important friend. Even as the ragged collection of vendors, many with children and some not more than children themselves, tried to entice her with polite calls of bargains, she continued walking.

"The poor things," Swag's client said, returning only a small smile to a little girl who held up a mosaic of the New York skyline fashioned from shards of glass glued to a piece of cardboard. "The poor little things, they really have nothing."

"If you gave them a franc, then they'd have enough to eat for two weeks," Swag said, noting that her hand didn't move toward the lizard purse.

The woman paused slightly, scrunched up her face and said, "But Monsieur Swag, if I give them money, then they become beggars, no? Is it not better that they sell their little things rather than beg?"

The little girl was in front of them now, not quite blocking their way as she took small dancing steps back with their forward progress. She wore a filthy I Love New York T-shirt. She was moving the mosaic up and down anxiously, hearing Swag put in his pitch to close the sale for her. "*Très joli, très joli,*" she chanted. "Bon marche, très bon marche! Seul trois bucks!"

Lorette smiled, amused at the young girl's persistence and street-French. "Oui, very pretty, and very cheap," she said agreeably.

"Then buy one," Swag offered, already knowing the answer. "That's not even a franc."

"Hey, for you folks, three bucks," the little girl said, then paused. "Okay, straight up, only two and a half, 'Merican."

The woman smiled broadly at this, finding genuine humor in the prospect of purchasing such a thing and shaking her head at the same time. "But what would I do with it? Can you imagine?"

Hearing this exchange, the little girl drifted off, back toward the hotel, where a blond gentleman in a poplin suit and French running shoes was crossing the street. A group of children had gathered around him, dancing with impatient excitement. He was smiling down at them as he ran a hand through his blond hair, pretending to think hard on the choices held in the dozen, dirty upstretched hands in front of him. The children recognized the sham and began to laugh and shout louder, sounding almost like children at play. Then the man reached into his pocket to pull out a handful of coins. With the other hand he pointed quickly to a dozen or more of the handicrafts, one from each child, that he wished to buy, all the time looking across the plaza at Swag and his client.

As Swag and the woman approached the curb, her hand strayed casually along the raw silk of her jacket and toyed with the platinum and diamond pin newly purchased from Arturo. She had not bargained for a better price. Knowing where the pin came from only fired her desire to have it.

She'd paid in Banc Suisse traveler's checks, counting them out in a neat row along the polished surface of the table with precise movements before countersigning each one with a gold-nubbed fountain pen. Arturo had watched anxiously, his gray tongue poking over the thin gray lips, sweating each pen stroke as she filled in the date. She carefully crossed the sevens, European style, before rising from the table. She left the checks where they lay for Arturo to gather up.

The traffic moved haltingly before them. Swag and his client waited for the light to change. Where was the husband? he thought again. What was he doing now? Waiting for his pretty young wife to return? Telling himself that he was lucky to have her, at any cost, because she loved him? No, that wouldn't be it, Swag decided. If a man could afford her, then he wasn't the type to fool himself.

How much did one like her cost? Swag wondered, watching the line of cars creep by in front. But he already knew the answer: If you had to ask how much, exactly, then you couldn't even afford the down payment.

The light turned from red to green, and they began moving across the street. In front of them was the looming tower of the Bahamian Commonwealth Bank. A great white structure that held not only ten floors of Caribbean bankers, but thirty or more branches of foreign banks. Swag could still remember when it was the GM Building. There had been a showroom on the bottom floor, displaying a polished selection of Detroit steel on revolving pedestals. Before that the site had held the Savoy Plaza Hotel.

You would have to look hard to see the changes of the last ten years. Old movies and memories showed the same landscape of skyscrapers and shops. Only now they were shabbier. The whole city had the look of a failed franchise. From Wall Street to midtown the buildings were see-throughs, empty cathedrals of commerce. Strange now, Swag realized, to even think of them filled with people. At night you could look out on the familiar skyline and know that the shells of the buildings were lit by charity of a federal government.

Nobody ever ventured into the upper reaches of the buildings, save for those anonymous changers of bulbs, who wandered hunched under duffel bags brimming with flourescents. It was rumored that they worked at night, better to see what needed changing. Swag always pictured them moving like ghosts through the rank smelling mazes of broken drywall and the litter of abandoned offices.

A half-dozen people approached from the opposite corner, and Swag steered her gently by the elbow, away from the herd and out toward the yellow line of the crosswalk. Swag felt it before he saw anything wrong.

A dark suit broke away from the small group of crossing pedestrians. He could have been a banker, he was dressed like one. But he was walking quickly, his left hand already unbuttoning the suitcoat. His face was drained white by the flood of adrenaline, and his eyes pinned on the woman, who was chattering away.

In an instant Swag sized him up. Dirty-blond hair, a solid six-foot-two or -three, maybe 200 or 210 pounds.

Swag grabbed her hard by the elbow, and she let out a little cry as he pulled her back to the center of the crosswalk, putting himself in front of Lorette, putting the pedestrians between the two of them and the dark suit.

But it was already too late. By the time Swag pushed his client back and reached around to the back holster for his gun, the dark suit had broken into a determined half run, his hand moving up high inside the jacket in a singular reach of a shoulder-holster draw.

The woman stumbled back a step and then came forward, not seeing the dark suit's approach. She was right at Swag's shoulder, blocking his gun hand. As she moved out from behind him, uncomprehending, the dark suit brought the matte-black Glock out from the downslanted holster.

The crowd scattered at the first sight of the gun, leaving Swag and the girl in the open.

"But Monsieur Swag—" she began, her voice close in his ear and the scent of her perfume in his nose.

They were the last words she would say. The dark suit fired twice. Not ten feet away as he came to a stop. The first blast blinded Swag as he dodged right, his left hand seeking the girl's waist to push her back behind him as he brought out the Browning.

The gunman fired in a two-handed combat stance—legs apart, elbows slightly bent—and his aim was good. The first shot hit the girl high on her left cheek and took off half her face, from the top of her jaw to the hairline. The woman's head snapped to one side with the force of the impact, and she toppled back in a short half step. Reflex brought her left hand up to her cheek as she began to fall. Then she staggered left and away from any cover Swag may have provided.

The second shot caught her just below the first, punching her back across the yellow line of the crosswalk and against the rear bumper of a taxi stopped in the intersection. The slug severed the tips of two fingers of her upraised hand before smashing through teeth and flesh.

Swag felt the fine spray of warm blood and heard the screams of the frightened and scattering crowd. He brought the Browning up, thumbing the safety off as he drew down on the dark suit.

As the girl crumpled to the ground, the dark suit, still in combat stance, turned, catching Swag in the Glock's red-tipped front sight. But Swag fired first, hitting the gunman square in the chest. The dark suit staggered back a step and caught hold of a car's hood with one hand. As he brought the gun up in his other hand, Swag shot him again, this time in the stomach. The gunman doubled over, knees bent together, his gun hand clutching at his stomach at the center of the crosswalk.

Swag waited for the dark suit to fall, but the shooter didn't go down. Groaning, he painfully unbent and tried raising the pistol. When Swag shot him again in the stomach, the impact sent him turning in a kind of awkward two-step, and he staggered around the front fender of the car.

As the gunman dropped on the other side of the car, Swag got a good look at his shirt. There were no blood-stains, just the neat little holes where the nine-millimeter slugs had punched through.

Swag moved cautiously around the front of the car, looking for a head shot. The driver had long vanished beneath windshield level, and Swag heard the doors' electronic locks click shut as he passed in front. But before he was halfway across the hood, the gunman reemerged up the street, rising slowly at the rear of another car. He had crawled or duck-walked his way back, up Fifth Avenue, nearly to Sixtieth Street and a side entrance to Central Park. Then he pushed himself off the back fender and began to run. He started slowly, in a painful doubled-over trot, then picked up speed as he advanced between the stopped cars.

Swag caught him again, once in the back as he dodged between two cars. The gunman fell, his free hand searching for purchase along a cab's open window as he continued up Fifth Avenue.

Car horns sounded far back in the line of halted traffic. Swag turned to see what was left of the woman. Her body lay sprawled nearly at the center of the street, her legs awkwardly out in front of the lifeless form, as if she had decided to just lie down in the middle of the street. Most of her head was sprayed across a taxi's trunk and rear window.

Swag followed the gunman's path up the center of Fifth. If the dark suit broke to the left, then the wall that bordered Central Park would slow him down. If he broke to the right, he'd leave himself open on one of the side streets.

Whatever else this guy was, he was one tough bastard. With each step he seemed to gain speed as he made his way up between the stopped cars.

Swag broke into a full run. When only five car lengths separated the two men, the gunman looked over his shoulder to see Swag gaining. Then the line of cars began to move, creeping forward slowly as drivers maneuvered around the girl's body. When Swag was three car lengths back, the gunman turned in a panic, then pushed off the rear fender of a limo and headed for the side street, vanishing around the corner on 63rd.

Swag cut across between the next two cars, rising slightly as he climbed over the fenders to see the dark suit halfway up the street, heading toward Madison Avenue. Beyond him, at the intersection, Madison Avenue was jammed with cars and pedestrians. If the dark suit made it to Madison, he was home free.

The three or four people on the street ducked down between parked cars as Swag rounded the corner on 63rd. The guard in front of the New York Academy of Sciences retreated behind the heavy steel doors of the converted town house as Swag ran by, Browning held at shoulder height. Traffic on the side street was light, a few cars lined up, waiting for a break in the traffic jam on Fifth.

When the dark suit was within twenty yards of Madison, he turned again to see Swag gaining. Bringing his gun up, he fired two quick rounds, then cut between the solid row of parked cars and dodged in a serpentine run to the north side of the street. As the gunman passed a window of a street-level boutique, Swag threw his arms over a car's roof, brought the gun down in a two-handed position and fired. He'd been aiming for the gut, hoping to slow the blue suit down. But the shot went low, drilling into the gunman's left hip and knocking him to the ground against the marble steps of a town house.

So you don't have armored legs, you bastard, Swag thought to himself as he cut into the street.

Moving in a crouch along the line of parked cars, Swag raised his head above the sleek roof of a Mercedes coupé as the gunman fired again. The shot turned the car's rear window to dust.

Three car lengths ahead Swag came up for another cautious look and saw the dark suit had limped forward to come to rest, sitting against the corner boutique's plate-glass window. Two mannequins in expensive originals peered down at the wounded man with pouting lips and stylized poses. He was sweating badly and holding the oozing hip wound tightly with one hand. In his other hand was the gun.

As Swag came up on him from between two cars, he saw the dark suit tilt the gun to release its magazine, then fumbling, replace it with another from an inside pocket. Scanning the line of cars along the side street, he moved the gun in perfect line with his sight. Seeing nothing, the dark suit rose painfully up on one leg. Using his free hand for support, he leaned hard against the plate glass, leaving a trail of bloody palm prints as he hobbled backward toward Madison.

When the gunman was within ten feet of the corner, Swag came up fast from behind a small import. Behind Swag was an iron fence bordering a brick building of a private bank. The dark suit beat him to the draw. The first shot smashed through the window of the import, then chinged off one of the iron posts of the bank's fence behind Swag.

The second shot sliced smoothly through the front driver's door and out the passenger side, inches from where Swag crouched. The sonofabitch had changed to jacketed rounds.

Swag inched forward so that he was even with the front wheel well. Then he came up quick again, using the hood as a support. The dark suit fired twice more. Both armor-piercing slugs bored through the side panels and flattened against the engine block.

Swag's first shot hit the gunman high on the chest, knocking him back against the plate glass. The second shot went high, opening a neat hole in the glass and knocking the arm off one of the mannequins.

The gunman returned fire, but his shots went wild, taking huge gouges of brick off the imitation colonial building. Madison Avenue had emptied out, no pedestrians or cars. Swag rose to his full height and began pulling the trigger as fast as he could. Brass cartridge casings pinged off the hood of the import as his gun exploded again and again.

Five of the eight rounds struck the gunman, the others punched through the glass. The sixth shot caught him square in the chest, knocking the gun from his hand. The eighth shot finished the job, taking his good leg out from under him and sending him falling backward against the window.

The bullet-riddled window gave way under the sudden blow, and the gunman fell sideways through the window with a crash of shattering glass and sudden alarm bells. Writhing at the feet of the stylish mannequins, he looked up just in time to see the large wedge of green-edged plate glass fall from its precarious position above and slice through his neck.

chapter four

It was a question of jurisdiction. That's how Swag saw it. And like everything else in town, if you didn't buy something or steal it, then it was handed out on a first-come, first-served basis. Officially, street shootings were NYPD territory, but with the city quiet, the provosts were swooping down on every high-profile crime they could snatch off the police band. If there was a photo op, then the provosts were there.

Now Swag was curious to see how it would turn out. A dead guy in a boutique window could bring out a platoon of provosts and reporters.

But the store's alarm had been wired direct to the local NYPD precinct. A couple of rookies answered the call, the siren and lights of their radio car going like a Christmas toy loaded with new batteries. They stepped from the blue and white unit, one after the other, guns drawn and spreading out, just like they'd learned in the academy. They had answered the call expecting a smash and grab, and driven into a major crime scene to find their key suspect drinking Evian water from a plastic bottle offered by the boutique's owner.

Down on Fifth, where Swag left his client, Bammer's men would be picking up the pieces. It was only a matter of time before they began listening to witnesses and the police band to arrive at the boutique. That's when the question of jurisdiction would come in.

"Drop it," the nearest uniform said, moving in slowly.

"Drop what?"

"Drop the water," the other put in. "And get down on your knees, ankles crossed, fingers laced behind your head." Then to the boutique owner, "You too, sister."

Soon Swag was sitting in the back of the squad car, listening to one of the uniforms try to radio for the crime scene guys and coroner. Looking through the patrol car's clouded window, he judged the traffic on Madison. Rubberneckers had jammed it up good, slowing to catch sight of blood. A tour bus had diverted from its set route and now lingered in between the crosswalks at the center of Madison and 63rd, providing thirty German tourists with a nonscheduled photo op as the driver feigned a flooded engine. There would be some hefty tips for the driver; Germans, Swag suspected, were all closet death junkies.

"Dispatch, this is 402, request 10-83 forthwith, corner of East 63rd and Madison," the rookie said into the mike. "Possible DOA, over."

Dispatch came back with a 10-9, and the uniform repeated the code.

When the dispatcher repeated her request again, the rookie began cursing.

"Hey pal, been on the job long?" Swag asked, feeling the pinch of the cuffs as he leaned forward in the seat.

"Long enough to know you're in a world of trouble," the uniform snapped. "Now just sit back and be quiet."

"But not long enough to learn your codes," Swag said. "You just called in that you're taking a meal and need the coroner, Deceased Confirmed Dead at Scene. That's a nice touch, they'll like that over at Dispatch."

"Goddamnit," the uniform cursed, then began pounding the dashboard. "Damnit."

Between the static layered cross-talk, Swag could hear the radio's subculture. Cops on air for four or five words, no identification, just nicknames. Cops arranging to coop, or meet down by the docks to exchange information, or make plans for that night. All in a code that even other cops didn't understand and didn't question. Not much had changed, nothing really, since Swag was in uniform.

"Hey, that's okay," Swag said, hoping to settle the kid. "It'll give the provosts something to think about. Now, do this. Give her a 10-1, over the set. It means you can't copy. Then key in 10-85, DOA. Get your sergeant and the Crime Scene Unit. Use the keyboard, it'll take the provost's Com-Center longer to relay it out to the field."

The kid hesitated for a second, not certain if the suspect was out to help him or get him shitcanned. When he saw his partner walking back to the car after making sure the guy was dead, he turned to Swag and said, "What were those codes again?"

"Give it to me," Swag said, leaning forward so that the uniformed officer could put the mike to his mouth.

Swag gave the message, just as he had told the rookie to do, then added, "Irish pronto to West 36."

Detective Sgt. Patrick O'Neal and the provost's men arrived on the scene at the same time. By then Swag had talked one of the rookies into getting him a coffee—light, no sugar—and removing the cuffs. In order to justify the coffee, the rookie was making a half-hearted attempt to weasel a confession, saying, "So, why'd ya do it, huh? He owe you money or what?"

"You gotta get the other uniform over here to play bad cop," Swag said. "Otherwise it won't work." Then he took another sip of his coffee.

"You know, we got enough to lock you up now. Throw you right into the system," the uniform answered. "That shirt alone should earn you two years, minimum."

Swag studied the shirt casually. Across his chest a group of pigs, apples jauntily tucked into snouts, were dressed like hula dancers against a backdrop of an erupting volcano. "What? You don't like the shirt?" Swag asked, sounding hurt.

"Buddy, whatever else you did today, putting that shirt on is a fashion crime," came the rookie's answer.

A large crowd had gathered now around the body, still lying in the window. The other rookie was busy trying to keep them back by saying, "Keep moving, nothing to look at, nothing happened here."

Then the provosts piled out of the new green and white Land Rover and took over. The rookie never had a chance as the six uniformed provosts pushed him back into the crowd, relegating him to spectator.

A few of the bystanders, crime scene Fellinis, were filming the area with handheld video cameras, panning from the revolving lights of the patrol car to the bloody corpse in the window. The local news would pay a few bucks for the tape.

"You can make it easier on yourself, ya know," the uniform offered to Swag as he watched O'Neal's grim approach. The detective sergeant reached into his back pocket and clipped the badge he withdrew onto his shirt pocket.

"I'll tell you," Swag said, as O'Neal, hands now in pants pockets, slightly stooped, came closer. "It started with a girl, the most beautiful girl you ever saw."

"Yeah?" the rookie said, leaning over the backseat, anxious now to hear the details.

"She was," Swag said, pausing significantly, "Swiss."

O'Neal came over to the patrol car. From the look of his large wrinkled face, the Irishman was not happy. At the boutique's broken window the provost's men had taken control of the scene and were hustling gawkers with threats and the butts of their Steyr automatics.

"Get that suspect out of the goddamned car," O'Neal said wearily to the rookie. Behind him one of the provost's boys was closing in, but the decision wouldn't even be close. Swag was in official NYPD custody.

The young man complied, trying to uncoil himself from the front seat, then hustling around to open the back door. "I was just questioning the subject, sir."

"That's fine," O'Neal said, "now you keep those stormtroopers back until the crime scene guys and bus get here."

Then O'Neal began walking Swag to his twelve-year-old-unmarked detective's unit. It was, as department cars always had been, a Ford.

"Sir?" the rookie said.

"I'm taking custody of this suspect, officer."

"Sir, you're taking the perp?" the patrolman asked in a disbelieving voice. "What about the provosts?"

O'Neal waved him off impatiently. "You drive back to the station, I'll meet you there," he said, walking across Madison to where the battered Fury was double-parked.

"Sir?" the rookie called after them, but O'Neal ignored him. Taking the keys from his pocket, he opened the door, ushered Swag into the backseat, then started the car and steered out into traffic.

Swag, still in the backseat, waited for O'Neal to speak first. O'Neal tapped the siren and swung the car in a wide turn across on 65th. When he reached Second Avenue, he turned again. Now they were heading downtown. Traffic was lighter on Second and the lights were green. They were making good time, O'Neal driving aggressively.

"So, what's the deal?" Swag asked. "Taking me down to the docks, maybe work me over for a confession?"

O'Neal grunted, hunching over the wheel in his sweat-stained shirt. "I should, you know," he said at last. "I really should. But Christ, when I heard that call, I thought my mind was going. Like going back ten years. Calling in the numbers and all backward."

When they reached 42nd Street, he swung the car left and headed toward the East River. He cut through the red light on First with another touch at the siren and headed downtown under an elevated section of the FDR Drive, which ran along the river. When he reached 34th, O'Neal pulled up between two limos in the heliport's parking lot. Beyond the chain-link fence a slick copter was taking off, its engines whipping back the hair of two uniformed attendants who stood nearby under the floodlights. The copter lifted itself lazily, then tilted its nose slightly toward the water and skimmed off over the darkened river, heading for Kennedy or LaGuardia.

O'Neal turned slowly and, Swag thought, tiredly, bringing one elbow through the opening in the caged partition. "So what's the deal?" the cop said.

"The guy back in the window," Swag answered, "he flaked my client."

"That Swiss twist back on 59th, she was yours?"

Swag said, "Yeah, she was mine."

"Christ, Bammer's guys were all over the scene when the call came in. They were picking fragments off a cab's windshield with tweezers. What was it?"

O'Neal had once been the best homicide detective in the city; before that he was the best patrolman. But all that was long before Bammer's boys arrived. Now he was doing Past Burglaries. Interviewing television*less*, jewelry*less*, and joyless victims. It was all paperwork; even the victims knew they'd never see their shit again. What they got was a printout from a pocket computer listing the stolen items and an identifying number. Now, just talking about a murder brought back the old O'Neal.

"Coulda been anything," Swag answered. "Political, maybe. Wasn't a kidnapping gone wrong. The guy was a real pro, though, came right up and started shooting. Shot right past me, like he'd been programmed. A cool bastard—definitely not off the street."

O'Neal reached into his shirt pocket for a cigarette. Even in the dark Swag could see the blue of the Gitanes box. Opening the pack's flap, he went for a lighter. Then he remembered that department cars weren't equipped with them, and began digging in his pocket for a lighter.

Swag beat O'Neal to it, producing a pocket lighter and putting a flame to the Gitane.

"You want one?" O'Neal asked without much enthusiasm in his voice. With Gitanes and Gauloises going for twenty bucks a pack, Swag didn't blame him for the half-hearted offer, but took one of the French cigarettes anyway.

They sat there smoking in silence for a while, enjoying

the cigarettes and listening to the cross-talk on the unit's radio.

"Run it down for me," O'Neal said.

"We're crossing Fifth and the guy shoots the girl," Swag began. "I shoot him a couple of times. He gets up and runs up Fifth. I chase him, shoot him a couple of more times, and he goes through the window."

O'Neal exhaled a long column of smoke, turning his head slightly toward the opened window on the passenger side. "What was he wearing, a vest?"

"Either that or he's Superman," Swag said, flicking an ash onto the floor. "But I'll tell you, I was shooting some big loads into him, 147-grain jacketed hollowpoints. He should have went down."

O'Neal let out a long sigh, then took another drag on the Gitane. "Takes you back, doesn't it? Remember that maniac Cirelli dropped over on the Deuce, what, it must be eight years ago?"

"The one outside the peep show?" Swag answered. "I remember he shot him four times with a .38 and the guy kept coming."

"We were the officers on the scene," O'Neal said somewhat dreamily. "Show up on an 'officer needs assistance,' and there's Cirelli shaking like a leaf, still holding his piece on the guy. And the maniac dead at his feet. Four holes in the dead guy's chest. Real nice grouping, is what the IAD shoo flies said. Remember that?"

Swag inhaled on the Gitane, wondering how a cop like O'Neal could afford Gitanes. "That was a while ago," he said.

"And you're there trying to calm Cirelli down, while I clear the skels away. I'll never forget what one of them said. He said, 'Motherfucker, I wanta get me some' a what he was doing. That shit's Bruce Lee quality."

Swag threw the last of the cigarette out the window. "Turned out the guy wasn't doing anything. He was just nuts."

"Used to be fun, being a cop," O'Neal said, then flicked

his cigarette out the window. The radio's constant static hiss mixed with the sound of cars above them on the FDR. "Interesting anyway. Tell me, you ever miss it?"

Swag looked over the partition at his ex-partner. Even in the dim light of passing cars and the glare from the heliport's lamps, he could see that O'Neal had aged ten years in the last three. "Sometimes," Swag said. "You know, the way it used to be." Then Swag saw the white patch of skin on O'Neal's forearm. Scar tissue, he thought, then he knew where O'Neal got the money for French cigarettes.

"Who'd you sell it to?" Swag asked.

"What's that?" O'Neal asked, then answered his own question by rubbing the shiny round patch where his tattoo had been. Swag remembered it as a vivid "To Protect and Serve" banner above an angry eagle wearing an NYPD cap.

"The eagle," Swag asked. "Who bought it?"

O'Neal smiled a bit and kept rubbing his arm. "Dr. Shinozaki's World Famous, would you believe it?"

Swag did believe it. Dr. Shin's buyers were everywhere, searching out the best tattoos they could find for the museum. What had started out with a collection of *irezumi*—full-back tattoos—of yakuza mobsters, had grown to include American exhibitions of death row prisoners, veterans, circus freaks, anything with a little style. Now, O'Neal's eagle was flensed, cleansed, and lieing next to full-back yakuza specimens in a glass-topped tank in the Tokyo museum.

"Paid fifty francs," O'Neal added quietly.

"They've gone for less," Swag said. "You got a good deal."

"Well, I best be taking you in, boyo. We don't send you through the system, the provosts will put out a warrant," O'Neal said. "We'll charge you with something. Get a long court date."

"ROR?" Swag asked, wanting to be released on his own recognizance.

"Sure, upstanding guy like you, roots in the community," came the answer. "Give you some time to move. They'll process you through central booking and arraignment, shouldn't take all night. That is if you don't let some young P.D. plead you to Murder One."

"No problem," Swag said.

"And if you weren't lying, then you're clean."

O'Neal started the car and eased it back out of its parking place.

"And if I wasn't?" Swag asked.

"Lying?" O'Neal asked.

"Clean."

O'Neal cut the wheel left and began heading up toward the precinct, moving along the shantytown set up under the FDR Drive. "Then I was figuring on putting you on one of those helicopters out to the airport. Ireland still doesn't have extradition."

Farther down river, just above Houston Street, a black Mercedes limo with ceramic tiles protecting the tires came to a smooth stop in the top of the East River Park, a narrow park stretch of green bordering the river. The uniformed driver stepped quickly as he emerged from the car, then opened the rear door. Inside was his employer, sitting next to the wounded Johnny G.

The driver nodded once to the gray-headed man in the back, then grabbed Johnny by the shoulder and eased him out. The wounded man was much heavier than the driver expected, and the form fell clumsily to the ground. The driver said, "Shit," and looked down on Johnny, partially illuminated by the car's inside lights.

Johnny wasn't dead, but it felt that way to the driver. The drug they had given him, a synthetic form of the *Gonyaulax tamarensis* shellfish toxin, had rendered all his voluntary muscles, including those in his eyes, paralyzed.

The world tilted and swayed for Johnny G. as the driver bent and lifted him off the ground in a fireman's carry. Johnny's eyes hurt, dried out from not being able to blink, and everything seemed a little out of focus. Behind him a car door shut. Then they were moving toward the river, the driver walking along the narrow footpath. Old newspapers, a plastic cup, a condom, were strewn along the ground.

Johnny wanted to cry out, but couldn't. It felt as if his body was shot full of novocaine. He had no way of knowing that he was the first person outside of a Zurich lab to experience the drug.

The world tilted again as the driver eased Johnny off his shoulder and over an iron railing. Briefly, Johnny could see the uptown skyline through the trees—the old Citicorp Building, now some Jap bank, the 59th Street Bridge, and the nearer lights of the heliport.

The driver grunted slightly, then Johnny G. was falling back away from a starless sky. He didn't feel the cold shock of the water as he hit. Then the river's water covered his eyes and lapped up into his mouth and nose. Above him, he could make out the dark form of the driver, looking down impassively as he pulled a comb from his pocket and drew it through his hair. When the current turned Johnny over, face first into the river, the driver walked back to the limo and shut the door.

The smoked-glass partition hummed down and the gray-haired passenger said, "Very good, Roger. Do you suppose I can still make my reservation at Le Cirque?"

The driver cut a quick glance at the car's clock. "Just barely, sir," he said, shifting the idling car into gear.

In a fashionable restaurant on East 63rd, a blond man in a tan poplin suit and French running shoes sat across from a young blond woman less than half his age. They were eating what he liked to call "eye-talian spaghetti" and what she called "pasta."

The young woman marveled at how the man ate effortlessly without losing a speck of the Bolognese sauce to the regimental tie or tan material of the suit.

"Well, what do you think?" the young woman said after the conversation had reached a lull.

"Good eye-talian," the man replied, then reached for his wineglass. "What do you call this wine again?"

"It's an '88 Bordeaux, *deuxième cru,* Jim Bob," the young woman said. "From the Haut-Médoc region."

"Mighty tasty," the man answered, and took another sip.

The young woman took a sip as well and found the wine not too tannic. "So what do you think?" she said. "About Ms. Lorette?"

"Mighty pretty girl," Jim Bob answered, putting the wineglass down. "Damn shame."

"Leaves us high and dry," the young woman said. "Maybe we should call the European section in? Coordinate and cross target on that end."

Jim Bob frowned slightly at the young woman's use of agency slang. "No good," he said at last. "If it's running like I think, them old boys in Switzerland, they got eight ways from Sunday of plausible deniability. They'll sit back grinning like fat possums under a front porch in June. You know what I'm saying?"

"I'm sure I don't, Jim Bob," the young woman said. "But Ms. Lorrette's still dead. We're back where we were last week."

"That Swiss girl, well, she was only one part of the enterprise," the man said. "I figure we'll just have to follow old Swag for a while, see where he leads us. Meanwhile, you keep that appointment over at the Carlyle."

The young woman nodded in agreement and said, "Jim Bob, don't say 'girl,' it's not politically correct."

The man smiled broadly at this, then reached for the wineglass again. "Darlin', you know this ol' boy ain't nothing, if not politically correct."

chapter five

THE WHEELS OF JUSTICE rolled twenty-four hours a day
down on 100 Centre Street. They churned out cheap justice, blindly dealing trash-time plea bargains, full loads, and
probation sentences all with the same tired and uneven precision of a bankrupt machine shop.

Judges, Assistant D.A.'s, and public defenders worked in
round-the-clock shifts, processing those unlucky or stupid
enough to get caught. When the jail adjoining the courts
jammed up, they shipped the raw material of justice in from
Rikers Island and the two dozen jail barges anchored in the
river.

The blue, white, and orange Corrections Department
buses formed a permanent line, backed up three blocks to
Pearl Street, past Foley Square and the noble architecture
of the Manhattan Supreme Court and U.S. court. Marble
and granite buildings, done up like Roman temples. Wide
steps led up through their Corinthian-pillared entrances
and marbled halls, which echoed with the sound of expensive shoes and the whispering voices of high-priced lawyers,
hushed in the presence of top-shelf justice.

Defendants, with bar-coded docket numbers sealed in
plastic around their wrists, looked out at the buildings
through the tight weave of the buses' iron window gratings
as they waited to disembark at the soot-blackened gray marble of the Criminal Courts Building. No ripped-off faux-
Roman influence where they were heading. Just a couple

of blackened towers studded with the gray steel of dripping
air conditioners.

Suspects often waited days for processing through central booking, weeks for arraignment, and sometimes years
for trials. Public defenders no longer went back into the
holding pens for pretrial meetings with their clients. D.A.'s
and ADA's built reputations for speed, not cases. Both fed
off a stack of files—yellow for felony and blue for misde-
meanor—that the last shift left for them on their tables.
Fastened to the top of each file was a computer-generated
case briefing, no more than two or three paragraphs long.
The summaries began with the docket number and ended
with acceptable plea bargains.

Then there were the other courtrooms. Rikers had
twelve. Bellevue five. And each prison barge had its own
courtroom. This was the annexation of justice. Trials and
arraignments were held in what were once used as day-
rooms, cafeterias, gyms. Judges sat at steel-gray govern-
ment-issue desks, while prisoners could gaze down at the
Formica surface of what was once a cafeteria table and read
the ancient graffiti, while their lawyers pleaded them out.
One of the prison barges even held court, on sunny days,
on the roof, once a cyclone-fenced exercise court topped
by razor wire. The judge sat beneath a nylon halo of a bas-
ketball net, and everyone got some sun.

It surprised no one that the D.A.'s and public defenders
were often in agreement. Their summaries had been prepared by the same computer, printed on the same paper
and stamped by the same hollow-eyed court clerks. It was
these summaries that they read prior to each case. Neither
police officers nor the provost's soldiers—Bammer's men—
appeared in court; they read the trial results on computer
screens or on posted printouts in squad rooms. Law
enforcement officers' testimonies were supposedly available
on tape, but requesting such material could land a suspect
far back in line. One in a hundred trials used the tapes,
fewer went before juries. This was a world of all-purpose
courts and the imperfect algebra of cut-rate justice. In these

shabby brown courts justice wasn't blind or wise. Her eyes
were bloodshot and her brain numbed by endless cups of
coffee and the endless sorrow of it all.

And Swag had heard the stories, everyone had, of those
skels lost in the system by misplaced paperwork and computer errors. Those men and women were the institution-
ally damned. They would board the buses daily or
weekly—*sometimes for years*—on the way to their ten-
minute arraignment and plea. Those were the ones who
grew old in transit, eating their meals of baloney and cheese
sandwiches, fruit juice and bruised apples. Often they slept
on the buses' straight-backed seats or in the tiled holding
pens, waiting for appearances that would never come.

Then there were the rumors of tourists caught in the
machinery of the system, never to be heard from again.
They moved like bar-coded specters from Rikers to holding
pens to barges, then back to Rikers to repeat the process,
their accents falling away into jailhouse slang. Embassy officials—like Kansas tourists caught in some Times Square
nightmare of three-card monte—hunted for them futilely,
always one step behind the system's constant shuffling.

Now, as Swag approached the court in the backseat of
the radio unit, he saw the Corrections Department buses.
They were lined up past Pearl Street, feeding from two lines
of vehicles that stretched around Horgan Place. There were
more than forty of them moving in a creeping double line
guided by blue police barricades.

It was hard for Swag to remember when they weren't
lined up. At one time he might have said throw all the prisoners into the barges and let them drift out to sea. Now
he only stared, like everyone else amazed that one city could
have so many unlucky sonsofbitches.

Sidewalk shysters in tattered suits shouted up at bus windows, looking for clients. For a hundred bucks they'd plead
your case with annoying theatrical flourish, maybe getting
you the same time that the public defender would.

Street vendors were selling soft drinks through exagger-
ated straws, which they poked through the screened win-

dows, along with loose cigarettes at a two dollars per. Relatives moved patiently up and down the line, shouting the names of sons, daughters, husbands, and cousins.

"Pretty amazing, isn't it?" the uniformed officer asked.

Swag rolled slowly past the lines of buses, turned at the side of the courthouse, passing under the skyway that connected it to the jail, and turned onto Baxter Street. Across the way was a small park. Up the street was Chinatown, where the all-night restaurant signs were lined up on either side.

Swag shot a glance at the rearview mirror and saw that the officer driving couldn't be more than nineteen or twenty. This was the only kind of justice the guy had ever known.

"Pretty amazing that it works at all," Swag said.

The uniform climbed from the front seat, grabbing Swag's paperwork as he came out of the unit. "Looks like you got a free ride," he said. "How'd you move through so fast? Real VIP treatment, huh?"

"I have friends in the department," Swag said, taking the bar-coded folder.

"Yeah, I heard," the officer answered, hustling to keep up with Swag as he moved toward the courthouse's rear entrance. "It true that you used to be a cop?"

Swag and the uniform moved quickly between the parked cars and approached the door, which was guarded by a sleepy corrections officer. A greasy paper bag and battered thermos rested at his feet. "Long time ago," Swag answered, flashing the yellow folder at the guard.

"So, what happened?" the young cop said, following Swag through the door, past the metal detector, and into a tiled hallway. "I know you didn't do your twenty."

Swag started down the metal stairs, worn smooth with age, then down a hall that would lead him to a service elevator and the chambers of a very special judge. "The usual bullshit," he said, finally answering the young cop.

"Yeah, I know what you mean," came the answer.

And Swag knew that the young uniform didn't have a clue.

It was well after dawn when Swag, released on his own recognizance, came down the five steps in front of the courthouse. The only thing that changed in the gray light were the stenciled numbers on the buses. A mime was working an early morning crowd of city employees.

Hell of a world, Swag thought. Almost six hundred thousand people jamming the criminal courts, and all the lawyers and mimes were running around free.

The idea of mandatory jail time for mimes and lawyers brought a smile to his face, but it quickly vanished when he spotted the three near the bottom of the stairs. Two sidewalk shysters had cornered a young ADA against the marble veneer. "Two years probation, max, then you'll get your fuckin' money," one of the lawyers said, speaking in a harsh whisper.

The ADA was shaking his head, looking for an opening between the two. But they closed ranks. The kid couldn't even get the edge of his briefcase between them.

The other lawyer threw away what remained of a cigarette and stepped in closer, crowding the ADA. "See what that says, kid," he said, pointing to the spot above the prosecutor's head.

The ADA twisted around to eyeball the slogan carved into the building's marble veneer.

"'Good Faith is the Foundation of Justice,'" the shyster read to the prosecutor, blowing a long stream of smoke into his face. "Now how 'bout showing some good faith, whattaya say? Our boy can't make no money if he ain't on the street."

Swag tried not to listen as he passed the arguing trio and went down the five steps and into the street. He tried not to think of the lawyers as he passed. He had seen their kind before. They'd hook in clients on the courthouse steps, accepting a ring, a bracelet, even a hot telephone credit card number in payment. Then they'd stand up in front of the judge in their shabby suits and plead the guy out or try for reduced bail. Usually they'd mumble their way through it, except for one line, which they all spoke with resounding clarity for the record: "I'm representing Joe Shitoutofluck *for purposes of arraignment only.*"

It may have been the courthouse or the fatigue. But as he stood on the curb, blank-faced and numb, he remembered the last time he'd gotten caught in the machinery of the system. Back then, he'd been a part of the machinery—a cog with an attitude.

He could still see the bodies. The memory of it was as vivid as when he first arrived at the crime scene, gold shield hung on the pocket of his new suit. The uniform on duty waved him through the tangle of cars and vans in the parking lot.

Chilled in the predawn air, a fresh shiver ran up his spine when he wound his way through the mobile news vans, reporters, and gawkers, and stepped over the plastic crime scene ribbon, between two of the thirty or more RMP's, EMS buses, and unmarked units parked with their high beams and emergency lamps on.

This was going to be a bad one. But he already knew it was bad by the C.O.'s voice on the phone. The borderline panic in the voice pulled him out of a sound sleep. He already knew it was bad when he rolled out of bed and into his clothes. Now it was just a matter of degrees.

When he got to the edge of the water, he knew that this one was right off the scale. Eighty-seven bodies bobbing gently in the current, bunched in like so much river refuse between the two piers. It didn't look like eighty-seven to Swag then. It looked like two hundred. Bleached faces, hands, floating up in the river. They rose and fell in an eerie rhythm of the lapping water. Thin pools of scum had formed between them, beer cans, plastic milk jugs, chunks of Styrofoam coolers were trapped between legs and outstretched arms.

The harbor patrol had positioned a dozen launches between piers 81 and 83, effectively containing the corpses as their spots ran over them in slow probing and crossing bands of light. More lights poked out from the parking lot, playing over the dark water, searching for bodies.

Both piers were parking lots. At one time home to the Day Line and Circle Line tour ships, the only reminder now was the partially submerged ship tied next to the Circle Line pier, its white, green, and red bow pointing toward the scattered lights of Jersey across the river.

There must have been seventy-five or more cops on the scene, not counting those who were keeping the press back, and maybe thirty EMS guys. And not one of them said a word.

The Zone Commander, Casey, arrived, then the crime scene guys, lugging their aluminum cases.

"Jesus Christ," Casey whispered from nearby.

The crime scene guys fanned out, with their video and still cameras.

Swag turned away from the water. Across Twelfth Avenue, past the burned-out sixties facade of a failed hotel, he looked over the crowded midtown skyline. The Empire State Building dark, its upper floors shrouded in clouds.

He turned back when he heard the whump-whump-whump of the police chopper coming up the river. The copter banked right and took up a position above the boats, adding its searchlight to the mess.

Then someone started up a portable generator and the halogen floodlights snapped on, illuminating the entire sickening scene.

It's going to fall apart fast, he thought. Already there were swarms of uniforms trampling over the crime scene. Destroying any kind of evidence. Then he heard the two-note sirens of the provosts, walking their way down 42nd Street.

Another chopper, a provost, joined the NYPD chopper at the far end of the piers. Each kept a respectful distance, not even their lights crossing as they hovered above the water.

He saw the third chopper come in from the center of the

river. It came in fast and low, like an attack ship, its rotors churning the water, forcing the NYPD and provosts' choppers to veer off, left and right. Swag watched as the chopper headed straight for him, passing no more than a dozen feet over the water. When it was fifty feet away, it pulled up, banked right, then made another pass over the water. As it passed overhead, the television station's call letters were clearly visible. So was the cameraman, strapped into the opened doorway.

Colonel Bammer arrived at the crime scene with a seven-car motorcade. They swept into the parking lot in neat military fashion, the television lights following their arrival. Bammer, surrounded by a phalanx of a dozen men, Steyrs at the ready, broke through the yellow crime scene ribbon, the press following in his wake. Not even dawn yet, but he looked bright-eyed and awake. His uniform was freshly pressed, every bit of brass gleaming, and not a hair out of place.

He strode right up to the edge of the water, his face devoid of all expression, waited for the cameras to position themselves, then turned. His mouth had formed itself into a thin grim line of determination. He held the pose while the rest of the cameras fired up. Then he spoke.

"I will not have this in my city," he said. "We will find whoever is responsible for this slaughter and punish them."

"Who'll be conducting the investigation?" one of the reporters called.

"It will be a joint investigation between the Provost Command and the NYPD," Bammer answered. "A joint investigation, which, I might add, will demonstrate the new era of cooperation between our two forces. Major Tancloe here will head our task force. I remain certain that the NYPD can find someone with the qualifications to head their end."

Feeling a strange lightness at his back, Swag turned and instinctively felt for the Browning Hi-Power. The gun and holster were missing. Both had been lost in the system.

He bought a coffee from a street vendor and hailed a taxi.

When he gave the cabbie the address, the man turned, opened his mouth, then saw something in Swag's dog-tired bloodshot eyes that made him think better of asking the question.

Four city units were parked on the small promenade near the Manhattan Bridge. The flashing lights from the EMS bus and two police units cut the gray dawn light steadily. Nearby, parked closest to the river, was the coroner's black station wagon.

A blond man in a blue jogging suit and French running shoes stood downriver. Braced against the black iron rail, he moved through a series of stretches.

A few civilians, residents of the cardboard shantytown, loitered about, peering over the side into the choppy lead-colored water. A gurney waited near the Medical Examiner's black station wagon, the dark form of a body bag neatly folded at its center.

As the blond man approached casually, he could see the NYPD emergency services diver fasten the wire noose around the dead man's chest, just under his arms, and give the signal for the other cops to switch on the portable winch.

The dead guy turned in the water, stretched to his full length; then the pant leg, which was caught on a piece of submerged piling, ripped and he broke free.

"Another floater," the skel closest to the blond guy said. "Been a lot of them lately."

The blond guy nodded and moved closer, getting a good look at the body as it came dripping over the railing. Neither the medicos nor cops made a move to touch it until it hit pavement.

The blond guy watched the floater intently, noting the wound at the knee. Then he looked up the river, calculating the current and thinking that there was no way to tell where he went in. Not with all of the pilings and piers that could stall the stiff's progress downriver.

"Nice shoes on that one," the skel remarked with a knowledgeable nod. "Most of them don't have nice shoes."

The blond guy nodded back slightly, then looked out over the river, lost in thought. Around his right wrist was a crude brass bracelet, formed from a piece of bent rod and inscribed with a series of sawed-in markings. He had purchased it the day before, with a dozen other trinkets. The other items he'd discarded quickly, yet he kept the bracelet, finding its solid weight pleasant—almost familiar.

"Why'd you think that is, anyway?" the skel insisted.

"What's that, friend?" the blond guy asked, turning for the first time toward the ragged speaker. He spoke in a slight southern drawl.

"Why'd you think guys that jump in the drink don't have decent shoes?" came the response. "I been around, I seen guys in Guccis go outta windows. A man in a pair of Ballys is just as likely to put a bullet in his head as one in Florsheims. But show me a floater, I'll show you an example of crappy footwear. Else they take 'em off. Shitty pair of shoes, they'll take 'em off for they go over the side. What sense is that?"

The blond man turned, almost too quickly, when he heard the sound of the body bag's zipper. Then an attendant slammed the rear door of the coroner's station wagon.

"So, what sense is that?" the skel insisted. "You tell me."

"I don't know," the blond guy said. "Not a clue." And then he began jogging uptown.

chapter six

THE CAB MADE THE TURNOFF at 23rd Street and cut over to
First Avenue. When they came to a stop in front of the East
33rd Street entrance to the Medical Examiner's Office and
City Morgue, the driver gave Swag a sidelong look, as if
daring him to venture out of the car.

But Swag needed no prompting. This was familiar territory—as familiar as the dull force of habit that brought
him here in search of answers. It was no longer a matter
of who; the guy who waxed his client, Lorette, was dead.
The question was, who the fuck was that guy? If he didn't
figure out who'd flaked his client, and do something about
it, he'd be unlikely to get any new business anytime soon.
Bottom-feeders like Johnny G. shot tourists in hotel rooms
for a living. Guys in suits didn't gun down Swiss ladies on
Fifth Avenue. It just wasn't done.

The street in front of the morgue was empty. The building itself had that drab style and worn look of neglect of
an unimportant government building. Later, luxury tour
vans filled with tourist death junkies would arrive. At one
time the city's "Death Museum" had been closed to the
public. Back then, visiting pathologists, cops, and even an
occasional mystery writers' group waded through formal
requests for a chance to view the exhibits of fatal oddities
that included the clothing of a man struck by lightning in
Central Park and a cross section of a perfectly preserved
esophagus clogged by an equally intact jumbo shrimp.

Now European travel agents booked the tours hosted by perky bilingual blondes.

Once Swag had seen a Japanese family walk through. He remembered that the father had taken a picture of the two kids, their tongues out, pretending to choke in front of the shrimp exhibit.

A long row of empty gurneys lined each side of the wide tiled hall leading to the Medical Examiner's lab. An ancient guard dozed at the door, sleeping comfortably in a straight-backed chair. Swag knew that it must have taken years of practice to fall asleep perfectly straight, one leg resting casually over the other. Swag saw no reason to wake the man.

Inside, the M.E.'s lab was a cavernous green-tiled room filled with a dozen perforated stainless steel tables, each one with a hard-rubber cushion at one end and double water taps at the other. Above each table was a digital scale, a high-intensity light, and a small video camera.

Cranen, the M.E. himself, was busy escorting a slight red-haired man around the room. He spoke in a tired monotone, as if performing an autopsy, stopping briefly at each point of interest. Swag watched as the two men made their tour, the redhead reaching out tentatively every once in a while to touch a carefully arranged lineup of instruments or one of the porcelain buckets that hung from each scale.

Cranen was a fat man with short little legs. Just the right height for his work, Swag thought.

The two men, Cranen and his guest, had nearly completed the tour before they noticed Swag standing just to the side of the door. The little redheaded man looked nervous, but Cranen looked nothing at all. Whispering something to the visitor, Cranen stepped from behind one of the steel tables and approached Swag in a not quite casual walk.

Swag remembered when Cranen was an assistant M.E. who weighed each restaurant lunch, new pair of shoes, and after-work cocktail against the mortgage, the car payments, and the wife's ceramics class. He was an honest civil servant back then, with an office full of glazed owls, crooked pottery, and a hopelessly cluttered desk. Swag didn't need to check a calendar to know that was a long time ago. One look at Cranen was all it took to know that the M.E. had been on the hustle for years.

Just the clothes Cranen wore under the white lab coat were worth more than the city paid him in a year. French linen suit. English cotton shirt. Italian tie. Swag couldn't tell about the shoes, but they had the warm sheen of expensive leather. The three-carat stone he wore on his little finger wasn't bad either. Under the bright lights of the morgue, the big emerald shone clear and flawless. The ring was a hard act to follow, but the watch strapped to the pathologist's wrist did a good job. It was a gold Rolex President with enough diamonds set into its face to make telling time a pain in the ass.

"How's business?" Swag asked, coming slightly away from the wall and keeping his eyes on the redhead.

"You're not a cop anymore," Cranen said, his face tightening up as he moved directly in front of Swag.

Swag ignored the pathologist, reached for a cigarette, and remembered too late that he was out. "In early. Is that newfound diligence or you got a little side action going? What's he doing, buying or just sightseeing?"

"What do you want, Swag?" Cranen said, not about to be bullied. "Unless you got a badge, get the fuck out."

Looking past the pathologist, Swag gave the redheaded man a big smile. The redhead shifted uncomfortably, first on one foot, then the other. "Hey, how's it going, pal?" Swag called across the room. He could feel Cranen begin to panic as the threat of losing the death junkie client grew into a wallet-thinning fear. No doubt Cranen had already spent the money in his mind, and it wasn't on his long-gone wife's ceramic class either.

The redhead mumbled something and focused all his attention at the floor.

"What do you want?" Cranen repeated, his eyes darting from Swag to the redhead then back again. The redhead looked as if he would bolt at any second.

"Yo, pal," Swag called. The redhead brought his eyes up slowly.

Swag made sure to look right at the redhead, right in his pale watery eyes. "Yeah, you," he said, his voice loud enough to echo in the tiled room. "You got a cigarette, I just ran out."

The redhead shook his head and mumbled something else Swag couldn't hear.

"Yeah, I know what you mean, bad for your health. Ask Doc Cranen here, lungs'll crumble like a dry sponge."

"What do you *want* Swag?" Cranen said. His voice wasn't hard anymore, it was almost pleading. There was money at stake here, maybe even a lot of it.

"You got a little side action going here, Doc?" Swag said again, still smiling pleasantly past Cranen at the redheaded death junkie. But the guy wasn't looking back, he was staring at the door longingly, calculating his escape.

"That happens to be one of my associates from Great Britain," Cranen tried. "Highly respected in his field. It's an exchange program arrangement. Perfectly legal. Not that it's any concern of yours anymore."

Swag cut his stare away from the redhead and put it on Cranen. Not smiling, he said, "If he's a pathologist, I'm Dr. Kil-fuckin'-dare. What's the admission to a private performance, huh? Or maybe you just let them alone with the stiffs in a nice storeroom?"

"What is it?" Cranen said in a hushed voice. "Tell me now or get the hell outta my morgue."

"There was a woman brought in last night," Swag said. "Mid-twenties. Multiple gunshot wounds to the head. Name was Lorette. Swiss, I think. And a man. Probably a John Doe. Late twenties, early thirties. Blue suit. Fell through a window up on Madison."

Cranen thought back for a moment, then remembered. "So?"

"Do 'em now," Swag said. "Both of them."

"Provost men are handling the cases," Cranen said, panicked. "Their team needs to be here."

"They can watch the tape," Swag answered. "Administrative mix-up. It's happened."

Now Cranen was shifting nervously. "Not two in one day it hasn't."

"Do 'em, Doc, or you've given your last performance."

"Christ, it'll take all morning," Cranen protested.

"Skip to the good parts," Swag suggested. "Wound analysis on the girl, identifying marks on the John Doe."

Cranen pondered this for a moment, then said, "You're going to owe me for this, you realize that?"

"You got box seats to the next subway series," Swag answered.

Cranen didn't answer; rather, he walked back to the redheaded death junkie and began speaking in a low voice. The man nodded his head several times before Cranen turned back.

"We'll begin with the girl," the pathologist said. "Why not be a good boy and go fetch her, last locker nearest the door."

They stored the bodies down the hall. Swag knew the way. The large room was lined with steel lockers, a thermometer and temperature controls above each door.

By the time Swag wheeled the gurney into the lab, Cranen had pulled on his gloves and had the redhead from Britain sitting on a plastic chair near one of the stainless steel tables. Nearby another gurney held an assortment of tools; scalpels, saws, probes.

Cranen pulled the plastic sheet from the girl and took a professional moment to study the wound. There was nearly more wound than head. The entire left side of the girl's skull, right down to the jaw, was gone, exposing a good portion of brain and jagged bone. Dried blood covered it all.

The death junkie leaned forward to get a better look.

"Be a good fellow, then, and give a hand," Cranen said.

Swag pulled on a pair of gloves from the box then positioned himself at the girl's feet, and the two men lifted her from the gurney to the stainless steel table.

"Made a damned mess of her," Cranen said, reaching up to turn on the tape and overhead lamp. "I shall have to ask both of you not to talk or intrude in any manner."

Swag reached up and turned the audio switch to the camera off. "I'll tell you what, let's make this one confidential," he said. "You can put in the sound track and subtitles for the provost guys later."

Cranen glanced back, annoyed, but didn't protest.

The woman's dress was a bloodstained mess. The pin Arturo sold her and all the woman's jewelry were gone. Swag cast a quick look under the gurney's compartment that held personal effects. It was empty. The medicos had given her CPR, all right—Cash, Purse, Rings.

"What killed her?" Swag asked.

Cranen looked up slowly from across the table. "Somebody shot her in the head."

"Excuse me, I say, pardon me, old boys."

The voice, an uppercrust English accent, was so unexpected that Swag nearly jumped. It was the redhead. The man was still sitting in the chair, but was now leaning far forward, one finger slightly extended.

"I say, but isn't it procedurally correct to remove the clothing before—"

Swag wasn't sure what expression came into his face but whatever it was, it shut the redhead up.

"Let's see what we have here, shall we," Cranen said, giving the body a quick once over. "Female, Caucasian, twenty-five to twenty-eight."

"Look closer," Swag said.

Cranen didn't have to be told what to look for, bending in close, examining the uninjured hand under the magnifying glass. Between her fingers he found what he was looking for. Gently placing the hand back on the table, he turned her head so that he could study the hairline of the uninjured side. "Female Caucasian, thirty-three to thirty-five," he began again. "Signs of recent—and quite expensive, I might add—surgery and collagen treatment apparent at hairline and fingers. Weight approximately 105 pounds, wearing a . . ." Cranen checked the bloodstained label in her jacket, "tan Chanel number. *Quel dommage.* What a pity."

Then, rising up, Cranen gently lifted the girl's ruined hand in his own and looked down on it as if he were examining a ring. "Third and fourth digits severed," he began, looking up at Swag, challenging him to deny it. "At second knuckle. Wound consistent with defensive gesture. She saw who shot her."

"So, what was it?" Swag asked. "You've seen gunshots before."

Cranen leaned in closer to the girl, moving his head slightly to examine the wound. "Shotgun maybe. Close range."

"No, it was a pistol."

"You're telling me now?"

Swag didn't answer.

Cranen bent closer to the body, then without looking lifted one of the probes from the worktable. With his other hand he pulled a clump of blood-encrusted hair away from the wound and examined the damage it had hidden.

"No gunpowder or stippling," Cranen said. "You say it was a pistol?"

"Ten, fifteen feet away, that would explain it."

Cranen grunted but didn't look up. He was now caught up in it. Whatever he was now, once he had been good at his job. Ten years ago Cranen was fast, thorough, and smart. He could dig into some poor dead bastard and pull out the one piece of evidence that put the guy who killed him away. And put Cranen up on the stand in court, and he was everyone's favorite uncle, loosening up the jury with small jokes and giving nothing back to the defense lawyers. Now that old crafty magic was coming back after years of tagging, bagging, and bragging.

He washed what was left of the girl's head quickly and thoroughly with gauze and soapy water, then examined the wound again.

"Curiouser and curiouser," he said, putting the last piece

of bloody gauze down and picking up a probe. After he'd poked around the wound for a minute, he put the probe down and reached for a scalpel.

Cranen made a pair of twin incisions, one behind the girl's right ear and the other far back, where the wound stopped and flesh started again. Then he cut around at the nape of her neck, just below the hairline. When he pulled her scalp forward, it came up and over her eyes in one piece, revealing the delicate marbling of her skull.

"This is a strange one," he said, studying the girl's oddly hairless skull. He spoke more to himself than Swag. Then he reached for the saw.

The saw was stainless steel, not much larger than the electric clippers a barber might use, with a minutely serrated circular blade at its end.

He began cutting at the back of the head, the blade grinding through the bone. When he had cut around to where the bone ended in a jagged line of the wound, he gently lifted the top of her skull off. It came away from what was left of her brain with a slight, sucking sound.

The girl's brain was splotched with blood. A large section was missing from the wound. Swag could now see the extent of the wound and why Cranen's practiced eye had thought it was the work of a shotgun. There was too much damage; clearly a third of it had been blown away. The girl was dead before she hit the ground.

The death junkie fidgeted nervously, his shoes tapping out a soft tattoo on the floor.

"Ah," Cranen said, as he carefully placed the top half of the shattered skull on an empty section of the worktable. "A handgun you say?"

Swag nodded, but the pathologist paid no attention. He picked up a pair of long tweezers, then probed the wound.

The redhead mumbled something and retreated from the room, keeping his eyes glued to the sight as he backed out through the door.

"You were working for this lady?" Cranen asked, still working the tweezers into the soft, bloodied folds.

"Yeah," Swag said.

Cranen rose up slightly, extracting something with the tweezers. "Well, my friend, somebody wanted your client dead very badly."

Cranen stretched erect as he held the tiny object up to the light, examining it through squinted eyes.

Swag bent slightly toward the pathologist, looking at the dark metal sliver fastened between the stainless device. "What is it?"

Cranen held out the tweezers, out of camera range, offering Swag a look. "Not common ordnance," he said. "Not at all."

"Glasers?" Swag asked. But the small sliver was more like a knife blade than the pellets used in Glaser rounds.

Cranen thought about this, then said, "No. Too small. Her brain's riddled with them. Keyhole effect—they get in there and bounce around. *Beaucoup* damage. This is something new. Not a flechette, but like one."

By the time the redhead returned, Swag had wheeled the girl back into the locker and brought out the dark suit. Like the girl, he had been stripped of any jewelry he may have had, though Swag doubted even a wallet would have identified him.

"This one's easy, he died of blood loss," Cranen said. "A window you say it was? Well, it severed his carotid."

Swag looked at the dark suit lying out on the table, nearly as pale as the sheet that had covered him. The gash across his neck had done more than cut through his carotid, it had nearly taken his head off.

"Let's check him out for scars, tattoos," Swag said.

Cranen, changing his gloves, said, "You want your money's worth, eh, boyo?"

First they pulled off the blood-stiffened suitcoat, which didn't have a label. Cranen guessed it to be Italian. Underneath was a blood-soaked shirt, but even with the blood, Swag could see the Browning's work. Nine neat holes, just where he knew they'd be.

Cranen carefully loosened the tie, then slowly began to

unbutton the shirt. As he peeled it back, the slugs rolled down across his stomach and clinked across the table.

The death junkie let out a slight gasp. And so did Swag. The dark suit wasn't wearing a Kevlar vest. The bullets had ripped into his skin, leaving nasty little punctures at the center of large bruises, but they had not penetrated.

"Who's been at him?" Swag asked.

"Nobody," Cranen said.

"Emergency team, maybe?"

"No chance, my friend," Cranen said. "I'd be able to tell from the stains on the shirt. And the tie. Nobody's tampered with our friend here. Whoever shot him just wasn't close enough."

Swag helped lift the corpse to remove the shirt. More bullets, this time from his back, clinked out. "Fifteen feet close enough?"

"Don't be moronic," Cranen snapped back as he bent to pick up one of the half-flattened hollowpoint slugs. "These are what, nines. Some blunt trauma is all."

"Cut him," Swag said.

"Why not, in for a penny, in for a pound, eh?" Cranen quickly stripped the blue suit's clothes off and picked up a fresh scalpel. The hip shot had smashed into him square in the pelvis, shattering the entire left side. Swag could see now that there were no scars, no birthmarks, no tattoos.

The pathologist paused for a moment, the blade hovering above the corpse, then began the chest cut, bringing the scalpel down in a practiced movement at the collarbone of the left shoulder. He moved the knife quickly, using his right hand to smooth out the flesh. Swag knew that there'd be two cuts, one from each shoulder, then a longer one right down nearly to his equipment.

"What the . . ."

Swag looked up to meet Cranen's steady gaze. "What is it?"

The scalpel had come to an abrupt stop, after less than two inches.

Cranen brought the blade away from the small gaping incision.

"What is it?" Swag repeated.

Cranen didn't answer; rather, he moved the scalpel down, just above the pubic bone, and began to cut. The blade came up an inch then stopped.

"What is it?" Swag asked again.

"Don't know, never saw anything like it," Cranen replied, stepping back from the corpse. "You say he was shot at close range?"

"Close enough."

Cranen moved forward and began cutting again, this time using a lighter stroke. Swag watched as the pathologist pulled back the skin to reveal the implants. Between the man's skin and muscle was a tight dark green mesh, from well below his belt line to high up on his chest. It was divided into symmetrical sections, like the underside of a turtle.

"Kevlar?" Swag whispered.

"Or something like it."

The two men stared at the green implanted mesh. Behind them the redhead lifted himself from the chair and walked from the room. Neither Swag nor Cranen noticed.

Finally, with a slightly shaking hand, Cranen folded back the two flaps of skin, smoothing them into place as best he could. "Leave," he said, pulling the sheet back over the corpse.

Swag looked up at him.

Cranen switched off the light then peeled off the gloves. "You heard me, get the fuck out," he said. He wasn't mad, he was scared. He was as frightened as any man who has spent twenty years cutting into bodies could get. Nothing Swag could threaten him with could scare him more.

"What, what is it?"

"I don't know who these people were," Cranen said, walking away. "I don't want to know. I just want you out of here. Whatever you're into with this, it's out of my league."

Swag was halfway down the long tiled hall when the two orderlies came off the elevator. They were wheeling a gurney with a body bag strapped to it. Both were laughing, kidding around at the end of a long shift.

Moving out in front of the gurney, Swag offered the two white-suited attendants the best smile he could and bummed a cigarette. As the orderly raised a lighter to the cigarette, Swag said, "Long night, huh?"

"You got no idea," one said. "*Beaucoup* pickups, running our asses all over town, and this crazy floater." The orderly patted the black plastic affectionately where the leg was. "Every day they get dumber and dumber."

"How's that?" Swag asked, curious now.

"This sorry sack of shit wants to off himself, right?"

"Happens," Swag said, inhaling a lungful of smoke.

The other began now. "So he kneecaps himself, then jumps in the river."

"Can you imagine?" the first put in.

Swag froze there, the tiles seeming to shift in front of him as he remembered shooting out Johnny G.'s kneecap. "You said 'kneecaps himself,' right?"

"Yeah, so what?" the first said, edging the gurney forward, running it into Swag's leg.

"Let me see him?" Swag said, reaching for the zipper on the front of the bag.

The first said, "See him? Hey man, this ain't that kind of place. Go buy a ticket to the museum."

"Let me see the damn stiff," Swag said, pulling the zipper down. "I think I know him."

Swag only had to pull it down eight inches or so to see Johnny G. staring up at him, worse for the wear and tear of East River water.

"So, you got a name for him?" the first orderly asked.

"How you know he did himself?" Swag asked back.

"Detectives found a note in his pocket, sealed in an aspirin bottle. You know him or what?"

"No," Swag said, moving out of the way. "Never seen him before."

chapter seven

THE NEXT DAY was hot, maybe even hotter than the previous one. Moist air drifted in from the ocean and hung over the city like a load of wet laundry. It was the kind of day that cops hated. Not even noon and the temperature was pushing eighty. When it got hot like this, the kids screamed just a little louder. Wives were just a little more shrill. And husbands became bigger assholes. Swag knew that the heat always bumped the statistics up a notch. By night the precincts and hospitals would be filled with the statistics bleeding over the floors.

Swag's Hawaiian shirt was sticking to his back by the time he reached the corner. His pants seemed loose, but it didn't surprise him. They'd been fitted for a gun he no longer had, but he was about to remedy the situation.

Flagging a taxi down on Second Avenue, he slid into the back seat, feeling his shirt attaching itself to the already sweat-slick vinyl.

The taxi ride downtown didn't help the heat much, and neither did the driver. He was one of the chatty types who was still taking his cues about New York cabbies from old movies. Maybe he was popular with the tourists. The French, it was said, adored Jerry Lewis. The driver hadn't gone two blocks before he starting talking about the weather, opening with the timeless "Hot 'nough for ya, pal?" then easing into "It ain't the heat, it's the stupidity." When Swag didn't laugh, the cabbie waited a few blocks, marking time by talking sports, and then repeated it. By the time they crossed 34th Street, he'd said it twice more, determined to get a reaction.

"That's a good one," Swag finally offered. And the cabbie laughed, and didn't repeat it again.

Stepping from the car on the corner of East Tenth Street and Avenue A, he surveyed the scene. What was once the New York Boys Club was now a provisional police station. The street was nearly deserted except for a few kids drinking beer and leaning against the shell of an abandoned car. There were two boys and a girl. The girl kept saying, "It's too hot, it's too hot," and danced away as the boys tried to grab her.

This was the tattered edge. Across Avenue A, the buildings, even the government-built projects, had begun to crumble into themselves. The streetlights were permanently darkened. Fewer and fewer people were to be found. A handful of political extremist factions fought nightly over the falling-down buildings, trying to expand their territory east and west. They organized house-to-house battles at night, liberating the five- and six-floor walk-up tenements with their sooty facades and railroad-flat apartments. They stormed the narrow entranceways, clattered up rusting fire escapes, and launched campaigns across tarpaper rooftops. They were like children, playing at war.

The groups formed uneasy alliances among themselves. But no sooner would the sporadic gunfire end in a minor victory than they'd splinter off into more extreme groups. At one time, announcements of battles in this part of town had been dutifully faxed or phoned in to the newspapers and television stations. Rebels wearing bandannas across their faces took time out for interviews in which they launched into long diatribes on Marx, Engels, and McDonald's. At first the provosts had deemed those fighters a security threat, but then Bammer realized that their airtime fell off when the public's interest in them waned, and besides, they only killed one another.

But the kids were what scared Swag the most. They

weren't even like kids anymore. They crawled out from under the jagged edge of plywood boarding of some sky-scraper squat and worked the street all day at a thousand hustles that could put food in their stomachs. Tough little bastards, the street was all they knew. Their uniform was ragged gimme T-shirts, baggy German jeans, and plastic shoes. They carried butterfly knives or homemade shivs wrapped in wire or tape. There were legions of them, and every single one had the same flat dead eyes that sent a cold chill through Swag. And grim. They were all as serious as death on a bad day. In ten or twelve years, maybe sooner, they'd own the street.

Halfway up the block, toward First Avenue, Swag cut down a short flight of stairs and rang the buzzer next to the cracked wooden door of a basement apartment. Bolted to the other side of the door, he knew, was two-inch-thick steel plating. The windows to his left, beyond a tight row of steel bars, were painted red and yellow, the paint peeling away from the thick Lexguard ballistic glass.

When he got no answer, he rang the buzzer again. Something clicked into place at the center of the door, and Swag shifted slightly so that his face was aligned with the peep-hole. After a slight pause, the door buzzed open and Swag stepped inside. The big man was already walking away by the time Swag swung the heavy door shut.

Longford was an easy six-six, though it would be hard to measure because he walked, sat, and probably slept in a marked stoop. His close-cropped hair was gray, the color of burnished steel. Swag had never seen him wear anything but his green workshirt and matching pants. They were more than just a little too short in the legs and sleeves, but were crisply pressed, like a uniform.

Swag followed the hulking shape down the narrow hall and through another steel-reinforced door. The inside of the basement apartment was cool. Longford wasn't one to deny himself anything. Somewhere there would be a great beast of an air conditioner churning away, its power drawn from the provisional NYPD headquarters up the street.

Behind the second door was the shocker, a brightly lit room, as clean as an operating theater.

One entire wall of the room was taken up by a long workbench. It was three-inch butcher block, with two one-foot squares of steel inlaid into it, along with three drill presses, a lathe, two vises, and a large sander. On the wall above the workbench there couldn't have been less than two or three hundred files, punches, reams, hacksaws, chisels, and hammers. They were arranged on the wall with such precision it looked as if Longford had used a micrometer. Under the table were a dozen identical steel tool chests. No doubt their contents were laid out with equal care.

Next to the bench were a half-dozen gray metal tanks up on racks, each over its own neat line of gas jets.

Swag was grateful that Longford wasn't bluing or finishing. The room would stink then, with the heated chemicals sending off fumes that could crush your eyeballs, despite an elaborate ventilation system. The remaining walls were covered with books. Hundreds of books all written on one subject—guns.

There were two other rooms, both smaller. One was filled with handloading equipment. The primer hand tools and the single stage and progressive presses, with their empty tanks above them, were arranged in a tight row beneath two full shelves of loading manuals, two digital scales, and long rows of Winchester, Hercules, and Accurate powders. A long line of neat drawers were filled with bullets. Along the opposite wall ran a steel trough, twenty-five feet long, that Longford used as a test range.

Swag knew that Longford slept in the third and smallest room. This room, barely larger than a closet, held only a bed.

By the time Swag came in through the workroom door, Longford had already reseated himself in an armless swivel chair and was leaning over the workbench. As Swag walked closer, he could see that the big man was working on a pistol's takedown lever, his large hands gently filing along its smooth surface. The remainder of the gun lay disassembled to the side.

"I lost the Browning, Long," Swag said.

The slight filing sound stopped, Longford's big fingers still poised above the small part. Through the material of the big man's shirt, Swag could see the muscles in his back visibly tense under the dark green shirt.

"You lost the Browning," Longford said without emotion. Long was a man unaccustomed to speaking; Swag had never heard him speak about anything but guns, let alone idle chatter. He was a man whose fingers did all the talking for him.

Longford carefully set the file down and turned to face Swag with that long, basset-hound face. "The Hi-Power."

"Yes, the Browning," Swag said.

"And you lost it," Longford answered, now rubbing the bridge of his nose with two fingers. "The one I made for you?"

"I said yes," Swag replied. Suddenly he felt like a schoolboy sent to the principal's office.

"The one with the custom sights, beveled magazine, ambidextrous safety, ported chamber, ultralight alloy slide, titanium and fiber trigger at, uh, three pounds." Longford had customized maybe a thousand guns in his life, and he remembered every one.

"I seem to remember that being the one," Swag said. He felt more ashamed now; Longford had put a lot of work into that old Browning. In another age they would have called the big man an artisan. Maybe he'd be building clocks or furniture, Swag thought, something that did more than punch holes in people.

"That's a shame," Longford said sadly. "It was a beautiful weapon. May I ask who is in possession of it now?"

"The police," Swag answered.

From under the big man's heavy lidded eyes a glimmer of hope flashed. "Ah, perhaps you can buy it back?"

"Went into evidence at precinct level," Swag said. "Probably back on the street in a service holster."

The faint hope faded in an instant. "Clanging against a baton and mace cans, no doubt," came the sad answer. "Thrown into a damp locker after the shift."

Swag thought it better to change the subject, before Longford became too morose to do business. "I need another one," he said.

"Another Hi-Power?" the big man replied. "Two months, maybe three. They're a lot of work."

"What do you have out of the box, Long? I need a piece."

Longford shifted nervously in his chair, a look of obvious annoyance crawling over his face, tightening the loose bunches of muscles. Swag would have sworn that he saw the gunsmith shudder. "Out of the box, did you say?"

"Well, maybe a touch here and there," Swag answered quickly. "But something I can be proud to own." He was playing to the big man's vanity now. Longford was a strange one, for sure. Nobody knew where he came from. He just sort of appeared one day, as everyone in New York does. Soon word was spreading that there was a guy downtown, turning out the best iron in town, maybe even in the world.

"There is something that may be your style," he said. Lifting his great bulk from the chair, he walked heavily into the adjoining room. When he returned, he was carrying an automatic. He held it two-handed, at the top of the slide, offering it to Swag.

Swag took the gun and hefted its weight. Like the Browning, it was perfectly balanced, its weight seeking the center of his hand. Also like the Browning, all traces of factory stamping, right down to the trademark triangle and Colt logo on its side, had been thoroughly erased. "What is it?" Swag asked, "Colt Delta?"

"That's the way it began life," Longford said, "a Colt Delta Elite 1911." He took a step closer. "You've got a rebeveled magazine well; custom three-point sighting; aluminum and steel trigger, three-pound pull; lowered and flared ejection port; and a recrowned barrel."

"See that, almost right out of the box," Swag said, pulling the slide back and testing the action.

"There's also a new recoil spring, and I replaced the recoil buffer," Longford said. "Out of the box, you get a plastic buffer."

Swag didn't answer; he was busy moving the red-tipped sights along the wall of the gunsmithing tools. Then he released the magazine, saw that it was indeed empty, and snapped it back.

"There's some modification on the hammer, makes it lighter, and I clipped the coils from the magazine release spring for speed," Longford continued. "The feeder's been polished and treated. There's a new custom sear, and I removed the hammer and magazine safeties. You don't need them, do you?"

"Naw," Swag said, feeling more than a little uneasy at this. "Never use them."

"I didn't think so," Longford said without a trace of humor in his voice. "But try to avoid dropping it, please."

"Anything else?" Swag asked, sighting again along the wall. He racked the slide and dry-fired at the wall. The action was smooth through the entire throw.

"Well, those neoprene grips, they're new."

Swag lowered the gun. He knew Longford wasn't running through the modifications to jack him around on price. It was a matter of pride. "Anything else?" he asked.

"One more thing," Longford said, gently taking back the pistol and releasing the magazine. "The magazine, it's custom, holds nine rounds, 10mm, .40 caliber, not eight."

"You have the ammunition?" Swag asked.

Longford didn't answer, rather he walked, hunch-shouldered, into another room. When he returned, he held a small plastic box of cartridges. "These are eleven grains of number seven with a 180-grain jacketed hollowpoint," Longford said. "They're hot loads, but you'll hit what you aim at."

Swag removed one of the cartridges and turned it over

in his fingers. "Will it go through a vest?" he asked, thinking now of the dark suit.

"Probably not," Longford answered. "Not the new twenty-six layer ones."

"What will?"

"For the ten?" Longford asked, then answered his own question. "Teflon will penetrate. Glasers will, if you want to shoot plastic. Full metal jackets and a hotter load, but you'll be trading for accuracy. And providence doesn't shine on those who overload."

It was the first nearly human thing Swag had ever heard Longford say. "'Providence doesn't shine,' Long?"

"No it doesn't," Longford replied, falling back into the robot routine. "You can't have the ten if you intend to ruin it."

Swag took the ten, the ammo, an extra magazine, and an inside-the-pants custom holster. He wasn't sure if providence would shine on him, but something better, because the gun nearly wiped him out. He needed cash, and he needed it soon. Even with a long trial date, there was a lawyer to hire.

"You can take care of the paperwork on this," Swag asked, turning to go. "I want it street legal."

"Consider it done," Longford replied, moving back to his workbench.

As he stepped out of Longford's place he came up the stairs to see that four boys had joined the original two drinking beer against the side of the car. The girl had taken off her shirt to reveal a kind of halter underneath. She was still taking sips off the boys' beer and dancing around, happy to be the center of attention. If she wasn't careful, she'd end as a headline.

It started very much like the beginning of an old and not terribly funny joke. "You see, these two guys walk into a bar and sit down . . ."

They were both wearing dark suits.

When the bartender asked them what it'd be, they both

said soda, and he charged them four francs apiece, hoping to get them out fast. But they ordered two more, and two more. And all the time they tipped well, maybe even a little too well.

"Say," the bartender said, leaning over the mahogany, "we don't get many of your kind in here."

"No," one of the dark suits answered.

"And at these prices, it's not surprising," the other said.

"What exactly is your kind, anyway?" the bartender asked.

They could have been cops, looking to bust him. But somehow the bartender didn't think so. He'd been dealing black-market cigarettes, fencing boosted appliances, and changing money for so long, he could spot a cop half a block away. And anyway, these guys had kind of a funny accent.

"We're businessmen," the first one said.

The conversation was interrupted when one of the bartender's steady clients came through the door, spotted the two suits and took off in a determined and patently felonious walk. The fact that he was carrying three German-made toaster ovens stacked in his arms didn't bespeak legitimacy either.

The bartender, casting a worried look of loss at the door, said, "Businessmen, huh? What kind of business are you in, exactly?"

"Yours," the first dark suit answered. "We would like to buy this bar."

"Sorry, but it ain't for sale."

"You are the owner, then, Mr. Douglas Dresh?" the second guy said, smiling.

"Hey, who wants to know? Just who the fuck are you guys to come in here and start askin' questions, huh?"

"We represent your new partners, Mr. Dresh," the second dark suit said.

"What the fuck are you talkin' about, partners? Gimme a break, huh," Dresh answered. "Who sent you around, those Italian scumbags? Tell them this ain't 'seventy-eight no more." He was leaning over the bar, both hands flat against the wood, getting right in the first dark suit's face. But the guy held his ground, not leaning back on the stool so much as a centimeter.

"Mr. Dresh, you will pay ten percent of the gross proceeds of all black-market and stolen goods transactions to an account whose number we will provide. Wire transfers will be made in amounts not totaling over twenty-five thousand dollars."

The bartender was smiling now, a nasty stony smile filled with bad teeth and gray gums. "You guys have to be kiddin'," he said, leaning farther over the bar. "What kind of lame, half-assed shakedown is this?"

"Mr. Dresh, we are sincere, please believe that," the first guy said. As he spoke he took hold of Dresh's wrist. At first it seemed like a kind of pleading for sincerity, until the bartender realized that he couldn't move his hand up off the bar.

"Do you understand, Mr. Dresh, ten percent," the second guy said then.

Dresh tried to pull his hand up off the bar again, using the other to help, but he couldn't budge it. He was about to swing on the guy, when the other one brought out a seven-inch Tanto knife and plunged it through the back of Dresh's hand, pinning him to the wood.

Dresh screamed then, feeling his knees go weak as he tried to move his other hand. But the other hand wouldn't come up from the bar; there was a big meaty hand pinning it to the blood-soaked mahogany. And there was a Glock 9 pushing his chin up.

"Is it clear to you what we want, Mr. Dresh?" the first guy said.

"Yeah, yeah, it's clear." His voice rasped.

"Then it's a deal?" the second guy said, pulling the knife from the bar and ruined hand and wiping the blade across Dresh's jowly cheek.

With the Glock still touching his chin, Dresh grabbed

a bar rag and wrapped it around his hand. "It's a deal, okay? Ten percent?"

The first dark suit pulled the gun slowly away, then placed a business card on the bar, far away from the widening flow of blood. "Understand, we do not expect full cooperation immediately," he said. "These things, we know, take time. Relationships must, what is the word, mature?"

"Sure, we'll be pals in a couple of weeks," Dresh answered bitterly, fighting through the pain. Looking down, he could make out the name of the company, Euro-Zeitech, S.A. The number listed was a Swiss bank on Grand Cayman Island.

"Understand, we must be certain there is no misunderstanding," one of the dark suits said.

Dresh lifted his eyes from the card. "Come up to the house Sunday, we'll have a couple 'a beers and watch a Jap golf tournament."

The first dark suit seemed not to hear him. "But you must ask yourself some questions before you think of fighting us, no?"

"Yeah, and what would that be?" Dresh asked as he examined the bloody rag.

"You must ask yourself this," the first guy continued, "is your son, who is nine and attends P.S. 129, and your wife, who is forty-one but says she is thirty-nine, worth ten percent?"

The black Mercedes limo was sitting in front of the Carlyle Hotel when one of its two phones buzzed.

The driver, picking up the handset, gingerly said, "Yes. Very good." Then he replaced the receiver on its cradle and buzzed down the partition.

In the backseat a well-dressed man with nearly white hair was holding what looked like a platinum pen between the fingertips of both hands. When he gave the cylinder a half turn, a small jade fish rose from the center of the one end. The man held the cylinder to his mouth and pushed down on the top of the fish briefly, sending a nearly imperceptible mist from the jade figurine's mouth into his own. He then turned the cylinder again, and the green fish vanished into its platinum case.

"Alpha Team just checked in, no substantial resistance from the target—a saloon owner named Dresh. We're on schedule," the driver said as he hung up the phone. "They have a half-dozen more meetings today."

"And the others?" the gray-haired passenger asked.

"They're in the field, all twelve teams," the driver answered. "All on schedule. By the end of the month crime will pay ten percent less."

The passenger seemed not to hear this last comment. "Keep contact with the Fishers comm center. I don't have to tell you that I'd be interested in knowing of any communications regarding the operation on the police or provost bands," he replied dryly. "Likewise, I'd like a hardcopy of any related reports that go into their computer systems. Add hospital records to that if possible."

The driver nodded, not needing to make a note. Then he turned, just in time to see the gray-haired passenger once again administer a spray from the cylinder into his mouth. "You do too much of that shit," the driver said.

A look of mild annoyance spread over the gray-haired man's face, then he felt the first tingle at his lips and tongue. As he sat back in the seat, a warm flush rushed through him in the air-conditioned interior of the car. It was very much like a charge of adrenaline. His chest tightened slightly and the burled grain of the car's maple trip came into sharper focus. As he put the platinum receptacle away, a private euphoric smile crossed his face.

"You know nothing about it, Roger," the man said, amused.

"I know you do up enough to keep Tokyo stoned for a month," the driver replied.

"They have a saying, you know," the gray-haired guy said mildly. "Those who eat fugu are stupid, but those who don't eat fugu are also stupid."

"But what you're doing is synthetic," the driver said. "About as close to puffer fish as an aspirin."

"Yes, a poor substitute, indeed," the gray-haired guy conceded. "When we get to Japan, I'll take you to the best *chiri* chef in the world."

"No thanks," the driver replied. "I don't like playing Russian roulette with half-cooked fish liver."

"That's the difference between you and I, Roger," the gray-haired guy said, then opened the car door and left.

The driver watched his gray-haired employer walk into the lobby through the car's tinted glass, and thought: That isn't the only difference, boyo. I didn't lose a cornea, kidney, a shitload of bone marrow and both balls at some Monte Carlo baccarat table.

chapter eight

RAFFLES WAS A NEW hotel, built by British money to replace the one in Singapore that they lost to the government there. The owners had spared no expense to imbue it with that unique brand of clubby elegance that history books told them was popular a hundred years before. To this end the developers had leveled nearly a full block on Park and 53rd, then erected the four-story thing. They built it to look old, then filled it with first-rate replicas and second-rate works of original art dating back to the Edwardian era. The imported staff of service personnel was urged, under penalty of dismissal, to yield neither British accents nor manners and to refer to America, if at all possible, as "the colonies." The idea was to out-Connaught the Connaught.

The tourists, particularly those from Britain, enjoyed it all immensely.

The only position of importance held by an American was, oddly enough, that of Senior Guest Representative. To reach Lucas Lancaster one had to inquire at the front desk, then walk across the marbled floor to where the concierge stood guard behind an Edwardian writing desk, and then ask for Lancaster again. The concierge would then "ring up the assistant manager," who would meet Mr. Lancaster's visitor at the front desk. The assistant manager would then ever so politely inquire as to the nature of one's business with Mr. Lancaster. If one gave a suitably vague response, then the concierge would be required to "ring up Mr. Lancaster directly."

Swag had seen Lancaster maybe thirty times, and the entire ritual never varied, despite the fact that Lancaster had never once refused a visit from the ex-cop.

Now, as Swag followed the blue-suited concierge down the long paneled hall to the staff elevator, he decided to broach the subject. "You remember me, don't you?" he asked.

"Sir?" the concierge replied.

"Look, Jeeves, every time I come in here, you bust my balls. What is it?"

The concierge began, "Sir, I would never presume to . . ."

Then Swag broke in with, "Bullshit, Jeeves."

". . . cause one any undue discomfort."

When they arrived at the elevator, the concierge pressed the button but remained standing next to Swag.

"So what's your story, Jeeves, huh?" Far from being the proper English servant, a little bit of nastiness was leaking from the concierge. Swag could almost smell it. Maybe it was the way he stood, perfectly still, feet just so far apart, his center of gravity not up in his chest, but bunched down much lower. It was a brawler's stance. Or maybe it was the set of his mouth, which was crooked, like the jagged end of a broken bottle.

Then the elevator door opened before the concierge could answer, and the attendant took them both down.

They went to a basement sublevel and walked a corridor of unpainted cinderblock walls and dropped fluorescent lighting to a gray steel door. The concierge punched the number for the combination lock and ushered Swag in.

Inside, a half-dozen women sat at terminals. The terminals were split screen, allowing the women to monitor guest bills, then to enter debit requests directly from European banks. The money, like that reaped at most of the foreign hotels, never flowed across the Atlantic. Rather, it was deposited directly into the hotel's home country account.

Often, Swag knew, the guests' accounts were prepaid tours with additional escrow funds set aside specifically for an American holiday. The idea was to bring as little money as possible "across the pond."

Behind the double line of typists was another portal. The concierge knocked softly before opening the door and presenting Swag to Lucas Lancaster, who just then was sitting behind a desk saying, "No, I said 'Wykeham caning.' No, it's not a person's name, it's a school." Then, taking notice of Swag, Lancaster held up one finger. He'd be off in a minute. "No, a public school. He wants to be spanked. Do you understand now? Spanked with a headmaster's cane?"

Lucas Lancaster had the intense dark eyes and pale skin that came from having an Irish father and an Italian mother. And he had the street smarts of someone who dropped out of high school in the eleventh grade and made good. The day after he quit school, he took the F train from Brooklyn to Manhattan. For a week he walked the streets figuring out who had the money and where they went. He took a job polishing the brass awning posts in front of a Fifth Avenue apartment building. It was in this job that he learned the manners of the rich.

Later he changed his name to Lucas Lancaster and discovered his special talent: finding anything anybody could want in New York. His understanding of the world, that everyone is on the hustle, was also particularly appealing to European concerns whose home-grown staff was known to fall over themselves needlessly at the sight of an old name or worthless title.

Lancaster dropped the finger and began playing with a crystal paperweight, testing its heft. "No," he continued, "I don't give a damn what they did at P.S. 124. Look, honey, you're the pro, just use your best judgment, okay?"

And then Lancaster was off the phone, motioning for Swag to come farther into the oak-paneled office. As the concierge retreated, Swag heard the man say "Bloody fookin' arsehole," the accent moving, for just a second, from Mayfair's Berkeley Square to the Liverpool docks.

Lancaster raised an eyebrow, motioning Swag into a facing chair. "Don't fuck with my concierge, Swag," he said, clearing a portion of desk in front of him of papers. "That's one mean tea bag."

"Where'd you find him?"

"Don't look at me," Lancaster replied, holding his hands up. "Some of the London boys found him. Former SAS out of Belfast. Dishonorably discharged, or whatever they do when they show you the bricks."

"What'd he do?"

"The way the home office phrased it was 'overzealous,'" Lancaster explained. "Guy's one cup short of a place setting."

Swag leaned slightly forward, studying Lancaster. "What do you use him for?"

"Haven't decided yet," Lancaster said, now sifting through papers. "Just so long as he doesn't start whacking out guests, I'll be happy."

Swag didn't know how to approach the subject, so he began dancing around it. "Business pretty good, huh?"

Lancaster smiled broadly; business was obviously good.

"Shit, you work in this place long enough, it makes you want to put a title in front of your name, a number after it, and marry a cousin. They got me wearing double-breasted suits. Dunhill, ya like it?"

Swag knew that Lancaster wasn't going to cut him any slack; he'd have to come out and say it. "I need an assignment," he said.

Lancaster stopped fiddling with the monogrammed buttons of his suitcoat and laid his hands neatly across the nearly empty desk. "I thought you were booked at the Plaza?"

"My schedule opened up," Swag answered. "You have anything?"

Lancaster gave Swag a long hard look that had ten miles of tough Brooklyn street smarts in it. "Opened up, huh?" he said. "That little trophy with her brains scattered across Fifth Avenue wouldn't have been yours?"

"She was a two-week job," Swag said.

"And what did it last? Twenty minutes?"

"Maybe a little more," Swag answered. "But I won't be sending in a bill."

"No references from the family either, I bet," Lancaster replied with a chuckle. Then he turned serious. "What was the deal there?"

"What'd you hear?"

"Just what I read in the papers," Lancaster lied. He was the type who got his news from every source in town, except the papers. "Wife of prominent Swiss banker gunned down by unknown assailant. That it was the 123rd robbery murder in the last two months. How it was bad for tourist business, but a fluke. And the police are investigating, arrests are expected soon. You know, usual bullshit."

"What'd you hear about the shooter?"

"Papers said he got away," Lancaster answered, a slight smile opening across his perfectly capped teeth. "Then there's a rumor that he had an accident. Up on what, 63rd and Madison?"

Swag took a cigarette from his pocket and lit it with a lighter off Lancaster's desk. "It was a hit," Swag said, blowing smoke up to the air vent.

This bit of news seemed to take Lancaster by surprise. "Bullshit, who hits a thirty-five-year-old third wife?"

Swag thought on this before answering. "A forty-two-year-old second wife?"

"Or a husband, huh?" Lancaster mused quietly.

"What'd you know about him?" Swag asked.

"Ziggy Lorette?" Lancaster answered, as if the question were way out of left field.

"That's the husband's name, Ziggy?"

"Sigmund, officially," Lancaster corrected. "German-Swiss, lives in Zurich. He's fifty-five or -six, third or fourth generation of an old Swiss banking family. There was money going way back, but more, a lot more, after World War Two. They say his old man, Ziggy Senior, had a nice little sideline going. Kind of a delivery service over the Alps."

"For which side?" Swag asked, amazed at Lancaster's knowledge.

"What do you mean, which side?" Lancaster asked, annoyed. "It's after a war, so you got English, Americans, Russians, and the French running around liberating everything that isn't tied down. Then you got the Gestapo fucks who would've stolen a hot stove then come back for the smoke. And being neutral—"

"What about Ziggy Junior?" Swag asked, clearly impressed, but tired of the history lesson. "He dirty?"

"The apple doesn't fall far from the tree, does it?"

"I asked if he's dirty," Swag said, not caring now if he blew the chance for an assignment.

"Word has it that Junior ain't none too bright," Lancaster said. "He has a plant in Italy, makes bathroom tile. Owns a piece of a fast-food chain in France. Telecommunications in Portugal. You know, Common Market stuff, but spread out, under one holding company, Lorette-Defour."

"Amazing," Swag said.

"What?" Lucas said, smiling. "Typical bullshit."

"That you know it," Swag answered.

"Yeah, well, like I said, he plays fast and loose," Lancaster continued, shaking off the compliment. "And he's got expensive tastes, less one, if you count yesterday. But he's a player."

Swag leaned slightly over the desk, bringing the cigarette out of his mouth. "What's he moving, under the table?"

"The only thing left," Lancaster said with a smile. "Money. He moves money around. The kind of money that you don't want anybody to know you've got. Third world paper, American dollars, and easies." The street slang for European currency—easies—sounded strange coming from Lancaster.

Swag stubbed out the cigarette and rose from the chair, thinking.

"Hey, what about the assignment you came in for?" Lancaster called when Swag was nearly to the door.

Turning, Swag said, "You got anything?"

"Look, Swag, give it a couple of days, just until the fortnight tour cycle's through," came the smiling answer. "I'll fix you up, okay?"

This was a patent lie that Lancaster wasn't doing anything to conceal, which meant Swag couldn't even question it. But a couple of weeks would be enough time to check out Swag's story. If it was a hit, then perhaps Swag couldn't be faulted; *anybody can flake anybody.* But if it was a random occurrence, then maybe Swag was slipping. And, as Lancaster well knew, dead guests were bad business, even when you were running an eighty percent occupancy rate.

Two men in dark suits entered the Little Flower Restaurant in Chinatown at exactly two in the afternoon. One had a meticulously trimmed head of hair and calm features. The other had hair cropped so close, his head resembled a well-tanned skull. His eyes, which were slightly sunken, moved mechanically around the room.

It wasn't often that anglos ventured into the place, and then the service and quality of the food was such that the same ones never returned.

It was a basement restaurant and the two men had to negotiate four steps to reach its door. They walked past three customers, who sat near the door reading Chinese newspapers—and walked directly to the older man at the back table.

The two men bowed to the old man, who was fat and wore a plaid cotton shirt and black pants. And then, oddly, one of the dark suits began speaking in perfect Cantonese.

The three men near the door turned and rose, but the old man pushed them back into their seats with a slight motion of his hand. Then, with the same hand, he motioned the two visitors to sit.

When one of the dark suits began speaking again, it was in hushed reverential tones. The old man's eyes opened wide. When his mouth came open in anger to say something, the speaker pointed to the front window, where the legs of two more dark-suited men were visible.

The three customers up near the door were openly staring now. It had been years since Chow Chi had dealings with Americans, and then, those were Italians from across Canal Street. And these, definitely, were not Italians.

When the old man made to rise again, the dark suit said something else, and looked at the gold watch on his wrist. It was 2:05. Four blocks away a bomb exploded in a basement gambling parlor, killing thirty-four gamblers and employees. The explosion was so strong that it blew the reinforced steel door up the narrow stairway, across the street, and through the window of a Hunan restaurant.

The old man did not hear the explosion.

By the time the man in the dark suit began speaking again, three men, feeding currency through an automatic bill counter, were instantly killed and the money destroyed when another bomb in the back of their import/export storefront on Catherine Street detonated in a fiery explosion that killed three passersby with shattered glass.

The old man turned white when the sound came through the humming of the restaurant's air conditioner as a hollow thud. Chow Chi was about to say something, but the dark suit beat him to the punch. Looking at his watch again, he informed the old man in the most respectful manner that a Beemer with three of his young enforcers, ranking members of the Ghost Shadow gang, had just been ambushed in Queens. All three teens were dead.

The old man sat there, hands on the red and white checkered table, listening to this anglo speaking in flawless Cantonese. The anglo spoke quietly, like a teacher, paraphrasing a parable of the Chinese philosopher Chuang-tzu. "The king keeps a sacred tortoise wrapped in cloth, in a box in the temple. She has been dead for three thousand years," he said, his words coming patiently in the singsong Cantonese. "Would this tortoise have rather died and left behind her bones to be held in honor? Or would she have rather lived and trailed her tail in the mud?"

The old man stared at the anglo for a long time, not speaking. It was an imperfect parable for what the anglo was asking. He had known the answer from earliest childhood, yet he did not reply. His reply, the one the anglo wanted, was meant to shame him. Yet, what were they offering him, peace in exchange for money? The very idea was nearly laughable, as if he were a timid shopkeeper.

Somewhere far off a phone was ringing.

When the skinny cook appeared, he was holding a cordless phone, which he handed to the old man. The old man listened intently, his eyes widening, then narrowing in grief as he heard the news of his son and grandson's death in the explosion.

The dark suit nodded in sympathy, as if he were about to order up flowers and march in the funeral procession.

"Go away. I will trail my tail in the mud," the old man said quietly, finishing the parable.

The anglo nodded again, slowly, then reached into his pocket and produced a business card with a number for a Cayman Island banker. He rose then and bowed respectfully in his leave taking. By the time the two men reached the door, all four telephone lines of the Little Flower Restaurant were ringing.

chapter nine

COLONEL MORTIMER BAMMER SAT at his customary table in the Oak Room of the Plaza Hotel, staring at his own image on page three of the *Post*. The picture was that of himself and five enlisted men, conducting a house-to-house on 128th and Lenox Avenue. He was out in front of the small group, wearing neatly pressed fatigues, while the enlisted men followed, their faces obscured by Lexan visors, their bodies bulked out by the weight of armor-plated vests. Contributing to the contrast was the old Dan Wesson .44 Mag. that Bammer held at shoulder level. The old wheel gun set him off nicely from the futuristic Steyr rifles the enlisted men carried.

LAW EAST OF THE HUDSON, the headline read. Never mind that the colonel had arrived after the actual search and never entered a single building. Going into a building up there was worth your life. Forget about some lunatic with a gun, those places were breeding grounds for TB.

But that didn't matter, the photo op was what mattered. Bammer's private creed had always been, "Heroics make dead men. Pictures make heroes."

Studying the newsprint photograph more carefully, he thought that he looked a bit like Westmoreland in the early years. Then he thought, no. But goddamn if he didn't look like Patton—and not that tired George C. Scott Patton either, but the genuine Blood and Guts article. The kind of guy who could even make a bit of a paunch seem dangerous.

Colonel Bammer's military bearing was part of a carefully cultivated style that photographed and taped well. And he enjoyed seeing his own image staring pointedly away or engagingly toward the lenses of newspaper and video cameras. The firm chin, the unblinking steely eyes, the rigid posture, they had taken him far. *Right to the damned top.*

Of course, he knew what the enlisted men said about him. They said he used Preparation H for lip gloss. This he believed was merely the grunts' jealousy talking.

In the vaulted, dimly lit room, Bammer could hardly see the shadow that fell across his own printed image. But when he heard the dry cough, he slapped the paper down and jumped up suddenly to face his gray-haired guest.

"Colonel Bammer," the man said, nodding. It wasn't a question.

"Sir," Bammer replied in acknowledgment, now seeing that his visitor was not alone. Another, larger man with dirty-blond hair stood behind him, eyes moving steadily about the nearly empty room.

"So good of you to see me," the gray-haired guy said. "I appreciate the time you've taken out of your schedule."

As if I had a choice, Bammer thought. "No problem at all," he answered, aware that the guy was going to try and bullshit him from the jump.

A waiter appeared at the opposite end of the table, napkin folded over one arm. The gray-haired man smiled, moved lightly around the table, let the waiter pull out the chair, and sat with fluid ease. The waiter removed the artfully folded napkin and laid it across the gray-haired one's lap.

Bammer had chosen the Oak Room because it was intimidating. The darkly stained wood, the high ceilings and heavy silver made it more like a church than someplace to fill your stomach. But now he saw that his visitor was at ease in these surroundings, and knew he had a problem. He had felt the first alarms go off in his gut the minute he got the call. Even the name Catherwood sounded like trouble. Then there were the other calls—six of them—and all from Washington. "Extend Mr. Catherwood every courtesy," is what they said.

The waiter didn't travel to the other side of the table, and Bammer sat down and bounced his chair forward. "Nice place," he tried, putting on a smile. "And they tell me the grub isn't too bad either."

Catherwood offered only the slightest smile, then said, "Yes, so I've heard."

Bammer studied the visitor now, trying to offer the same slight smile back. But the guy must have been wearing five thousand francs' worth of clothes on his back, and he kept staring across the table with those two little, gray-green eyes. It was the eyes that got to Bammer. They were a cold gray, only slightly darker than the whites that surrounded them, and nearly the same color as his hair. And the face; it was totally impassive, maybe even a little bored. There wasn't a line on it. The guy must have been forty, but if he dyed his hair, he could have passed for twenty-five.

What the good colonel had no way of knowing was that his visitor was in fact blind in the left eye—the cornea long vanished into some Dutch clinic, replaced by plastic. The face too was not his own, rather the product of German surgeons. Not even the bored attitude was natural. Embedded beneath the skin of his upper arm, like contraceptive implants, were five silicon tubes that leaked a powerful dose of a psychoactive antidepressant, an experimental treatment to cure a gambling addiction.

"This is our latest operation," Bammer said, handing the paper across the table with considerable pride. "Not bad, huh, front page, right hand column."

Catherwood took the paper hesitantly, studied the photo of Bammer, then refolded the tabloid to reveal the headline: MORGUE DOC MURDERED, accompanied by another photo, of a dozen provost men combing Cranen's autopsy room for clues.

The colonel saw that the headline held Catherwood's

interest, and said, "Shame about the M.E. Looks like a black-market hit. We'll get the scumbags, the people who did it."

"Really," Catherwood answered, putting the paper down. "How, precisely, can you tell, about it being related to the black market?"

Bammer could sense Catherwood warming up, showing some interest. "Well, when we searched the office, my men found videotapes. 'Death tapes,' we call them. You know, for tourists. Death junkies."

"And there is a market, or should I say, audience, for such things?"

The guy had no accent, Bammer thought. It was a television voice. Too perfectly American to be real.

"Hell yes, a big one too," Bammer said loudly. "You wouldn't believe what he had in there. He had a tape that was supposed to be the Elvis autopsy. Real lame, some guy with a Bronx accent trying to put on like he was southern, going 'This is the King' and 'Gawd rest his immortal soul,' then slicing into some fat fuck with glued-on sideburns."

"Fascinating," Catherwood replied with a vague air of repulsion. If Colonel Bammer had been more attentive, he would have seen that the disdain was directed at him.

"That ain't all," Bammer continued. "We found names and numbers. You know, bio-chop shops from here to Baltimore. Garage clinics. Even a place that fences boosted hair. He was selling every-fucking-thing he could slice off, extract in a hypo, or put a saw to."

"Extraordinary," Catherwood said as he exhaled, then raised his glass to take a small sip of water. "It is reassuring to know you have the situation under control."

The colonel beamed happily. "One week, max, and whoever did that to the doc, his ass is mine."

"Reassuring indeed," Catherwood said.

"You bet," Bammer answered obediently. Then noting the bodyguard, he leaned forward, elbows on the table, toward Catherwood. "You don't need him here. You saw my two men just outside. Nobody without a reservation or a damned good reason gets past them."

Roger, arms folded across his chest, twisted his mouth into a small smirk as his eyes continued to scan the room.

Catherwood looked up at his bodyguard, knowing that the man's fingers were centimeters from the Seecamp auto-pistol slung under one arm or the Walther P-38 under the other. Before Bammer's men had flipped their safeties off, Roger could have killed every living thing in the dining room.

"Roger here," Catherwood began, almost apologetically, "he's more of a driver than a bodyguard. But he's coming along nicely. Isn't that so, Roger?"

"Yes sir, Mr. C.," Roger answered, not breaking the rhythm of his sweeping gaze. If Catherwood had the blank voice of a television announcer, then Roger's was that of a machine. It was the voice at the other end of the telephone that told you the line had been disconnected.

"Jeez, a driver," Bammer said. Even under the imitation Armani suit, Roger seemed better built than any driver Bammer had seen. His face was bland and tan beneath a good haircut, the eyes fixed in the middle distance, unblinking. "If you want, I'll assign a couple of men. Real pros, you know, I could dress them up nice for you."

Catherwood made eye contact with the waiter, who immediately started across the room. "That won't be necessary," Catherwood said. "Roger is wholly adequate. Isn't that right, Roger?"

"I try, sir," came the deadpan reply.

Two menus appeared. In recent years the Oak Room had expanded both its menu and its kitchen. Catherwood took his time studying the menu, concealing himself from the colonel behind the large leather cover. When he finally put the menu down, he turned his attention back to Bammer. "Now, please be so kind as to tell me about this Swag person."

"Him?" the colonel replied, more than a little taken aback. "He's a punk."

"I take it you don't hold him in high regard, then?"

"Fuck no, I mean, hell no," Bammer answered. "Swag's no big deal. He's one of those Oddjobs; the city's full of mutts like him. Just a tour guide, really, with a pistol. If he's breaking the law, we haven't caught him yet."

Catherwood focused his full attention on the colonel now. "And nothing distinguishes him from the others? I understand he was a police officer at one time."

"That's the rumor," Bammer answered, shifting uncomfortably. "He keeps a low profile. Except for his shirts. He wears those loud Hawaiian shirts."

"How interesting," Catherwood said. "I also understand that he's under indictment, waiting to stand trial."

This was a piece of news the colonel didn't know, but he decided to brazen it out. "That's the rumor."

You mean you don't know?"

"Mr. Catherwood," Bammer said, stiffening, "I have better things to do than keep track of every piece of scum moving through the system."

"Yes, indeed, Colonel," Catherwood said. "But it was my understanding that your department would provide full cooperation."

Bammer could feel whatever slight edge he thought he had slipping away, and he didn't like it. Not at all. Whatever Catherwood was, political hatchetman or just an errand boy with manners, he didn't want to give up a fucking thing to him. But here he was, sitting across the table from the little prick, who was staring at him with eyes the color of chipped tenement paint.

Finally Bammer said, "If Swag's in the system, I'll pull him. Deliver him up to you like room service."

Catherwood's face twitched with annoyance. "He is not, as you put it, 'in the system.'"

"If he's on the street, then it'll take longer," Bammer said. "How you want him? You want this guy in plastic?"

"I want him alive, Colonel," he said definitively.

Bammer tried to smile, but it didn't work. "Then you'll

have him alive, Mr. Catherwood. Alive and kicking. But tell me something. Why you so interested in this guy?"

Catherwood nodded slightly to the waiter, who started back across the room to take their orders. "No, I'm afraid that's restricted."

Bammer felt the hairs on the back of his neck rise at the word restricted. *Restricted from who, goddamnit?* Nothing was restricted from him. Not in his town! And not in his fucking hotel!

Bammer changed gears. "Some pretty impressive people called me, or at least their assistants did. Told me you were coming, told me I should grease the skids a bit. Get the lay of the land. Offer you every courtesy."

"I understand," Catherwood replied. "I'm grateful for their assistance. And for yours as well."

"Let me ask you something, are you a spook or what?"

The uniformed waiter stood by Catherwood's side, waiting for the conversation to end. "Hardly," Catherwood answered, his voice a good-natured half laugh. It was almost human, put on for the benefit of the waiter.

"You mind telling me exactly who it is you work for, then?"

Catherwood opened the menu again, reviewing it briefly. "Oh, I'm afraid you wouldn't know them, Colonel," he answered without looking up. "They're from California."

Across town two men, the president and executive vice-president of Reliable Toxic Industries, Inc., were shackled to the pillars of an ancient warehouse. They were the sole owners of a waste disposal company in Elizabeth, New Jersey. The company consisted of a hundred-by-two-hundred-foot lot, three ancient Peterbilts with milk tankers, and several broken-down Yale forklifts. The company specialized in waste placement, jobbing out hazardous chemicals to lots in Jersey City, Secaucus, and Newark. Most of the stuff they handled was French and Italian, which meant it was particularly *hot*. But they managed to bump the bottom line up by sending out tankers with twenty or fifty thousand gallons of the stuff on rainy days. Drivers were instructed to open the valves and drive south down the Turnpike or Route 1 & 9.

The two owners were tough Jersey boys and weren't afraid of showing it. And they stayed tough, claiming at one point to be "totally legitimate businessmen." They were tough right up to when they found themselves chained to the wall of the warehouse while two guys in dark suits slipped on new yellow slickers, the kind fishermen use.

When one of the men in yellow waterproof clothing fired up a plasma welder and pulled on a pair of goggles, the president began to reconsider the offer. By the time the other one lowered his goggles and pulled a machete from its canvas sheath, the offer seemed generous, and he said as much. So did his partner.

But the guys in yellow slickers couldn't be sure how sincere the two men were. What they did was begin on the president's face and let his partner watch. By the time they left the warehouse, Reliable Toxic Industries was solely owned by the vice-president and funded by a consortium of venture capitalists incorporated under the name Daimyo Enterprises, Ltd. Daimyo would allow operation of Reliable Toxic to continue as usual.

chapter ten

THE FRONT PAGE of the *Post* hit Swag like a fist between the eyes. He saw it at a newsstand on Lex a couple of blocks from Raffles. But he didn't buy the paper. He didn't need to read the story. It was enough to know that Cranen the M.E. was dead.

Losing a client was hard luck. Johnny G. turning up dead was coincidence, maybe. But Cranen getting whacked crossed the line into paranoia. And Swag didn't need a paper to tell him that.

What he really needed was a drink, and some information. And he knew that he could get both at Jimmy Gyp's.

Jimmy Gyp's was over on First Avenue. Like most bars in the city, the place had a history. Jimmy Gyp's past wasn't the stuff of legends, just a bit more tangled, and almost tragic.

Originally owned by a retired cop pensioned off on disability, the bar's juke had at one time boasted the best selection of Gaelic folk songs on the Upper East Side. When Jimmy Gyp dropped dead behind the Guinness spigot, a couple of Long Island kids came in and took it over from his widow. It was said the price paid was top dollar, which didn't surprise anyone. Before Jimmy Gyp's wife became a widow, even before she became Mrs. Jimmy Gyp, she was a barmaid who had been known to short anyone foolish enough not to count their change. Legend had it that she could count sixty in change off a roll of five ones, then apologize sweetly for the mistake. After she became Mrs. Gyp, she took to settling disputes by launching her five-foot-two frame over a length of beer-puddled mahogany with a Galliano bottle clutched in her hand. She often explained that she preferred Galliano because the tapered neck of the bottle fit her hand better than the sawed-off Louisville Slugger that rested near the speed rack.

The kids who bought the place didn't know Jimmy Gyp, but liked the name. What they knew about bartending wouldn't fill a shot glass. After a year the place still wasn't making money. Bartenders, waitresses, and managers all robbed the place blind. And sometimes late at night, when a few of the remaining regulars gathered at a back table, they could imagine hearing Mrs. Gyp's phlegmy, three-pack-a-day laugh echoing up from her Naples, Florida, condo.

Then Carlo Bagatelle paid a visit.

Carlo was an operator who ran jukes, pool tables, and video games. He came through the doors at midday, just as a nattily-dressed liquor salesman was leaving. "How you boys doing?" he asked, studying the juke. There was still a column of Irish crap on the right, and four of the title strips on the left side were missing. Everything going to hell, he thought to himself.

"Everything okay with the music, the pool table?"

From outside, the sounds of a high-rise construction site could be heard. One of the Long Island kids came around the bar, long-faced, and started spilling out a tale of woe.

"Hey, don't worry 'bout it," Carlo said. "The drop here on the juke and pool table is what, three, four hundred a week?" Actually, Carlo knew the weekly average was $348.17 for the last six months. He also knew this was nearly entirely made up from the bar's lunch shot of beer-and whiskey-drinking hard hats.

The kid continued on about how no big spenders were coming in. Carlo nodded slowly, and what he thought to be, sympathetically, as he eyed the shelf of bottles over the kid's shoulder. Two bottles of Jameson's and one of Jack still had the liquor store's white price stickers. And he'd go three-to-one that the vodka and maybe even the gin in the speed rack had the same stickers. Some bartender had gone into business for himself, bringing in his own stock.

Christ, he thought, that bit's a fuckin' antique. It belongs in a museum. Carlo knew that most of whatever money was going across the bar was walking out the door in a bartender's pocket.

Putting on his best Dutch Uncle smile, Carlo leaned over the bar and said, "I been in business a long time. And I learned one thing. You gotta spend money to make money."

Before he left, he gave the two kids a loan for fifteen thousand. The interest was two and a half points under prime, to be paid back out of the juke and pool table take. But that didn't matter. In two months the construction site emptied out; it would be a year before the building filled with tenants. The two kids would never be able to make the juice on his loan, new interior or not.

In six months the store was Carlo's, though on paper it was owned by his half-wit cousin, an optometrist from Queens. The first thing Carlo did was put in a bank of six pay phones. Later he would brag that he was "running every crooked piece of shit out of the joint," which wasn't much of an overstatement. But that was when times were good. Things had changed. And they had continued to change steadily, for the worse.

Way back when, the neighborhood east of Second, above 75th, was wide open. The bars belonged to the players, the hustlers, knock-around guys, and the thrill-seeking dilettantes. Then the good times rolled for a decade, and everyone was scrabbling for a piece. Sixty-dollar-a-month railroad apartments were snatched up at one thousand per and crammed with bright young things from Smith, Vassar, Brown, and Stanford.

The back rooms got knocked down for space. And the hustlers and players left for points unknown, squeezed out by sushi bars, trendy saloons, and real estate developers. The smart ones saw themselves outclassed by the thieves who called spaghetti pasta and served it up for $22.50 a plate.

Everyone was leveraged to the max; the landlords, the developers who threw up the high rises, and the bright young things. Then when the shit came down, starting with the end of the Federal Reserve, the whole game fell apart. The city took over the unbought high rises on tax defaults. The sixty-dollar-a-month railroad flats that were renting for a grand emptied. And the bright young things went back where they came from—Connecticut, it was rumored.

Before the last Paul Stuart suit and cashmere sweater was packed, the players, hustlers, and knock-around guys had returned.

Swag came through the doors into the dim light of Jimmy Gyp's. A couple of guys at the end of the bar moved their business to a back table when Swag slid onto a vinyl stool. The bartender looked like a boxer gone to seed, which in fact he was.

"How's it going, Swag?" the bartender asked, making a show of wiping down the dry mahogany. "Beer?"

Swag reached into his pocket and brought out a roll of bills, peeled two off and laid them on the counter. "Carlo around?"

The money was U.S. and didn't impress the bartender much. Nobody would sell out for U.S. currency, even a bartender. It was easies or nothing. Pulling down on the tap, the bartender said, "You see him here?"

Swag took one of the bills from the bar and put it back in his pocket. "I might if I went downstairs."

Setting the beer down with more force than necessary, the bartender said, "You have an appointment?" Then he scooped up the remaining bill.

"What? Carlo's an executive now?"

The bartender returned with the change and snapped it down on the bar. Swag noticed the coins were pesos, and pushed them to the inside lip, then looked over at the house phone. There were four lines, one was lit.

"If you can't fold it, then it ain't a tip," the bartender said, pushing the coins back across the bar.

Swag took a drink of the beer. "You think that up by yourself, Jerome?"

That's when Carlo came up from the office. He was a little guy with elevator shoes and a thinning head of black hair that was going gray. Maybe he was sixty, but he looked older than Swag remembered. He emerged through the back door, just slightly behind his two bodyguards. All three wore suits that had seen better days, but not many of them. Business, Swag supposed, had not been good for Carlo in a long time.

Sliding off the bar stool, Swag walked straight into the bodyguards' hard stares. When one of the guards made a move to step forward, between Swag and Carlo, his boss held him back with one hand.

"What? You got business here or what?" Carlo said, now stepping out from between the two larger men.

"Just want to talk," Swag answered, moving forward himself.

"You got a beef, you tell me in front of the Johnnies," Carlo said. Both of his bodyguards were named Johnny; he'd never bothered to number them, which, Swag supposed, might have cut down on some confusion.

"No beef, Carlo," Swag said. "And no need for the Johnnies."

"What then?" Carlo challenged. "You trying to put the bull on me? This some kind of fuckin' shakedown?"

One of the Johnnies moved a hand toward the lapel of his worn sharkskin suit.

"No shakedown, no nothing, Carlo," Swag replied. "Just want to buy some information."

"You looking for something on the boys, forget it," Carlo said. "Where you get off anyway? You ain't a cop no more."

"Carlo," Swag answered slowly. "There aren't any more

boys, no more wiseguys, no more Cosa Nostra, mafia, it's all gone."

It was true, but it had been no headline-grabbing Fed prosecutor who did the wiseguys in. When the stock market crashed, most of the dons got wiped out, even the ones who stuck to the blue chips and triple A bonds. Those with money in Switzerland, Belgium, or the Bahamas, were never heard from again. In the old country aging capos turned their backs on America as they would any bankrupt proposition. Those left behind, their American capos, *con-siglios*, lieutenants, crew bosses, soldiers, and enforcers, did not fare well.

Now the fear—the mob's most valuable asset—was gone. And with it vanished the power and the respect they fed off of. Even the lowest of enforcers had grown fat and soft by the time the dollar went south for good. In the streets the young and hungry jackals had replaced the made guys. Youngsters with flat dull eyes, who never expected to see twenty-five.

One of the Johnnies moved closer, chesting Swag back a step. "Call him off, Carlo, or you'll be down to one Johnny," Swag said, feeling the muscles tighten at the back of his neck and down his back.

"Johnny," Carlo ordered, "go get this man his beer. Bring it to the office."

Swag followed Carlo and the other Johnny to the back of the room, past the pool table piled high with empty beer cases and a burned-out lighting fixture. As they passed the two men sitting at the back table, Swag heard one say to the other, "So the Emergency Room guy, the doc, he sez, 'Jesus Christ it's da worst busted nose I ever seen on a livin' person,' and I say, 'Youse don't get out to Bay Ridge much, huh?'"

The other guy started laughing then. It was a laugh that sounded very much like a toilet unclogging.

Carlo, Swag, and the Johnnies went down the stairs to the cellar office. The basement itself was stacked high with empty beer cases. Rows of empty liquor bottles sat on shelves. A small table held a plastic funnel and gallon jugs of cheap scotch, bourbon, and vodka. Several empty bottles of top-shelf liquor waited nearby to be filled.

"Business isn't good, Carlo? You started hashing the stock?"

"They're killing me, my friend," Carlo said in a weary voice. All the bluster had drained from him. Suddenly he was just another tired old guy in a losing business. "It isn't like it used to be."

"No, it isn't," Swag answered, glad that Carlo and his boys had been caught in the switches with everyone else.

Carlo stepped through a small door and Swag followed. This was his workroom. The door opened into an expansive space filled with video poker games. Dozens of the machines lay partly assembled along a cluttered workbench. In another area of the room a weasel of a technician worked on the circuit board of a video mah-jongg game.

"Still running pokers, Carlo?"

"Pokers! Now they're after my pokers, the miserable fuckin' bastards!"

Carlo was halfway to his office door before Swag spoke again. "Who's that? Who's after the pokers?"

"Everyone, punks, rat-bastard punks," Carlo spat, turning around. "Two hundred games on the street and they don't even pay for the Johnnies."

"Carlo, everyone doesn't want your pokers," Swag said. It was like talking to a child. Swag was about to turn and leave when the other Johnny came up behind him with his beer.

"Bullshit, they don't," Carlo said, turning in challenge. Then to the tech he said, "Gene, gimme that fuckin' thing."

The tech reached under the bench, pulled out a large portable radio and handed it to Carlo.

"Bullshit, they're not after me," the old capo muttered. "Look at this. Gene, turn that thing on."

The tech switched on a nearby poker game. Jacks, queens, kings, and aces rotated in slot machine fashion down across the video screen in attract mode.

"Bastards, look at what they're doing to me," Carlo said. When he pushed the radio's On button the screen went blank, then immediately fired up again.

"What is it?" Swag asked, now fascinated. Someone was stealing from Carlo, but he didn't know how.

"It's a fuckin' machine of doom, the bastards," Carlo said.

Without anyone asking, the tech cut in. "It's a transmitter. Let's go with a five-second burst of high frequency, knocks out the machine. These old games, they're set on a thousand-turn repeating cycle."

Swag stared at the tech, still not understanding.

"They've been working in teams," the tech continued. "Three or four to a team. A man outside resets the machine with the transmitter, then two or three others pump dollars into the machine, counting the hands. You know, winning hand on six pull, six hundred and twenty-ninth pull, one hundred and forty-second pull."

"Then the high rollers came back later," Swag offered as the tech nodded. "They reset the machine, and he bets heavy on the winning hands."

"That's about it," the tech said.

"Your locations aren't happy with this," Swag said to Carlo, knowing that locations paid winnings out of the cash drawer.

"Happy? You sonofabitch, happy?" Carlo fumed. The thought of being beat by the street infuriated him. In a vein-popping rage he threw the radio down, smashing it on the concrete. Swag saw that the inside was filled nearly completely with batteries bound together with black tape. A large antenna of copper wire had been wound around the periphery. In one corner was a fist-sized section of layered circuit boards Swag assumed to be the transmitter.

The Johnnies looked mournful at the sight; maybe a little too mournful, Swag thought. Like maybe they'd want one for their own.

"Nothing to do," Swag said.

"I can screen them, partition the motherboard off with a tempest shield. Elastomer, you know, plastic, or else metal," the tech said. "But this is my last week. I'm history. I got an offer from a German firm."

They went through into the office then, Carlo kicking the bits of smashed plastic with the toe of his battered Gucci as he went.

Carlo took a seat behind a desk cluttered with liquor invoices. And Swag took the one next to it. The two Johnnies stood near the door, looking as if they too wanted to work for a German firm.

"So what're you looking to buy?" Carlo said, getting comfortable in the chair, pretending it was like the old days.

"Information," Swag said. "Somebody hit one of my clients."

"So, it wasn't me," Carlo said, as if that were a possibility.

"Somebody also flaked Cranen over at the morgue, and put Johnny G. in the river."

The Johnnies shifted uncomfortably.

"I read that thing about the M.E.," Carlo said. "So what are you, back on the job?"

Swag shook his head slowly. "It's worth two hundred marks to me to find out who did them."

Carlo thought about this for a second before answering. "No, you ain't on the job," he said. "You're looking after business."

"That's right, Carlo, I'm taking care of business," Swag said.

The wheels behind the aging mobster's eyes turned, sorting through files he held in his head. "That M.E., Cranen, he was dirty from way back," he answered at last. "Johnny G., he was the one who was the ex-con, all busted up, right? He was probably into some shit, tried to beat someone on a deal. And I don't know about your client."

"Anything going around on the street?" Swag asked. "Who's doing your collecting now, the Johnnies?"

Carlo looked up at his two bodyguards, asking the question without saying anything. Swag turned in his seat to see them shake their heads.

"So, nothing," Carlo said. "What's it to you anyway? I

can understand how losing a client could get you, but those other two scumbags? What's the deal?"

"Maybe I've been working too hard. Maybe I'm getting a little paranoid," Swag said. "I'm looking to connect the dots."

"A little paranoia never hurt anybody," Carlo said. "It's dangerous out there, you know. Nobody respects nothing no more."

"Getting hard to make a dishonest dollar, is it?" Swag asked.

Carlo, caught up in a philosophical moment, ignored the remark. "There's eight million scumbags in the naked city, my friend," he said. "Any one of 'em'll fuck you over."

"I'm outta here, Carlo," Swag said.

The old man snapped out of his reverie and eyed Swag closely. "So what you looking for?" he asked. "Something that puts these people together? Whataya got so far?"

"Just a feeling," Swag said. "Like I said, maybe I'm getting paranoid. It's just a feeling I get when everyone I know starts getting killed."

Carlo laughed and picked up a pen with a beer's name stamped on it. "I remember your last feeling. Youngest and most decorated detective on the force. And you blew it, *bigtime*."

Swag got up to leave, but Carlo motioned him back down.

"You boys remember that?" he asked the Johnnies.

Behind him Swag could feel the Johnnies shrug, not really caring.

"Swag here was a big man on the force," Carlo went on. "When it fell apart, people were getting whacked left and right with the new gun laws. But this one time, there were what, seventy, eighty floaters over on the West Side."

"Eighty-seven," Swag said, not wanting to hear the story again. Eighty-seven floaters bobbing up and down in the water like empty beer bottles. Swag could still remember what it looked like, the way they were packed in between the boats and the pilings. It took two hours to haul them all out. Sea gulls had landed on some of them.

Carlo continued for the benefit of the Johnnies. "Right, eighty-seven stiffs. All kinds, you know, from Harlem, the Bronx, downtown, even a couple of lawyers. All floating like dead fish, you know, real amateur stuff. And everyone's saying, 'It's the Colombians,' 'It's the gangs,' 'It's organized crime.' But not our boy here, he goes off in another direction. How'd you know where to look?"

Swag hadn't thought about it in a long time. He didn't want to think about it now, but he answered anyway. "They weren't professional," he said. "Didn't weight the bodies, no stab wounds to release gases, just dumped them like trash."

"See that," Carlo said to the Johnnies, "wasn't professional."

"And they weren't all dirty—most of them were, but not all," Swag said. "Six of them were brothers or cousins of dirty guys. They killed the wrong guys."

"No shit, that's not what the papers said," Carlo answered, more than a little surprised. "You'd think it was the FBI's Most Wanted floating up against that Circle Line. So anyway, Swag here, he figures it out. Goes after the perps. And who do you think they are?"

The Johnnies shrugged again, still not really caring.

"They're a bunch of Colonel Bammer's boys, his elite guard," Carlo said. "Now this is the part I know didn't make the paper, but I just happened to get a transcript of all that grand jury's proceedings, out of a personal interest you might say. When Swag here goes into the grand jury, he's got some young assistant D.A. in his corner. The real D.A.'s a drunk, so you two hotshots got the indictment past him. You're maybe looking for Chief of Detectives at thirty, and he's looking for an end run around his boss and a shortcut to the big office."

"I was just doing my job, Carlo," Swag said.

"Anyway, they both thought they was gonna be heroes," Carlo continued for the Johnnies. "Only thing, Bammer's got a ringer on the grand jury—some corrupt little guy, but smart—shit, he took Swag and that kid prosecutor apart like a cheap watch. They start pressing about the initial investigation, asking what he based your charges on. Tell him what you said. Go on, tell the Johnnies."

"They don't want to hear it," Swag answered.

"And he said 'Swag,' right? That's cop talk for 'Scientific Wild-Ass Guess.' And for that whole week of grand jury testimony, the ringer keeps calling him Mr. Swag."

"You taking this anywhere, Carlo?" Swag asked, making a move to leave.

"A history lesson for the Johnnies is all," Carlo said. "You should read those transcripts sometime, they're a scream. 'Mr. Swag, isn't it true, then, that you coerced evidence from this individual, this Lenny Kingston, known as 'Rat Fuck' Lenny?' They're hysterical."

Swag didn't need to read the transcripts. He could remember them clearly enough, right through to the part where the ADA jumped ship.

"They handed you your ass, didn't they?" Carlo boomed. "Shit, they wanted to *indict you*!"

Swag got up to leave. Carlo was painfully right. But Swag was younger then, and Bammer was new to the post. He didn't know Bammer had the grand jury in his pocket. Even later, after they'd squeezed him off the force, Swag had thought Bammer was just covering for a bunch of renegades in his ranks. It took a long time for him to realize that it was the colonel himself who made up the list and gave the orders.

"Look, I'll see you around, Carlo," Swag said, moving through the doorway.

"Sure kid, sure you will," came the laughing answer. Retelling the story had improved Carlo's mood, but not Swag's.

Outside the office, the tech had cleaned up the shattered radio transmitter and was desoldering a PCB, plucking the chips up off the board one at a time.

"So, you're going to work on the fruit machines," Swag said, pausing at the workbench. "Where you heading?"

"Cologne," the tech answered, bending low to the nearly barren board.

Swag stepped out of the bar, back into the intolerable heat. What little information he now had just wasn't clicking. There used to be some sense to it, he remembered. The city made sense. The very worst of it could be explained in the unforgiving algebra of the street. You could understand the pieces of it—broken down into precincts, vics, perps, skels, addicts, whores, hustlers, wackos, ratboys, dealers, players, shooters, snitches, and the hundred thousand variations on a hundred thousand themes. As bad as it got, there was a formula of greed and need. That's what police work used to be. They said he had a natural talent for it, like the guy who could multiply four-digit numbers in his head. Find the motive, the stressor, the money, the drugs, the witness. And find them fast, before it all vanished in the wind. The old-time cops knew it better than anyone. Nothing could surprise those old guys back then, he thought, except the future. Nobody was ready for what came next.

A block down, Swag put a couple of coins in the pay phone, dialed the M.E.'s office and asked to speak to the acting M.E. Maybe he could pick up the trail there.

A bright young man's voice came on the phone.

"Yes, my name is Chris Rollins," Swag said. "I believe you have a friend of mine there under a John Doe?"

"Would you like to come down and make an identification?"

Swag said, "Can you tell me if anyone else has? He had a lot of friends."

"Could you describe him please, and I can check."

"White male, approximately six-one, wearing a dark suit," Swag tried. "I understand he was the victim of an attack on 63rd and Madison a few days ago."

The line went dead for a moment; then the young man's

voice came over. "Sir, I show no records that fit the description."

"They shipped him to Hart Island yet?" Swag asked, realizing his error as soon as the words were out of his mouth. A citizen wouldn't know the name of New York's Potter's Field.

"Sir, I'm reviewing the printout for the last month," the voice said. "To tell you the truth, I have no John Does under sixty for the last weeks, male or female."

Swag hung up without saying good-bye.

It seemed to Swag that he stood there for a long time, watching the traffic on First Avenue pass. Finally he dug more coins from his pocket and dialed another local number. The phone on the answering machine came on; it sounded like it was a long way off. He'd always thought of the voice as one you might have once heard on a southern interstate, coming in clear over the AM radio to announce bargains at the local Chevy dealership or a men's apparel store. It was a folksy drawl filled with bits of Oklahoma, Arkansas, and wry amusement.

Swag listened carefully to the message. When the beep sounded on the other end, he hung up. He wasn't at all surprised by the recording. If you knew Jim Bob's number, then you ought to know how to find him.

chapter eleven

THE SAN REMO APARTMENTS WERE LOCATED at an excellent address on Central Park West. The building's sinister twin towers were a monument to expensive views and quirky thirties architecture. Topping each tower was a miniature Roman temple—columns and all. Emery Catherwood lived near the center of the south tower. No doubt he would have preferred a townhouse, something on the East Side. Something in limestone with neo-French ornamentation. Something with the exuberance, if not excess, of the Gilded Age.

But the San Remo was reputed to have the best security. Four guards at each of the two front entrances and another four in back, all with automatic weapons. And, unlike most private security forces, the San Remo's men knew how to fight.

Catherwood had the triplex paneled in rare African and South American woods, each darkly stained and polished.

Now, sitting by one of the windows that faced Central Park, he switched on an ornate Tiffany lamp over a writing desk. From a small cherrywood box he lifted a coin. Battered on all sides, it was more of a fragment than a complete piece. "Roger, what did you think of our Colonel Bammer's personal guards?" he asked, his voice soft in the quiet room.

Roger, sitting in a large wingbacked chair, checking the action of the Walther, said, "Not much."

Catherwood turned the coin in his hand, examining the owl etched into it. "And the colonel himself?"

The Walther automatic went "chick-chick" in the silent room, and Roger said, "Less."

"He is rather crude," Catherwood said, still squinting at his newest prize. It was an Athenian four drachma coin; an expert in London had dated it at 440 B.C. "Can he be trusted, I wonder, our Colonel Bammer?"

"I wouldn't," Roger said, slipping a laser-sighting device onto a mount on the Walther. "The guy's an asshole."

Catherwood went "Ummmm," then said, "That isn't quite the way I would phrase it."

"Still true, he's a wrong guy," Roger replied, leaning back in the chair, waiting. In his life he had spent a good portion of his time waiting. He was used to it. Waiting and listening were part of his job, but not the good part.

"And the other, this Swag person?"

This took Roger a little longer. "Don't know enough about him."

"But your initial impression is . . .?" Catherwood let the question hang.

"Maybe dangerous, maybe a shooter," Roger said, flicking on the laser's power button. "I'd give you odds on him over anything Bammer has."

"And you base your assessment on . . .?" Again Catherwood left the question only partly asked. He was holding the coin up between two fingers, examining it under the light.

"Just that he took out your boy, body-armor implants and all," Roger replied without much thought, "and that could make your hit on Lorette . . . complicated." Roger brought the Walther up fast; the minute red dot of the laser halted precisely at the center of the small coin, quivering and turning its ancient gold into blood red. "It's real easy to keep score."

"But is he a team player?" Roger asked, examining with some displeasure the reddened coin.

"I'd say no," Roger answered, keeping the laser site on

the coin as Catherwood turned it slowly between his fingers.

"Then we must make him a team player," Catherwood said. "I wish to recruit him. Is that understood?"

"I think I got the gist of it," Roger answered, still keeping the beam of light on the coin.

Catherwood, bored with his bodyguard's answers and cheap gunslinger tricks, changed the subject. "In the ancient times, Roger," Catherwood said, lowering the coin as Roger switched off the laser, "temple priests, endowed by strange gods, consecrated the money their people would use."

"Sounds like an idea," Roger replied, settling deeper into his chair as he slipped the Walther into a shoulder holster.

"Money was an act of faith, as holy as anything else in their lives," Catherwood continued.

"Seems to me a lot of people were praying a few years back," Roger answered.

"Come here, Roger, look at this coin," Catherwood offered.

"I've seen it, sir."

"The Athenians, *they* had democracy," Catherwood said, more to himself than Roger. "Democracy, art, culture, literature, advanced financial institutions."

Roger studied the toe of his shoe, looking at a recent scuff mark. Then he pulled a small comb from his pocket and began working it through his hair. "All that good stuff, huh?"

"Yes, all that good stuff," Catherwood said, only slightly put off. "Do you know what happened to them?"

"They got their asses kicked," Roger said flatly. "All the men were killed, women raped, all their good stuff got boosted. Think I need a haircut?"

Catherwood came up short at this, lifting his gaze from the coin. "Exactly, Roger, how do you know this?"

"You're talking about the Athenians, not if I need a haircut, right?" Roger said, slipping the comb back into his breast pocket.

Catherwood shot Roger a stern look and said, "Just for the sake of argument, let's assume I don't share your obsessive fascination with your hair."

"Well, how many Athenians you see lately?" Roger replied. "I mean happy ones."

Catherwood ignored this, put the coin back in its box and clicked the brass clasp shut. Then he moved around the side of the desk. Outside, Central Park was growing dark. The few people who still ventured into it for relief from the summer heat were drifting toward its boundaries. "They were conquered by the Persians, their democracy replaced by an oligarchy," Catherwood said, looking across toward the East Side. "Have you ever thought that perhaps the natural evolution of democracy is oligarchy?"

"All the fuckin' time," Roger said, lifting himself out of the chair and aiming himself toward the spiral staircase. "I'm gonna get a sandwich. You want anything?"

"No, no thank you, Roger," Catherwood answered, without turning from the view. The double pane of glass through which Catherwood gazed was slightly tinted. Between the two thick panes, inset into the sill, was a small amplifier that produced a random frequency up through the glass, as a countermeasure for laser bugging. Under the exotic woods the walls were lined with aluminum. In the bookcase a small unit ran hourly spectrum analysis checks on the room.

Catherwood placed the tips of his fingers on the thick pane and felt reassurance in its thickness. Bringing a hand away from the pane, he reached into the pocket of his coat, drew out the small platinum cylinder and gave it a half turn, exposing the jade fish, then released a mist of fugu toxin into his mouth.

Roger was halfway down the staircase before Catherwood turned from the window. "Roger," he called, "where on earth did you locate that videotape? The one the good Colonel Bammer mentioned."

Roger backstepped two stairs so that his face barely protruded above the thick fringe of a Persian carpet. "You mean that Elvis thing? It was already in the M.E.'s office. He was a wrong kind of guy too."

When Roger was down the stairs, Catherwood turned back to the glass and studied the view for a long time. The drug was already working, tingling across his chest and down his arms, making him feel as if he were floating over the twilit park.

Then he picked up the phone and dialed a number from memory. A phone rang at the other end in a weathered mansion on Fishers Island. You couldn't find Fishers Island in any guidebook, and the ferry service, when it ran to the rustic beaches, included signs that vigorously discouraged the curious. Those who built summer homes there had always cherished the privacy money can buy. Guests now arrived by private launch or helicopter.

When the phone was answered on the second ring, a crisp male voice said, "Yes?"

Catherwood answered, "Line four, please."

Then both men switched their phones over to a scrambled mode.

"I shall require additional assistance," Catherwood said.

"Yes?" the voice on the other end replied. "How many men, sir?"

"I should think four would be satisfactory."

"Yes, sir," came the voice, and the line went dead.

Twenty-two floors below Catherwood's expensive view, a lone man wearing jogging shoes sat in the park on a small folding camp stool. He was sixty, but still had blond hair and an unlined face. Traits he credited to good genes, rather then good living. To one side of him was a black nylon athletic bag, containing a cheap notepad, a paperback book entitled *Birds of North America*, and an IAI Automag IV. The stainless steel barrel of the big .45 glinted up from the inside of the canvas bag.

On the other side there was a small Styrofoam cooler containing the last can of what was a six-pack of Jax beer, floating in a puddle of melted ice. In front of him, mounted on a tripod, was a $60\times$ spotting scope. It was aimed directly at the San Remo.

Swag spotted the boys as he made his way to where Jim Bob sat. They were coming down the asphalt path from the clearing when Swag entered the park. There were five or six of them. No more than sixteen or seventeen years old. Instinctively Swag felt the muscles of his neck tense, and thought of the gun resting in the holster.

As they moved forward in a bunch, Swag expected them to try to crowd him off the path. They were of a type. They'd be looking for weakness; eye contact, a flinch; a sudden move off the path. Then they'd demand money, counting on intimidation to carry off the shakedown. They'd be looking to get paid.

But then Swag noticed they were walking fast, almost running. As they approached Swag on the path, the small group broke apart, allowing him to pass, then cast nervous glances back over their shoulders.

As he cleared the bike path and came into the clearing, Swag caught sight of James Robert Spurock, Jim Bob. Even from the back he could be no one else, not dressed in the faded tan poplin suit and French running shoes.

Swag was maybe five yards away when a pretty blond woman with close-cropped hair and a pair of tight blue running shorts jogged by. He turned to admire her legs, thinking she looked vaguely familiar, and that's when Jim Bob leaned over, brought the .45-caliber Automag up from the bag and turned smoothly in the chair. He did it in one fluid motion, fast, but not too fast. The shiny gun came up shielded by one poplin-clad leg. Swag didn't see the gun until it was pointed at his stomach. When Jim Bob saw it was Swag, he brought the gun down and smiled.

"Thought I had some more visitors," Jim Bob said, not the least apologetic.

"Like the ones who just left?" Swag asked, coming closer.

"Fine fellas, real polite," Jim Bob said. "Reaffirms my belief in the youth of America."

"That piece wouldn't have taught them any manners, would it?"

"God help me, but I love and appreciate those new handgun laws," Jim Bob said.

Jim Bob lifted himself from the chair. He didn't move like any sixty-year-old Swag had ever seen. He moved better than most forty-year-olds. Jim Bob attributed his agility to an obscure form of martial arts that was painfully pretty to watch, unless, of course, the fighter was snatching an opponent's eyes out of his sockets with two fingers.

"The new rules haven't cut down on crime."

"See now, there's the cop in you showing through again," Jim Bob said. "Of course there's still crime, but manners have greatly improved. Would you care for a beer? How'd you find me?"

Swag shook his head no, seeing there was only one left. "I was a detective, Jim Bob," Swag said, moving in closer. "I detected."

"Got the message on my machine, huh?"

"Couple of tea-bag bird watchers over at the boathouse saw you," Swag answered. "I assume you haven't written anything down in that book, the Bird Registry they call it?"

Jim Bob reached down and grabbed the can from the icy water. "Nothing to report yet," came the answer.

"Bird watching, Jim Bob?" he said.

"I've been known to watch a hawk or two," Jim Bob said. "Out at my uncle's farm."

"That farm wouldn't have been near Williamsburg, would it?" Swag asked, slipping the question in slyly and with a smile. Then seeing it wouldn't break through, said, "Camp Peary, maybe?"

Jim Bob smiled back slightly at Swag's mention of the CIA training facility. "Adair County, Oklahoma, in fact."

"That's a long way from Peary," Swag tried.

"A real pretty drive, though," said Jim Bob, only half rising to the bait. Then, before Swag could ask another question, he said, "There's a nest of peregrine falcon up in that south tower," pointing with the hand that held the beer.

"Saw a red-tailed hawk the other day. And a broad-winged hawk. Never drop below five stories. They live off pigeons and sparrows. Swoop down on 'em real pretty."

Swag didn't believe it for a second. Jim Bob wasn't dirty, but he wasn't exactly a citizen either. Swag suspected he was with Langley, NSA, NIC, DIA, or some vague acronym out of Washington. Whatever he was doing, Swag was pretty sure it came under the heading of Domestic Intelligence.

Ten years ago, when Swag was working a homicide, he picked up a Dutchman for questioning. It was a routine hit and run. The Dutchman, who was probably drunk, had run a Korean kid on a motorcycle off the FDR Drive. It was a lock—a ground ball—as they used to say. The paint on the Dutchman's dented car matched the paint on the Honda. And there were three eyewitnesses, all eager to testify.

But the Dutchman remained cool. Yes, he wanted to remain silent. No, he didn't want an attorney. Yes, if he needed an attorney, he could probably afford one. But what he really wanted was his phone call.

Twenty minutes after the Dutchman hung up the phone, Jim Bob appeared at the precinct. First he talked with the desk sergeant, then with Swag. After that it took one phone call from Jim Bob to get the Dutchman kicked free.

"Now I don't want you to have any hard feelings here," Jim Bob had told Swag. "You can be sure that where that Dutch fella's going, he won't be drinking and driving and running Korean folks off the road."

After that Jim Bob popped up once or twice a year. Outside the Waldorf Towers, a load of dry-cleaning over his shoulder. In front of the U.N., wearing a tourist's goofy fishing hat with a camera around his neck. Once Swag saw him in a newspaper photo when the president of Dubai was in town. Jim Bob was standing in back of the president, wearing press tags around his neck and holding up a pocket tape recorder in the crush of journalists.

Over the past year or two it had become a game between

them, Swag trying to get Jim Bob to break cover, and Jim Bob smoothly wiggling his way out of every question. It would be just like him to study up on birds before setting up shop in the park.

"So you've been out here watching flocks of hawks," Swag said, moving toward the scope, bending down to have a look.

"Kettles," Jim Bob said with some authority, taking a long pull on the beer. "You put a bunch of hawks together, then you have yourself a kettle."

Swag looked down through the eyepiece. The Roman temple of one of the San Remo towers came into view. But there weren't any hawks. "I lost a client," he said, eye still to the eyepiece.

Jim Bob took another pull from the beer, brought the can away from his mouth and wiped his lips across the sleeve of the jacket. "Heard about that," he said slowly.

And Swag thought, here it comes, the patented hick act. Jim Bob is putting on the shucking and pshawing country boy. Listen to it long enough, you'd swear he was sitting around the porch of the general store, whittling a piece of pine with a Barlow knife, spitting out tobacco juice in between long shavings. Put him in Port Authority or Grand Central, he'd attract every hustler and low-rent con game from Houston Street to the Bronx.

"Well?" Swag said.

"Heard she was real pretty. Swiss, was she?" Jim Bob said, each word coming out slower and slower. "You got the shooter, did you?"

"Yeah," Swag answered. "And who hit the M.E.?"

Spurock took another pull from the beer, taking his time and swallowing slowly before he answered. "Damn if we don't live in strange times," he said at last. "Pretty Swiss ladies gunned down in the streets, tying up traffic. Medical Examiners, *public employees, no less*, murdered on the job."

Jim Bob knew, but he wasn't talking. It was the way he said it, talking slow, using a lot of words. You could listen to him for an hour straight, then walk away and realize he hadn't given up a scrap of information.

"Tell me who's behind it," Swag demanded. "Tell me about Bammer and his men. Did they wax my client?"

"They're not soldiers," came the fast response. "Those old boys, they're just another gang. And not a real bright one at that. All their hounds ain't barking, if you get my meaning. It wasn't them that killed that Swiss miss."

"Okay, it wasn't Bammer," Swag said. "Who was it? Tell me something I don't know."

"Here's a fact. Know why they turn off those top lights in the Empire State at midnight?" Jim Bob asked cryptically, then not waiting for an answer, said, "Back in the forties, one night more 'n two hundred birds flew into her. Attracted by the light. Happened again in the fifties."

"Right . . ." Swag said, waiting for him to continue. New York history had become a popular fad, the more obscure the better. Every paper and magazine in the city ran feature stories on New York history. Even Swag was picking some up.

"Back then it was just the biggest, brightest thing around," came the answer, and Jim Bob threw the can into the cooler with the other empties.

"You telling me anything in particular here?"

Then Jim Bob did it. The change was sudden and dramatic. The big, loose-limbed, easygoing country boy vanished and someone else took his place. This new demeanor bunched all the muscles up in his arms, stiffened his jaw and straightened his back. His feet, in those French running shoes, were planted solidly on the trampled grass. It was a stance of inflexible authority. When he spoke, the voice was not one of anger, but one of authority not accustomed to being questioned. "You just lay low there, friend," he said. "Put on some *un*colorful shirts. Make yourself scarce for a month or two."

"Can't afford to," Swag said.

Jim Bob kept his eyes fastened to Swag, the left one just slightly squinted, and said, "You can't afford to do nothing but exactly what I say. And you remember what I told you about those birds. You don't have any more idea of what you're into than they did. Myself, I make it a personal policy to stay clear of big things I don't know anything about."

At that moment, off the southeast corner of the park, Colonel Bammer was talking to his second-in-command. The colonel was leaning back on a white divan in his Plaza suite, boots leaving smudges across the gold-trimmed brocade. Before him, at parade rest, stood Major Tancloe.

"Major, there's been renewed interest in a certain ex-cop with a penchant for loud shirts," Bammer said. "I believe the man who has acquired this sudden interest is an old acquaintance of yours."

"Yes, sir?" the major replied.

"Name Catherwood doesn't ring any bells for you, does it?"

"No sir," the major answered immediately.

"Weird kind of guy," Bammer said. "I myself believe he's a Fed. Maybe some shoefly out of Internal Affairs. A paper shuffler."

Tancloe didn't answer. An answer wasn't expected.

"There's no need to bring up that whole business again," Bammer continued. "Unless you have any particular love for grand jury investigations, accusations of murder, and bad publicity."

"No sir," the major agreed.

"Find our old cop friend and terminate, Major," Bammer said. "Finish this business once and for all."

"Yes, sir," came the crisp response as Tancloe turned and headed for the door.

"And, Major," Bammer added, almost as an afterthought, "it should be an accident."

"Yes, sir."

"That means no official ordnance."

"Yes, sir," came the answer, and then the major was out the door.

chapter twelve

Swag spotted them the next day as he was walking down Park Avenue. They moved at an uneasy pace, not more than half a block back. And not talking to each other. What tipped Swag off was the way they walked side by side with no conversation as they edged through other pedestrians. They weren't tourists, and they didn't have the beaten-down look of office workers. But they were on the job, that much was certain. Their eyes remained straight ahead, not exactly fixed on Swag, but not far off him either.

When Swag stopped in the front of a Mercedes showroom to peer in through the plate glass, they crossed the street. In the dim reflection of polished glass, Swag watched them slow their pace. Half a block back they came to a complete stop, then stared across the traffic toward the Benz showroom.

Amateurs, Swag thought. He turned the corner toward Madison and cut into an office building. It took less than three minutes for them to pass the door at a hurried walk.

Swag got a good look at them as they moved by. Their suits were identical, except for a slight variation of color. The one on the inside was dark blue, the other dark gray. Both were about six feet, 190 pounds, and by the way they walked, Swag would guess that most of it was muscle. They had close-cropped light brown hair. But what struck Swag wasn't that they were walking fast—almost marching, in crisp military precision, one-twenty steps per—but that

they were nearly identical, both in their specific appearance
and their utter blandness. A police report would have read:
between thirty-five and forty; medium height; medium
build; brown hair; tan complexion. The kind of description, Swag knew, that would be of no help in identification.

Raffles was two blocks up Park. Swag emerged cautiously from the building's lobby, doubled back down the
street, then turned the same corner and continued up Park.
It wasn't that there were two of them. What triggered a
slow panic in him was that they both wore dark suits. *Cheap
European dark suits.*

Swag passed between a pair of uniformed doormen into
Raffles' lobby and waited. If the two men were still on him,
then he couldn't bring trouble into the hotel.

Two bars adjoined the lobby: one was called Guards, the
other, Brooks's. Both named after London clubs—
franchised deals, done up cheap for the colonies. Swag
crossed the lobby and made for Guards, the less pretentious
of the two.

Before Swag had gone four steps he felt a hand at his left
elbow. A strong handful of fingers tightened painfully
around his elbow as the concierge came up alongside. "'Ere
now, mate," he said, leaning over and showing a big smile.
"Where you off to, then?" All the London plumminess had
left his voice; that was apparently reserved for paying guests.

Swag shook the hand free and turned to face the concierge.
Instinct brought the big tea bag into a fighting stance, feet
apart, hands loose and slightly out from his sides.

Now it was Swag's turn to smile. Keeping his hands
down at his sides, he said, "Let's do it, pal. Right now."

The big man's hands and arms relaxed, like a machine
winding down. But the smile didn't come back to his face.
"Mr. Lancaster has instructed me to inform you that your
services are no longer required," he said in a parody of an
uppercrust servant's accent. Then, dropping back into the
Liverpool speech, "Figured there was something bent
about you, 'e did. Reckon my hunch was bang on."

"He tell you that personally?" Swag asked. "That you were 'bang on,' mate?"

"Let's just say I got the word, I did," came the answer. "Now, folla me, mate, or you'll be following your own arse out the door."

But Swag held his ground. "Phone down to him," he said.

"Sorry, old boy," the big man said, reaching out for Swag's elbow. "But Mr. Lancaster's appointment book is filled for today, it is."

Swag, moving a step back, said, "Ring him up 'old boy,' or you'll have a scene guests will write home about."

It took a second for the concierge to make a decision, then without saying a word he crossed back to his desk. After he punched in the number, he said a few words Swag couldn't make out, then handed the phone over the desk with a nasty little smile of crooked British teeth.

"Swag, what the fuck are you doing here?" Lancaster asked. There was a new tension in his voice—he could barely speak. "Leave."

"What, what is it?" Swag asked, straining to keep the panic out of his own voice.

The phone went silent for a long time. Then Lancaster said, "I don't know what it is. It came through from the home office when I tried to book you for a job yesterday."

"What, that Swiss that got whacked?"

The phone went silent again. "No, something else. They wouldn't even talk about it. But they sent a memo in the overnight from London, then called again today. Then I get this bullshit advisory from the Provost Command Center, saying you're under investigation. I swear, it's like you killed the fuckin' Queen Mum or some shit. This whole thing is hinky. Just leave the hotel. And put what's-his-name back on."

Swag handed the phone back over the desk to the concierge, who listened for a second and said, "Very good, sir." Then he put the phone down and came around the desk.

"Now, if you'll allow me to escort you, sir," he said, the nasty smile still in place.

When they were halfway to the doors, the big man grabbed Swag's elbow again. Swag pulled it away as two elderly tourists shuffled in front of them. By the time the two tourists had passed, Swag turned again to face the concierge.

"Bleedin' fookin' arsehole," the concierge spat, moving in. "Move your bum along now, 'fore you do yourself a mischief."

"I'm moving," Swag said, turning his back. "Just keep your hands off."

As Swag approached the door, the crisp uniformed doorman swung it open and a blast of summer heat rushed in. The concierge made another grab for Swag's arm. That did it. As the thick fingers closed in just above the joint, Swag backstepped, brought his own arm sliding back and grabbed the concierge's arm, digging his fingers into the pressure point at the wrist.

The Jeeves mumbled something as Swag brought a boot heel down across his instep. The arm came free of Swag's grasp as the concierge stumbled backward. Swag felt one meaty fist connect at his back in a quick kidney punch, but there wasn't much force to it. He turned with the blow, grabbed the Jeeves by the knot of his tie and propelled him out through the still open door.

The two doormen went for the holstered weapons hidden by the red tunics, but Swag was faster. In one movement he turned the concierge around, putting the struggling man between him and the two doormen. Then he grabbed the Jeeves by a handful of thinning hair and smashed him face first into the plate glass.

A thick splatter of blood bloomed from the concierge's mouth and nose and spread in a greasy smear across the glass. Swag yanked him to the side and heaved the dazed thug into the nearest doorman. The uniformed attendant stepped back quickly to avoid messing his costume with blood.

"Bloody fookin' arsehole," Swag mimicked as he turned and began walking up the street.

They caught him just as he turned the corner onto 55th. Three of Bammer's boys. They were dressed in plain clothes and driving an unmarked unit. It was a Volvo. One in the front, two in the back, they cruised slowly along the curb, looking more like a carload of Jersey City gang-bangers than cops. But then, none of Bammer's men ever looked like cops, in or out of uniform.

"Neat little trick you got there," the driver called.

Swag, without turning, said, "Just keep following me, I'll show you another."

"Swag, what action you got going?" the driver called. He drove with one arm draped out the window. The other hung casually over the wheel.

Swag kept walking. He was halfway up the block toward Madison. When he reached the corner, he'd turn left toward downtown, leaving them a choice of backing off or driving against traffic.

"Hey, word up, Swag," the driver tried, creeping alongside. "The man wants to talk to you."

"Try that down in front of a school," Swag called back, now turning to face the driver. "If you hurry you can make the junior high up in the Bronx."

"Better listen up, *freund*," the driver tried, affecting German. "Business *can't* be good since that lady got whacked. And it ain't gonna get better."

Swag stopped, came off the curb as the car inched to a stop, and bent to the window. "What man?" Swag asked.

"Very important gent," the driver said. "Says he got a job for you."

Swag saw the checkered grip of a Luger wedged under the thigh of one of the backseat passengers and a little Ingram automatic peeking out of the other's shoulder holster. Lugers weren't standard issue, and neither were Ingrams. And the front rifle mount by the dash wasn't holding a standard-issue Steyr, but a battered Daewoo assault rifle. Whatever business these boys were on, it wasn't official.

"This wouldn't be Colonel Bammer, now?" Swag asked.

"Bammer?" the driver said. "Hell no, this is a little free-lance we dug up for you. A real sweet deal. *Verstand*?"

"And all you boys want is a little taste," Swag offered.

"That's right, yeah," the driver agreed hurriedly. "Just a little taste. *Bitte*."

The two in the backseat began nodding their heads anxiously. Swag turned, studying the street, thinking it must have been Bammer who told them to start with the German. German was a good language for cops.

Swag raised himself from the window to walk away and saw one of the dark suits rounding the corner at Park. Turning his head, he saw the other coming toward him from Madison. They were walking slow and looking directly at each other.

When Swag looked back toward the car, one of Bammer's men was inching his hand toward the Luger pressed under his leg. Failing to get Swag into the car, they'd settle for a little drive-by action. The traffic was light enough so they could pop Swag as he leaned against the car, then drive off up Madison.

The two dark suits advanced steadily. Swag could see their faces clearly as they looked into the distance, careful to avoid eye contact. They both had that tight-skinned startled look of extensive plastic surgery.

When the dark suits were thirty feet away, and the provost's Luger had nearly cleared his leg, Swag pushed himself suddenly back from the car, grabbing the rear door handle with one hand and the Colt from his back holster with the other.

"Okay," Swag said, and yanked the back door open, showing the provosts the Colt. "Let's go, now!"

He was already pushing the plainclothes with the Ingram over before any of them knew what was happening. In their perfect world Swag would have sat between the two goons in the back or up front, where they could point a gun at the back of his head. Or even better, he'd be sprawled dead on the sidewalk with a crowd gathering around him as they headed up Madison.

That had been the plan. But now they couldn't figure what had gone wrong.

The driver turned, a question half formed on his lips, but stopped short when he saw Swag's 10mm pointed at his head.

"Drive," was all Swag said as he pulled the Luger from one of the backseat companions and the Ingram from the other.

As they pulled out into traffic, Swag lowered the gun so that it was pointed at the driver through the seat, and moved it to his left hand, away from the goon on the seat next to him. When they passed, one of the sidewalk dark suits stole a sidelong glance at the car as it made its way down the street.

"Hey, what's the deal?" the driver said, turning as he approached Madison. "We're all friends here, right?"

"Yeah," Swag said, turning to look out the back window. "You're all on my donor card for a kidney. Turn right on Madison."

They eased into Madison, Swag's Colt still pointing at the base of the driver's spine. The two goons sat motionless and quiet in the backseat while the driver cautiously negotiated the midday traffic of taxis and hired limos. When they reached 77th, Swag ordered the driver to stop. He didn't take his gun off the driver until he was opening the door and stepping out of the car. Then, hoping they wouldn't follow on foot, he doubled back to 76th and ducked in the Carlyle's side entrance. The narrow entranceway to the lobby was dark, cool, and quiet. It smelled of fresh-cut flowers and old money.

Security was on him before he hit the tiny lobby with its marble desk. You could say a lot of things about the Carlyle, but the place didn't lack for class. Three security men eased in from all sides. The tallest one, the team leader, wore a hand-tailored blue suit with covered buttons. The tortoiseshell frame of his clear glasses held the earpiece.

When he stopped Swag, it was with a sad little smile—an undertaker's professional grimace, filled with a manufactured sympathy at the cruel turns of life and inequitable judgments of fate that are beyond the capacity of mere mortals to comprehend. It was a smile that said, You've been screwed pal, nothing personal. Now hit the bricks.

"Sorry, Swag," the group leader said in a librarian's whisper, and Swag could almost believe that he had genuine regrets.

"What's the deal, Sheldon?" Swag asked, finding his voice lowered to a whisper as well.

"No deal," Sheldon answered, making the word deal sound vaguely disreputable. "You're no longer welcome on the premises."

"Where'd the word come from?" Swag asked.

Sheldon made a hand motion at shoulder level that sent the other two men melting back into the shadows, then adjusted something in his inside breast pocket, probably a communications microphone.

"The word came down this morning," Sheldon said, easing Swag toward the wall. "It was an official memo. Something to do with you being part of an ongoing provost investigation. Came from a certain suite at the Plaza."

"And unofficially?" Swag asked.

Sheldon looked anxiously over his shoulder. For just an instant he squirmed uncomfortably. "I tell you, but you owe me one," he said, voice dropping lower.

"Who's squeezing me, Sheldon?" Swag said, nodding.

"As far as I know, it's policy," Sheldon said. "You're officially a suspect in a shooting. Which is kinda odd, if you ask me, 'cause the papers said that the shooter you waxed got away."

"You know anything about that Lorette woman?" Swag asked. "She ever stay here?"

"A courier came couple days ago," Sheldon said. "Swiss diplomat, cultural attaché. But maybe not all that neutral."

"A Swiss spook?" Swag asked. "Come on, you have to do better than that."

Sheldon came in closer, bringing his head down to study the flowered pattern of the thick carpeting. "More like a mailman, actually," he said, lips barely moving. "For enough money he'll carry a little something through customs with him in the dip. Deposits for certain banks too sensitive for wire transfers. Maybe a contact name. Stock tips. The usual low-grade stuff."

"So, what's this got to do with me?"

"Well, he comes in like clockwork once a month," Sheldon said. "Makes his drop, then disappears into the bar. Has one drink, bitches about the price, and leaves. Couple days ago he comes in, makes the drop, and proceeds to spend three hundred francs in the bar, then checks into a two-thousand-franc suite."

"So, he made a score," Swag said.

"Some score," Sheldon said. "He holes up there for two days, ordering room service like a man that wasn't paying for it. We're talking girls, two, three, four a day—specialty acts—triples, just for a start. And we're talking tailors. We're talking every high-ticket entrée on the menu, and bottles of wine that carry their own insurance policy—"

"You're talking shit, Sheldon," Swag interrupted.

"Details, okay," Sheldon said. "I thought they might be important. Anyway, the guy doesn't leave the room. But he uses the hotel messenger for a delivery to the Plaza. Want to know what room it was?"

"Lorette's?" Swag asked, already knowing the answer.

"*Voilà,*" Sheldon said. "Next day your client gets wasted."

"He didn't do it," Swag said.

"I didn't say he did," Sheldon shot back. "It's just funny is all. Coincidence, right?"

Swag waited for more, Sheldon was definitely on a roll.

"Anyway, the day after he gets two visitors," Sheldon continued. "One right after the other. First, a weird-looking guy, then a little blonde number."

"They together? What were they?" Swag asked.

"They weren't together, not as far as I could tell. And I don't know what they were," Sheldon offered. "The weird-looking guy was gray, like Warhol with good skin. Not European, not American. The blonde, she was a snappy number with short hair. Pretending to be a working girl."

"How do you know she wasn't?" Swag asked.

"Shit, you can tell," Sheldon said. "Even if I didn't know every high-ticket pro above 52nd. You know, she didn't have dollar signs and an exchange rate running across her eyes."

"What was in the envelope he sent to Lorette?"

"Who says we looked?"

"Let's call it security precaution against terrorist letter bombs," Swag suggested. "Or we can call it an accident. Maybe the letter got too close to a leaky can of freon and you couldn't help but see what was in them."

"We'll call it security," Sheldon said. "Corporation papers and a printout for companies called Euro-Zeitech, Daimyo Limited, and about a half-dozen others. They're not publicly held, in case you were wondering. Incorporated in the Caymans, Isle of Man; Bahamas; Gibraltar; all tax havens, and a few others with secrecy laws. So they're dirty. Believe me—I get paid to know these things. The interesting part is, if you read the papers carefully, you'd see that they tied into Lorette-Defour, a supposedly legit operation run by your former client's husband, Ziggy."

"Anything else?" Swag asked. "Give me a topper."

"He stays another two days, charges up a total of fifteen thousand francs in big-time room service, *beaucoup* gratuities, and assorted services," Sheldon recited. "Not to mention a few hundred francs in calls down to D.C. He checks out five minutes after two wire transfers come through. The first was from Euro-Zeitech—Caymans, I think. The second is a Fed fund, drawn off an American firm, King's Secret Hosiery, out of a D.C. bank. And I'll give you any odds you want that King's Secret is some front operation for the Feds."

"There a punch line?" Swag asked.

"How's this for a punch line—he uses one money transfer to pay the tab and factors the other off on the street to a guy I know at a twelve point discount. Know what currency he converts to?"

"Is there a prize if I guess right?" Swag said.

"You won't," Sheldon said confidently. "Mexican pesos and Canadian dollars. No bargaining, no nothing."

"What does it mean?"

"I'd say the courier was peeking," Sheldon said. "Looking for a stock tip, found out something else. Maybe something that could embarrass a certain Swiss banker with a wife who just happens to be in New York and not just for the shopping. Then maybe the courier went into business; looking to sell the information or blackmail some people. Those checks were the payoff. Shit, who lays off that kind of money on the street, unless they don't want it traced? The point is, people don't spend honest money the way he did. He was definitely working a squeeze on someone."

Or a couple of someones, Swag thought to himself. "You talk to anybody about this?" Swag said.

"Naw, it doesn't mean anything," Sheldon said. "Except maybe to you, right?"

Swag was about to say that it didn't mean much to him either, when the manager strode over, moving quickly down the narrow hall.

"Sheldon, excuse me, will you please," the manager said, dismissing the security man. Then to Swag, "Sir, your protection services are no longer required. I shall have to ask you to leave at once. I'm afraid the retainer we paid last month will be your last."

Carlo Bagatelle was shuffling through bills at a back table, a pair of bifocals perched at the end of his nose, four or five stacks of blue, pink, and white invoices spread out in front of him. He was upstairs, because he hated the office. Two hours behind the desk in the basement was like jail time.

The two Johnnies sat at front tables near the window, watching the traffic and plotting between themselves. And somewhere in the background, coming over the sound system, a young, thin Sinatra was singing.

Carlo looked up when he heard the knock at the door; the bartender was late as usual. Outside, the late afternoon was slanting through the windows, but he could make out the profiles of two men in dark suits.

There was another knock at the door, and Carlo lifted his head again. "Will you get that, somebody?" he shouted from the shadows of the back.

One of the Johnnies put down his drink, J&B rocks, turned to the door and waved the men away. When they knocked again, the Johnny shouted, "We're closed, okay?"

But the two men didn't move. Rather, one of them knocked again.

"Jeez, will you get rid of them!" Carlo called, looking up and seeing the two forms in the doorway. From the suits, the haircuts, and the large bag one carried, Carlo made them as liquor salesmen. "Tell 'em we don't want any."

Lifting himself wearily from his seat, the Johnny walked over to the door and shouted, "We're closed."

One of the men made a motion, indicating that they should open the door.

Grimacing, the Johnny opened the door a crack and said, "Look pal, we're fuckin' closed. Okay?"

When the Johnny saw the gun, a matte-black Glock come up, he did a quick side-step and tried to push the door closed. But the other dark suit, the one with the bag, had already put his shoulder into the effort. When the door flew open, it pushed the one Johnny back, just as the other was coming off the bar stool.

The two men entered the bar, the one with the Glock leading the way.

"Let's all act like adults now," the guy with the Glock said. "And not do anything stupid."

The guy with the bag turned and relocked the door as the two Johnnies nodded and took a cautious step back.

The two men were both nearly identical in height and dress, their faces bland, nearly expressionless.

"Now, what's the problem?" Carlo began, rising up from behind the bills. Then he saw the gun and sat back down.

"Carlo Bagatelle?" the man holding the gun said.

The Johnnies were backing up, moving into the dim light at the back of the room as the guy with the gun directed them.

"What's the deal here?" Carlo said, showing remarkable calm. "You holding me up? You fucking with the wrong guy."

The Johnnies were now behind Carlo, not pretending not to be scared.

"You're Carlo Bagatelle?" one of the men said. Carlo noticed that he was holding a suitcase, what they used to call a Gladstone bag.

"Yeah, I'm him," Carlo answered. "Now what's the deal here?"

"We understand that you have a problem," the one with the gun said. "A little trouble with your video poker games."

"What? You guys looking for work?" Carlo spat. "You ain't going about it the right way."

"As we understand it, you've been experiencing some shrinkage of profits."

Carlo sat motionless for a second, trying to figure the angle. The way they were dressed, they looked like a couple of junior executives. Except for their eyes, and the way they carried themselves. Their eyes were cold and unblinking. And the way they stood, taller than any working stiff stood. Carlo recognized them as muscle almost immediately. They were the kind of guys he'd hire, if he could afford anything better than the Johnnies.

"You are Carlo Bagatelle," the guy with the briefcase said; it wasn't a question.

When he couldn't come up with an answer, Carlo said, "Yeah, so what?"

"We've taken care of the problem for you," the guy with the gun said.

"Bullshit!" Carlo hissed in a whisper. "Who are you guys? Whoever you are, you don't know who you're fucking with."

"The next time you collect, you'll notice a twenty-five percent increase in your gross," the guy with the bag said.

"You should consider that twenty-five percent a service fee," the other continued.

"What? This some kind of bullshit scam?" Carlo answered angrily. "You don't know who you're dealing with here. *I'm a made man.* You know what that means in this town?"

"Not a thing," the guy with the gun said as he brought the gun in close to Carlo's face. "Not a fucking thing."

"How'd I know you took care of any problem I got? Not that I'm saying I got one."

"Proof?" the guy with the gun asked, a smile coming to his face. "Would you like proof?"

There was something about the smile, and the way he offered proof, that rattled Carlo. Something that took him back to the old days, when he was on the other side of the table and holding a piece on some poor bastard.

Then the dark with the gun nodded to the one with the bag, and the one with the bag opened the brass clasp and turned the Gladstone upside down.

Three human heads—two men and a woman—tumbled from the bag, thunked across the table and stained the invoices with blood. Two rolled off on to the floor. The third landed in Carlo's lap.

"Holy fucking shit!" Carlo shouted and pushed his chair back fast, sending the third head rolling off his lap and under the table.

"As we mentioned, you should consider that twenty-five percent a service fee," the guy with the bag continued as he relocked the clasp. "It's non-negotiable and payable each month."

"Payable till when?" Carlo asked, in shock.

"Payable till forever," came the answer.

chapter thirteen

SWAG WAS ON THE MOVE, careful to avoid a pattern. For three days he'd covered his trail, checking in and out of cheap hotels and staying clear of his usual haunts. No doubt Bammer's boys were looking to disappear him, and those guys in the dark suits, whoever they were, were dodging him. Somewhere, just out of Swag's field of vision, there was a connection between the provost's hit squad and the dark suits, but Swag couldn't see it. All he knew was, ever since he'd been looking into Lorette's death, a lot of people had taken a lethal interest in his health.

It had been a while since Swag made it down to Times Square. The Deuce, that short forlorn strip between Sixth and Ninth Avenues, stretched across the center of the island like an unbandaged wound. Each year the ancient movie theaters slowly crumbled deeper into themselves, their tar-paper roofs rotting, while the sleek glass and steel towers of a real estate redevelopment deal stood darkened; victims of optimism, ego, and bad timing.

The new buildings now stood nearly completely empty, with street level entrances sealed over with poster-laden plywood. It was rumored that the buildings were filled with skels, hundreds of them, who trekked up fifty stories or more of darkened stairways to paneled offices designed for captains of industry. But Swag knew this to be fantasy. Even the homeless avoided these buildings.

What had begun as an effort to turn the Deuce into a

billion-dollar shopping mall had ended in an embarrass-ment of failed style and thievery.

But gone now were the second-floor boxing parlors, their walls plastered with ancient posters, the turn buckles of the rings layered with duct tape. Gone also were the dubious employment agencies, the bad-attitude Kalderash fortune tellers, cut-rate camera shops, pizzerias, tailors, and most of the peep shows.

There was history on the Deuce, but little of it good. The big theaters with their gold leaf and plush seats were now vacant except for rats. The years had turned the Deuce from naughty to gaudy to disreputable, and then into a kill-zone, where yellow plastic crime scene tape hung like bunting from lamp posts and parking meters and snaked along unswept gutters.

Almost until the very end, before the fall, writers of guidebooks felt compelled to call the strip colorful, as if a tourist strolling down the Deuce some summer eve might catch a precious glimpse of some real-life guys and dolls. Jaded tourists once sought titillation in the triple-X video stores or followed the barkers' welcoming chant of "Pussy, pussy, pussy."

Later, when the dollar sank and Europe's Common Market opened up, when the violent year began, the South American drug importers moved their franchises to Europe and the Pacific Rim. Suddenly, under martial law, everyone was sentenced to mandatory detox and the street ran red with the blood of unsated need.

Now, only a handful of sex shops remained. Squatting forlorn and brooding in the shadows of the vacant sky-scrapers, they had become obsolete in a city whose major industry was vice. They catered to the most budget-conscious skin tours, counting on cheap prices and nostalgia. Buses with their darkly-tinted windows began parking along the street at ten in the morning and flowed in an orderly fashion until just past midnight. None of the passengers, shuffling back toward the buses with paper sacks of sex toys and videos, ever looked all that happy.

Swag cut across Sixth Avenue, walking fast in the hot summer rain that cooled nothing. The sky was already dark at three in the afternoon, and the colored lights and neon bled out across the rain-slick street.

World of Peeps was the last of the old time establishments. Leonard "Money Shot" Sadowitz, who owned the joint, had once been hailed as a pioneer of porn, being one of the first to make the transition from the old 8mm loops to video. But he had not changed with the times. Back in '81, when a stylish Dutch couple arrived with a Vuitton suitcase loaded with wares featuring twelve-year-old starlets, Leonard hadn't waited for the first scene to end before he excused himself and lumbered into an adjoining office to make a call to lower Manhattan. The couple were never seen again. Their hotel bill went unpaid.

When the system collapsed, Money Shot bought out his silent, bent-nose partners downtown for a song and continued on, changing nothing.

Now Money Shot was hunched over a raised counter, wearing a canvas change apron. He sat like a fat bear in the back of the darkened store. Surrounded by broken neon and dusty sex toys, he counted one-franc tokens for the peep show booths and breathed pine-scented disinfectant for twelve hours a day.

As Swag came through the door, wiping a length of wet hair from his forehead, Money Shot slowly lifted his red-rimmed eyes up from his counting and rubbed the bridge of his nose. "Officer, my old friend," Money Shot said without any enthusiasm at all. "What brings you back? Nostalgia, true love, what?"

Behind the old bear was Nicky, a one-armed recovered junkie who had once worked as a kind of lab rat. Nicky was a former street tester, injecting himself with whatever mid-level dealers were offering that week. When his left arm became infected from a dirty spike, he waited three weeks before going into the Emergency Room. By then the arm was swollen to more than three times its size. It was the arm that made him a celebrity. After they drained the pus, the intern shined a penlight down a strangely graceful tunnel of putrefying flesh and saw the gray of his bone. That was good and bad.

They'd have to amputate, said the just-summoned chief of surgery, but they'd like to buy the arm for the teaching hospital. It would, he explained, benefit science, and how did two hundred dollars sound? Nicky made a telephone call to Money Shot, who came down and negotiated $850 while Nicky drank a cup of coffee, light with five sugars, that the intern had brought him. "You ain't dealing with some scumbag here, Doc," Nicky said as he emptied a sixth sugar into the coffee. "I got myself *representation*, motherfucker." What neither of them knew was that the hospital planned to film the operation for use on a teaching video disk. Nicky saw the set-up and video techs as they wheeled him into the operating room. Groggy from the anesthesia, he raised up on the gurney and said, "Fuck, we didn't get film rights."

Now Nicky was clean, and the story of his arm was the stuff of junkie legends. When he saw Swag, he raised his stump in a half greeting as he maneuvered a wet mop to sweep out a load of crumpled tissues from one of the dozen video booths. "How's it going," he called, letting a smile work its way over his pockmarked face.

"Hows by you, Nicky?" Swag called back over Money Shot's shoulder.

But Nicky didn't answer, lost in his recovered junkie thoughts.

"Lucy working?" Swag asked, moving closer to the counter past a small herd of Japanese businessmen sorting through opened cardboard crates of ancient videos. *Sararimen*, Swag thought, probably won the trip in a company contest. They all wore the same small red and white button as a badge of company loyalty.

"Lucy?" Money Shot said, then checked his watch. "She's working. Second booth up on the left. You want some tokens?"

"When's her break?"

"Not for a half hour," Money Shot answered in the same impassive voice. "You want some tokens?"

Lucy had originally come from some small midwestern town. When Swag first met her, she was working a West Side hotel, singing in the lobby's lounge and waiting for a record producer or movie director to recognize the talent that all the folks back home said she had.

When he saw her again, maybe a year later, she was turning tricks in that same lounge. She wore a conservative business suit, cut just short enough to tip off potential customers as to what business she was in. From there she drifted steadily downward, as if pushed by some gravity felt only by whores and hustlers. Another year passed, and Swag saw her on the stroll over on the West Side. She was holding a paper coffee cup in front of a Smiler's deli and winning five bucks off another hooker by singing "Memories" straight through. When Money Shot offered her a job, it was a half step up and away from a popcorn pimp named Staten.

It didn't take her long to set up shop as message center along the Deuce. She claimed that it was because of her trick memory. She had over four hundred songs in her head; remembering that "Deebs will be at the new place next Wednesday at six" was a piece of cake compared to learning all the words to "MacArthur Park" or "Candle in the Wind."

"Give me five," Swag said.

Money Shot counted out the small brass tokens with the warning, "Doesn't buy much time anymore."

The jack booths formed a single line along the narrow balcony. Each booth had two glass-fronted curtained doors. A mechanical divider and a floor-to-ceiling window separated the two sections. Two or three of the girls, wearing what may have once been provocative underwear, sat on bar stools in front of their booths smoking and casting derisive sidelong glances at a small huddled group of Japanese tourists.

From inside Lucy's booth Swag could see the distinct

flash of a camera. When a double-breasted businessman, Nikon slung around his neck, hurried from the booth and down the stairs to buy more tokens, Swag moved in front of the waiting group, edged into the customer's side of the booth and slid onto the torn vinyl seat of a bar stool.

There was a phone handset hung across a coat hook on the wall, and Swag picked it up.

She began speaking before the sheet-metal partition had completely risen. "So what are you shooting, 400 ASA," came the bored voice through the line. Although they were less than three feet away, separated by only a half inch of scratched plastic, her voice sounded distant. "You're wastin' ya time with that flash. Step the speed down to one-sixtieth and open up to F2. Polarizing filter wouldn't hurt, if you want to see anything."

When the partition was all the way up, the lights in Swag's side of the booth went out and a line of sixty-watt bulbs clicked on in Lucy's side, framing her in the center. Swag looked through the stained and smudged glass to see she was dressed completely in white, from the patent leather pumps to the frilly push-up bra. She was holding her phone handset between a raised shoulder and ear, and bending her head forward to light a cigarette, still not looking up.

Lucy was on the wrong side of thirty-five and had no illusions about it. Swag knew that she had maybe five more years before that partition stopped creaking up. After that, Swag couldn't guess what she'd do.

"No thanks," Swag said. "I'll work from memory."

"Ah, shit, Swag, it's you," she said, smiling slightly around the cigarette. "What are you doing here?"

Swag pulled a pack from his shirt pocket and lit his own cigarette, filling the small booth with smoke. "Still taking messages?" he asked.

"Now and again," came the wary response. "You want to leave one or take one?"

"Take one, unofficially," Swag said and inhaled on the cigarette, watching Lucy's response. She didn't owe him a favor, not a thing. He was counting on a dim sense of nostalgia to pull the information out of her.

"Who you want to know about?"

Letting out a lungful of smoke, Swag said, "Me."

Then the metal creaked down and the phone went dead.

Swag put another token in the slot and waited for Lucy to reappear. When she came back into view, she was frowning. "I haven't heard anything, honest."

"Any of Bammer's guys been around, talking maybe?"

"Usual bullshit," she said, letting out a thin stream of smoke toward the ceiling. "Heard Lenny bitching about it."

"What, about tourists? Anything?"

"Nothing, Swag, really," she said, letting the hand with the cigarette drop to her side. "What're you worrying about?"

"I think someone's trying to freeze me out," he said. It was the first time he'd mentioned it to anyone. But it sounded true. "They flaked a client. Swiss lady."

"Hey, that was you," she answered, perking up. "I read about her in the paper."

And then the screen came down.

Swag dropped his last three tokens in and waited as the sheet metal rose noisily along its grooved path.

This time Swag saw that Lucy was bending low to talk. Her hand held the phone tightly to her ear as the screen came up. "Who shot her?" she asked anxiously.

"A dead guy," Swag said.

"I read that he got away," she said. "Heard she was staying at the Plaza, that true? Was it a nice room?"

"It was great," Swag answered without much enthusiasm. "You haven't heard about anything weird going on? Anyone get disappeared? Any strange scams?"

"There's never anything new," Lucy said. "There's a crew running the pigeon drop up near Columbus Circle. And you're asking if there's anything new?"

"Lucy, for old time's sake?" Swag asked. "What's the strangest thing you've seen, say in the last month?"

Scrunching up her face, pretending to think hard, she said, "You know, there is like one strange deal from a few days ago."

"Yeah?"

"Couple of kids from downtown," she said, looking around as if the details were written on her side of the booth. "They came in a while ago, with schematics for this radio that'd make the right someone a piece of change. I steered them to a guy I know."

"Keep going."

"He came around to thank me for the steer, but said it was the most fucked up thing he'd ever seen, a directional antenna, weird frequencies. Specs Xeroxed from a school pad. Anyway, he takes a quick look at it. And says, 'You ain't gonna hear much.' He said the frequencies were so low. I mean *real low*."

"And they told him it was a transmitter, right?" Swag offered.

"How'd you know?" Lucy asked, clearly impressed. "The kid said, 'Look again, asshole,' and it was a transmitter. Only no circuits for a microphone—no input at all—nothing but a big-ass transmitter with two frequency settings and this directional antenna. My friend figured it was something to jam microwaves."

"When did they pick it up?" Swag asked.

"Who said my friend built it?" Lucy shot back. "And it can't have nothing to do with you anyway. Besides, the kids are gone, I heard, left for California."

"You hear about Carlo?" Swag said.

"Heard that someone was taking down his machines for *beaucoup* change," Lucy answered coyly. "And that he was about to bust a vein over it."

"Then you know not to fuck around with him," Swag cautioned. "No ideas about making one of those things for yourself."

"Did I say I made one?" Lucy replied sweetly. So sweetly that Swag knew she was lying.

"Don't mess with him, Lucy. Those machines and the

Johnnies are all he's got left," Swag said. "You hear what I'm telling you?"

"Yeah, sure, Swag," she answered without concern. "It's nice of you to warn me, honest."

When the screen came down again, she reached behind her in a quick motion, brought out a popsicle stick and jammed it between the worm scar and tracks, stopping its descent. From somewhere above an electric motor began grinding and then fell silent.

"Neat trick," Swag said. "You'll burn out Money Shot's motor, though."

Lucy leaned down just below the screen's edge and said, "Naw, it's on a clutch kind of mechanism. Who do you think is head of maintenance now?"

"So, Lucy, what do you know about computers?" Swag asked.

"Enough to know I don't know shit," came the answer. "What kind?"

"Banking, the kind that move money," Swag said.

"Swag, I don't want you to take this the wrong way," Lucy said. "But the way you look, the only money you're gonna be moving is from your left pocket to your right."

"I want to trace a company," Swag said.

"European or domestic?" came the reply.

"Could be both," Swag said.

"Maybe I know a guy who knows a guy," Lucy said. "How much you want to spend?"

"That depends on what you can set me up with in the way of work," Swag answered, then dropped the cigarette and ground it out with his boot toe.

"I know a couple of guys moving gray market liquor that need some protection. The work might cover my end."

Swag leaned forward at this news. "What are they into?"

"It's that Maker's Mark stuff," she answered in a lower voice. "From Kentucky, real top shelf. You know, bourbon."

"I mean, is it a legal deal?"

This got a small laugh, but when she saw that Swag didn't share the joke, she said, "First you ask for a connect on an international bank thing, then you want to know if a small-time operation is legit. But you know, as a matter of fact, it is."

"What's the deal on it?"

"Like I said, it's bourbon," she explained. "A hundred cases. The load was supposed to go out to some little country in West Africa, originally shipped in wooden kegs or whatever and bottled over there. The President for Life was queer for the stuff or something. Couldn't get enough of it. Had it bottled there with his picture on the label. Riding a horse, no less."

From above the motor began whining in a higher pitch. Then Money Shot's voice boomed up over the P.A. system. "Mechanic to the main level," he said in a bored tone. "Mechanic to the main level."

Lucy let the cigarette fall and exhaled deeply. "I swear I don't know what the fuck I was thinking when I fixed that thing for him," she said. Then, opening the door of her side of the booth, she yelled down, "What the fuck is it? We got a thing going on here?"

Money Shot didn't use the P.A. when he answered. "A gentleman says that selection twelve in the video booth is jumping around. It makes his eyes hurt when he looks at it."

Lucy rolled her own eyes and shouted back, "Tell him not to look at it, then."

When Money Shot answered this time, it was on the P.A. "Mechanic to the main level, mechanic to the main level."

Lucy, with her door still open, shouted down, "I'll get to it in a minute," as the businessmen went "*Oi! Oi! Oi!*" Hey you!

Fixing the businessmen in a cold stare, she added, "*Domo sumimasen*, okay?" Very sorry.

Money Shot and the businessmen all quieted down. Closing the door, she turned back to Swag and said, "Fuckin' multiplexer, piece of shit. Distribution, impedance, all shot to shit. I don't know, maybe it's shorting out, or that one-armed prick, Nicky, is sloshing water on units again."

"So, what happened to the order?"

"You don't read the papers much, huh?" she said. "The President for Life's term came up. Somebody voted him out with a car bomb. Anyway, the shipment goes through three or four brokers, everyone making a little. Now, there's two guys ready to move it off the Brooklyn dock, and need some protection. It's a grounder."

The motor changed pitch again. It seemed to be running faster.

"Needs oil," Swag said.

"You wouldn't believe what I've been using for oil around this place," came the frowning answer. "Anyway, my end's ten percent."

"Ten of what?"

"Of whatever you negotiate," Lucy replied sweetly. "And don't get fast with me on this thing either. Believe me, it'll get back to me."

Lucy gave him the phone numbers and released the popsicle stick from its resting place. The sheet-metal divider came down quickly and Swag left.

Downstairs, Money Shot was unpacking a box of yard-long sex toys.

"You turn that on, all the TV reception from here to Jersey goes out," Swag said, stopping at the counter.

"Whoever turns this on won't be watching no TV, my friend," Money Shot replied as he rose from the half-empty crate. "Six C-cells. Like one of those old-time cop flashlights."

"Lot of horsepower, huh?"

"You bet," Money Shot said, then leaned back and shouted, "Hey, Nicky, what'ya say we get Lucy to rig one of these things up for an arm, huh?"

Nicky didn't answer, but behind Money Shot's back he propped the mop in the crook of his good arm and gave his boss the finger.

"He's flipping me off, right?" Money Shot said, chuckling in a somewhat sinister manner. "Bet you a franc I can tell you what hand he's using."

"I'll give you a franc," Swag said. "Go buy yourself some new jokes."

"Know what I'll never understand?"

"What's that, Leonard?" Swag asked, not wanting to go back out into the rain, and intrigued at the thought of Money Shot pleading ignorance to anything. Ask the guy about Jimmy Hoffa, he'd tell you how he was Marilyn Monroe's personal sex slave.

"Twenty-five years I'm in this business," he said, raising one of the devices to drive his point home. "And you'd think everybody who wanted one of these things would have one by now, no?"

"Planned obsolescence, maybe," Swag offered.

"Naw, these things are made to last a lifetime," Money Shot shot back, and just to emphasize the point, he began pounding it across the chipped Formica countertop. "See? These babies are built to last."

Swag was nearly to the door when Money Shot hit the switch on a cassette player that blared a barker's cry in Japanese out over the P.A. It was Nicky's bored voice, shouting *"Chimo! Chimo! Chimo!"* which Swag knew translated roughly to mean, "Shameful hair."

chapter fourteen

HE WAS ALMOST TO Sixth Avenue before he saw them. Two men leaning against the side of a mobile catering truck parked near the New York Telephone building. It was the same pair that had followed him to Raffles the day before. They were taking cover from the rain under the truck's blue-and-white-striped canopy, holding the space by munching on greasy eggrolls wrapped in waxpaper sleeves. Their raincoats weren't exactly identical, but close enough. Swag could also see that they were both wearing dark suits.

Swag passed the two guys and got a good look at them as their eyes pointedly avoided him. They stood in a vaguely military fashion, one just behind the other, ready to cover his comrade's back. The one facing Swag was wearing court glasses—the kind of tortoise frames with clear glass that defense attorneys put on clients to give them the appearance of a studious nonviolent personality. But the glasses did little to offset the sharp angles of the guy's face or his unblinking predator eyes.

The other guy was a little heavier, but not much. Swag saw that one corner of his mouth drooped slightly, in a kind of half frown. Neither held an umbrella, and their hair was wet. Their skin shone waxy, almost plastic, in the gray light.

As Swag passed, he nodded to them quickly, but they kept on studying the ground. Who are these guys? he thought to himself. Even Bammer's boys weren't *this* bad at following someone, or this evil-looking.

Stopping at Sixth and 42nd, he looked ahead, surveying Bryant Park and the library beyond. Traffic was light across Sixth and on 42nd. The rain had taken care of the pedestrians, and only a few cars and cabs were on the street.

When he crossed Sixth, he could *feel* one of the men break away and begin following him. Casting a sidelong glance up Sixth, he saw the other, the one with the glasses, cross 42nd and head for the corner.

Swag began walking quickly now, edging past the corner and toward the park. Fifty feet or so up the block was a subway with a newsstand next to its entrance. When he stopped to buy the *Times*, he could see one of the suits crossing Sixth. The other one was on the opposite side, walking slowly under the cover provided by the Grace Building's archway.

As he headed down the subway's stairs Swag pulled the gun from its back holster and folded it into the *Times*. Then he waited, his back against the iron gate of the closed subway station, his finger around the Colt's trigger. Beyond the bars of the gate was an empty token booth and the IND line's platform. The sharp smell of urine drifted up from the floor of the entrance and darkened station.

It didn't take more than twenty seconds for the dark suit to appear. He was running, afraid he would lose Swag on the subway. When he saw Swag leaning against the closed entrance, he came up short, mumbled something and began to turn.

"Not another step," Swag said.

The guy froze, his back to Swag.

"Come on down here," Swag ordered. "Get out of the rain."

With his hands up, at shoulder level, the dark suit turned and came down the steps. "Excuse me," the man said, "is this what they call mugging?" He spoke with a vague accent, something from one of those cold countries, Danish maybe, or another Scandinavian language.

Swag took a step closer, grabbed the guy by the shoulder and turned him toward the wall. The dark suit fell into the position immediately, hands above his head, legs spread. "Yeah, that's what they call it," Swag said.

When the paper fell from around the Colt, Swag held it in close, at the small of the guy's back. Then he patted him down, one-handed.

"I have money, take it," the dark suit said, trying to sound helpless. "Please, do not hurt me."

"Why are you following me?" Swag asked as he ran his hand up the man's leg from ankle to belt loops.

"Is this not the entrance to the Number One?" the dark suit asked.

When he got to the chest, Swag felt the bulge of a weapon. Slipping his hand in, he pulled the big gun from the holster.

It was a Glock 9. Remembering the girl's wounds, he released the magazine and stuffed it into his pants pocket. Then he jacked the shell from the chamber and threw the pistol through the bars. The gun clattered and echoed in the darkness.

"Do not shoot me, please," the man said, his voice flat. "I am just a tourist."

Swag looked for a passport but found only a wallet in a breast pocket. He drew it out, thick with bills. It was a cheap eel-skin number, and there were at least four hundred francs in it. Not travelers' checks, cash. But no credit cards, and no papers, just a picture of a pretty woman and two blond little girls set against a backdrop of green trees and blue sky. The picture had been in the wallet when the blue suit bought it.

"Who do you work for?" Swag asked.

"I am just a tourist," the man said, and then made his move. The strike was so fast that Swag barely saw it coming. The guy did a sort of pivot on one foot, bringing his arm snapping back and turning in one lightning motion. Swag's gun hand blocked the blow, sending the steel barrel into his face, splitting his lower lip and numbing his arm down to the elbow. The force of the strike sent Swag backward, smashing him into the steel barred gate. The gate gave a little against the padlocked chain, then bounced him forward.

The hand struck again while the dark suit was still in motion, hitting solidly against Swag's shoulder and sending him to the ground. Swag wasn't done falling on his ass when he looked up and saw the guy complete a turn and assume some stiff-fingered maiming stance with his arms bent out at odd angles. He seemed a little surprised to see Swag down. The next strike wasn't from the hands. The dark suit spun out in a kick that landed just below Swag's shoulder, lifting him up and propelling him sideways against the tiled wall.

This guy's gonna kick you to death in the subway, Swag thought to himself. Then, before the next kick could land, Swag brought the Colt up and fired.

The blast echoed through the deserted entrance as the jacketed slug passed through the guy's hand. A thick spray of blood splashed across the tiled wall, which cracked and sent the bullet ricocheting out into the street.

The guy looked at the bloody remains of his ruined hand—the blown-out palm where bone was showing—like it was a mosquito bite. He frowned slightly, dropping the hand to his side, and made his move to kick again.

Swag fired again as the dark suit brought his foot up. The 10mm round punched into his chest, throwing him off balance against the steel handrail. He staggered back, his heels catching on the first step, then began pulling himself upright with his good hand. As he came up again he snaked out another kick, which went high.

Shit, Swag thought, another one of these fuckin' guys with a Kevlar gut.

When the guy stumbled forward and threw another kick, Swag fired again and got lucky. The slug hit in the solar plexus, sending the suit back against the wall.

"Who the fuck are you people?" Swag asked, then shot him again in the stomach.

The guy grunted as the bullet smashed into his gut and sent him doubling over.

Time was running out and Swag knew it. Switching the gun to his left hand, he moved in on the guy and brought him upright by the neck, then slammed his head against the steel bars of the closed entrance and jammed the barrel of the Colt right under his chin.

"Who are you guys?" Swag demanded then, pushing the dark suit's head back with the Colt's barrel.

"I am a tourist," came the strangled answer.

Instinct or luck brought Swag's head around then. At the top of the stairs was the other dark suit. He was halfway down the stairs before he saw what the deal was.

Keeping the first guy on the bars, Swag brought the gun up and shot low. The bullet caught the second dark suit in the shin of his left leg, snapping through the bone, spilling him down the stairs and sending the glasses flying from his head. By the time he hit the bottom, the toe of his wing-tipped foot was bent forward, nearly to the knee. And he was reaching for his shoulder holster.

Swag shot him in the shoulder, released the first guy and bent down to retrieve the gun from the holster. It was another Glock.

The second guy said, "Please do not kill me."

"I know," Swag answered, "you're a fuckin' tourist."

Swag kept the Colt trained on the second guy, who was not sweating and moaning, and turned back to the first guy on the bars, who had worked his shot hand up to his mouth and was biting at a bloody finger. Then Swag realized, no, he's biting a ring.

"Who are you people?" Swag demanded, bouncing the man's head off the bars, then bringing his forearm across the guy's throat and forcing the hand away from his mouth in one motion.

As the bloody hand fell away from the mouth, the guy smiled the biggest "fuck you" smile Swag had ever seen. It was all capped teeth and pink gums. A second later he began to shake. That's when Swag smelled it; the scent came through the guy's wet breath, through the urine stench of the entranceway. It was the smell of almonds. Cyanide. Swag felt all the neck muscles tighten and spasm beneath his arm before the guy's head flopped down.

Swag took a step back, letting the dead guy drop to the floor. "Who are you people?" he demanded, his voice coming out in a sharp bark as he bent to haul up the second suit.

The wounded man staggered back against the bars, his good foot wedged in the armpit of his fallen comrade, his bad one dangling off at an impossible angle, barely attached beneath the bloodied chalk pinstripe of the suit. His face was white from blood loss, and Swag knew that the guy had maybe half a minute before he went into shock.

"Talk to me," Swag spat out, holding his new captive by the throat and pushing the barrel of the Colt in the soft spot between the jaw and ear.

"I'm a tourist," the guy said, then punched out in a three-fingered maiming move. It was a short jab with his left hand, but there wasn't much power in the punch. Swag felt it coming and stepped into it before he could fully extend his hand. It knocked the breath out of Swag, but before the guy could grab hold of any muscles, Swag sent the barrel of the Colt cracking across his head.

"Who do you work for, scumbag?" Swag demanded, getting right in the guy's face. But the dark suit never flinched. His face twisted and sweat-soaked from pain, he looked right back at Swag with wide-open eyes.

The guy's good leg started to give out then, and Swag wrapped his hand tighter around the thick neck, pinning the back of his head between the narrow bars.

"Who pays you?" Swag spat into the man's face.

"I do not understand," the man said, then began dropping his shoulder for another punch.

Swag took a quick half step back, then, using both hands, banged the guy's head between the bars. The arm went limp and his eyes rolled back, unfocused by the sudden blow.

"Who pays you?" Swag repeated, then banged him against the bars again.

The guy's head lulled and came up slow, stunned by the

blows. The square metal bars behind him were stained with blood.

"Talk to me," Swag said, moving in close again, so that his nose was almost touching the nearly unconscious man. "Start talking or I'll pound your goddamned brains out."

Then, suddenly, the guy's eyes and mouth popped open in surprise. There was a muted snap and his head lolled forward. Behind him appeared the face of another man on the other side of the bars. It was a perfectly smooth and calm face framed by an excellent haircut. The guy was wearing a blue LaCoste sport shirt and a small, slightly amused grin.

An instant later the dark suit was dead weight. Swag struggled back and sideways as the body fell toward him to reveal the entire man standing behind the bars. He was holding a thin, clear plastic rod, twirling its six-inch length in his fingers carelessly. It was no wider around than a pencil, and exactly the same diameter as the perfectly formed hole at the base of the dark suit's skull.

"How's it going, ace?" the guy said as he casually dropped the plastic stick. "Are we having fun yet?"

Swag, trying to free himself from the body, raised the Colt and said, "Hold it right the fuck there!"

As the body fell, the stranger behind the bars said, "Know how to get to Carnegie Hall?"

Swag said "Hold it" again as the guy slipped calmly and smoothly out of sight, close to the wall on the other side of the bars.

Stepping over the two bodies, Swag stuck the gun through the bars and stared into the darkness. Somewhere underground, on the level below, a train rumbled through. From the shadows of the station there was an echoed laugh, and the stranger in the LaCoste shirt and good haircut called out, "Practice!"

Just a few blocks east, up 42nd Street, close to the river, a young woman with short-cropped hair sat at a computer terminal. Although the sealed room was windowless and had layered walls of two-foot-thick steel and polymer, the computer's terminal and monitor were encased in a box of heavy plastic, which extended out from the screen in a narrowing cowl that guarded any displayed material from the prying eyes of both humans and microwaves.

The keyboard too was specially constructed with the same shielding plastic, as well as a layer of soft rubber beneath the keys, which dampened any clicking.

The room was empty, save for the computer, high-speed laser printer, shredder, and two ergonomically designed chairs. In one corner of the room Jim Bob sat in one of the chairs, legs spread out in front of him, folding a piece of printout paper again and again. "How long you figure?" he asked, keeping his eyes on the meticulous folds.

"Putting it through encryption now," the woman said. "Then it'll transmit." Punching down on a half-dozen keys, she turned, swiveling the chair around, to study Jim Bob. "I coded it 'Flash.' The crew will relay it out from the European desk, then directly into the Euro-Zeitech account."

"And it'll be clear enough for those old boys to notice right off?" Jim Bob asked.

"I've done everything but hang a sign on it," the young woman said. "If they look at all, they'll see it. There'll be a stir in the San Remo."

"Yup, darlin', I expect there will," Jim Bob said.

"What about the Amcit?" the young woman asked.

Jim Bob frowned, partly at the task of accomplishing a difficult fold and partly at the young woman's use of agency slang. It was a habit he'd have to break her of. "Now, what American citizen would that be?" he answered.

"That Swag character," came the response. "The one with the shirts."

"We'll just sit back and watch him for a spell," Jim Bob said, stopping his folding of the paper. "See which way he comes up on this thing. I don't know what he knows and what he don't know."

"And if he comes up on the wrong side?" the young woman asked.

"Then that's a damn shame," Jim Bob answered without a second's pause. Then he smiled and made a precise reverse fold to form the delicate origami crane's head.

The young woman stared at Jim Bob intently, thinking that for all his easygoing country charm, he wouldn't hesitate for a second to do what needed to be done. Just the way he said "damn shame" made it sound like the death sentence it was.

Jim Bob was thinking about how they folded paper cranes for luck in Japan. Folding a thousand cranes would change your fortune, they said. But the way Jim Bob figured it, he only needed a little luck at this point.

The young woman smiled back, a little weakly perhaps, when Jim Bob held up the angular bird between two fingers. "How clever," she said, forcing a smile on her face.

"Know what this puts me in the mood for?" he said, rising, then crossing the room to present the woman with the paper bird.

"Sushi?" she answered hopefully, as she turned the crane between her fingers.

"Fried chicken," Jim Bob answered with a broadening smile. Then he teasingly added, *"Tsuru no hitoke,"* which the young woman knew meant not only "the crane's voice," but also, "the boss has the last word."

chapter fifteen

LONGFORD OPENED THE DOOR with a worried look on his face. "The Colt, you haven't lost it?" he asked. It was a nearly human voice of concern, the kind someone else might have used when asking whether a relative or close friend had died.

"I haven't lost it," Swag said, stepping inside and reaching behind his back to produce the gun as Longford closed the door.

The gunsmith gave the weapon a cursory look without reaching for it, nodded grimly, and walked mechanically down the hall.

"I need you to check something out for me, Long," Swag said as he entered the brightly lit workroom.

"A firearm?" Longford asked. That was the way he talked. Longford would never say the word gun. It was always firearm, weapon, or brand name.

"A bullet," Swag answered, pulling out the clip he had taken off the two dead dark suits the day before.

Longford took the clip and studied it for a minute, turning it slowly over in his large hands. "It's a clip from a Glock 9. Factory standard. Almost new."

Swag followed him to the workbench and asked, "What about the cartridges?"

Longford pulled a jeweler's loop from his shirt pocket and thumbed one of the cartridges from the clip. "It's a nine millimeter. Federal Hydra-Shok," he answered quickly, turning the cartridge every which way, "147 grain hollowpoint."

Swag leaned as close as he dared without disturbing Longford. "Anything else you can tell me?"

"Ah, 950 or so feet per second," he began. "Good grouping with the right gun. If you hit somebody with it, you'll get good expansion, maybe two centimeters. Decent soft-tissue penetration to say, thirty-eight, forty centimeters, and good permanent and temporary cavitation."

"That's it then, this is off the shelf?" Swag asked.

Longford continued to stare at the cartridge through the loop and said, "Well, yes, oh, now this is interesting."

"What's that?" Swag asked, bending in low again.

For a long second the room fell silent except for the humming of Longford's fluorescents and the air conditioner. "I don't know," he said, pausing a long time between each word. They were not words he spoke often if ever.

Longford rubbed near the indented crown with his thumb. There, barely visible to Swag, was a slight black scratch. It could have been a speck of oil or even a pencil mark, but it wasn't.

"What do you think?" Swag asked, bending impolitely closer. Longford didn't seem to mind. He was studying the bullet in earnest now, his concentration intense as more and more minute "imperfections" revealed themselves under his jeweler's loop.

"This wasn't made by Federal," Longford said at last. "It's a custom load, made to look like a Hydra-Shok. It's a nearly perfect counterfeit, if it wasn't for that scratch made by the magazine . . ."

"What'll it do?" Swag asked.

Then Longford did something Swag had never seen him do. The man smiled. It was a tight little smile, nearly mischievous. "We can find out," he said, and led Swag to the test range.

Longford's test range was kept in the loading room. It was an enclosed trough, twenty-five feet long, constructed of two-inch armor plating and lined with a high-density puttylike material. On one end was a small viselike contraption that held the pistol, and on the other a pair of clamps that could hold whatever Longford decided to shoot at. Built into the floor of it was a chronograph that read projectile speed and relayed the data to a display near the front. Built into the back was a device that monitored impact.

Longford found a Glock, secured it to the front of the range, attaching it so that he could fire it remotely. Then he lifted two Manhattan phone directories, bound together, from a pile on the floor, and secured them in place at the opposite end of the range. When he closed and bolted tight the three armored sections that comprised the top of the range, a little grin was twisting the corners of his mouth up.

"Should penetrate to the R's, I would think," he said. "Somewhere around Rivera." Then without ceremony he pulled down on the lever that fired the gun.

Swag could barely hear it fire.

Longford seemed to play it for whatever it was worth then. He began by opening the section nearest the Glock, which was still intact. When he lifted the next panel, the smell of powder filled the room. But when he opened the last door, both men stood by in shock.

The bullet had penetrated far past Rivera. In fact, it passed Zzzyrmidgeonski, Leon B. at 548 West End. Leon was the last residential listing in the second book that year. The cartridge tore through just under his name and through the six blue-page listing of government offices with a hole the size of a fist. Scraps of paper, some still smoking and resembling what's left after a firecracker explodes, covered the bottom of the range.

"What was it?" Swag asked.

Longford meticulously removed the bound telephone books, laid them on the floor of the range, and felt along the high-density material behind where the books had been anchored. He pulled his hand away quickly, a slick pinprick along his index finger.

Without saying a word, he left the room. When he returned he was holding a small flashlight and a pair of delicate-looking needle-nose pliers. He bent over the back section and, using the flashlight against the gray lining, extracted a tiny piece of metal from the material.

"What was it?" Swag asked again.

"Explosive round," Longford answered. "Maybe something like the old Devastators. But look, see this?" Longford held the small piece of metal up to the fluorescent. It was shaped like a double-edged serrated knife, ending at a nasty little point.

"A piece of the bullet?"

"Exactly," Longford replied. "They used to make multistrike cartridges, seven or nine layers, called them wafers. They stacked them."

"That's what this is?"

Longford thought on it a second, then carefully laid the small fragment on top of the gray box and fished out another piece from the back of the range. This one was identical to the first. "No, these were bundled, I guess you'd say," he said. "Held together vertically. But that's just a guess."

Swag peered over at the tiny sliver. "How good a guess is it?"

"As good as anybody's," Longford answered. Then he carefully placed the fragment lengthwise between the pliers' jaws and squeezed. It didn't bend, it shattered.

"It's not lead, huh?"

"Some kind of brittle alloy," Longford said. Then, almost forgetting, he bent down and read the chronograph. What he saw made him let out a whistle. "This thing was traveling over fifteen hundred feet per second when it hit."

"Is that fast?"

"Not for a .44 Magnum or .50-caliber machine gun," came the dry answer.

"Who would make it?" Swag asked.

"It came out of a lab," Longford said, still studying the fragment. "A few years ago I heard that some companies— Battelle, Dynamit Nobel, Heckler and Koch—were experimenting with nitramines. You know, RDX, HMX. Trying to match them with thinner casings."

Swag didn't know, and he said so.

"Compressed propellants and more room for them," Longford said. "They were talking ten, fifteen percent increase in charge. But this is beyond that. Propellant may even be contained in the projectile."

Longford was talking as if he were in some college lecture hall, but what he was saying was scaring the shit out of Swag. "What's your general take on it?" Swag finally got up the nerve to ask.

Longford paused, rubbed the bridge of his nose with one hand and asked back, "Are the people you're currently antagonizing using this, may I ask?"

"Yeah, they are."

"Then try to make some new enemies," Longford said. "This didn't fall off a truck in New Jersey. Whoever made this is very sophisticated—not only to manufacture it, but to disguise it as a street-legal load. I wouldn't want to see anyone unfortunate enough to meet up with one of these."

"I have," Swag said. "It wasn't pretty."

"No, I imagine it wasn't," Longford replied quietly. "May I have the others, to study?"

"Sure," Swag said, "knock yourself out. Just be careful with them."

Longford paused, dug his hands deep into his pants pockets and said, "I was just about to offer the same advice to you."

"Both of them?" Catherwood whispered as Roger leaned down toward the table.

"Yes sir," came the reply in a quiet voice.

Catherwood and Roger were in La Grenouille, on 52nd, near Fifth. The long rectangle of a dining room was filled with flowers that stood out brightly against the sea-green walls. Catherwood, sitting at a high-backed banquette in the exclusive front room, clicked the heavy fork to the plate and looked into space for a long time.

Roger, still standing next to Catherwood's table, leaned down again and said, "Sir?" to break the silence.

"Sit," Catherwood said. "Tell me about it."

Roger, now dressed in a knock-off Armani suit, slid into the chair across from Catherwood. Between them was a small vase of bluish flowers, which he shifted to the side to better see Catherwood. He didn't like sitting with his back to the door, any door, but the mirror behind Catherwood was a comfort. "One killed himself and I killed the other," Roger said. "The one I eliminated was wounded, his leg nearly shot off." Catherwood picked up the fork and gently sliced through one of the pile dumplings—*les quenelles de brochet*—artfully arranged on the plate. The wine sauce ran over the fork's tines thickly, like gray blood. Catherwood said, "Please, confine your report to a general accounting— just the essential elements. I have no interest whatsoever in visceral details. And, please, do try to be professional."

"Just the facts, huh?" Roger said. "Okay, we continued high-visibility surveillance on Swag for two days, with yours truly working backup. On day one he eluded the operatives by hitching a ride with an unmarked provost radio patrol unit. Bammer, by the way, denies his men made any contact with the subject. Though he claims to be continuing his search. On the afternoon of the second day, the subject confronted both operatives. One self-terminated when confronted with an eminent ass-kicking. The other, effectively rendered both useless and a potential security threat, was terminated in the field before such threat could be exploited by the subject. Following these actions, all evidence of the operatives and encounter were covered by means too lengthy to include here."

Catherwood chewed at the dumpling for a long time, as if chewing over the facts that Roger had just relayed. "And this person, this Swag fellow," he said, picking up the fork and positioning it under what remained of the dumpling, "he has received no formal training aside from the local police academy?"

"That's right," Roger answered, hoping that Catherwood would at least let him order dinner. But as Roger well knew, Catherwood was of that rare breed who could eat while others watched, or eat alone, and still enjoy the food.

Catherwood ate the rest of the small morsel, enjoying the way the fluffy rice mixed with the fish taste and delicate wine sauce. After he had swallowed the small portion of dumpling, he put the fork down and asked, "Did he seem agitated?"

"He wasn't relaxed," Roger answered as the waiter came and refilled the crystal water glass in front of him. Dropping his voice, he said, "Our guys apparently got in a few licks, but nothing that did any good."

"Obviously," Catherwood answered, slicing into another dumpling.

Roger took a long drink of water and watched Catherwood chew his food.

"Tell me," Catherwood asked, "did he seemed panicked? Was he operating under the influence of adrenaline and fear? Was there undue amount of stress on his part?"

This took about two seconds for Roger to think about. "No, he lured your boys into a trap. Subways have colored lights at the entrance, green for open and red for closed. It's a pretty good guess he knew this and your boys didn't."

Catherwood let a small smile play across his lips as he finished chewing. "Interesting fact," he mused. "About the lights. I wasn't aware."

"When was the last time you were in a subway?"

Catherwood smiled a little wider. "Roger, there has yet to be a first time."

"So, what do you want me to do?" Roger asked. "You want me to bring him in?"

Then Roger watched as Catherwood finished off the last dumpling. A waiter came almost immediately and removed the plate. Roger marked his approach in the mirror behind Catherwood.

"No, not just yet, Roger. And under no circumstances should you attempt direct contact of any kind. Is that clear?"

"He's flaked three of your hotshots," Roger argued. "Those boys don't come cheap."

"No, Roger, indeed they don't," Catherwood said. "And neither do you, I might add. Now, be so good as to tell me, how are things progressing in regard to the primary timetable?"

"Good," Roger said. "Funds from the eastern corridor operation should start hitting our system by the end of next week. The work's been a little damp, in say eighty percent of the targets, but there's been no organized response."

"You say it's been 'wet?'" Catherwood replied, his interest aroused.

"I said, 'damp,'" Roger answered. "Fatality rate is still way below the projected numbers."

"And the authorities are hearing what?"

"They're hearing random assaults by assailant or assailants unknown," Roger answered. "Now, do you mind telling me, what the deal is here? Does this Swag character fit one of your pysch-profiles or something? If you ask me, he's a wild card."

The waiter brought a small raspberry tart and set it in front of Catherwood. A cup of coffee also appeared. "I wasn't aware that I asked you," Catherwood replied irritably.

"Well, yeah. But the guy falls into the game off the street," Roger said. "We know zip about him. Then you start rattling his cage. So what's the deal?" Roger asked, watching Catherwood lift a small fruity portion of the tart out from its crust and bring it to his mouth.

Catherwood set the dessert fork down and leaned slightly forward, opening his mouth as if to speak. The action brought Roger forward as well, leaning over the white linen tablecloth, expecting some clue as to the operation, and knowing that he had not given Catherwood the whole story. Swag had gotten a good look at him and would remember the face. Roger didn't doubt it for a second.

"Roger, please don't presume to *say* anything further. Your opinions, such as they are, only serve to muddy the waters of clear thinking," Catherwood scolded. "Have you taken the time to think why I should instruct you to conduct *high-profile* surveillance?"

A waiter passed by then, saw that Roger's water glass was empty, but didn't bother to refill it.

"This Swag is a creature of the environment," Catherwood explained. By the tone of his voice he might have been talking to a child. "All of our existing intelligence and observation tell us he is a person of formidable ingenuity and resources. More so than the recently departed Jonathan G., our first, and may I add, less then successful, attempt at local recruitment."

"Sure. So?"

"It might take years, if possible at all, to raise our own people to his level of feral intelligence."

Roger pulled the comb from his pocket, gave his hair a couple of swipes, then replaced the comb. "If any of them live long enough."

"And he has a penchant for corruption—the grand jury transcripts indicated as much."

Roger waited, knowing what was coming, then asked, "You really want to hire him, don't you?"

"Either hire or eliminate," Catherwood answered. "For the time being, Roger, you'll continue parallel surveillance. I want you to oversee these operations yourself. Keep our Mr. Swag out of harm's way."

"You want me to babysit him?" Roger said incredulously.

"Act as his guardian angel," Catherwood answered. "Though I doubt very much he needs your assistance."

"Not from the way he handled your three boys."

The tart didn't quite suit Catherwood, and it remained on the small plate, hardly eaten. "My boys," he said softly then. "What were their names, if you recall?"

Roger thought for a moment, then said, "The first was called Ward, the other two Dunlop and Kirby."

"Quel dommage," Catherwood sighed. What a pity. Then he added, "Ward, Dunlop, and Kirby. Those were not their actual names, I take it?"

"Does it matter?" Roger said.

"I suppose not," came the answer. Then, "Roger, be a good lad now and bring the car around."

chapter sixteen

THERE WERE FOUR BANKS where Swag kept his money: Japanese, Swiss, German, and American. All of them were small private institutions that charged negative interest and heavy service charges. Preferred customers, those with two million dollars or two hundred thousand of Europe's Common Market ECU currency, did their business in hushed and paneled offices over cappuccino.

Swag, like the rest who fell beneath the mark of fiscal significance, waited in lines marked off with velvet ropes to get at their cash. But he could have kept the money under a rock at the bottom of the harbor, for all the good it did him. All four banks had sealed his safety deposit boxes and frozen all accounts, pending an ongoing investigation. It was, as the tellers needlessly, and somewhat nervously, explained, all perfectly legal and in accordance with Section 18 of the Banking Act of '94. It was, Swag knew, useless to argue.

"Does it say exactly why I can't get into the account?" Swag asked the teller at the last bank.

"I tol' youse," the young girl said. "The account is temporarily frozen under a Section 18. That's a federal order. The gov'ment shut youse down. Youse think I'm lying to youse or what?" Her voice was heavy with Brooklyn.

"Okay, does it say who froze it?" Swag asked. "What agency? Anything?"

"Look, there's a light blinking on my screen that says ya

don't get no money," the girl shot back, holding her ground as she leaned over the marble counter. "Youse ask me, the fashion police shut youse down for wearing that shirt. Now, I'm *très* sorry, really, but I got people waiting."

"What? Now you don't like my shirt?" Swag asked, looking down its front where a half-dozen or more parrots were riding a school of dolphins through blue white-capped waves. The parrots wore little cowboy hats and six-shooters, tiny reins dangling from their beaks. Swag pulled a handful of material away from his chest with both hands and asked, "What? What's wrong with the shirt?"

Swag turned around once, slowly, to give the teller the full effect. He didn't want her to miss the lasso rope script that spelled out *Aloha Buckeroo* across the back against the azure sky.

The girl made a face as she gave the shirt another appraising look. Then, noticing the minute sheriff's badges pinned to the parrots' feathery chests, said, "Mister, that shirt's a crime against nature. Next!"

Swag left the bank and headed downtown. He had an appointment to meet Norman Bubere, the computer guy Lucy set him up with. Swag had heard of the guy before, but never actually saw him. In fact, he had never met anyone who had actually seen him. According to everyone, he moved around—sometimes sleeping in four-star hotels, sometimes in down-and-out dives. The rumors went that he'd been spotted sleeping in telephone booths at Grand Central.

Now Swag was on his way to meet him at the old Vista Hotel. A one-time fashionable address for European and midwestern money men, it sat on the edge of the financial district and was now the choice for low-level Euro-hustlers.

Bubere wasn't hard to spot. Camped out in the old lobby, he was as out of place as any one person could be in any one place. He was maybe forty and fat, wrap-around two-dollar sunglasses and a week's growth of uneven beard covering his moon-shaped face. He looked like a well-fed beetle. A large roll of white stomach protruded between the baby-blue T-shirt and the white patent-leather belt. He was wearing greasy Campbell plaid gold pants that ended in a pair of tattered black Chuck Taylor Converse All-Stars. With his legs crossed, as they were, Swag could see that Bubere wasn't wearing any socks.

A pair of pricey personal stereo headphones covered his ears.

Swag missed his mark at first, saw the shirt and kept walking. When he crossed again, he saw the two shopping bags, crammed with rags, packages of junk food, and the tops of printed circuit boards.

Bubere was sitting next off to one side, partially hidden by lobby foliage, and drinking a brown concoction out of a large brandy snifter. When Swag approached, he saw that there were at least half a dozen maraschino cherries riding high atop the drink.

"Norman?" Swag asked, when he was nearly on the guy.

Bubere didn't answer at once, rather, he nodded to the plush-covered seat next to him. Swag sat down, moving away a shopping bag.

"Nice shirt, really," Norman said.

"I'm glad you like it," Swag replied. "Can you help me?"

"Help a guy with no money?" Bubere said. "That's charity, isn't it? Better see the Red Cross."

"Who said I don't have money?"

"All four of your banks," Norman replied, still staring straight ahead, his head bobbing faintly to the music. "I ran you this morning." Then he took a drink from the snifter.

"That's going to change," Swag said. "Soon."

"Not under a Section 18 it's not."

"Look, I just hooked up with something, some delivery work," Swag said. "You can check with Lucy."

Bubere lifted his glass again, opened his mouth wide and let six cherries float in. A good portion of the drink, which Swag assumed was Coke or Pepsi, flowed out the sides and down the T-shirt. He seemed not to notice. "Okay," he said finally. Then put the drink down.

"Great," Swag said. "Where?"

"Right here," Bubere replied, signaling for the waitress.

When the waitress came over, she was smiling. "Is everything satisfactory?"

"Check," he said.

Bubere pulled an obscenely fat wallet from his pocket, removed a pink rubber band from around the outside, and dug around in a two-inch-thick pile of credit cards. Swag caught a glimpse of at least ten American Express cards, from green to platinum. There were a stack of Barclays, Diners, Visa, and maybe five Eurocheques.

All dead babies, Swag thought. With that much bogus plastic a guy could live for years.

The waitress took the platinum Amex that Bubere offered, read the name and said, "Thank you, Mr. Keynes."

When she handed it back, Swag saw that the name embossed into the plastic was John Maynard Keynes. Bubere tipped well—forty percent—and the waitress smiled more broadly. "Thank you, Mr. Keynes."

"In the long run, we're all dead, right?" Bubere said, and rose heavily from the chair.

Bubere had a small room in the hotel. The room looked out on the water, but the view didn't matter. The first thing Bubere did was close the shades. "This is a good place," he explained. "Phones have their own modem jacks."

Then Bubere emptied a bag across the bed, spilling out an ocean of refuse that ended in a small lap-top computer. "Look," he said, sorting through the trash and pulling out a small printed circuit board.

Swag looked; the board was heavy with chips, some of them two inches high. The board wasn't factory made, and from the looks of the contact points, it was constructed to fit something big.

"You want to buy it?" Bubere asked. "I'll give you a good deal."

"What the fuck is it?" Swag asked back. Some of the chips were stamped in Japanese, others in German. The one labeled in English near the center read "TSD Proprietary."

"If you don't know, you got no business trying to find out," Bubere said, then threw the board carelessly back on the bed.

He took his glasses off then, revealing small moist eyes that were surrounded by circles dark enough to have been painted on, but weren't. "Let's get to it," he said, picked up the lap-top and walked over to the phone. "What you want to know? Who shut you down with the banks?"

"That'd be nice. But first I want a corporate trace on a company called Euro-Zeitech," Swag said. "Subsidiary of Lorette-Defour, out of Zurich."

"Piece of cake," Bubere said. "I'll go in through Euronet-DIANE."

Swag watched as Bubere clicked away on the keyboard for a while. When he leaned back, he indicated that the information was on the screen: the complete holdings of Lorette-Defour, sixty companies. Not one of them named Euro-Zeitech.

"Try again," Swag said. "Could it be hidden in there, owned by one of those subsidiaries?"

"Shit, Australia could be hidden in there," Bubere said. "Do they operate in the States?"

"Yeah, can you find it?"

Bubere didn't answer. Instead he set his pudgy fingers back across the keys, and in a couple of seconds the screen began to scroll with more names. "Okay, here's what I'm doing, sports fans," he said, keeping his eyes glued to the screen. "I'm going into Euronet's billing system, accessing Lorette-Defour's file. If they talked to anyone in the past month, any substantial bank like, I'll know about it."

The screen filled with French. Swag could pick out city names between the lines, Zurich, Frankfurt, Tokyo, Barcelona, and Paris. After that the screen scrolled too quickly.

"Oh, now, lookie at this, your friends did some business with some leading banks in the Isle of Man, Channel Islands, and Antilles-Netherlands," Bubere said, stopping the screen. "Tax-dodge city."

"Sounds about right," Swag said. "Can you get in?"

"Let's check those governments' files on corporate and trust registrations," came the response. "Those secrecy laws aren't what they used to be."

Three minutes later Euro-Zeitech came up on the screen, listed as incorporated in the Isle of Man, but with fifty-one percent owned by Lorette-Defour. And seven discretionary trust subsidiaries. All incorporated in the Caymans.

"Anything else?" Bubere asked. "Don't be shy."

"What do they make?"

"Judging from this, they make money," Bubere replied. "Not too specific on how. But it's all nontaxable."

"Can you find out?" Swag asked.

"Let's see what they have by way of address," came the answer. Then, "See that, it's an electronic office. Used to be they had mail drops down there for corporate headquarters. But those were too labor intensive. Now they just stick the works on a big-ass mainframe. Run their businesses off a piece of rented database, invoices, credit, the works. Saves a trip down for the executives. And keeps collateral records out of the banks. Okay, in we go."

Bubere began clicking at the keyboard again; there were a dozen screens with menus and graphics, then they switched over to computer code. "Okay, here's what you got," Bubere said. "You got a company in the Caymans taking in small money from the U.S., over the CHIPS wire—EFT—Electronic Funds Transfer. Let's see, two, three, four New York banks, and one in Jersey. Not more than two or three thousand at a time, then spinning it off to what, ten, twelve, fourteen little companies in the Caymans, Antilles-Netherlands, Luxembourg, and Channel Islands, Madeira, the Isle of Man, and Mexico."

"Is it legit?" Swag asked.

"The process is. But the money, not likely," Bubere said. "No way to explain the money, it's all just under the Fed's regs for reporting. But I'm not tracing it through those little fucking companies. They could be doing anything, buying Russian glass, UCIT bonds, positions on silver futures, then selling it back to another one. They could be making low-interest loans to one another. But it all filters back to someplace. I'll tell you this, though, it's moving fast. There's coded instruction that it shouldn't sit for more than a day, pending exchange rates. My guess is that it's heading to Switzerland, through the back door. Saves a lot on taxes."

"Fuck the taxes," Swag said. "What else are they doing?"

"Let's see," Bubere replied, and began clicking away. "We're in the electronic office's utilities now. They send wire transfers, generate telexes for other wire transfers to other banks. A bunch of encryption code you can't afford what it'll cost for me to get into."

The columns of files continued to scroll across the screen as Bubere clicked away. "This is a real nice little program they got here," he said at last. "It isn't what you get when you just rent space. Someone went through a lot of trouble to design this baby. If they're moving money with three or four more like it—which is what it looks like—nobody'll ever be able to put a trace on them. It would take years. And they've put a logic bomb right at the fucking center, probably triggered by the money manager from a modem."

"What is it?" Swag asked. "What's the whole system?"

"It's a Maytag," Bubere said. "You know, for washing money. A big-loan model too. A guy could drop two, maybe three hundred million a week in there and it would vanish, then come out in the Alps, clean as the driven snow."

"What makes that much money?" Swag asked.

"Twenty years ago, American multinationals did. Nothing American anymore," Bubere answered, still glued to the screen. "Hey, look at this!"

"What'd you find?"

"Look at this fucking thing," Bubere said, chuckling at a block of numbers and letters that filled the screen. "Somebody's tacked on this raggedy-ass utility on the clock."

"What does it do?" Swag asked.

"It's what they used to call a 'salami slicer,'" Bubere said. "It steals. This one's set to extract random percentages before the transfers are logged on in the system. Then it shoots them out to, what . . . six, eight, ten numbered accounts at banks in Switzerland, Luxembourg, Haiti, and the Caymans without keeping a record. And wouldn't you know, none of the account numbers match those in the system. Somebody's skimming."

"How much?" Swag asked, finally presented with something he could understand.

"From what it looks like, it's anywhere from one half to one two-hundredth of one percent," Bubere said.

"Not a whole bunch of money."

"It is if you're doing a hundred million a month," Bubere answered.

"Trace the money back to New York," Swag instructed.

Bubere tapped in a line of digits and the screen went black. Then he tapped in a line of six-digit numbers which appeared with another line of four digits just below it.

"See that top number, that's the initiating sender, the Cayman bank. Those others are banks in the U.S. First two digits of top line is city or state, last four is the bank. Bottom line is Fed district and instructions to receiving bank."

"Any reason I should know this?"

"Sit back," Bubere said. "You'll get an education. Now we know what bank it's going to, right. Watch this, because this is why you're paying top dollar. A typical schmuck would try to get on-line through the wire transfer key code, Zeitech's personal code. But the banks monitor and record each entry, even inquiries. Somebody would know we've been there. And you can't get in through the Treasury side, because they got encryption up the whazoo. Would take about twenty-two hundred years. But a bank, being the cheap bastards they are, operate on one big network. The same system that's keeping track of personnel files is moving their money."

"So?"

"So, they've got the security of a paper bag," Bubere answered.

Bubere typed again, and the screen went dead. Then it came back on, blank. A form appeared, then another, and another. "We're in the money-transfer room at the bank uptown. Logged on to the supervisor's screen."

"Now what?" Swag said.

"We wait for the guy to get up and take a piss or something," Bubere said, leaning back. "Then we can access the whole system. If he doesn't log off, like he's supposed to."

It took half an hour. When activity on the screen ceased for a couple of minutes, the hacker made his move.

Bubere said that they had maybe eight minutes on the system. It was more than enough time. "See, now this is interesting," he said after a few keystrokes. "There's money coming into the U.S. clean. But it's not going into a corporate account. It's a personal account, guy named Emery Catherwood. Address listed is the Grand Caymans. No local address. And what have we here—transfers from those original banks in the Maytag. Chump change."

"So, somebody's sending a shitload of money out, but only a little is coming back in?" Swag asked.

"That's it," Bubere said. "But you missed the point. If your buddies at Euro-Zeitech are sending dirty money out, then they're sending clean money back in. Get it? Once cash hits a U.S. bank, it's supposedly clean. My guess is, this isn't investment capital. It's salary. This guy Catherwood is running a branch office. Something with real low overhead. He's operating out of pocket, you know what I mean?"

A group of numbers began running across the screen without Bubere touching the keys.

"Whoops, somebody's back at his desk," he said, then Bubere typed in, WE'RE WELL ARMED AND WE KNOW WHERE YOU LIVE.

The typing stopped and Bubere logged off.

"What about that salami slicer you found?" Swag asked.

"Somebody's stealing, is what about it," came the answer.

"They're stealing from their own company?"

"Happens all the time," Bubere said. "Look, nobody checks the standing instructions on money transfers. Banks don't even *pay out* the interest unless you got a sharp money guy. It's a game they play. You know, who worries about twenty-four hours' worth of interest? And once the registration agent sets up those offices, nobody looks at the software. Not unless you're real paranoid, like a rabid accountant type. You want a printout?"

"Will it help?" Swag asked.

"Take the test key codes for the wire transfers," he said. "You never know, they could be useful."

"Sure, print them out," Swag said.

Bubere gave Swag a sly look and entered the commands. While the small unit hummed, he turned from the screen. "You have any idea who these guys are?" he asked.

"I thought that's what you were going to tell me," Swag said.

"I just told you what they do," came the answer. "But you should know this, there aren't too many people who can set up a system like they got."

"Who can?" Swag asked.

Bubere thought about this for a long time, scratching seven or eight different places as he thought. "Actually, nobody can. Who would want to?" he said at last. "It's too big to be profitable except for really serious fucking amounts of cash. If your friends are running a scam, then it's a huge one."

"What about the government?"

"What government?" Bubere snorted derisively. "Government's a buncha gray-haired fucks each happy to be stealing enough to make their kids' lives easier and maybe take the little woman to Paris twice a year. This is an ongoing business you're peeking into. A start-up with some heavy capital."

"So?" Swag asked.

"So, this," Bubere shot back. "If you're peeking just for yucks, then you're at risk of being leaned on, big-time. That's the least that could happen to you. But if you're thinking of dealing yourself in or jamming them up, then you'll end up dead."

"You think so?" Swag asked, more than a little annoyed at Bubere's casual attitude.

"Hey, people die all the time," Bubere answered as he ripped the printout from the unit.

"How do you want to be paid?" Swag asked as they were pacing up.

"We'll do a money transfer," Bubere said, jamming his stuff carelessly into the shopping bags.

"How do I reach you?"

"You don't," Bubere said. "Just make sure you're covered when that Section 18 lifts."

They were in the elevator and heading down before Swag asked, "Anybody ever stiff you on one of these deals?"

"Once," Bubere said, nodding his head in time to the music on the headphones.

"What happened?"

A small grin appeared on Bubere's face and he turned his wraparound shades in Swag's direction. "You don't want to know," he said.

As Swag was pushing through the revolving doors of the lobby, Roger, dressed as a telephone repair man, was just closing the door to the hotel's PBX telephone switching room. Behind him was a dead security guard, a victim of bad luck and a strategically injected hypodermic Roger had stabbed him with. In the cheap plastic briefcase Roger carried, a small lap-top held on hard disk every keystroke that Bubere had made upstairs.

chapter seventeen

THE NEXT DAY, Swag walked out on the street and saw a cabbie eating his lunch behind the wheel of a White Star cab. When Swag raised his hand, the driver put his lunch aside and switched off the Off Duty sign.

The White Star cab took Swag over the Brooklyn Bridge. Swag hated Brooklyn almost as much as Jersey, but that's where the liquor distributors Lucy had told him about were, operating down by the docks that lined the East River. At least there weren't any toxic sites in Brooklyn. While Jersey had become the world's carcinogenic dumping ground, Brooklyn had turned into a brownstone barrio. Each morning a ragged parade of beggars, street vendors, dishwashers, piecework drones, and porters trekked across the three bridges, the price of even a subway too costly. The parade began before dawn, in darkness.

Now, at noon, the bridge was nearly empty, even of traffic. At five or six the pedestrian walks would fill again and continue late into the night.

The cabbie eyed Swag nervously in the mirror as he pulled off at the Cadman Plaza exit and swung the car around under the Brooklyn Bridge. "You sure you know where you're going, pal?" he asked.

Swag leaned back in the seat and took a pull on a cigarette. The wind had blown through the open window when they were on the FDR and the bridge; now, as they slowed down, he could feel the stale press of the noon heat again. "Yeah, make this turn here," Swag instructed.

"Shit, you're heading me toward the fuckin' river," the driver said, making the turn anyway.

"I said Brooklyn," Swag answered.

"Yeah, but I thought you meant Park Slope," came the whining reply. "The docks. There's nothing down there anymore."

Swag didn't answer. A pack of dogs, eight or ten of them, trotted into the street, and the driver slowed. It used to be that the dogs were just pets turned out. Some of them, back then, still had collars. And you could see some pedigree, Dobermans, shepherds, maybe even a boxer now and again—at least pieces of pedigree anyway. But that was three or four generations back. Now they were more or less all the same, dull brown, a little over knee high, and uniformly filthy. And mean; they were mean bastards now, living off garbage scraps, rats, and the occasional skel.

"Look at this, will ya," the cabbie said, edging his arm back in the window as they moved through the intersection. "It's like a fuckin' Tarzan movie out here. They ripped a little kid up last week, ya hear about that?"

"Rats will do it too," Swag said, watching the dogs round the corner. "Worse."

They were moving parallel to the bridge. This was an old section, the narrow streets running at imperfect lines between the rows of buildings. When they made the next turn, the river came into sight, the skyline looming across the water in a tightly-packed line of glass and steel.

"Rats, no shit," the driver said.

Swag took a last draw on the cigarette and dropped it out the window. They were in front of the warehouse now. It was the bottom floor of an ancient brick factory, the windows covered with gray tin. Only a few of the original steel shutters were left, rusting on their hinges. These had been pried closed and chained.

"Here," Swag said.

The cabbie flicked the meter's flag down, took the fare,

and eyed Swag as he stepped out. "See you later, buddy,"
he said, and gunned the taxi away down the street.

The door to the warehouse was open. Taped to the front
was a yellow and red sign that read, TRESPASSERS WILL BE
SHOT, and then in smaller letters: "Survivors Will Be Shot
Again." Beneath the store-bought sign was a smaller hand-
lettered one that read, *Ring Bell*, and Swag did.

The door opened almost immediately to reveal a tall guy
with black hair. He was maybe thirty and rail-thin. He had
a tough-guy look that Swag figured he'd probably learned
from television. He was dressed in what had come to be
known as "the Full Jersey." It was almost a uniform from
Newark to Cape May: Cracked imitation leather shoes with
rubber soles; Korean double-knit golf pants, and a factory-
second poly T-shirt advertising a Portuguese feminine
hygiene spray. The one this guy wore was puke green and
bore the slogan for a company that manufactured stuffed
toys: THE LUSHIEST PLUSH was emblazoned from sweat-
soaked armpit to sweat-soaked armpit. Thirty years ago
you would have seen the outfit in magazine stories about
third world countries on the brink of the sixth revolution
of the year. Now Jersey was the third world, Liberia on the
Hudson.

"You the guy that called?" he asked, sizing Swag up.

"Yeah, I'm the guy that called."

The black-haired guy looked past Swag, then yelled into
the warehouse, "Who left the fuckin' door open again?"

From inside another voice answered that it must have
been the Chinese food kid.

"I gotta do everything 'round this place," the black-
haired guy complained to Swag and closed the door. Then
he turned and started back into the warehouse, leaving
Swag standing just inside the doorway, thinking about
what kind of deal Lucy had hooked him into.

The heat rose ten degrees when Swag stepped into the
warehouse. A short hallway, paneled in stamped plastic
with a wood-grain finish led into the warehouse's main
office. There was a small maze of painted partitions with

the glass busted out of them. Through the glassless openings, Swag could see the darkened warehouse beyond. A small light burned in one of the farthest offices, where a man was seated at a desk.

When Swag reached the office, he saw that the second guy looked enough like the first to be his brother. Both were variations on the theme. Like the other, both his shirt and pants were drenched through with sweat. This one was sitting behind a gray metal desk littered with Chinese take-out containers. He was reading a comic. It was an English version translation of *The Machi Man*. A long-time favorite in Japan, the comic was building an audience in the States. Swag always wondered who read those things. Now he knew.

"So, sit down," the guy behind the desk said, laying the comic book out in front of him so that Swag could see it. The room smelled of sweat and garlic chicken.

"There isn't a chair," Swag answered.

This caught the guy, who Swag took to be the boss, a little off guard. "Frankie, go get the man a chair, will ya."

While Frankie was out finding a chair, the guy said, "Yeah, well, I'm Joey, that's Frankie." Then, holding up the comic, "You ever read these *manga*, items? They ain't bad."

Swag shook his head as Frankie came back in with the chair.

"I got all of 'em," Joey said. "These things are gonna be worth money someday. You're the guy that knows that chick over at the stroke shop, huh?"

"So, what do you have?" Swag asked, his voice flat as he watched Frankie shuffle around to stand behind his brother. As he walked, Swag could see the small automatic strapped to his hip. There was an autoloader shotgun resting in one corner. It was a nice family portrait; their mother would have been proud.

Joey smiled and said, "Right to business, huh?"

"I'm on my time now," Swag answered with a shrug. "You want me to start the clock? We can sit around and bullshit."

Joey seemed to enjoy this. His smile widened. "Hey, Lucy said you were pro," he replied. "Okay, here's the deal. We got one hundred cases—cases, mind you, of primo bourbon. And every fuckin' one is presold; all we got to do is make delivery."

"Hotels, bars, who you delivering to?" Swag asked, reaching into the pocket of the blue-green Hawaiian shirt for a cigarette and lighter.

"I don't know if that's any of your business," Frankie put in. "And it won't be, unless we decide to hire you."

Swag wanted to ignore him. The kid was talking just to be adding something. Though they looked almost identical, it wouldn't be hard to tell them apart. The younger one, Frankie, was the one with the bad attitude and no brains.

He leaned over the desk next to his brother, knuckles pushing down on the scarred Formica, and said, "You're working for us, not some other way around. Remember?"

"You got a phone here?" Swag asked, flicking a length of ash on the floor.

Frankie was straightening up now; leaning on the desk was hurting his knuckles. "Sure, why?" he asked.

"Why? Because I'm calling a cab. I'm out of here," Swag said. "You boys have a good time delivering your liquor."

Frankie made to lean back down on the desk, then stopped short. "What? What is that, some kind of fuckin' threat, scumbag?"

"No threat," Swag answered calmly, getting up. "It's what it is, bonjour."

"Bon-*fuckin'*-jour my ass," Frankie said, leaning down on his palms. "You don't come in here and bust our fuckin' chops."

The kid was close to making a grab for his gun. The tension level in the room was rising fast. Either they weren't legit, like Lucy said, or someone else was riding them. Both were jitterbugs; the younger one was just wrapped more tightly.

"Look now, guys," Joey said, pushing his brother back

rom the desk. "We're all a little wound is all." He was
miling. Sweat ran down his face.

"You guys have a phone or no?" Swag asked, dropping
the cigarette and grinding it out.

"Look, we've been working hard, me and Frankie here,"
Joey said. "Been living in this fuckin' dump for a week, protecting our merchandise while we set up the deal. Suppose
you just tell us why you want to know?"

"It's the way I do business," Swag answered. "First, I
want to know where I'm working. I don't go through that
tunnel to Jersey."

"Hey, we're from Jersey," the younger one, Frankie, put
in, set to defend his home state.

"No shit," Swag answered. "But I don't care if the
Carlyle moved to Newark. I don't go through that tunnel.
Second, if you get burned on this thing, I get burned. I
have to know who you're supplying. And third, and this
is key, you better have the goods, and it better be legit. If
this shit fell off a truck somewhere, or if it's from a bust-out
operation from some joint out on Long Island, I'm gone."

Joey wiped the sweat away from his face with one hand
and smiled. "See that, all a misunderstanding," he said.
"We're delivering to midtown, already have the orders
locked. And I got bills of lading, liquor authority and broker transfers, anything you want to see. This is one hundred
percent square. Trust me."

Frankie seemed to relax somehow; he faded into the
chipped paint and broken glass of the wall, twitching a little
with residue anger, but under control. If it was true, about
them living in the warehouse for a week, then they probably were a little nuts. It was ninety outside, and with the
sun pounding down on the steel roof, the temperature
inside the warehouse was 103, 104, easy.

Swag thought about it for a second, lit another smoke,
and said, "Okay, let's get to it."

"Great," Joey said. "What you want to see first?"

"The paper," Swag said.

It was there, just like Joey said. The whole story was laid

out in bills of lading, bills of exchange, even a letter on con
sulate stationery from the African President for Life, whose
term came up. It was like Lucy had said, the liquor had
moved around a bunch, but never off the Brooklyn docks.
When the money on the deal got too small, all the brokers
backed off, and that's when the Jersey boys made their
move. Swag supposed it was their first.

The two brothers watched and sweated as Swag read
through the paper. He was on the last transfer, which gave
the two brothers possession of the merchandise, when he
read the words "Payment received cash—D-marks," at the
bottom.

Swag put the papers down on the corner of the desk and
said, "Who's the banker?"

Both brothers stiffened at this; then Joey said, "Who says
we got one?"

"What'd you do? Go to the street for it?"

"Hey, pal, that ain't your business," Frankie cut in.

"It is if your money's a six-for-five deal off the street,"
Swag replied.

The vig on those deals would grind down a profit to
nothing. Swag had seen it happen before. Small-time oper-
ators taking five large in one week had to pay back six grand
the next, hoping for fast turnaround. The smarter ones
moved around, buying francs, marks, pounds, against dollars, playing the market and hoping to cut their grand-a-
week interest from tiny moves on the exchange rates. But
more than one operator was caught, hustling to just pay
the juice, as deals stretched from one week to four, then to
six. Moving too slow meant watching the vig eat up the
profits. If the deal fell through altogether, then it got ugly.

Joey wiped more sweat from his face and looked at Swag
with the expression of a trapped animal. "Swear to God
we've had the merchandise a week," he said. "We don't
move this shit soon, we're out of the game."

Swag lit another cigarette and said, "Let's see it."

The liquor was stacked on wooden skids in the back of
the warehouse inside a small cage, its thick wire mesh

reaching nearly to the high ceiling. Inside the cage, between the stacked cartons of bourbon, were two sleeping bags, a Coleman lantern, and a stack of *Machi Man* comics.

Swag looked over the merchandise and said, "What kind of security you keeping here?"

"See them two doors," Joey said, pointing to a pair of sliding doors big enough to drive a truck through. "We got both of them rigged with shotguns. That fan up there, it ain't working cause its frame's wired from a city two-twenty power line. And we welded that other door shut. Nobody's coming in here."

It wasn't the best security Swag ever saw, but it wasn't the worst. "Your banker know where you are?" he asked.

"He saw the stuff at the other place," Frankie said. "Nobody knows where we are. And we ain't gonna be here long anyways."

Swag leaned against the cage and dropped the nearly burned-out cigarette. "Good thought," he said.

"You ain't dealing with amateurs, pal," Joey sneered.

chapter eighteen

THEY MOVED THE LIQUOR at night. Frankie left shortly before sunset and returned, grinning behind the wheel of an ancient step van. Then the three of them worked like stevedores into early evening, loading the back end, leaving a small channel down the center for Frankie, who'd be riding in back with an old H & K 9 assault rifle with taped stock and trigger, pointed at the twin doors in the rear. Swag would ride shotgun up front. The boys had bought or borrowed a Franchi Law-12 gas action autoloader, which he'd keep in the doorwell, within easy reach. Joey would have the other shotgun in his doorwell.

The city was full of take-out artists. If they couldn't get you in an empty alley, they'd do it right out on the street. Working in teams, they'd come up from behind, two on each side, and stick a gun through the window. No talking. No threats. Just one shot to the side of the driver's head. It was a low-rent game, strictly for bottom-feeders. They'd have their guns silenced with an empty liter soft drink bottle. The bottle, taped to the barrel, killed the flash and suppressed the noise. Swag had once seen this close up, in a movie theater. A guy in a raincoat came up behind a couple and put the Diet Coke bottle over her ear. "Hey Dena," he said, "it's the real thing." Then fired. The thin farting noise was muffled further by the sound of Hollywood gunfire. Nobody even turned from the screen, as her brains blew out over her date's popcorn.

By the way the truck's springs sagged under the weight of the liquor, Swag wouldn't have taken odds that they'd make it up the bridge's ramp, but somehow they did. With gears grinding, they picked up the Brooklyn-Queens Expressway and headed toward the Manhattan Bridge.

"You know how it works," Swag said, running through the drill again. He had to yell above the sound of the gears. "If that back door opens without anyone pounding on it three times, you start shooting."

"We've been through that part, pal," Joey said, his hands spread out across the big wheel.

"Yeah, we ain't retards or nothing," Frankie called from the back.

Both were higher than kites, loaded up on adrenaline, greed, and bargain basement pharmaceuticals. Joey, his pupils widened like opened manholes, kept cutting his gaze from the road over to the left, to ogle the lights of the city. None of them saw the three cars that were following. Two of them were Plymouths, the third a dark blue Benz.

When they hit the bridge, neither brother was talking. They didn't open their mouths again until they were rattling up Sixth, toward their first delivery. That's when Swag spotted the two Plymouths following. Then one of the Plymouths turned off at Canal, heading uptown through a maze of twisting side streets. The remaining Plymouth followed the step van up Sixth. He never saw the Benz, which hung far back in the light traffic.

Swag would have preferred dropping twenty-five or fifty cases at each stop. But none of the bar managers would trust the brothers for more than the lowest possible quantity. According to the order list that Frankie had flashed, each stop would deplete the truck by only three or four cases. The run would last all night.

The first stop was a piece of cake, with Joey ringing the bell to the service entrance and fetching the bar manager. Four or five porters followed the stiff-faced manager down, and they unloaded the cases. The bar manager paid in cash and didn't ask for a receipt. He'd get a receipt later, from a legit distributor.

It went like that all night, with the truck pulling up in front of second-and third-rate hotels and the bar manager coming out in shirt sleeves to inspect the merchandise, breaking open a case at random and inspecting the label. For many of the hotels it was the first top-shelf liquor they'd seen in a long time, and they didn't care where it came from. Mostly, they just worried about the labels.

"Easiest money you ever made, isn't that right, pal?" Frankie said after they'd completed four or five stops.

"It isn't over yet," Swag answered.

Frankie laughed. "Fergitabout it. We're golden. The provost woulda given us an escort if we asked."

Swag turned, a sharp panic clutching at his insides. "What do you mean, escort?"

"He means we spread a little money around," Joey answered. "You know, smooth out the bumps and the humps."

Swag could have strangled both of them, right there. "You fuckin' idiots," he spat. "Bammer's guys'll take you out before anyone!"

"Hey, relax," Joey said, putting a hand on Swag's shoulder. "Ain't no big deal."

Swag shook off the hand and stared straight ahead as the van rumbled uptown.

By four in the morning the rusted bed of the step van was nearly empty. Frankie lay sprawled out against a small pile of liquor cases, the shotgun across his lap. Joey was showing signs of fatigue. He'd been wrestling with the truck for nearly eight hours, double-clutching and grinding the gears on the floor shift.

"So what do we have, three more stops?" Swag asked, casting a quick look in the cracked side mirror. The Plymouth was gone again. He'd spotted it three hours before, but now he told himself that he was imagining things.

Frankie shifted lazily in the back of the truck. "Yeah, and you're going to love these," he said.

"It's what, the Chateau, the Madison, and the Fleet-street," Swag said, listing off the three hotels that appeared on the list. All of them, he knew, were in midtown, not three or four blocks from each other.

"Not quite," Joey said.

Swag, worn-out from a night of loading and unloading boxes, said, "What's not quite?"

They were turning now, cutting west across Broadway, low in the Twenties. "The last deliveries are for the clubs," Frankie called out from the back of the truck, his voice barely distinguishable above the racket of the truck's clatter.

The news hit Swag with a jolt. He hated that part of town, parallel to the river, along either side of the West Side Highway. From Fourteenth Street up were the after-hours clubs, sex clubs, gambling clubs, bare-knuckled fight rings, and basement dogfights. Once that had been the center of meat packing and distribution in the city. Now only a hand-ful of those operations were still in business.

The buildings remained. The new joints in this section of town were a far cry from the tony town-house retreats in the East Seventies or West Sixties. In this part of town folks took their vices seriously. Things that even the pro-vosts couldn't stomach thrived in the smaller West Side clubs. Everything went right to the limit down by the water.

Degenerate gamblers had been known to sign markers that would put their wives to work in back rooms and hotels for months. And "You bet your life" wasn't just an expression down there, not with kidneys going for six thou-sand francs on the black market, wholesale. Marrow brought almost as much, Swag knew, but that was a high-odds proposition, at twenty thousand to one that they'd have a match with a buyer. So nobody bet on the come for marrow. "Roll the bones with a marker for marrow," went the street wisdom, "and you'd end up with some chop-shop doc slicing into your back or lifting a cornea." And once they got you under the gas, nobody ever got up and said, "Hey, I said just *one* kidney."

Some of the bars had closets of snuff video that sold out in weeks. And it remained one of the last of the city's hold-outs for bootleg pharmaceuticals, now a capital offense in any quantity. Nobody ever carried anything small into a bar down here, except now Swag was carrying two small-timers with him. And out on the outskirts, that was the worst thing you could do.

"Hey, tell me if I'm wrong here, but you didn't say any-thing about the clubs," Swag offered. They were heading down the West Side Highway now, making good time in the light traffic.

"We forgot, okay," Joey said from the driver's seat.

"And besides," Frankie added, "when we told two other guys, they turned the job down."

They turned left off the highway and headed across Little West Twelfth Street. The first of the hustlers came into view, leaning against the corner of a building. A young guy with ripped jeans and a leather T-shirt was smoking a cigarette, balancing it precisely on his lower lip. He looked as if he was waiting to have his picture taken. Across the street his female counterpart walked down the broken sidewalk in front of a meat-packing plant, wriggling her hips in a rolling and well-practiced motion.

"We didn't tell you about the clubs?" Frankie said, grin-ning. "Gee, I thought we did. Whyn't you tell him before now, Joey?"

"It musta slipped my mind or something," came the laughing answer.

"This is bullshit," Swag said, looking again in the sideview and seeing the Plymouth turn the corner behind them.

Frankie's laugh turned into an amused giggle, and his laugh was soon joined by Joey's laugh—just a couple of boys from Jersey getting over on a New York hotshot.

"Relax and enjoy it," Joey said, "this is the best part." Then he turned the van left again, heading it back uptown. "Hey, would you look at that." Ahead of them another woman came into view, appearing out of the shadows of a loading dock. She wore a long cloth trench coat, high heels, and not enough underneath to wear to a beach.

Frankie scrambled up to the front to take a look at the door-whore as they passed. The whores down here either worked in the doors and alleys or plied their trade car-hopping. They'd tell their Johns to keep driving—"Both hands on the fuckin' wheel, lover." Another ten bucks bought a parking spot near the docks or under the West Side Highway.

"Hey baby, we'll catch you on the trip back," he called through the open passenger window. The girl smiled sweetly and shifted the nylon strands of the blond wig out of her eyes.

"You try your luck with that," Swag said, "she'll take you apart in about six seconds."

"I heard dey hide razors up their poontangs, bro," Joey said. "You think that's true?"

"No, but dey'll hide a knife between your ribs," Swag said, mimicking the accent. A gun, even a little one, carried felony weight for working girls. A razor was something you shaved your legs with. And they were good with blades. There wasn't a pro on the stroll down here who couldn't hold a single-edged razor blade or sharpened nail between their teeth. If a John was lucky, they'd go for the eyes. The unlucky ones got it across the throat.

They were turning often now, as Joey searched out the place down the narrow streets. When they turned a corner onto Washington, the abandoned freight overpass came into view, like a shadow above the street. It was under the rusted blackened steel of the elevated freight tracks that Joey found what he was looking for—the club known as the Chateau. The place was half concealed down a flight of stairs in the basement of a wholesale meat place. To get to the club, patrons had to pass a surly doorman, walk down a flight of stairs, then through a long hallway lit by red bulbs. The Chateau's specialty was bondage and discipline. But what bothered Swag was that there was only one entrance.

A small line of limos were parked out front, the uni-

formed and armed drivers waiting patiently for their customers to conclude a night's pleasure and head back to the
uptown hotels.

Joey pulled up behind the last limo and turned off the
engine.

Frankie was up front now, crouching just behind the
gearshift, his eyes gone wide as saucers. Two tuxedoed men,
wearing leather masks with zippers for mouths, lounged
against the outside walk smoking casually. "Will ya look at
that," Frankie said, pointing to the two men. "Look at
them freaks. They got some money. Don't tell me them
freaks don't have no cash."

"Get in the back," Swag said.

A limo pulled up behind them and two women wearing
riding outfits and carrying crops strolled past. They
stopped a moment by the door to chat with the men in the
black masks, then vanished into the red glow of the doorway.

"Hey baby, you looking for a horse," Frankie called out
the open window. Then to Joey, "This place is wild. I think
I saw it in a magazine once. Let's hang here for a while and
check it out."

"Pick up that gun and get in the fuckin' back," Swag
ordered.

"What's your problem, Jack?" Frankie shot back. "Look,
this place is cool. All those drivers aren't sweating it."

Swag turned on his seat, nearly coming out of it to grab
a handful of Frankie's shirtfront. "Nobody's gonna take out
a tourist or a driver," he said pulling Frankie closer. "And
nobody's going to care if they fish a couple of punks out
of the river tomorrow. Now get in the fuckin' back and do
your job!" With the last word, Swag pushed back and
released the shirt so that Frankie stumbled and fell across
the remaining cases.

"You're just uptight, man," Frankie said. "Tell him, Joey,
tell this guy who's paying him."

But Joey never had a chance to answer. Swag turned to
see a red dot quivering on his cheek. When Swag pulled

him forward, Joey resisted, jerking back, thinking Swag was putting the bull on him.

The first shot plinked through the windshield and ripped through his throat, the second into his chest. Swag felt the third bullet plow through the air just under his nose and drill a hole in the side of the van. As Swag dived for the floor, he caught a glimpse of the Plymouth through the shattered window. It was parked across the street. The rifleman was firing from the passenger side, resting the silenced weapon across the roof.

Joey lay twisting across the floorboards trying to talk, but it came out in a wet gurgle. The oxygenated blood foamed between the fingers that clutched the wound at his throat.

"What the fuck, man," Frankie said, and began working his way to the front.

Swag grabbed the Franchi autoloader and slipped between the two seats. When Frankie had made his way up, unarmed, he looked down at Joey and said, "Aw man, oh goddamn, man. Shit!"

"The doors! Cover the back doors," Swag spat, pumping a shell into the chamber.

But it was too late. As Frankie turned toward the back, the double doors burst open. When he heard the sound, Swag jerked the handle to the passenger door up and rolled out on the sidewalk. Frankie vanished in a hail of automatic fire that coated the dashboard, seat backs, and front windshield with his blood and chunks of flesh. The sound of the automatics was deafening in the steel truck, and as Swag hit the sidewalk, he heard their bursts echoing off the buildings.

Then the metal of the half-opened door puckered in a jagged hole near Swag's arm as a high-powered round from the silenced rifle tore through it.

One of the shooters came around the side of the truck, and Swag opened up on him with the Franchi. Two double-O loads ripped the gunman's legs out from under him, and a third took the top of his head off before he hit the ground.

Swag wedged himself between the curb and the truck, and rolled under the truck facing the rear. Just behind the rear double tires, he saw the unmistakable polished shoes of a provost beneath the cuffs of nonofficial khakis. Firing off a round in the prone position, the pants burst into a shredded bloody horror that sent the shooter falling nearly straight back, firing a quick burst from his weapon.

That's two, Swag thought to himself. There were probably four. If they called in another car, then maybe there were eight.

Edging around, he saw another pair of provost shoes double-timing it along the side. Swag sighted along with the trotting feet, fired, and sent the gunman into a spill.

From the rear of the van someone called, "He's under the truck." Swag turned and saw the feet, ruined at the ankles, being pulled away.

Across the street another silenced automatic sent a ten-round burst along the cobblestones, tracing a jagged path from the front to the rear tires. The jacketed shells bounced and skidded, chipping the smooth stones as Swag covered his face with an arm.

Swag fired twice in the direction of the gunfire, but the shooting had already stopped. Everything was quiet for a second, then Swag heard it. The van's worn suspension creaked, and the drivetrain lowered by a fraction of an inch. Crepe soles inched their way across the van's bed above him.

Instinctively, Swag tried to pull the shotgun up, found that he couldn't and gently laid it down. Twisting his right arm back behind him, he pulled the Colt from its back holster and placed the barrel silently against the nearly rusted-out floorboards above him.

Tracing a line between the drivetrain and exhaust pipe with the gun, Swag held his breath, trying to judge the position. When he heard the click of a safety coming off, he began firing. He fired blindly, tracing the gun up the passenger side of the drivetrain at the center of the truck, then skipping over to the driver's side. Above him someone jumped, crashed against the metal side, then screamed.

Swag fired two more rounds up through the rusting floorboards near the side of the truck. A burst of automatic fire ripped through the floorboards in a random pattern. And then there was the heavy thud of a body falling.

"Scooter!" someone called from across the street.

There wasn't an answer. Swag began counting rounds. Five from the Colt, which left four. And four from the shotgun, which left another four.

Then Swag felt it coming down across the back of his neck. Reaching behind him, he wiped a hand across the back of his neck, then brought his fingers up to his face. Even in the dim light he could see it was blood, but it smelled like liquor. The grooves of the cargo area had been turned into small rivers of blood and bourbon. Now he could feel it soaking through his pants and his shirt, leaking where he'd fired the Colt up through the floorboards. The strange mixture was trickling down across him and the ground, like a transmission with a blown gasket.

"Scooter!" came the shout from across the street.

And then another voice, closer, "Hey, Scoot-man!"

"Scooter's fucking dead," Swag called back. "I shot him in the balls." Immediately he wished he'd kept quiet. It was like a signal. A barrage of full-auto gunfire ripped along the cobblestones just under the truck on the street side as Swag quickly edged himself back behind the rear tire and toward the curb.

Scooter was apparently well-liked. Probably a real good guy, Swag thought. Maybe even clean-up hitter at intrasquad softball games.

The rear tire blew with a long wheezing expulsion of stale air. Swag inched himself forward as the bullets chipped at the stones and dinged into metal around him.

The front tire went next, and Swag felt the hot exhaust pipe lower across his back as he scrambled to the curb side. And then there was something else. Suddenly his back and arms were cool and wet as the thick smell of gas filled the air. Some of the rounds had hit the gas tank. Miraculously it had not exploded, but now he was soaked with high-test.

The gunfire stopped, and a voice across the street shouted, "Hey, come outta there. We just want to talk."

Swag was nearly to the curb. A thick puddle of gas had run down from the tank and was soaking through his pants. His legs and arms were covered in it. He knew he couldn't fire again, the muzzle flash would send the whole truck up. And if they opened up again from across the street, he was also dead.

"Hey, you still—" a man called, but was cut off.

Someone else shouted, and then there was the sound of a windshield blasted out by a silenced weapon.

It was a lame trick, Swag thought, wanting him to think someone else was firing on them. Joey or Frankie perhaps. But while they were playing games, he had some time. Creeping backward, he brought his feet, then legs, and finally his head out from under the death trap at the curb side.

As he rose slowly, he tucked the Colt into the front of his belt and listened. He could feel the gas drying on his skin, the blood turning sticky across his neck and arms. There was the sound of a car starting as he made his way to the front of the truck. Then he heard wheels struggling for purchase along cobblestones.

Peeking around the foreshortened nose of the step van, Swag saw a Plymouth fishtailing out of sight around the corner. Three thick trails of blood stretched from where Swag had shot the men in the legs to where the Plymouth had been. Slumped over the hood of another, nearly identical Plymouth, farther back, was a man with most of his head blown away.

As he moved out in front of the van, Swag looked quickly to the windshield, nearly opaque with blood. The tempered safety glass barely hung in the frame around the gaping bullet holes.

Swag crossed the street cautiously, shotgun raised and ready. A quick look back showed the ruined side of the van. At least fifty rounds had done their work from driver's door to the rear. All were at chest level.

People were edging out now behind him. Limo drivers and partygoers from the Chateau stared wide-eyed at the carnage. They wore black leather vests over bare chests, leather G-strings, and thigh-high boots. A fat man dressed in jockey shorts and a dog collar took a red ball-gag from his mouth and gaped slack-jawed in mute horror at the scene, while the leather-corseted woman who held his leash grabbed at his arm at the elbow for support.

"Harv, what—" she began, but the fat men shushed her with an upraised hand.

In the distance a two-note provost siren grew louder. Then it was joined by three more sirens. They were moving fast, covering from the West Side Highway and from the East Side.

Up the street, under the tracks, there was a muzzle flash and a hissing report. It wasn't a gun, silenced or otherwise. Swag felt the hot wind as the projectile passed fifteen feet to his right, moving fast at shoulder level. By the time he turned, shotgun up, the thing, whatever it was, had smashed through what remained of the van's windshield. A second later the insides of the truck exploded in a flame so hot that the bloodied windshield began to melt almost immediately.

The crowd from the Chateau let out a collective "ahh," like it was a fireworks display, then inched back.

Up the street a car pulled out from its parking place. The van's gas tank blew then, covering the van in bright orange flame that licked greedily at the steel sides and lit up the street, illuminating the faces of the Chateau's clientele in pulsing detail. The dimpled bullet holes in the van's side glowed brightly, through an inky smoke.

Swag, feeling the scorching heat at his back, moved aside as the Benz passed. Its window was pulled down maybe six inches, and he caught a brief look of the top of the driver's head. It was only a second, by the fire's pulsing light. But Swag thought he recognized the haircut.

chapter nineteen

Roger, lying across a divan, stretched his legs out and crossed his ankles lazily as he watched Catherwood look at himself in the mirror. "Four of them," Roger said, turning his head slightly to make eye contact by way of the four-paneled mirror that was folded out from the walk-in bedroom closet.

Catherwood arched a skeptical eyebrow and shifted his weight from one custom-made shoe to the other. He was standing on a small wooden stool, pantless, as an ancient Chinese tailor measured his waist with a tape measure. "Tell me about it, Roger," Catherwood instructed.

Roger picked up one of the samples of cloth from a low table and studied it casually. "Now probably isn't the best time," he said, then put the swatch of material down.

"Nonsense," Catherwood answered. "Mr. Chen, here, doesn't speak a word of English. Isn't that right, Henzen?"

The old man seemed not to hear; rather, he brought the tape around and began measuring Catherwood's left arm.

Roger cast a skeptical look from the tailor to his boss. Catherwood was wearing one of those Battistoni shirts, the kind that never wrinkle because they button between the legs. Wondering how Catherwood took a piss, Roger began his report. "He was under the van most of the time," he said. "He took three of them out with a shotgun, the third, by firing up through the floor, probably with a pistol. It was a regular amateur hour, as far as the provosts performed."

Catherwood shifted again as Henzen moved from one side to the other. "And how many were originally sent after him?"

"I counted seven," Roger said. "One drove what was left of the wounded away. The remaining two were terminated by yours truly to expedite his escape. Like you instructed, I was his guardian angel."

The old man finished with the left arm and moved to measure Catherwood's waist, which was unnaturally slim, almost like a woman's. "I take it that you performed that last function with your typical aplomb."

Roger didn't answer; rather, he watched the tailor. Watched his face, around the eyes. The way the muscles contracted, making him squint, just for a second.

"Do you intend to answer me?" Catherwood said. "Did you or did you not terminate two of Colonel Bammer's men?"

"They were terminated," Roger said at last, reluctantly. "I did it."

The tailor moved the tape down from Catherwood's waist to his left thigh. He had written nothing down: he didn't need to, the information was stored indelibly in his memory. "Very good, then," Catherwood sighed. "Hand me that phone if you will."

Roger rose, picked the cordless handset of the phone from a cherrywood night table and handed it to his boss. As he watched Catherwood punch in the first six digits, first the area code, then exchange, which were 516–788, Roger casually hit the power-off switch on the base unit.

Catherwood wheeled his head around from the sight of his own reflection. He was frowning, pulling that thin-lipped patrician mouth into a scowl, but looking more like a spoiled child than a pissed-off adult. "Roger, what on earth do you imagine you're doing?"

"That's not a secure line, sir," Roger said, meeting the gaze with a blank look.

The childlike scowl faded. Indeed, Catherwood had forgotten, but he wasn't about to let on. "It will be secure, as soon as I tell them," he said authoritatively.

"You're the boss," Roger said, then flicked the switch back on before retaking his seat on the divan. Almost immediately he began combing his hair.

When the male voice came on the other end, Catherwood said, "Line four please, your end only."

"Sir?" said the voice.

"I said line four, single-end voice encryption," Catherwood repeated into the phone. He wasn't speaking loudly, not actually shouting, but his voice was stiff.

"Sir, that is outside policy," the man on the other end said.

"Jupiter transfer," Catherwood tried.

"Sir—" the voice on the other end began.

"Goddamnit, I said Jupiter transfer. For your sake, don't make me repeat myself."

"Sir—"

"You have exactly two seconds to patch this call into Jupiter section."

Roger couldn't help but smirk. His expression didn't go unnoticed by Catherwood, who shifted and waved the Chinese guy off as the ancient tailor was about to measure the inseam. When a phone rang off the coast of Florida on a small island named Jupiter, Catherwood smiled.

The phone rang three times. Then a young lady with an English accent picked it up and said, "Yes." Her voice was Kensington through and through.

"This is New York," Catherwood said.

The girl said, "Yes." She stretched the word out, somewhat incredulous, a fact not lost on Catherwood.

"I need four more," Catherwood said. "By tomorrow."

"I believe you have misdialed, sir," the girl said.

"Young lady, I have not misdialed," Catherwood said, his voice rising. "I need four more by tomorrow morning. Is that clear?"

The girl began to say something that began with "Sir." But Catherwood had hung up.

"Way, *way* outside policy," Roger said as he slipped the comb back into his pocket.

"Roger, take this damn thing," came the terse response. "And don't ever question my authority again. Is that clear?"

Lifting himself from the divan, Roger walked across the thickly carpeted room and placed the phone gently back on the bedside unit. "As clear as an unscrambled call, sir."

Catherwood loosened up a little and said, "Roger, do you believe yourself to be indispensable?"

The tailor began to measure the inseam then. When he had the tape measure up along the inside of the leg, Catherwood said, "On the left side," and the old guy nodded slightly.

Roger, seeing this, carefully put down the swatch of cloth he was studying and said, "No one is indispensable."

"Just remember that, then," Catherwood replied, and stepped down from the stool.

The tailor folded the small step-stool together and moved with a slight hunch toward his thin sample case. Catherwood slipped back into the trousers that hung on a wood hanger by the closet's door.

"And while we're on the subject of security," Catherwood said. "Have you noticed anything strange as of late?"

"Strange?" Roger answered. "What kind of strange?"

"I've heard a rumor," Catherwood answered, "through unofficial channels, that a shadow operation's been launched. A security fail-safe, as it were."

"That's interesting," Roger answered. "Those fat cats in Switzerland getting a little nervous, are they?"

"Cautious perhaps," Catherwood answered, slipping on his suit coat. "Understandably, I suppose. There's a great deal at stake. But you haven't heard or seen anything? Perhaps that intuition of yours? A feeling that you're being followed?"

"Nobody's said anything to me," Roger replied.

"Very good, then," Catherwood said, adjusting his tie. "More than likely it's just office gossip."

Roger watched Catherwood as he turned from the mirror, a small self-satisfied smile on his face.

Checking the wafer-thin Blancpain platinum watch, Catherwood said, "We may just make my lunch at the Four Seasons. Bring the car around, Roger. If that doesn't represent a breach of security. Show Mr. Chen out, will you?"

"Sure, why not," came the reply.

As they walked from the bedroom, Roger slowed his pace to that of the old man, lagging just a step behind him. Then, walking through the gleaming kitchen, empty now of the cook, he led the old guy through a steel door that opened into a drab, concrete alcove where the service elevator was housed.

Punching the button, Roger said, *"Nin wan on."* Good afternoon to you. He spoke it with a distinct Mandarin accent.

The old guy turned to him, slightly surprised, and replied with the more familiar, *"Wan on."*

"This'll just take a second," Roger said casually.

When the old man nodded, he sealed his death sentence. Roger reached around and grabbed him by the head, one hand under the chin, the other at the forehead, and twisted. It hardly took any effort at all; the neck snapped with a sound of dry twigs as the old guy dropped his sample case and stool.

By the time the elevator arrived, Roger had already secured the corpse in the walk-in freezer, the dead man's belongings piled next to him.

Down on the lake in Central Park, a sixty-year-old blonde-haired man in khaki pants and a madras shirt rowed a wooden, yellow and red boat. Pulling effortlessly at the oars, his French running shoes wedged along the boat's dry bottom, he smiled across to the pretty young woman seated at the stern.

She wore a sleeveless, white cotton dress that exposed her

long slender arms, tanned by the sun. She was blonde, her hair cropped short, and there was a light dusting of fine blonde hairs on her arms that Jim Bob found intriguing. He also liked the way her hair, partially covered by a straw hat with a pink ribbon, was cropped at ear level. Just right to set off her slender neck.

On the seat between them was an open wicker picnic basket, which revealed rows of plates and silverware, neatly strapped to its lid. The basket had beeped twice fifteen minutes before, but Jim Bob kept the young woman from looking under the rows of smoked turkey sandwiches, macaroni salad, and cold fried chicken.

Now she was pouting slightly, eager to see what treasure the machine had revealed. Jim Bob was eager too, but she was just so damned pretty, the way she scrunched her mouth up and fidgeted.

"We should check, don't you think?" she asked.

Jim Bob pulled hard on the oars, sending the boat into the middle of the lake. "*Come live with me, and be my love, And we will some new pleasures prove. Of golden sands, and crystal brooks,*" Jim Bob recited, "*with silver lines and silvery hooks.*" He spoke it easily, as if saying, Pass me a beer from the cooler. The old poem fit his accent as if some good ol' boy from Oklahoma and not a seventeenth century English cleric had written it.

"Poetry?" she said. "You have to be kidding."

"Don't they teach you youngsters anything anymore? Where was it, Smith?"

But he already knew it was Vassar that she had graduated from with honors in economics three years earlier. He knew other things about her as well. She was twenty-five and her father was a middling-level official in the State Department, a career man in a white shirt and thick-soled shoes. He had moved from Korea to Austria to France, and finally to Japan. By the second post, he'd risen as far as he ever would, but continued slogging away in some dead end advisory role. The girl spoke five languages and was an avid skier. Somewhere in an Agency file was the notation that she had so impressed the instructors at Austria's Sankt Anton ski school that they offered to ease the government certification process in an attempt to lure her into the school as an instructor. It was an offer she laughed off, though she still kept the wallet-sized certificate of graduation with all stamps, official signatures, and photo.

She'd grown up in embassy compounds and American schools. The Agency had recruited her right out of college and put her to work in some black room cryptocenter—until she had a short but dramatic affair with a case officer. Then they sent her to school for ECCM (electronic countermeasures); ELINT (Electronic Intelligence); ELSEC (electronic security); she breezed through in just under two years. Now she was working as secondary agent, with Spurock in the P.A. or principal agent slot. And she's doing a damn fine job of it, Spurock thought.

"Vassar," she said. "And they told me to look out for you. Especially when you started reciting poetry."

"Lies, all lies," Jim Bob said, smiling. "Lies, and damnable ones no less. Who *exactly* told you?"

"I'm afraid that's classified under need-to-know information." She laughed. More of a giggle, Spurock thought, betraying her age. But that was okay. You didn't hear nearly enough giggling anymore. And then he thought, did they teach that now in some Agency school? Probably taught in something like Covert Unconventional Techniques for Enticement.

"It wouldn't be a certain senior NIO, now would it? What exactly did your informant say?"

"She said you were the best in the W.H. Division," the young woman replied. Then paused just long enough to see a smile form at the corners of Spurock's mouth, before adding, "At covert ops, that is."

Then she outright laughed, leaned forward a little and hooked her ankles together.

Spurock pretended to frown, then said, "Reach me over one of those turkey sandwiches and a Jax, darlin'."

The young woman's smile faded, her face turning serious

as she dug in the basket. Inside, among the wrapped sand-wiches, salads, and utensils, was a powerful scanner, pre-amp, and small voice-activated recorder. The antenna was set for the repeater on the San Remo. And its low-band directional antenna was aimed at the apartment in the south tower.

As she continued to dig in the basket, the young woman noted the six-digit frequency codes displayed on the scan-ner's face and the small, coded readout of the heavily mod-ified reel-to-reel.

By the time Spurock had put the oars up, she was han-ding him a wax-paper-wrapped sandwich and opening the beer.

"See anything interesting?" he asked, unwrapping the fat sandwich and watching her dig one out for herself. He could make out the gentle curve of her breasts in the scooped-out neck of the dress as she bent forward toward the basket.

"Two minute call on a cordless," she said. "Transponder frequency of 46.61 megahertz, unencrypted, 516 area code. That's on Long Island."

Spurock bit into the turkey sandwich, nodded, and began chewing slowly.

"Probably called his real estate broker for a summer rental in Montauk," she said, removing a sandwich for her-self.

Spurock swallowed and took a sip from the beer. "The recorder up?"

The young woman nodded, said, "Umm-hmm," peeled away a layer of wax paper and took a small, dainty bite from the sandwich.

"We'll just see then, I suppose," Spurock said, and took another drink of the beer.

Holding the partially-wrapped sandwich in one hand, she reached into the cooler and retrieved a lemon Perrier. "What about the civilian?"

"Which one?"

"Your friend, Jim Bob. You know, the Amcit, Swag?"

Spurock brought the sandwich to a stop midway to his mouth. "He's in the middle of it, that old boy is."

"What do you think's going to happen to him?"

"I don't know, darlin'," Spurock said.

"But if you had to guess?" she asked.

"Nothing good," came the answer. "Old Swag now is just into it pretty deep. Would you like to hear some Byron? *'She walks in beauty like the night/Of cloudless climes and starry skies/And all that's best of dark and bright/Meet in the aspect of her eyes—'*"

"Are you going to help him?" she interrupted, her green eyes opening wide over the top of her sandwich.

"I declare," Spurock said sadly, "it's a sorry state of affairs when pretty girls don't swoon over poetry. Where is it you suppose that the world went wrong?"

chapter twenty

COLONEL BAMMER WAS SITTING at his reserved table in the Palm Court at the Plaza and waiting for the music to end. Set up at one end of the restaurant was a violin, cello, and flute trio. The musicians were two long-haired women and a very anemic young man. They played every day, from noon until five, and always the same song without end. Bammer didn't know much about music. But he knew two things about this trio. The first was that they should get rid of the guy and replace him with another chippie. Then they should outfit the whole bunch of them in something that showed some leg. The dresses they wore now were down to their damned ankles. Bammer also knew that no song could last five hours, even one without any words. Yet the trio never seemed to pause. Over the last several weeks it had become his secret personal quest to discover just when one song ended and the next began.

Bammer took a small sip from his coffee and watched as one of his men walked across the room with an air of uneasy authority.

When the man, who Bammer now recognized as a lieutenant, paused in front of the table, Bammer made a quick motion with his free hand, indicating that he should sit.

"Sir," the young lieutenant said, pulling out a chair and seating himself. "I just left the hospital."

"Corbett, is it? Tell me about it."

"It's bad," the young man said, nodding grimly. "Sergeant Strengon lost his left foot. Hodge, the left leg below the knee. And Bingham needed a length of his lower intestine resectioned. Major Tancloe, Sergeant Danfield, Wakeman, and Scooter—I mean Schnabel—are dead."

"And that Hawaiian shirt-wearing renegade bastard is still out there someplace," Bammer added as he clicked his coffee cup down on the saucer.

"Yes, sir," the young man answered. "That's about where we stand now."

"Perhaps you can explain something to me, soldier," Bammer said, fixing the young man in a purposeful stare.

"I'll try, sir."

"Explain to me this," Bammer said in measured tones. "Tell me how one man, alone, can kill, wound, and maim six men."

"We got two of his accomplices, sir," the young man answered hopefully. "Two gray marketeers from New Jersey."

"Two gray marketeers from Jersey," Bammer echoed. "You're sure that wasn't too much of a strain on the combined resources of this department?"

"Sir, in all due respect, there was a third accomplice we were not aware of. This individual is the one who shot Wakeman and Tancloe."

Bammer raised his cup and took a long deliberate sip from the coffee, thinking of what to say next. "And who was this accomplice?"

"There's no way to tell, sir. He held a sniper position. Witnesses say he left in a dark Mercedes. License number unknown."

Bammer removed his hands from around the coffee cup and stared across the table at the young man. The lieutenant squirmed slightly under the cold gaze, which had its intended effect. "Let me tell you something, Lieutenant," Bammer began. His voice was flat, as if he were trying to control anger, but in reality it was fear he was fighting down. "This is the way it is going to be. You are to take nine men. You pick them. Put your nine men into three unmarked units. Then kill this sonofabitch. Do it in a drive-by, blow him up, dump him in the river, I don't give a fuck how, but do it."

"Yes, sir," the young man said promptly.

Somewhere far off the trio began a new number, faster, without missing a beat.

"Well, what are you waiting for?"

"There's one other thing, sir," the young man stuttered out.

"Yes, are you going to make me wait?"

"No, sir," the young man said. "It's just that maybe we aren't the only ones who have Swag under surveillance. There's something really strange going on."

Bammer stiffened, feeling the newly barbered hairs on the back of his neck stand up. He waited a long moment before speaking, wanting to be sure his voice came out right. "And what would that be?"

"Two days ago, when the major ran a check on his bank accounts, to track activity, well, it's just that the accounts were frozen. Under a Section 18."

Bammer relaxed a bit, feeling this didn't represent a threat. "That's pretty standard, isn't it? The man is involved in a felony investigation."

"Sir, the NYPD didn't freeze the accounts," the young man said. "Neither did the FBI, Treasury, or our headquarters. I checked."

"Follow the paper, then," Bammer ordered. "It takes a court order to freeze assets."

When the young man spoke again, it was in a hushed tone. "I did, sir," he said. "The order was signed by a federal judge in Wilmington, Delaware, and sealed."

"And did you call this federal judge from Wilmington, Delaware?" Bammer asked.

"Yes, sir," the young lieutenant responded. "He was unavailable, sir."

"Unavailable? We'll see if he's unavailable when I call."

"Sir, he checked into the Betty Ford Clinic the day after he signed the order. His clerk told me he was drying out."

Bammer took a sip of coffee and gazed across the room at the trio. "Isn't that the place where the patients clean toilets?"

"Sir, it's part of the therapy program."

Bammer brought his gaze back, fixing the young man in his best no-bullshit stare. "Lieutenant, understand this. If Swag isn't tagged and bagged inside of twenty-four hours, you'll be taking Betty's cure in the Port Authority crapper," Bammer said. "Tell me if this is not clear to you. It should be clear to you. I want you to think—no, I want you to dwell—on the prospect of taking the Betty Ford program in the Port Authority with a toothbrush."

"Yes, sir. It's perfectly clear, sir," the young man said. "Only one thing . . ."

"And what is this one thing?" Bammer sneered.

"Sir, what if whoever else is following this Swag is big," the lieutenant answered. "I mean bigger than Provost Command, bigger than our immediate jurisdiction? Is it wise to step over any lines? Maybe we could launch a cooperative effort . . ."

Bammer's mind flashed back to that guy, Catherwood. He was more sure than ever that Catherwood's questions about Swag could only mean he was investigating that mess with the grand jury. But with Tancloe dead, there was only one loose end to tie up: Swag.

"Sir," Corbett continued, "a cooperative effort, a task force, with another agency could benefit everyone concerned."

"Understand something, Corbett," Bammer replied slowly. "Nobody in this town has more authority than me. There will be no cooperative efforts. And there will be no task force. With this character dead, a tragic victim of street violence, all investigations will end."

The young man rose stiffly from the chair and brought his hand up into a salute.

"Corbett, one other thing," Bammer said.

"Yes, sir."

"Tell those musicians to play something that somebody

knows," Bammer instructed. "Like 'Moon River,' or that fuck song."

"That what song, sir?"

"You know, that song you fuck to," Bammer replied angrily. "Daa. Da-da-da-da-da-da-dada."

"The Bolero, sir?"

"Yeah, the fuck song."

Catherwood paused at the open door to the Mercedes limo just long enough to fix Roger in an unblinking stare. Then very smoothly, he bowed slightly and slipped into the car. Roger shut the door and moved up to the driver's seat.

Turning the ignition key, Roger thought to himself, He's pouting again. Just like a little kid.

And then, sure enough, the smoky glass of the partition came down and Catherwood said, "Your attitude is patently insubordinate. Additionally, do you know that you have cold-bloodedly murdered one of the finest tailors in the world?"

"No," Roger said, "but if you hum a few bars . . ."

"None of this is acceptable," Catherwood said. "Is that clear?"

"Sure," Roger said. "But you're the one getting sloppy. Aren't you curious how your boy Swag is doing?"

"Is there any change in his condition?"

"I put a couple of new boys on him, low-visibility surveillance," Roger answered, turning in the seat to face Catherwood. "He left one of his banks an hour ago, trying to talk his way back into the account. He wasn't happy about his accounts being frozen."

"I expect he should be low on funds by now," Catherwood said.

"Just what he has in his pockets. The guy's running on vapors."

"Very well, then, clean up his trail," came the terse response. "Eliminate every street person he's talked to in the last week. I want him scared and without resources. I want him brought in tomorrow for a chat. And why aren't you driving?"

"You haven't told me where to *drive to*," Roger answered, not bothering to screen the sarcasm from his voice.

"Sotheby's," Catherwood said, then whirred the partition up. As the smoked glass rose, Roger could see Catherwood pull the platinum cylinder from his pocket and administer a small dose of the synthetic tetrotoxin. His movements were hurried with the need for the drug.

"I should have known," Roger said to himself, and turned the big car out into traffic.

They cut neatly across Central Park to the East Side. Roger turned on Second and drifted down into the Sixties before turning east toward York Avenue.

There was a long line of limos out in front of the auction house, and Roger slid the car into the last place. When he opened the rear door, Catherwood rose gracefully from the seat and said, "Two and a half hours," without so much as a sideways glance in Roger's direction.

When Catherwood was safely deposited inside the building, Roger drove the car up three blocks and turned down a side street. Opening the briefcase on the seat next to him, he fit the handset of the cellular phone onto an acoustic coupler and picked up the handset mounted into the briefcase. Punching in the number on the cellular phone, he waited as the line rang twice and a man's voice answered with a businesslike "Hello."

"Line four," Roger said. "Cellular unit."

The young man said, "One moment please," and Roger punched three buttons on the interior of the briefcase. A small liquid crystal display at the top of the console flashed, WAIT. WAIT. WAIT, and then LINE SECURE.

"Yes?" the young man asked.

"Zermatt link," Roger said.

"Sir?"

"Come on, patch me through to Zermatt."

"I need coded authorization for that," the young man answered. There was a note of hesitation in his voice. In the year and a half he had been working on the island, he had never relayed a call to Switzerland.

"Shit, you're not going to make me say it, are you?"

"Sir, it's—"

"I know, procedure," Roger said. "Okay, here it is, 'Roger the dodger wants to talk to the codger.' Are you happy now?" Roger had dreamed up the password himself; now that he had to use it, he was sorry. He should have stuck to a number, like everyone else.

The line went silent for a second; then the man said, "One moment please." And Roger waited as the link and electronic security was enabled on the other end.

The next voice he heard was the old man's. It was an ancient voice, dry and breathy, but it still had a bit of a Midwest twang to it. "Do you know what time it is?" the man asked.

"You were sleeping?" Roger asked, his voice jovial.

"I'm an old man," the old man said. "Have you called to harass an old man in the middle of the night?"

"That's exactly why I've called," Roger answered. "How's the food?"

"The food is foreign, the people are foreigners."

"But you're close to your money."

"A cold consolation in this damn cold country," the old man offered with a dry laugh. "I want to return to Santa Barbara. Why precisely are you calling, my young irascible friend?"

"Your boy Catherwood is getting sloppy," Roger said, his voice changing now to a flat, businesslike tone.

"He is, now?" the old man said, his interest aroused. "Just how bad is the situation?"

"Not bad. He's begun moving some money. We've tied up a good portion of the unskilled service sector," Roger said, knowing that the old man would know that he meant gambling, prostitution, protection, waste disposal, and fences.

"Wretched businesses, all of that," the old man said.

"From a management standpoint they were in chaos,"

Roger replied. "I've run some spread sheets. Even factoring in the enterprise's percentage, they'll continue to remain profitable for the original principles. Textbook acquisition."

"And what of the others?"

"We've made some initial contacts in other market segments," Roger said. "Specifically, the storefront surgeons, the black-market people, and the money men," Roger answered. "Spreading good faith funds around. Not too far off the original timetable."

"Then what precisely is the problem with our Mr. Catherwood?"

"In my opinion, he's been abusing his management and fiduciary responsibilities."

"I should take that to mean, what?"

"He's getting careless with security," Roger said. "And careless with your money. Are you near a terminal?"

"Yes," the old man said, somewhat hesitantly.

"Okay, I'm going to transmit some information through. Have one of your numbers guys and an analyst look at the data. They can fix the problem at Center One in the Caymans office, but don't let them touch the code until you hear from me."

Roger inserted the computer disk in the encryption unit and transmitted. The line went silent for a long time. When the old man got back on the line, he said, "What the hell is going on here?"

"He's added some personal touches to the Center One software," Roger said. "Random amounts aren't registering as incoming funds. He's set up his own network, shadowing the one we're using for the enterprise."

"He's stealing from me?" the old man asked incredulously. "How much?"

"Not much, yet," Roger said. "When your boys on that end run the figures, they'll see wire transfers bouncing around the Caymans and Grand Duchy. Then to Bank of Tokyo, Credit Suisse, and Bank in Liechtenstein. Bank accounts are registered in Ms. Lorette's name. There's also a trust set up in Madeira."

"Why, that one-eyed, slippery sonofabitch," the old man said.

"Just another good reason for eliminating the Lorette woman," Roger added. "She must have been in on it. He'd need someone help him set it up. Use her to help establish his own shell corporations."

"Are you telling me she wasn't selling secrets of our little enterprise? That is what Catherwood mentioned as the reason for her elimination."

"Oh, she was doing that too, sir," Roger said. "Or trying to. She used a Swiss courier to bring the information into the States. I would speculate that she had a falling out with him. To the best of my knowledge, no information has changed hands, only money. It is also my understanding that the courier suffered a fatal heart attack on the plane back to Zurich."

"Quite extraordinary," the old man said. "You are a remarkable young man of talent, and, I dare say, ambition."

"That's my job," Roger said. "What should I do?"

"I'll call California, France, Frankfurt, and our people on the Rim. In the meantime, just keep driving his car. We shall deal with this thief."

"Yes, sir," Roger replied. "It won't be a problem, when the time comes."

The old man sighed. "It's all become so tedious. Sometimes I question the wisdom of our actions."

"You're a patriot, sir," Roger said. "Just remember that."

"I will strive to remember that, my young friend," the old man said. "And fear not, I will remember your loyalty as well. My associates and I can be very generous. And you can take that to the bank, as they say."

"I intend to, sir," Roger replied, then hung up.

The loft was on Walker Street, just off of Hudson. It didn't look like much from the outside. Just another building with weathered brick and a rickety fire escape. To look at the building you would think that the roof leaked and the plumbing was bad. On the ground floor was a storefront company that made zippers and another that sold offshore imports. The four stories held six units, five of which were empty.

In the front unit of the second floor, behind a gray steel door, 3500 square feet of gleaming polished wood floors and pristine white walls. Two small bedrooms led off the main room, and a kitchen ran halfway up one wall. The only furniture in the large room was a red leather couch near the center of the room, and two stools pulled up to the kitchen area.

Jim Bob, sitting cross-legged in the center of the room, looked across to the young woman and nodded. She bent toward the two small reel-to-reels between them. Because the Nigra had no speaker, she had transferred the tape to the larger, Japanese unit. In the last twenty-four hours Jim Bob had requested that the tape be played nearly fifty times.

Each time, Jim Bob listened to it the same way—eyes closed, head slightly upturned toward the ceiling fifteen feet above him. It was as if he were listening to a song he enjoyed; a tune he wanted to remember, note for note.

Catherwood's voice, remarkably lifelike, came from the small speaker. When he had finished talking, the young woman switched the recorder off.

"Want to hear it again?" she asked, her face serious, hand already on the rewind switch.

Jim Bob shook his head slowly and opened his eyes.

"What does it mean?" she asked.

Rising easily to his feet, Jim Bob crossed over to the kitchen counter and took a long drink of Evian from a liter bottle.

"The repeater work all right for you?" he asked, recapping the water.

"Fine," she said, rising from her cross-legged position and joining Jim Bob at the counter. "It's still on the roof, has approximately three weeks of power left."

"That's fine, then."

"Why don't you just once tell me what you think?"

Jim Bob turned to study the young woman. She was

frowning, and he hated to see a pretty girl frown. "Not much," he said. "Maybe they're getting careless. But that might not mean anything."

The young woman continued to frown disappointedly.

"What would you like it to mean?" Jim Bob asked.

"A code maybe," she said hopefully. "We could send it to the center."

"Naw, those ol' boys got better things to worry about," he answered, casually stepping away from the counter to run through an advanced t'ai chi routine that sent his right arm dancing out in front of him as he glided light-footed across the floor.

"In two months it's the only thing we've gotten," she said.

"So it's got to be important, huh?" Jim Bob replied with a smile. He shifted his attention to his left arm now, twisting and turning slowly; then he jabbed out in a graceful arc at some imaginary adversary.

"Well, it's got to mean something."

"Darlin'," Jim Bob replied, stepping into a complex series of slow moves that took him past the woman and halfway across the room, "it means exactly what it means."

chapter twenty-one

THE MAN WITH THE RAINCOAT walked into World of Peeps at exactly nine in the morning. It wasn't raining, but buttoned raincoats weren't an unfamiliar sight to Money Shot. Not at nine in the morning. Not even on sunny summer days.

"How many?" Money Shot asked, not looking up from where he was stacking tokens.

"Three, please."

Still not looking up, he pushed across a short stack of the square-edged tokens and raked in the francs.

The man took the tokens and walked stiffly up the stairs. A small group of girls dressed in underwear were loafing in front of the last booth, drinking coffee and listening to another girl tell a story.

The conversation stopped as the man made his way past the girls and went into the middle door. He had all three coins in the slot by the time Lucy reluctantly disengaged herself from the discussion and walked to her booth.

Looking up at the customer, she saw he had his right hand jammed deep in the pocket of the raincoat. Good, she thought, he's got a head start.

The customer nodded, then began unbuttoning the coat with his left hand.

"What would you like to see, lover?" Lucy said, not able to keep the boredom from her voice and hooking a heel across one of the stool's rungs.

"I am a tourist," the man said with a slight accent, as he unfastened the last button.

"We're all tourists in this town," Lucy answered, reaching around to unclasp her bra.

"Yes, this is true," the man said, and shifted the coat to reveal the gun. Then he very deliberately placed the silencer over the glass.

"Hey, what kind of shit is this?" Lucy said.

The man in the dark suit fired four times. The first shot widened the hole in the Plexiglas and knocked Lucy against the back wall of the booth as it ripped into her chest. The last three shots caught her in the chest and stomach as she slumped forward. The screen came down as she hit the floor, falling halfway out of her side of the booth.

By the time the gunman was down the stairs, the girls were already screaming. "Hey, that scumbag shot Luce!"

Money Shot, big and slow, reached for the sawed-off under the counter as he came off his stool. The gunman made a slight turn as he headed for the door and shot Leonard "Money Shot" Sadowitz twice, once in the chest, the second time in the throat.

There was more screaming then, and the sound of curtained doors slamming shut from above. Pausing, gun still at waist level, the gunman scanned the room as he backed toward the door.

A half-dozen feet from the double doors he turned, took two steps and caught a mop, heavy with disinfectant-laced water, across the side of the head. Dazed, he staggered back, raising the gun as he began to turn.

"You don't pull that bullshit on the Deuce, asshole," Nicky snarled, and hit him again with the mop, this time full in the face.

Blinded by stinging, pine-scented disinfectant, the gunman fired twice. The first shot went wild and to the left, scattering a neat stack of tokens from Leonard's counter, then plowing into the Formica-paneled row of booths, leaving a jagged fist-sized hole in the particle board underneath. The second shot caught Nicky through the cheek and

exploded against his bottom molars, taking out the left side
of his face and jaw. Momentum carried Nicky another step
forward; then he fell, face first across his mop.

By the time the girls began to emerge from their booths,
the gunman was crossing 42nd Street and heading toward
Sixth, in a fast walk.

Longford lay in an open ward at Bellevue, his left thumb
and index finger destroyed, the small stumps swathed in
thick bandages. His left eye was gone, and the socket covered by a patch of cotton and gauze. For two days he'd
watched the IV drip morphine sulfate into his arm and
wondered just who the hell had made the bullet that
exploded in his vise, and why. It must have had some manner of built-in self-destruct feature, triggered when the projectile was removed from the casing. Because when it blew,
it shredded the thick leather of the welder's gloves and protective goggles without any trouble at all.

More than likely it had been triggered by friction. Perhaps some manner of primer around the upper section of
cartridge. Quite possibly ignited by a turn of the projectile.
Of course. A turn, Longford mused through the half sleep
of morphine. Anything else would explode the projectile
in the chamber. A person would be shooting shrapnel. It
would ruin the weapon's barrel and expand the casing when
it was fired under normal conditions and wouldn't move
through the ejector port. The projectile itself was probably
hollow. Filled with propellant or an explosive. Or both.

Longford was interrupted from his musings by a white-
suited male nurse wheeling a cloth partition around his
bed. "Good morning, Mr. Longford," the nurse said, pulling a medication dispenser into the enclosure. "Time for
your shot."

"Ah, antibiotics. It isn't quite time yet, is it?" Longford
asked.

And the nurse, smiling, said, "Painkiller."

"Demerol?" Longford asked.

"You asked for it and we have it," said the nurse, filling

a hypodermic from a small vial. "Five milligrams of our finest."

"Demerol you say?" Longford asked, then noticed the faint outline of a compact Glock 9 in the nurse's front pocket. Definitely a Glock, Longford thought to himself, too big and boxy to be anything else.

"Firearms aren't allowed on wards, are they?" Longford asked as he watched the nurse professionally squirt a little of the solution into the air to remove bubbles.

"Definitely not," came the answer. "Now if you'll just give me your arm . . ."

Longford extended his right arm, and the nurse swabbed it with a gauze alcohol patch.

"Now, this won't hurt a bit," the nurse said, leaning forward with the needle, still holding his arm.

"Wait, please," Longford replied. "The other nurse said I could take my painkillers in a less conspicuous place. I bruise easily, you understand. She said the doctor approved it."

"Of course," the nurse said. "Now, if you'll just turn over."

Longford groaned slightly and turned on his stomach. "Silly, really," he said, letting the arm with the IV hand over the edge of the bed.

"I understand perfectly," the nurse said. He spoke in a perfect nurse's voice, like talking to a child.

"Oh, I don't even know why I bother." Longford could feel the icy touch of the alcohol swab on his ass as he reached under the bed.

"Now, this won't hurt a bit," the nurse said.

Then, turning back around suddenly, Longford brought up the modified .380 Beretta and fired in one motion.

The nurse fell back, dropping the needle as he crashed against the screen. Longford forced his feet off the end of the bed, pulling the IV from his arm in the process. To his surprise the nurse was scrambling backward, digging into his pocket for the Glock.

Longford shot him again in the chest, the unsilenced

weapon echoing through the ward. All around him patients were rising up, calling to each other and rolling to the floor to take cover under the steel-frame beds.

"Who are you?" Longford said, moving in on the nurse who had by now dug out the firearm and was rolling into a sitting combat position.

When Longford shot him the third time in the chest, the impact blew the nurse sideways and he scrambled to the other side of the wheeled screen. Still woozy from the morphine, Longford squinted his one eye to see through the scalloped material, but saw no shadow.

Then from the other side of the screen came a shot. The material billowed out slightly and darkened with powder burns. Longford felt the numbing heat of the bullet skin along his arm and explode against the wall behind him in a shower of plaster and institutional green paint.

The bullet had dug a narrow canal across Longford's upper arm, but had not detonated. He knew that it didn't hurt as much as it could have or would, once the morphine wore off.

Crawling up on the foot of the bed, Longford looked down and saw the tips of the white nurse's shoes moving along toward the left of the screen. He fired twice, the first shot flying off the thick tiles but the second plowing through the left foot in a blossom of blood. The nurse let out a scream and fell.

Someone nearby yelled, "You got him!"

Longford fired through the screen again, toward the leg, and heard another moan as the injured foot twitched in a small pool of gathering blood.

Five shots rang out from the other side, exploding off the end of the bed. Longford knew the gunman had three rounds left.

When Longford fired again, higher, the gunman moaned.

"You got him in the balls," a patient yelled from the other side of the screen.

The groaning continued as the gunman triggered off his

last three rounds, sending two into the thin mattress. The third rang off the bed's steel frame.

Longford climbed down off the bed and eased himself barefoot across the floor to the edge of the screen. Crouching low, the Beretta out in front of him, he pushed aside the screen. The gunman lay motionless, a pool of blood extended from his legs down, soaking into the crisp white uniform.

Longford walked barefoot through the blood to the gunman's head, reached down and retrieved the Glock. Then, kneeling beside him, he turned the dead man over. Not enough trauma to kill, Longford thought, not with a .380. And then he saw that the bogus nurse had his hand at his mouth. The small stone from the ring on his third finger was missing.

The ward was silent as Longford rose up, Beretta still in hand, his large ungainly feet cold on the tile floor. Blood was already drying sticky across his soles.

"Somebody get me a nurse!" Longford boomed, not seeing the pack of nurses' faces staring in through the double-door window panels at the end of the ward.

"You just shot one, buddy. Give it a rest, why don'tcha?" someone called back from the other side of the ward.

Norman Bubere was sitting at a corner table of the Harvard Club's library on West 44th, clicking away at a small lap-top computer. He liked the Harvard Club because it was cozy and the bathrooms were cleaner than those in Grand Central.

Bubere was wearing a filthy, light gray Hong Kong tailored suit, which only partially concealed a filthy T-shirt emblazoned with the slogan: NO MORE MR. NICE GUY—ON YOUR KNEES BITCH! Beneath, just above an expanse of exposed stomach, and in considerably smaller type, were the words, "Jersey City Dog Obedience School."

At his feet were a clutter of shopping bags, and on the table, numerous glasses that had once held a concoction of Coke, grenadine, and multiple maraschino cherries. Since his arrival that morning, more than one visitor to the library had inquired as to "that person's" legitimacy as an alumnus in good standing and to comment on his disgraceful attire.

A nervous manager had explained that, indeed, the computerized records indicated that Mr. Nodis was indeed an alum, class of '79, and his dues were fully paid up.

When the manager made another trip to the corner table, Bubere had just patched into New York Telephone's Packet Switched System, from where he could reach a certain airline's computer. Antigua, he had heard, was nice this time of year.

"Mr. Nodis, I believe there is a telephone call for you," the manager said. "And since you are currently engaging the library's only phone line—"

"Nobody's calling me, buddy," Bubere said, without looking up.

"I assure you, sir," the manager politely insisted. "There is a phone call. The individual indicated that it was quite urgent."

"Fuck off," Bubere said, and continued clicking away.

Twenty minutes later the manager returned.

"Mr. Nodis, you have a visitor," he said.

"What's the problem now?" Bubere said, looking up.

"You have a visitor, sir," the manager repeated. "He insists on seeing you."

Bubere thought about this for a moment, logged off the system and rose heavily to his feet. "Okay, where is he?"

"In the lobby, sir."

"Okay, be a good boy then and watch my shit," Bubere said. "Make sure it doesn't get boosted."

"Sir, I assure you—" the manager began, but the disreputable Mr. Nodis was already heading for the lobby.

When Bubere saw the guy in the dark suit rise smiling from a chair in the lobby, he did a quick turn to the left. By the time the guy was reaching into his coat for the Glock, Bubere already had his finger on the trigger of the Sokolovsky Automaster.

The guy took a step forward, still smiling, and said, "Norm!"

And Bubere shot him in the chest, without drawing the pistol from the custom holster. The guy staggered back, drew the Glock, and Bubere shot him again, this time through the throat. A spray of blood erupted from the exit wound, splashing across a moody, gilt-framed portrait of one of Harvard's more generous benefactors. Class of '10.

"Come on scumbag," Bubere said, pulling the big .45 from the holster and coming forward. "You want to fuck with me some more?"

But the guy in the dark suit didn't answer, even after Bubere kicked him solidly in the groin. The shot to the throat had taken most of the back of his head off in its upward trajectory.

When Bubere looked up, the manager was standing at his side. "Mr. Nodis, you—"

"Some shit, huh?" Bubere said, holstering his piece. "What kind of joint is this, anyway?"

The manager didn't answer; rather, he looked from the corpse in the immaculate dark suit to the ruined painting, and then to Bubere. His expression clearly suggested that the wrong person had been shot.

chapter twenty-two

THERE WERE SIX HOTELS called the Palace in New York, but the one downtown, on the Bowery and Bleecker, was by far the worst. The neglect of hard times and planned disaster of insurance temptation had miraculously spared the place, leaving it the sole business on a block of burned and gutted shells. The management had noted this fact early on, and made liberal use of available cheap labor to expand.

The Palace's domain soon extended through demolished walls to adjoining buildings. The hotel's catacombs of plywood, Sheetrock, tin, and scavenged wood stretched out for three or four buildings in each direction, offering hundreds of four-by-six rooms with their foam mattresses covered by stained rubber sheets. Halls were lit by bare sixty-watt bulbs from purloined city power; stairs were often not more than aluminum ladders propped through a jagged hole axed in a floor.

Little distinguished it from the line of three- and four-story buildings on the street, not even a sign. Only at night could the stairway entrance to the second-floor lobby be seen by a seventy-five-watt bulb that burned in the narrow doorway.

Swag was sitting on the edge of the bed, smoking and thinking. It was funny, if you thought about it. Here he was, feeling like a con in a basement holding pen. Until today he'd only had that view from the other side of the bars. The deluxe room was at the back on the third floor;

a five-by-ten cell, furnished only with a steel-framed bed
and lit by a single bulb. The dim light was caged in a wire
mesh on the ceiling, safe from theft or acts of violence.

Swag could feel it slipping away. The old bad-ass confidence that every cop needed, that told him he was the
baddest motherfucker on the street and gave him the cour-
age to go up on the roofs, into the basements, and through
the doors. And now it was leaking out of him like a slow
bleeding wound. He'd seen it happen before, but to other
guys. And he knew what happened when it reached near
empty. That's when they lost their nerve and started drinking hard, bullying, and batting their wives around. That's
when he'd seen more than one eat their gun. Swag knew
he'd have to force a play with Bammer or those dark-suited
bastards soon.

Down the hall two men were yelling, arguing in mur-
derous tones that threatened a gunshot at any moment. The
argument had erupted full-blown an hour before, its source
no doubt already forgotten as the two men screamed twin
strings of personal invective. Swag figured that if nobody
was dead by now, then the chances were good the men
would just wear themselves down, exhausting their bank-
rupted hate in the narrow hall.

When the men stopped arguing suddenly, Swag heard
footsteps. They came down the hall at a steady, determined
pace and ended with a knock on the door.

Opening the paint-chipped door, Swag found himself
peering into the dead, red-rimmed, rummy eyes of the janitor.

"You got a telephone call," the man said around a mouthful of broken yellow teeth.

"No I don't," Swag said, and began closing the door.

"You calling me a liar?" the man growled, and held the
door. "I know you ain't calling me no liar."

"I'm saying I don't have a call," Swag replied, hardening
his voice as he forced the door an inch or two forward to
close it.

But the old guy had more fight in him than Swag would

have thought, and the door stayed open against the increased pressure. "You ain't calling me no liar, Jack," the old guy insisted. "I say you got a call, you damn well have one."

Swag got a better grip on the door, thought about jamming it back on the old guy, decided against it, and stepped into the hall. "Where's the call?" he asked.

"That's better," the old man said. "Downstairs in the lobby."

Walking down the darkened hall toward the front of the hotel, Swag and the janitor passed the two men, now watching silently, and moved down the tilted stairs toward the lobby. This was the bottom, Swag thought, where those with nothing left to be snatched away held their ground like rabid pit bulls, guarding a last few possessions and the small change of vanity and pride.

"Let me hold a dollar," the janitor said, offering his hand out.

The lobby was like a thousand other flophouse lobbies, with the desk clerk sealed behind plastic at one end and a dozen men smoking and watching a raised, wall-mounted television. They stared transfixed in the dusty light, sitting on ancient furniture, as the canned laughter blared tinny from the set's small speaker. Across one wall were a couple of vending machines that didn't work, their coin boxes long pried from the fronts, the coin mechs destroyed in hundreds of failed attempts at tampering, and the goods going stale inside.

"If I have a call, you can have the dollar," Swag replied.

"You call me a liar again, I'll kill you," the old man said. "You're messing with a stone killer, and you don't know it. Stone icy killer, Jack."

"A stone killer," one of the television watchers called, mocking as the laugh track answered his joke.

"Don't be making no fun," the janitor shot back, searching the lobby with blazing eyes for the anonymous heckler. "I'll kill the lot of you in your sleep. Do it with a knife, you degenerate bastards."

Swag walked past the old man toward the desk, where the unshaven clerk was already poking the phone through the narrow money drawer at the bottom.

Picking up the phone, Swag put it tentatively to his ear and heard Carlo's voice yelling at him. "Jesus Swag, what the fuck you doing down there?"

"How'd you find me?" Swag asked the old mobster.

"Give me the dollar!" It was the old man, now right in front of Swag, hand upthrust, eyes blazing triumphantly.

"Hold on a second," Swag said as he dug a dollar out of his pocket and handed it to the janitor.

The old man scuttled off toward the sound of the television, holding the dollar clutched in his fist.

"What's the deal, Carlo?" Swag asked. "Are you at your bar? Why'd you track me down? How'd you track me?"

"Swag, there's some serious shit going down," Carlo said. "All hell's breaking loose."

"How'd you find me, Carlo?" Swag insisted.

"Shit, you don't have no idea what's been happening, and you worried about that," the mob boss complained.

"I know what's been happening to me," Swag said.

"Okay, okay," Carlo offered, calming himself. "That desk clerk, tell me he don't look familiar."

Swag looked at the pear-shaped clerk, who was reading a stroke book titled *Adventures of Dee Dee Candue*. A wet smirk was spread over his face as he read, moving his lips slightly.

When Swag didn't answer immediately, Carlo said, "It's Sallie Worms! Remember, he used to run a crew in Queens."

And Swag did remember. He remembered how Sallie Worms ratted out half the wiseguys in the state, after the Feds put him in the witness protection program.

But Swag couldn't believe it. Somehow he'd always thought the Feds moved the rats out to Idaho or someplace, where they ran sporting goods stores and carpet cleaning franchises. Again he let the phone go quiet as he watched Worms turn the page, smiling, then wipe a fat hand over his wet lips.

"Sallie told you I was here?" Swag asked, already knowing the answer.

"Look around, pal," Carlo said. "See any of your old friends?"

Swag looked, but the figures watching television were dim in the bad light. Across the room, he watched as the television zoomed in on a close-up of a perky dark-haired girl. "No, no, no, you're not exactly Jerry Lewis, *mon cheri*," she said. And right on cue the laugh track kicked in.

"The Feds *own* that dump," Carlo said. "The whole joint is filled with pensioned-off snitches!"

Swag looked into the bluish, television-lit gloom, but recognized no one. "Ah, shit," he said at last.

"Listen, Swag," Carlo said. "I'm just gonna say one thing to you: 'Daimyo Enterprises, Limited'—you ever hear of it?"

"Yeah, I've heard of it," Swag said, still searching the lobby for snitches.

"How 'bout Euro-Zeitech Corp?" Carlo asked.

"What do you know, Carlo?"

"I had my tech do a computer search on them. Then I called offshore. Them and about a dozen other companies, all of them cutouts, come out of one place, a Swiss holding company, Lorette-Defour," he said. "Run by a guy named Ziggy Lorette. Now, I know you've heard that name."

"What do you know?" Swag asked.

"They'll make us all fuckin' dead is what," Carlo said. "You know what I'm talking about? They got a bunch of suit and tie maniacs running around, looking for a piece of everybody's action. You know what I'm talking about?"

"No, but I sure as hell would like to," Swag said, feeling his grip tighten on the phone.

"Yeah, I bet you would," Carlo chuckled. "I'm sending one of the Johnnies to pick you up for a meeting. I got a proposition for you."

"What kind of proposition?" Swag asked, wary of anything Carlo had to offer.

"The kind I ain't gonna talk about over no phone," came the quick answer. "Meet a Johnny in the park at 23rd and Broadway in an hour. Up front by the statue."

Carlo hung up without saying good-bye.

Swag handed the phone through the divider to the desk clerk, started toward the exit, thought better of it, and turned toward the back door.

He was already crossing a vacant lot, to East Second Street, when the provost's car pulled up in front of the Palace Hotel. The three provosts took the stairs two at a time, causing enough of a disturbance to turn every head in the room away from the television. Sallie Worms raised his eyes slowly from his book in an attitude of a man in a seller's market.

"Whattya got, Sallie?" one of the uniformed men said.

"Maybe I got a guy you're looking for," came the unhurried reply.

"Give me a name," the provost said, leaning closer into the smudged glass.

"Call in the name Swag, uptown," Sallie Worms said. "One of the colonel's favorites put the word out on him a week ago."

The young provost radioed the name into the dispatcher, who patched him through to the Plaza. When word came back, Sallie Worms was smiling.

"What room is he in?" the young provost said.

"Ain't in no room, he left," Sallie replied, leaning back, away from the glass partition. "I know where he's going. Ten francs."

"Bullshit, ten francs," the young man said.

"Looks like you don't want to know too badly," Sallie cackled, grinning.

"Oh, I want to know badly," the young man said, then motioned his head toward the office door.

The two other provosts moved like clockwork as they came up on the door. One kicked it in, the other brought up his Steyr, cocked and on full-auto. The third kept the room of television watchers covered.

Sallie jumped at the impact of the door coming off its hinges. He came out of his chair and back against the wall. All the television watchers had turned now, but none moved from their seats, their eyes still glazed as this new drama began to unfold.

"Okay, now let's do this thing easy," the provost said, speaking through the glass as Sallie stared down the barrel of the Steyr.

"Hey, I called you guys, remember?" Sallie whined. "That's worth something ain't it?"

The provost leader didn't answer.

"Come on, boys," Sallie said. "I woulda called you before, but I didn't recognize the guy. He wears those flashy shirts now."

The leader stood there, a statue in the half light of the lobby, staring down Sallie Worms, letting the unspoken threat fill the silence.

"Okay, okay," Sallie said. "This one's on the house, just remember, you owe me one, okay?"

The leader still didn't answer, but rather made a quick motion with his head that caused the provost inside the office to back off a step.

Trembling, Sallie opened the sliding drawer of the ancient desk and pulled out a small tape recorder. Pressing the front button, he rewound the tape, then pressed another.

Carlo's voice said, "Meet the Johnny in the park at 23rd and Broadway in an hour."

When the leader turned back toward the stairs, the other two provosts followed, backing out slowly, covering their tracks as a dozen pairs of tired eyes watched.

"Just remember," Sallie called when the three men were at the stairs. "You boys owe me one! One hand still washes the other!"

Sallie was already sitting back in his chair and pulling it up to the desk when he looked up to see another guy standing in the still-open doorway. "Miserable fuckin' bastards," Sallie mumbled, putting the tape recorder away. "Now, who the fuck are you?" Sallie knew the guy wasn't a customer, he was dressed too good. Clean-shaven in a slick Italian suit and a good haircut.

"Just a guy," the guy said and smiled.

"Well 'justaguy,'" Sallie said, making it sound like one word, "fuck off."

The guy stepped into the room, still smiling. "Justaguy who wants to hear that tape," he said.

"You gonna pay me?" Sallie Worms asked, a faint flicker of free market hope lighting his eyes.

"Nope," the guy said.

"Then fuck off," Sallie spat back. "Another freeloader is the last thing I want."

The guy moved closer into the office. In out of the gloom of the lobby, the guy's partner, a man in a dark suit, stepped from behind a pillar. His vantage point gave him a clear view of the desk clerk's glassed-in office and the television watchers. On his face was an expression of boredom, as if he were waiting for a bus.

Sallie took it all in, his eyes darting from the dark suit in the office to the one in the lobby and back again.

The first wasn't smiling now, he was serious. "You know, the last thing that anybody wants is almost always the last thing he gets."

"What's that 'sposed to mean?" Sallie said, reaching across the desk for the Colt Commander hidden under a newspaper.

The gun came out of the shoulder holster before Sallie touched the chipped grip of his piece. "This," Roger said, and shot Sallie Worms four times in the chest.

Roger played the tape all the way through. When he finally turned, pocketed the cassette, and headed for the door, the dark suit fell in right behind him. Every eye in the room was glued to the television. On screen, a young man was sticking straws up his nose in a passable impersonation of Jerry Lewis.

chapter twenty-three

SWAG WAS HEADING UPTOWN on lower Fifth Avenue, heading toward Madison Square Park. Behind him was the Flat-iron Building and what was said to be the windiest corner in the city. Back at the turn of the century, Edwardian rakes loitered near the building, on the corner of 23rd Street, watching the wind blow women's dresses up above the ankles. Cops on the post would rouse the men along with a swing of the nightstick and the warning that became known as the "Twenty-three skidoo."

Crossing 23rd, Swag squinted into the gloom of trees. It was dusk, and he could just make out the silhouette of the park's statue of William H. Seward, Lincoln's Secretary of State. Swag knew that money was tight even back then, so the city used the body of Lincoln and stuck Seward's head on it. Before that the park had been a Potter's Field. Later there was a prison, and the anonymous and died-broke were planted uptown at 42nd where the city would eventually build the library.

When they built the old Fifth Avenue Hotel, back before the Civil War, 23rd was at the edge of the world. But the crooked pols set up shop in the downstairs sitting rooms. Ten years later Delmonico's opened for business, on Fifth and 26th, and the rich had already built their mansions and hotels in the area. And the city kept stretching north.

Now the six-acre park was just a park, a green crater surrounded by the gray granite and glass of office buildings.

Swag knew why Carlo wanted him to meet the Johnnies there. It was open, but not too open—the kind of place where you could see trouble coming. Carlo, Swag thought, was still crafty, even after all these years. But he wasn't crafty enough to freeze Swag out of the hotels and slap a Section 18 on him. Not only did he not have a reason; he didn't have anywhere near the juice.

No way could Carlo be behind it, Swag thought, the old mafioso just wasn't up to it. Suddenly Swag couldn't step a foot into any hotel without security showing him the door. And freezing bank accounts just wasn't Carlo's style. No, Carlo's style was sitting down with the guy for a good meal, then putting a bullet in the back of the poor bastard's head.

Now Swag had two francs and one cigarette in his pockets. Tomorrow, if he was lucky, he'd have a couple of bucks from a black-market exchange, which might get him through another day, and some information from the Johnnies.

He could see the money and cigarette guys ahead, spread out along the waist-high iron fence that bordered the park's entrance and center path. They were dressed in suspicious fashion, shiny suits and loud ties, all of them looking hinky as hell and not caring. In winter they'd be out there in wide-shouldered coats, warming their hands over trash can fires.

A couple of steerers ran over, just kids, ten or eleven years old, but dressed up in German sneakers and French gimme-shirts. "Hey man, what you want? We got it, no trouble. You want smokes, we got frog cigarettes, Gauloises, Gitanes." And another, "I got Jap smokes, Lucky Sevens, Sometimes, Partner, Misty Midnight Tiny, and Ten-der." Their chants filled the night air as they swarmed around Swag like entrepreneurial gnats, each one yelling out name brands.

"Who's doing currency?" Swag asked.

Two of the kids broke away, heading for the entrance and another customer. The remaining two guided Swag toward a small black guy tricked out in a tight sharkskin suit.

"You looking to trade some money?" the guy said, not

looking directly at Swag, but fixing him solidly in his peripheral vision. "I got yen, I got easies. What you looking for?"

"What's the exchange on francs?"

"Francs, oh, *très bien*, *très*, *très*-fuckin'-*bien*," came the answer. "Market closed what, an hour ago at say thirteen-seventy bucks to the franc," he said.

"Fourteen-sixty," Swag corrected.

The guy moved his head around, catching Swag in a hard stare, and said, "Still the same, we go thirteen bucks to all EEC today, you save on the tariff. Marks or yen, maybe we can work something out. If you have twenty, thirty, maybe we can do better. But I'll tell you, my man, just between you and me, you don't look like no Belgian dentist."

Swag reached into his shirt pocket and pulled out his last cigarette, straightened it, lit it, and said, "I want to change two francs."

"Two francs?" the guy answered. "You dissing me for two lousy francs? What you trying to do, pick up cigarette money?"

That was exactly what Swag was trying to do, but he wouldn't say so. "You want to go at twelve or what?"

"*Beaucoup* grief for chump change," the guy said, then reached into a side pocket to pull out a roll of dollars that once would have seemed impressive.

Swag handed him the franc notes, and the guy snapped off two tens and six ones. "Smoking's a nasty habit, man. Almost as nasty as that shirt. What are those things crawling around on there?"

"Palm trees," Swag said.

"If those're palm trees, how come they got faces?" he asked. "Wait man, I know those guys! What? They're carved coconuts?"

"Washington, Jefferson, Lincoln, and Roosevelt," Swag said. "Teddy, not FDR. You got a light?"

"Sure man," the money man said, and handed out a book of restaurant matches.

Swag had smoked half the cigarette when he saw one of Carlo's Johnnies coming across the park. He was moving in from the east and walking fast. The Johnny brushed by the steerers and came up the path, his eyes set straight ahead.

"This better be a friend of yours," the money guy said.

"Yeah, it is," Swag answered.

"Maybe he wants to do some business," the money guy offered.

When the Johnny reached Swag, he didn't bother to shake his hand. Rather, he gave the money guy his best tough-guy look. But the money guy just took it. Even for the Johnnies life had changed.

"So, you want to change some money?" the money guy asked, staring back.

"No, I don't want to change no money," the Johnny answered, still staring. But he was shooting blanks with the tough-guy act, and the money guy knew it.

"What does Carlo have for me?" Swag asked, dropping the cigarette and grinding it under his boot.

The Johnny didn't answer. He was too busy trying to stare down the money guy. When he saw it wouldn't work, he said, "We're havin' a meeting here, you mind or what?"

"*Excusé mois*, you greasy motherfucker, I don't mind," the money guy said, and moved off a few feet.

When the Johnny was satisfied that the money guy couldn't hear, he said, "Here's the way it is. Carlo said he wants to meet, up by the library."

"What for?" Swag asked.

"He says he's got work for you," came the answer. Then the Johnny pulled out an envelope. "Says this is for good faith."

Swag could see that there must have been an inch of bills in the envelope.

When Swag made no move to take it, the Johnny held it out farther and wiggled it a little like a fish lure.

"What's going on at the library?" Swag asked.

"Go up and find out," the Johnny said. "It ain't like nobody tells me anything. Here, take the fuckin' money, it's getting heavy."

Swag shook his head slowly. "Start talking," he said.

"Don't be an asshole," the Johnny said. "Take the money and go to your meeting." Then he pinned the envelope against Swag's chest with one finger.

Swag reached up slowly, tentatively, with his left hand and snatched the finger holding the envelope, bending it back with a loud snap as the payoff fell to the ground between them.

"Okay, now, we're going to play it my way," he said, drawing the Colt out with his right hand and holding it to the Johnny's stomach, poking it into him so he'd know it was there.

Releasing the broken finger, Swag reached up and felt inside the Johnny's coat. The shoulder holster was empty. Then he kicked at both ankles and felt no bulge.

"Start talking," Swag said, moving in close so that he was right in the guy's face. All around, the money and cigarette guys had ceased doing business to stare.

"I already did all my talking, you crazy fuck," the Johnny said.

"Where's the other Johnny?" Swag barked. "You guys are a matched set."

"He's back with Carlo," the Johnny said, holding his injured hand with his good one. "They just sent me to give you a message and money."

"Where's your piece?" Swag asked. "You forget it or what?"

"I thought this was gonna be a friendly meeting," the Johnny said plaintively, not really answering the question. He was the kind of guy who wore his piece when visiting his mother.

"Bullshit," Swag said, pushing the Colt's barrel deeper into the Johnny's gut. "You got about two seconds, then I'm gonna do you, right here."

"Okay, okay man," the Johnny answered, trying to back up but stopping as the back of his legs hit the railing. "Couple of guys came in, wearing suits, you know. They shot the tech, now they got Johnny and the old man locked in the walk-in freezer."

"What'd they want?" Swag said, moving closer, crowding the Johnny against the rail.

"They want you," the Johnny said. "They want you up at the library on Fifth."

"What's there?" Swag insisted.

"How should I know?" the Johnny moaned. "They walked in five minutes after Carlo hung up the phone from talking to you. They musta had a tap on it."

"What's up at 42nd?" Swag said, pushing the Johnny farther back over the railing.

"It ain't like they told me," the Johnny complained. "They just said to give you the money and send you up there."

"What about Carlo?" Swag said. "What did he want?"

"I tell you that, I'm signing the old man's death warrant," the Johnny complained.

Swag pushed the gun hard into his belly. When the Johnny began to fall back over the railing, Swag caught him by the soiled knot of his tie. "Right now, you're signing your own."

The Johnny looked around, as if for help from some of the money changers and cigarette guys. "Okay, okay, but you didn't hear it from me," he said. "He wanted to hire you. Carlo said to tell you that it's worth five thousand easies to blow them suits away. That was before them guys came in and the plans changed. He figured you'd whack those suits or they'd get you, and I should hit them. The suits gave me the money to give you."

"Does he know where they're from?"

"You're killing the old man," the Johnny whined. "Just as like you was putting a gun to his head."

"Carlo's already dead, you dumb fuck," Swag spat. "What'dya think, those guys are going to let him walk away?"

The Johnny considered the logic of this. It seemed to take a long time. "Carlo doesn't know shit," the Johnny said. "He figured you did."

Swag jammed the Colt's barrel farther into the Johnny's stomach and thumbed back the hammer.

"You think I'm lyin' to you here?" the Johnny said, bending back over the railing. "I ain't lyin'."

When the car pulled to a squealing stop at the side of the park, Swag turned. And that's when the Johnny's head exploded. Swag heard only the wet crack of bone as the Johnny's skull flew apart. The slug had caught him just above the nose.

The Johnny was still standing in his thin-soled Italian loafers. Swag released his grip on the tie, and the Johnny crumpled, falling backward over the iron railing.

Swag ducked low, snatching up the envelope in the process.

From somewhere behind him another shot was fired, taking out a chunk of the concrete near his left foot. Reflex brought his foot up as he grabbed hold of an iron rail and jumped over it to take cover behind a tree.

Whoever was shooting was after *him*, not the Johnny. Lying low to the ground, Swag brought his head around the tree. A shot bit into the bark, exposing a thick section of pulpy white wood.

The shots were coming from the Flatiron Building, and high up.

Turning, so his back was against the trunk of the tree, Swag saw them coming from the opposite direction. Four of Bammer's men, double-timing it down the path in loose formation. They were in civilian clothes, but two of them were carrying provost-issue Steyr automatics. The other two had handguns.

Swag came up in a crouch and ran, heading west across the park, crossing the path in two long strides and jumping a bench. Three shots whizzed by, hitting just ahead of him on the path, chipping concrete and gouging out a large divot of grass.

When he was almost to the railing that bordered the sidewalk along Fifth Avenue, he saw the unmarked Plymouth. Its doors opened and three more of Bammer's men rolled out, spreading out into neat defensive positions with small Heckler & Koch subs.

There was a trash can by the rail, and Swag turned it over, wedging himself between it and a tree. Two rounds from provost rifles chimed off the side, deflected by its curve. The three uniformed men with the submachine guns were moving in, fast.

Swag triggered off two rounds toward the submachine guns and watched as they fell back to the safety of the unmarked unit. Shifting uneasily, he fired twice at the four men who'd taken up positions behind trees on the other side of the guardrail.

Out in the street one of the submachines got on the unmarked unit's P.A. system and announced, "This is an official provost action. Please leave the park immediately. Please leave the park immediately."

The four men behind the trees were moving in. He could see them, one at a time, advancing in low, serpentine runs to closer positions.

Swag fired twice at the advancing men, but the ones hanging back put down cover fire, churning up dirt and chewing large chunks out of the tree at Swag's back.

"What do you want?" Swag yelled into the silent twilight. Someone was evidently even redirecting traffic around the park. Bammer's men were looking for a no-witness situation.

The windshield of the unmarked unit shattered, and the three men dived for cover on the opposite side. A silenced round, Swag thought, and something *big*.

The four men behind trees advanced again, one moving out from his position as the three others let go with short bursts. The guy was three steps out when he took a hit. The silenced round caught him in the side and sent him pinwheeling to the ground six or seven feet in front of Swag. During the fall his communication mouthpiece had come free, pulling the jack from the radio and opening the speaker so Swag could hear.

"Betty Ford, this is Liz Taylor, do you copy?" someone spat over the dead man's walkie-talkie. "Betty, we're taking fire here. Man down. Please advise."

"Liz, maintain position. Advance on word from Jerry Lee," the radio squawked back. Then, "Jerry Lee, do you copy?"

The radio let out a short burst of static, then went silent.

"Jerry Lee, do you copy? Come in Jerry Lee!"

Silence filled the park again. It was an odd quiet, devoid of even the sound of traffic.

"Betty, we're drawing fire here," the Liz Taylor unit squawked again into the nearby handset.

And Swag could see it, one by one the windows of the unmarked unit exploding as the silenced rounds slammed into the car.

"Jerry Lee, do you copy?" the Liz Taylor unit chief demanded, but no answer was forthcoming.

"Liz, come in, Liz," the radio squawked, then fell into silence.

Next, the unmarked unit exploded, its gas tank blowing with enough force to lift it off the ground, sending thick billows of black smoke into the sky above Fifth Avenue.

"Jerry Lee, do you copy, come in, Jerry Lee," the Liz Taylor unit chief barked. "We're drawing fire here, goddamnit. It's an ambush! Betty, come in Betty."

Swag turned from the burning wreckage of the unmarked unit to see four men, of what he supposed must have been the Liz Taylor unit, sprawled across the path. All were dead. He never heard the silenced fire.

Then, from the dead man's radio, Swag heard a voice, "Hullo, everybody, this is the killer speaking," which was quickly followed by the tinny sound of a cheap recording of "Breathless" that jammed all transmissions.

Swag crawled from the small space between the tree and the trash can. Colt still out, he worked his way across the glass-strewn grass, gingerly pulling himself along by his elbows. Near the western edge of the park, close enough to smell the burning plastic of the unmarked unit, Swag decided to make a run for it. He leaped up to find the silenced barrel of a Horstcamp .50-caliber sniper rifle pointed in his face.

Swag looked past the silencer, past the bi-pod and scope to see a provost sergeant's uniform. But it wasn't the uniform that held his attention. And it wasn't the good haircut either. It was the man, hand wrapped casually around the stock, finger on the trigger, that held his attention and brought his hands up. It was the same guy from the subway. And he was smiling.

"Almost bought the farm on that one, huh?" the guy said, outlined by the orange flames of the burning unmarked unit. He was still smiling, showing lots of white teeth. Behind him the fire sent its inky smoke into the darkening sky.

"There's witnesses now," Swag said.

And the guy turned, looking through the fire across the street to where people were starting to line up along the sidewalk. "You want I should shoot them?" the guy said. "You should have gone up to the library, like a good boy."

"You're not with the provosts," Swag said.

"You're right there, pal."

A White Star cab pulled up at the curb, and the bogus provost sergeant backed off, holding the .50-caliber rifle a little above waist level, the butt-plate jammed into his gut. Swag had no doubt that there was a shell in the chamber. No doubt at all. It wasn't an easy shot from twenty-five feet, but not an impossible one either.

As the phony provost backed smiling in through the cab's open door, more sirens began sounding. It was a smile of such utter confidence that Swag was almost willing to try for him.

When the cab pulled away, Swag jammed the Colt back into its holster and began running west across Fifth. He was nearly to the opposite corner when he saw the bike, a big-ass Harley Sportster. There was a thin guy dressed in denim, leaning back across the saddle and watching through the darkened visor of the full helmet as more provosts entered the park in a defensive serpentine pattern.

The guy must have just come out of the building, Swag thought.

Swag walked past him, then turned suddenly, drawing the Colt out. "You know what this is?" he asked, jamming the barrel of the automatic into the guy's back.

He was a little guy and the gun made him move forward a half step, straightening him up off the seat.

"I asked if you knew what this is?" Swag said, jamming the gun into his back and inching him out another half step.

The helmeted head nodded glumly but didn't try to turn.

"Take another two steps out," Swag said. He saw the keys were in the ignition.

The guy did as he was told without a word of protest.

"Now I'm taking the bike," Swag said. "Understand?" The man nodded again.

"Okay then," Swag said, and climbed on. "Here's a couple of bucks." He stuffed the envelope with the bills into the side pocket of the denim jacket just before he fired up the bike.

By the time he'd reached the corner, he was already shifting into fourth and keeping his eyes straight ahead, on the cab, hoping there was enough confusion that the driver wouldn't notice him. He dodged through the wooden barricades the provosts were just putting up across 23rd. A few shots sounded behind him, but then he was gone, moving fast through the stopped lines of oncoming traffic.

If Swag had looked back, he would have seen the helmeted and denim-clad owner of the Harley turn and lift the helmet's visor to reveal a young woman's face. She watched Swag run the police roadblock and then adjusted the communications piece at her throat.

"Jim Bob, your pal just stole the bike," she said.

"Well that's a damn shame," Spurock's voice echoed in her ear. "You have security turned on?"

"The way he's moving, the security system should be cutting off the fuel about now," the young woman said.

"I'll be swinging by in the van," Jim Bob answered.

"I'll be waiting," the young woman said, and removed her helmet.

The bike sputtered to a halt three blocks past the barricades at a red light. Swag stomped down on the starter pedal a half-dozen times before he noticed the small security keypad mounted to the right of the speedometer.

Up ahead the cab with the shooter was stopped at a light.

Behind him a platoon of provosts were double-timing it up the street, running between stopped cars, weapons drawn.

Another cab halted next to Swag and the driver gave him a small tough-luck-buddy smile. Swag brought the kickstand down and walked casually up to the cab's passenger window.

"Sorry pal," the cabbie said, pointing up to the sign that read Off-Duty.

Up ahead the line of cars were moving. "You just went back on," Swag replied, pulling the Colt and extending it through the open window.

"I guess you're right," the driver answered.

Swag jumped into the front seat and found himself saying the words of a thousand late-show movies, "Follow that cab."

The White Star was disappearing into traffic.

"Ya gotta be kiddin', pal," the cabbie said.

"Follow that White Star or I'll blow your fuckin' head off," Swag replied.

They rode up under the West Side Highway, dodging between cars as the taxi outpaced traffic. He couldn't be certain where the White Star was heading, but by the time they cut east in the mid-Seventies, he had a good idea.

When the White Star turned toward the park, Swag jabbed the cabbie in the ribs with the Colt, urging him to run three red lights. They pulled up along the curb a block back from the San Remo as the White Star stopped before the building.

The building's front provided little cover, and Swag watched as the shooter stepped out of the cab and walked casually through the south-tower lobby.

Ducking into the tiny south-tower lobby, Swag approached the first guard outside the door and backed him into the lobby, keeping the Colt low, but making sure the guard saw it. The shooter turned, and for a split second a look of panic flashed across his face, then he smiled. As if by reflex, his hands came away from his sides.

"You're making some kind of mistake here, buddy," the guard said.

"No I'm not," Swag answered. He led the guard behind the small desk in the marble lobby and relieved him of the Ingram automatic and the guard behind the desk of a Smith & Wesson.

"You too," Swag said to the shooter.

Without a word and without hesitation, the guy pulled out a Seecamp autopistol and then a Walther P-38. He did it casually, and with no remorse. Swag tucked the Walther into his belt while holding the Seecamp in his left hand and Colt in the right.

"Let's go upstairs," Swag said.

"I'm sorry, man, he just walked in and pulled the piece," one of the guards offered.

"No problem boys, we're old friends," Roger said, taking a tentative step forward, but making sure Swag could see his hands as they hovered completely motionless out from his sides. "But I gotta tell you, this is going to seriously affect your Christmas bonus."

"Let's go," Swag said, then motioned with the Colt for Roger to step in front of the guards as he steered them toward the elevator.

Roger pushed the button, showing no panic, and the old-time arrow indicator above the door began turning as the elevator began its descent.

"So, who are you with, Daimyo or Euro-Zeitech?" Swag asked, probing.

"Pretty smart guy," Roger said. "Pretty smart. But really, you don't know shit."

"I know enough to get me into the apartment to see whoever it is you take orders from, whoever it is killed my client Lorette, whoever put a section 18 on my bank accounts," Swag said.

The elevator door opened, and Swag hustled the three men inside. "Push it," Swag said.

Roger shrugged with an air of resignation and pushed the button.

The door closed slowly, but the elevator didn't move. "Try it again," Swag said.

Roger pushed the button once more, but nothing happened.

When Swag reached out, stepping momentarily between the three men to push the button, the door opened. Looking up, he found himself staring into the dead eye of a .38 revolver.

"Seen any packs of wild dogs lately?" the driver asked, reaching out with one hand for Swag's Colt. It was the same cabbie that had taken him into Brooklyn a few days before. Worse, it was the same cabbie that had just driven him uptown.

Swag handed the gun over, and all four of them came out of the cramped elevator.

"Like the sign says, 'All Guests Must Be Announced,'" the cabbie added as he pointed casually toward the small standing sign in the front of the lobby.

"Caught me while I was doing backup," the cabbie explained as he handed the Colt, Walther, and Seecamp over to Roger. "I checked out the action in the elevator on the security monitor."

"You guys own every cab in the city?" Swag asked, then suddenly realized he'd had no trouble finding cabs for the last two weeks. It was a run of good luck that began when he left the Criminal Courts Building to go to the morgue, and continued through his visit to Longford, and the gray-market guys from Jersey.

"A couple," Roger said. "Makes getting around a little easier. Ever try to get a cab in this town when it's raining?"

"You need me anymore?" the cabbie asked.

"No, I got it under control," Roger said, jacking the shell out of the Colt's chamber and releasing the magazine. Then to the guards, "Why don't you boys get back to work?"

"You're going to explain it to me, huh?" Swag said as Roger steered him back into the elevator.

"I'm just hired help, pal," the guy in the provost uniform said. "But believe me, you're gonna love it."

chapter twenty-four

ON THE RIDE UP, Roger handed Swag back the Colt and said, "Nice piece, too bad it isn't loaded, huh?"

"What if I just pounded the shit out of you right here, in the elevator?" Swag answered, reaching around to fit the Colt into its holster.

"No offense, but you're just not that good, pal," Roger answered flatly. "Welcome to try, though."

The old-fashioned elevator hummed around them, and Swag watched the numbers pass, from five to six. "I wouldn't want you biting your ring or anything, huh?"

A small amused smile passed across Roger's lips, and he said, "Ring-biting is for assholes. Jeez, can you believe those guys? Where'd they think they're going, the Valhalla Hilton?"

The elevator was passing eight, and Swag said, "They seem to think it's part of the job."

"Well, they're dickheads," Roger said. Then mimicked, "'I am a tourist,'" and broke up laughing.

"Good help's hard to find, huh?" Swag said, thinking about his next move.

"No, it isn't," Roger said flatly.

The elevator chimed open on the twenty-fourth floor, and Roger hung back, waiting for Swag to step out first. When Swag began walking to the right, Roger didn't stop him.

The San Remo was an old building with wide halls, thick

carpeting, and sconced lighting. As they reached the end
of the hall, Roger rang the buzzer, and a voice on the intercom said, "Yes?"

"It's me," Roger said. "I have a guest."

The door buzzed open then, and Roger nodded for
Swag to walk through.

A narrow hall led into a main room large enough to have
once been two or three apartments. It broke off into an L
shape that formed two sides of the south tower. A row of
ten windows lined two walls, offering a view of Central
Park at night and the East Side's lights on one side, and the
midtown lights on the other. The requisite brass telescope
stood on a wood tripod near the center window facing east.

Another wall was taken up by a bookcase filled with
leatherbound volumes. One section, fronted by leaded
glass, held maybe a dozen African and pre-Colombian arti-
facts. Little grimacing guys made of stone. Swag couldn't
guess how much they cost, but they must have been
pricey—anything that ugly had to be.

There were a couple of leather couches that faced each
other, a few chairs, a polished writing table and matching
chair. There was, of course, the standard marble fireplace
mantel and ancient portrait of nobility above it, both no
doubt illegal imports from Europe.

Off to the left an entranceway led to more rooms. And
a graceful wood and steel spiral staircase ran down to
another floor of the triplex.

The whole place was all very subdued, stinking of money
and good taste. It was the kind of apartment Swag had
come to think of as "generic rich."

"Nice place," Swag said.

"Hey, the man has got a lifestyle, know what I mean?"

And then the man appeared. Swag saw only the top of
him first, a perfectly gray head of thick hair. And then more
and more of him came into view as he climbed up the staircase from the lower level.

He was wearing a light gray linen and silk summer suit
and tie, looking comfortable in the dimly lit room. As he

came up off the final step, he did a short half turn toward
Swag and said, "Ah, what a pleasant surprise."

"Mr. Big, huh?" Swag said as he did a quick scan of the
guy.

"My name is Catherwood," came the answer. And then
to Roger, "I believe there is a platter set out, just in the
other room. Roger, if you would."

Roger walked from the room, toward another part of the
apartment.

"Well," Catherwood said, "I imagine you have all manner
of questions. Where would you like to begin?"

"Can I leave?" Swag asked.

"Ah," Catherwood answered, "not just yet. You have
been a significantly costly project. And, I believe that Roger
has just saved your life, for the second or was it the third
time. In light of this, you will extend us the courtesy of a
small portion of time, no?"

"Is that a question?" Swag asked.

"No," Roger called back from the other room. He wasn't
far away and he wanted Swag to know it.

"Lay it out for me," Swag said.

Roger returned, wheeling a cart that held a silver caviar
set-up, iced champagne, and three chilled, fluted crystal
glasses.

The three men walked to the leather couches by the fire-
place. It was not a short walk. And when they sat, it was
Roger on one side, blocking the way to the door, and
Catherwood sitting opposite.

"Okay, what's the deal?" Swag asked.

"Would you care to indulge?" Catherwood asked as
Roger poured the champagne. Swag noted it was a vintage
Louis Roederer Cristal. But what he first took to be caviar,
wasn't. It looked as if it were covered in fat, like a can of
uncooked ham.

"French caviar," Catherwood said, as Roger handed him
a piece of toast spread thick with the pearly mass. *"Oeuf
d'escargot."*

"Snail eggs," Roger said, watching in thinly disguised disgust as Catherwood chewed the delicacy.

"The very best," Catherwood offered after swallowing. "From the *Helix aspera* family."

"Looks great, but I'll pass," Swag said.

"In Tibet they offer these to their gods," Catherwood continued, then took another drink of champagne. "They symbolize eternal life."

"Okay, so what's the deal?" Swag asked again.

"'The deal,'" Catherwood answered as if he were learning a new language, "is that we would like to offer you employment."

"What?" Swag said. "Roger here having trouble fetching your wine and snail eggs?"

"Hey, lighten up, okay?" Roger put in. "Hear the man out, then make up your mind."

Catherwood pushed on, paying no attention to the exchange. "It would be in a managerial capacity," he said. "Something well-suited to your unique talents."

"Who are you people?" Swag asked. "You can start with Euro-Zeitech."

Roger shrugged and said, "The man's got a right to know," and poured champagne into the two remaining glasses.

"Euro-Zeitech is merely one link in the chain," Catherwood offered. "And not a very significant one at that."

"And Daimyo?" Swag asked.

Catherwood shook his head with an air of sad impatience. "Those entities and two dozen like them are of no real importance," he said.

"Okay then," Swag tried. "Who owns them?"

Catherwood took a drink then, but even as he lifted the glass from the low table between the two couches, Swag could see the gears turning in his head. "As you no doubt are aware," he began, "there is a small population of Americans living abroad. In happier times, these men were leaders of industry and finance. Many of them are descended from the best families, their names intertwined with our country's history. If I may quote the eminent social philosopher, Ayn Rand—"

"Fuck Ayn Rand," Swag said, cutting him off. "Talk faster or get more interesting."

Roger could barely contain a chuckle at this.

". . . These men fled with the collapse of their country. Fearing for their lives and the lives of their families, they were forced to leave. They now live in exile, scattered across Europe and the Far East."

Swag had seen the pictures in magazines and on television, everyone had. Americans lounging poolside or sitting behind massive desks in some estate's library. Paunchy CEOs who absconded in corporate jets. Movie and rock stars fashionably dressed and even more fashionably subdued. All of them giving interviews of their deep, heartfelt regrets. And always, the token bit of Americana in the shot. A New York Yankees cap. The oil painting of the Chicago skyline. Or something more subtle, like a miniature street sign from the Santa Monica Freeway. "And what do you miss most?" the interviewer would always ask. And then the predictable answer: "You know, I really miss cheeseburgers." Or pizza, or baseball, or shopping malls, or a thousand other mundane things. About the only thing they didn't miss was their money, which they had squirreled away years before in low-tax countries. Refugees sitting on twenty or thirty mil, deprived of cheeseburgers. Pity those poor bastards, Swag always thought, all the money in the world and they can't get a decent cheeseburger.

"They must be going through hell," Swag offered.

"I assure you, they would like very much to return to their homes," Catherwood continued, nonplussed, though forgoing the Ayn Rand quote. "To help rebuild America into the great nation she once was."

"The last time I checked, the State Department was still offering repatriation to all American-born citizens," Swag said. "Have them check with the nearest embassy."

"Unfortunately, it isn't quite that simple," Catherwood explained. "The task ahead is monumental. These men, my employers, require recapitalization. Patriotism is not enough. To face the challenge ahead, we will require substantial funds."

"And the money's coming from . . ."

"Out there," Catherwood said, motioning toward one of the windows. "Down there, on the street, is an engine of criminal commerce that generates the equivalent of sixty billion European Currency Units a year through goods and services. That is roughly equivalent to two of the smaller Common Market nations."

"You're talking about what, the black market?" Swag asked.

"Among other things," Catherwood continued, a smile of self-importance and condescension tightening his lips. "Millions of individual transactions, billions in currency changing hands. They used to say that the old stock market was efficient; it was a clunker compared to the marketplace of the street."

"What he's talking about is taking a piece of it," Roger said.

"A piece of what?" Swag asked.

"Everything," came Roger's answer. "Black-market imports, exports, policy money, gambling, whores, the dog-fights, bio-chop shops, storefront plastic surgeons, after-hours clubs, even the black-market money guys. Ten to twenty-five percent off the top, to start."

"Are you talking about moving in where the bent-nose boys left off?" Swag said.

"Ah, the so-called Mafia," Catherwood answered, pleased with the question. "They filed for Chapter 11 years ago and did not even know it. Ineffective and unsophisticated management, limited government cooperation, and organizational disarray. And bureaucracy, layers and layers of it. They weren't top-heavy, like so many other failed ventures. They were *middle-heavy* with management. And they drew indiscriminately from a limited employment pool, hiring relatives and friends, regardless of qualifications.

They promoted with disregard to basic performance standards. They were, in a phrase, sloppy managers."

"And you don't have those problems?"

"Not at all. We shall eventually be operating with near total government cooperation, unofficially of course," Catherwood explained. "We're structuring our little enterprise around a centralized and experienced senior management, and with an eye toward *complete vertical integration of product lines*. Concepts the families were too short-sighted to grasp."

"And it's not just New York either," Roger added.

"He's quite right," Catherwood said. "New York is our test market, so to speak."

"What happens with the money?" Swag asked. "This thing a charity effort?"

Catherwood smiled pleasantly, reached out, began to spread snail eggs over toast, then changed his mind and gobbled a small mouthful directly off the small silver spoon.

"Well, what are these patriots going to do with the money?" Swag asked again. "Buy savings bonds?"

Catherwood licked his lips and smiled. "A century ago, giants strode this country," he said, his voice unnaturally deep. "They were the Carnegies, Morgans, Vanderbilts, Goulds, Cookes, and Rockefellers. They were giants of vision and Goliaths of industry. They took a nation of uneducated, filthy immigrants and ignorant peasants, and built their dreams in steel and concrete. The power of a country was distilled in their words, deeds, and iron wills. They answered to no laws, save those of destiny."

"He always talk like this?" Swag asked, turning to Roger.

"Pretty much," came the bored answer.

Swag and Roger watched then as Catherwood withdrew the tiny cylinder from his coat pocket, turned it once, then sprayed the fine mist of synthetic *chiri* into his open mouth.

For a brief moment Catherwood closed his eyes, composing his thoughts amid the slow pleasure of the drug. Then he began speaking again. "Then came the pampering

social reformers. The trade unions. The bleeding heart politicians with their government controls. The great moral
movement to educate the so-called masses. Equality.
Opportunity, Freedom. They were never intended to be
more than slogans to attract cheap labor or pacify potential
malcontents."

"You don't care much for masses, I guess," Swag said.

"They destroyed this country, eroded the power of those
who built it," Catherwood shot back. "They propelled this
nation into social chaos. We seek to restore a rightful social
order, 'for out of chaos new worlds may be born.' That's
Nietzsche."

"Look, if you're going to sit around and quote Nietzsche,
then I'm outta here," Swag said.

"No you're not," Roger answered flatly. "Listen up."

"So who calls the shots in the new world—robber
barons?" Swag asked.

"Giants of vision and imagination will once again claim
their rightful place as leaders," Catherwood snapped back.
"There is a market of 350 million people in Europe alone.
They need shoes, automobiles, radios, clothing. And they
need them made cheaply. America is still rich in natural
resources that have never been tapped."

"You're talking about cheap labor," Swag said. "Sweat-
shops. Company towns. Draining off the oil, minerals, lum-
ber."

Roger was smiling broadly now, amused more than anything. "Look, let's clear this up," he said. "Europe's fucked.
They got unions, child labor laws, environmental protection
laws, minimum safety requirements in the factories, free
trade agreements up the whazoo. It's all overhead, right?
We don't have that problem here. We raise the money and
roll the clock back a hundred years or so. Then reopen the
factories, give the poor slobs a job. Keep 'em off the street
twelve or sixteen hours a day. Then pay them just enough
to buy a television and keep from running around bare-ass
naked. They'll kiss your fuckin' ass and want to read about
you in the magazines, right?"

"There'll be unions," Swag said. "And 'pampering social reformers,' and 'bleeding heart pols.'"

"Interesting you should grasp on that point," Catherwood mused. "But there won't be. We have learned from the mistakes of the past. There's no need to mention that communication is now instantaneous, and intelligence gathering sophisticated as to nearly an art form. Further, we are not bound by antiquated notions of Victorian morality."

Swag shrugged, barely suppressing a chill feeling of fear. These people were serious.

"And remember these two points, because they're crucial," Catherwood continued. "America is not expanding as it was more than a century ago. This city, this country, is morally, financially, and spiritually bankrupt. We are not building, in the proper sense of the word, merely harvesting."

"Somebody will blow the deal for you," Swag said. "Nothing this big goes down without someone noticing that something's up."

"The media and the leaders, we intend on controlling both, one way or the other," Catherwood said. "We live in an age of marvelous technology . . ."

". . . And accurate firearms," Roger finished.

"Looks like you have it sewn up," Swag said, and began to rise.

"Just get comfortable there," Roger said, easing Swag back down with a meaty hand. "I'll lay out the proposition for you. That is, if it's okay with Mr. Catherwood, here?"

Catherwood nodded and took another drink of his champagne.

"It's a little like this," Roger said. "We're looking for locals to run the operation on the street level. You don't touch money, just keep everyone in line. We thought we had our man with that Johnny G. character, but you shot him up."

"And then you flaked him?" Swag interrupted.

"He turned out to be a bullshit artist with nowhere near

the contacts and skills that he claimed," Roger answered. "He had it coming."

"Your unfortunate friend, if I may use that term, wasn't a team player," Catherwood offered. "Nor did his basic skills meet our standards. Not management material. We offered him the opportunity of a lifetime, and he persisted in dabbling with side ventures."

"And my client, Lorette?"

"She was to be his first assignment, kind of an audition," Roger said. "When you took Johnny G. out of action, we fell back on a hired suit."

"And where does she fit in?" Swag asked.

"Her husband's a Zurich banker. He was getting a little nervous and a little greedy," Roger said, grabbing for his wine and taking a drink before continuing. "He began negotiating for the sale of certain sensitive documents, using her as the bagman. Or is that bagperson?"

"Very unfortunate in itself," Catherwood added. "But then his courier had a sudden spark of entrepreneurial fervor. Needless to say, neither Lorette nor the courier are a problem any longer. And the husband has come back around to our way of thinking."

"We still haven't caught up to her contact in America," Roger said.

"But I assure you, we do not lack for resources," Catherwood said.

"So, you guys are the ones who froze me out?" Swag said, unable to keep the anger out of his voice. "For shooting that suit up on 63rd?"

"Consider it part of our recruitment process," Roger answered easily. "By the way, we weren't the only ones. Your friend, Colonel Bammer, he's got a wild hair up his ass about you. He thinks you're working with the Feds to indict him."

"It will be of no little concern to you to learn that all charges against you have been dropped," Catherwood added. "You may consider it a signing bonus."

"So what do you think?" Roger asked. Leaning back

comfortably in his seat, he began working a pocket comb through his hair.

"Who thought all this up?" Swag asked.

"As you've already discovered, we are not amateurs or dilettantes," Catherwood said. "Our timetable, objectives, and business plan have been charted out to the last detail. The original proposal, I believe, was developed in one of California's more reliable research organizations several years ago for implementation in South America, as a means by which to service their debt. It was brought to the attention of our sponsors last year."

"So, what do you think?" Roger asked again, putting the comb away.

"I think that someone out of the Rand Corp or the Hoover Institute or someplace like that sold a pack of rich Americans a load of shit," Swag said. "And here's a flash—you can call it whatever you want, patriotism, harvesting, or any other fucking thing. But you steal, then you're a thief. You steal from thieves, you're still a thief."

"We prefer to view it as tapping a natural resource," Catherwood answered dryly. "In any event, may we consider your answer as a sign of disinclination to join our enterprise?"

"Yeah," Swag answered, already knowing it was the wrong move.

"That's a pity, really," Catherwood added, rose from his seat and headed for the stairs without looking back.

"We have a dental plan," Roger said, smiling, "if that makes a difference to you."

"I just have one question," Swag said.

Catherwood stopped at the stairs, an eyebrow arched as he turned back to Swag.

"Which one of you is stealing?" Swag said.

Catherwood kept his eyebrow arched dramatically. "I beg your pardon?" he said.

"Someone's skimming the Euro-Zeitech account out in the Caymans," Swag said. "I was just curious which one of you it was."

Swag could feel both of them stiffen.

"Roger?" Catherwood asked, not knowing precisely how to finish the question. "What do you know about this?"

"I'm real sorry he brought it up now," Roger said, and drew out the Seecamp from its shoulder holster as he rose from the seat.

"Roger, what's the meaning of this?" Catherwood said. The gun was pointed at him.

"The meaning is that you fucked up, big-time," Roger said. "Now sit on the couch, next to your friend."

"This is insubordination," Catherwood said, walking to the couch. "I'd ask you not to forget who is in charge of this operation."

"Don't bother," Roger answered. "You wouldn't like the answer."

Catherwood had just sat down when the phone rang. Roger crossed to the small table, picked up the receiver, said, "Yes," and pushed a button on the console. Then he said, "Yes sir, I'm in a meeting now. I'll take care of it first opportunity."

Swag noticed that when he hung up the phone, he was smiling. "Good news?" Swag asked, thinking to himself that if he made his move now, he could be on him in two steps. Roger had maybe fifteen or twenty pounds on him.

"Pretty good," Roger said, still smiling. "I think I've gotten a promotion."

"Climbing the corporate ladder, huh?" Swag said, looking for an opening, a shot at the guy. He knew that as long as he kept him talking, he still had a chance.

"A shortcut," Roger answered.

"I demand to know the meaning of this," Catherwood spat out. "Immediately."

"That was Zermatt," Roger said. "You've been replaced."

"By whom, may I ask?" Catherwood said.

Roger smiled broadly. "Me," he said.

"Preposterous." Catherwood began to rise, but Roger stopped him with a shake of his head and a motion of the gun. "I demand to know what is going on," Catherwood said.

"As long as neither of you will be talking about it, sure," Roger said. "Your boy here found that nifty little program you tacked on to the Caymans computer. I took the liberty of passing the information to our friends in Switzerland."

"You must be insane," Catherwood said. "I would never—"

"Hey, you've been abusing your fiduciary responsibilities. I took the liberty of pointing it out. Nothing personal."

"You have gone utterly insane," Catherwood said. "I'll clear this matter up immediately."

"Decision's already been made," Roger said, sitting back down.

Swag had seen that expression and heard the voice a hundred times before. It was the voice of a double-cross. His eyes went from one to the other, thinking that he could throw the glass of champagne at Roger and go for it.

"I am not a thief," Catherwood exploded.

"It doesn't matter; enough people think so," Roger answered calmly. The grin was still plastered to his face. Then turning to Swag, he said, "Too bad about you, though. You have some style. And I'm not a bad boss."

"You treacherous bastard," Catherwood snapped. "*Enhonte sour-nois—*"

"Please, not the French, not the French." Roger chuckled, and clicked off the safety of the Seecamp.

Outside in the hallway Jim Bob pulled a can of menthol Barbasol shaving cream from a toolbox and applied a generous mound to his hand. He sniffed at it briefly, then applied the thick glob across the black wallplate that shielded the security camera.

Jim Bob and the blonde woman, both wearing utility company coveralls and hard hats, now moved freely about their work, using hand signals to communicate. They had already evacuated the other tenant on the floor and strung yellow Con Ed tape across the exit and elevator doors. Building security had been alerted to a possible gas leak.

The young woman eyed the steel-reinforced door to Catherwood's apartment carefully, noting the thick frame, the German manufacturer's name on the electronic keycard's slot, and the alarm's membrane keypad.

When the young woman shook her head, Jim Bob held up three fingers. The young woman gave him a quick glance, then pulled out the three suction devices from her toolbox. In less than half a minute she had the three devices positioned on the door, each holding an eighth of an ounce of plastique.

When she had finished, she armed the devices by pressing a small button at the suction cups' edge, nodded, and handed Jim Bob the small detonating unit out of her shoulder bag.

Jim Bob turned on the device and smiled. "This is my favorite part," he whispered.

When the young woman had taken a position away from the door, her back against the wall, she nodded again. In her hand was a Walther P-5, a 9mm cartridge under the hammer. Jim Bob had the .45 tucked into the pocket of his coveralls.

"Anybody ever tell you you look just cute as a bug with your eyes scrunched up like that?" Jim Bob asked the girl.

She shook her head and gave him a look that said, "Get on with it."

"Okay, here we go," he said. Taking a step away from the door and turning his back to the wall, he bent down, pushed the intercom button and waited.

"Yes?" a man's voice asked.

"We're from the government and we're here to help you," Jim Bob said into the speaker. Then he quickly took another step down the hall, braced himself against the wall, and pushed the detonator button.

The door blew off its top hinges, and half the wall around the jamb vanished. Jim Bob moved first, working point. Coming in low, he raised his foot and kicked the door off its last hinge and moved through the acrid smoke into the entry hall as he drew the .45.

Catherwood vanished in the confusion, retreating down the stairs of the duplex.

Swag didn't know what the explosion was, but he used it. Coming off the couch, he moved on Roger, who already had the small Seecamp pointed at the entranceway. Swag grabbed his gun hand with one hand and caught him around the neck with his other arm.

Roger did a little sideways dance, walking into the hold, and used the two inches or so of space created to smash Swag in the gut with an elbow. Then he brought the steel edge of the barrel up under Swag's chin. The blows threw Swag back, over the couch, as Roger turned again toward the source of the explosion.

As Swag shook off the pain, he refocused his eyes to see Roger stalking along the wall to the entranceway. That bastard turns on you with that thing and it's over, he thought.

Crawling back behind the couch, Swag came up slow on one knee and pulled open the leaded glass case that held the display of primitive statuettes. He pulled the nearest stone figure out and threw it, then dived back behind the other couch.

The statue went high and outside, cracking off the wall's wood paneling. Roger turned and laid down a four-shot burst into the wrong couch, the slugs tearing through the leather. Then he raised the barrel and sent three more shots smashing the glass case.

Peering out from one corner of his couch, Swag watched Roger take up a position along the wall, giving him a clear view of the entire room, particularly the short hallway that led to the front door.

Swag came up again, slow, shaking glass off his back; he reached up and threw another statue. This one hit Roger on the arm.

And suddenly Roger was running, Seecamp down, toward the couches. He covered the length of the room in

four long strides. Swag, not seeing the two grenades, concussion and flash, that rolled into the opposite corner, came
up fast and caught Roger square in the throat with a left.
But Roger's momentum carried both of them over the edge
of the couch, tipping it back as they spilled across into the
fireplace.

The concussion grenade blew out all the windows on one
side of the room in a hollow, deafening blast that Swag felt
down to the roots of his teeth. When the flash of the second
grenade hit, Swag had just pried the autopistol from
Roger's hands.

Even with the cover provided by the overturned couch,
the flash was blinding. Red and blue dots swam at the center of Swag's vision. Roger's arm came up, caught Swag in
the side with a rib-cracking blow, and pulled the gun back.
Swag lifted his head, felt the soft cushions at the back of
his head, then head-butted Roger square in the face.

The Seecamp came free again, and before Roger could
make another move, Swag had its barrel pressed against
one of Roger's eyes. "Don't fuckin' move, scumbag," he
said, and watched as Roger lifted his hands, palms up,
above his head.

Through ringing ears Swag could hear people moving
above. Keeping one hand on the trigger, he used the other
to lift the couch partially off his back.

"Anybody home?" Jim Bob called.

Swag looked up to see Spurock at the center of the graceful dots, out in the middle of the room, holding the .45 in
two hands, arms stiffly pointed down. He was wearing mir-
rored Raybans. Backing him up was a blonde woman,
frowning behind a pair of fashionable French tortoiseshell
shades. Even in the shades Swag recognized her as the maid
from the Plaza and the jogger in the park.

"Oh lordy, what do we have here?" Jim Bob said, moving
closer as he shifted to a one-handed grip. "You just get
yourself up off the fella, Swag. And let's get a good look
at him."

Jim Bob, the shiny AIA semiautomatic fully extended

and pointed at a spot dead center of Roger's chest, pulled the couch fully off of the two men with his free hand and helped Swag to his feet.

Swag took up a position alongside Spurock, keeping the Seecamp pointed directly at Roger's head.

The young woman lifted the shades up high on her head and moved to the staircase, proceeding on a slight nod from Jim Bob. "Darlin', whyn't you go fetch up that other fella," he drawled. Adrenaline, it seemed, brought out the Okie in him.

"He's gone," Roger said, brushing glass from his shirt-front and sitting on the newly righted couch.

"He ain't, unless he could fly," Jim Bob said, moving in closer. "Seems that your service elevator's out, stuck way down there 'tween four and five. Doorway to service stairs kinda jammed too."

The three men watched the young woman advance cautiously down the stairs, gun first.

Jim Bob took off his shades, casually slipped them into his overalls pocket, and studied Roger. "Now you, you're just a kinda mystery to me friend," he said, a smile breaking his lips. "But you do look familiar. A face in some grainy picture maybe—in what, the Middle East? West Africa maybe? One of them ceiling-fan countries. I do believe you're that fella who's forever standing behind some other fella with his head circled in grease pencil. Ain't that right?"

"I get around," Roger said glumly.

chapter twenty-five

ALL THREE OF THEM watched as the tips of Catherwood's fingers rose up from the graceful arc of the spiral staircase. They could have been the young woman's fingers, they were that long and slender. But then the sleeve of a suit coat and the head of gray hair emerged. Swag and Jim Bob let out a small sigh of relief.

The woman was holding the Walther P-5 on Catherwood, and he was holding his hands high above his head. His suit was disheveled and he was breathing hard. A small bruise was rising along his cheek. There wasn't a hair out of place on the woman's head.

She walked him across the room and sat him down next to Roger.

"Found him hiding in the bathroom," she said. "Very nice indeed, Jacuzzi, gold fixtures, whole nine yards. I guess the rich are different than us common folks."

"That a genuine fact, darlin'," Jim Bob answered, "they have nicer bathrooms."

The young woman briefly examined the little shiny .25 and tucked it into a pocket of her coveralls. Swag assumed it was Catherwood's. It had pearl grips with gold inlay.

"May I have a moment, please?" Catherwood said, tentatively letting his hands slide down from above his head and into his lap. "We're all businessmen here, of one sort or another."

"Is that what we all are?" Jim Bob drawled.

"I thought you guys were tourists," Swag offered, moving the Seecamp from Roger to Catherwood.

"Hear me out, please," Catherwood said. "I am prepared to offer all of you 100,000 francs, marks, whatever Common Market currency you prefer, simply for walking from this apartment immediately."

The room fell silent for a second as Catherwood began to smile.

"What about two hundred?" Jim Bob said at last, motioning with the .45.

Swag felt his chest tighten, then his fingers curling tighter around the Seecamp's grips. If Jim Bob and the girl were in on it, then he didn't stand a chance. But at least he could take two, maybe three of them with him. He would start with Catherwood's muscle, Roger.

"Very well, then, two hundred, but you must leave immediately."

"I'd like three," the woman said.

"Three? Well, that's an entirely—"

Now Swag saw what the game was. Not wanting to be left out, he said, "I'd like a million five."

Catherwood's smile faded; his chest puffed out a notch, and he said, "I assure you, I am not joking. I am making you people a legitimate offer. There is serious money on the table. I suggest that you think about it."

Jim Bob moved in quick then, laying the .45 along the side of Catherwood's nose, so that he was looking down the black tunnel, his good eye going a little cross-eyed in the process. "You listen to me," he said, crouching down low, so that he was speaking right in Catherwood's ear. "This is what's on the table. You give me a telephone number in Switzerland, your list of contacts in Europe and the Rim, or I'm going to shoot you through the eye."

Catherwood, trying to bluff his way out, said, "Really, such theatrics. It's beneath contempt. Do you believe this dreadful display, Roger?"

Roger, fingers laced behind his head, turned a little, studied the look on Jim Bob's face, and said, "Yeah, absolutely."

Jim Bob thumbed the trigger back and said, "This fuckin' round'll go clean through. Then I'll pitch your body out the window. Now, here's a start, the number begins with 001, 113."

"I would like to phone my attorney," Catherwood said. "Immediately."

"No lawyer is going to do you any good," Jim Bob said. "Now, just finish that number for me. Who's the contact in Switzerland?"

Catherwood brought his hand up and pushed the .45 away from his face. "I demand to speak to my attorney," he said. And then he began to rise up off the couch. "Your superiors, whoever they are, will hear about this treatment, of that you can be certain."

Swag moved in fast, raising the Seecamp and knocking Catherwood back down with a sharp blow to the jaw. "You listen to me, asshole," he said, joining Jim Bob in crowding the gray-haired guy. "You tell him what he wants to know or *I'll* put a fuckin' round through your head."

Catherwood rubbed his jaw lightly and looked up at the two men, still perfectly calm. "Really, such brutality," he said. "Do you actually believe for an instant that you intimidate me?"

Swag turned away from Catherwood and said to the woman, "Give me the envelope."

A look of puzzlement began to pass over her face, but before it was complete, Swag said, "Give me the fuckin' envelope!"

She began to say something then, but Jim Bob cut her off. "I'll get it," he said, and moved across the room to her purse.

When Jim Bob returned, he was holding a number 10 envelope which he handed to Swag, who put it in Catherwood's breast pocket. Then, smiling, he patted the thick envelope into place.

"And what should I presume this is?" Catherwood said easily.

"That," Swag answered, "is your goddamned death warrant."

"Really, such high drama, quite amusing," Catherwood said, and began to rise again. "Now, I really must insist that I speak to my attorney."

Swag pushed him back down in the seat. "Pal, you got a bomb in your goddamn pocket and you don't even know it."

"That's a financial statement from Credit Suisse," Jim Bob said. "And two faxes dated this afternoon, one from the Union Bank of Switzerland and one from Yamaichi brokerage. You lost three million easies in silver options on a margin call today."

"There's also a printout of that program you inserted in the Caymans account," Swag added.

"Do you honestly think anybody's going to believe these patently contrived accusations?" Catherwood answered. "They're complete and utter drivel."

Jim Bob leaned in even closer. "You think anybody is going to look any further after they find you on the sidewalk?" he said. "There's a certain Swiss banker, his name's Ziggy Lorette, he's very upset. He rolled over on you this morning. Your own people think you got a hand in the till. Now you tell me."

Roger was fixing Catherwood with a cold, dead eye, catching him in a white laser of contempt. "Separate them," Swag said. "And he'll talk."

Jim Bob, still holding the .45 against Catherwood's nose, reached a hand down and lifted the man up off the couch by the shirt collar. Then he walked him to the opposite side of the room.

Jim Bob and Catherwood talked in whispers for a moment, then headed for the stairs. No one in the room spoke while the two men were gone. It seemed like a long time to Swag, but then they came back up the stairway. Catherwood led the way, then Jim Bob, still holding the .45 in one hand. In the other hand was a digital computer disk.

"Got it?" the woman asked, her eyes meeting Roger's formidable stare. She kept the Walther trained on him, motioning it slightly for him to keep his fingers laced behind his head.

"Whole kit and kaboodle," Jim Bob answered, raising the disk slightly.

That's when the young woman turned, the beginnings of a smile forming at the corners of her mouth.

When Swag moved back a step to grab the sealed water bottle from the floor, Roger made his move. Kicking out, he connected solidly with the woman's wrist and knocked the Walther from her hand. The gun went low, sliding noiseless across the Persian carpet.

Swag triggered off a two-round burst from the Seecamp as he brought it up. The two rounds ripped through the carpet at Roger's scrambling feet, then the gun froze, empty.

The woman dug into her pocket for Catherwood's little .25, but Roger was already up off the couch and caught her in midair with a high kick, the heel of his shoe connecting solidly with her ribs and sending her tumbling backward.

In an instant Roger had the woman's Walther, rolled, and came up in a combat sitting position. He fired off two rounds. Jim Bob was pivoting quickly as he raised the .45. The first went just under his partially extended arm and smashed into Catherwood's chest.

Catherwood and Jim Bob began their descent at the same time, Catherwood's hands clutching at the spreading bloodstain on his chest, Jim Bob hitting the carpet and rolling left as the second round smashed through Catherwood's mouth and exploded out the side of his neck. He was dead by the time he slumped to the floor.

Jim Bob lay flat on his belly as he came out of his roll and brought the .45 up. But it was too late. Roger, believing he hit both Jim Bob and Catherwood, had already turned and taken aim at the woman, who was gasping for air as she pulled herself up off the floor.

Without thinking, Swag dived on Roger, coming at him from the side. It was like running into a wall. Roger turned quickly, trying to twist out of Swag's grasp. Swag brought his left foot around, tripped Roger, and they landed in a heap on the floor, with Swag on top. Roger struggled to bring the gun around, triggered off a round into the floor just behind the woman, who was now on her feet. The round sent her dancing away in a wide circle, clear of the Walther's line of fire. Roger twisted again, and brought the gun around, catching Swag on the jaw with the top of the slide, blinding him for an instant and knocking his hands free of the gun.

Jim Bob fired off a round; the big .45 slug plowed into the carpet, inches from Roger's head. Swag recovered quickly and brought his hands back up to the Walther's barrel, trying for a grip.

As Roger tried to roll away, he drew the gun back, the sudden movement jerking Swag's finger across the trigger guard over Roger's finger.

The Walther fired again, jerking in both men's hands and sending the girl into a crouched run to the side as the bullet streamed past her head.

When Jim Bob fired another round, it missed Roger by a good foot, but sent him rolling sideways across the floor, twisting Swag's finger out of the trigger guard.

Roger jerked an arm back and turned, so that he was now facing Jim Bob, who was moving fast out from under the Walther's sights.

Swag brought his right hand up and grabbed, catching Roger's ear. He jerked violently downward with all his strength just as the girl kicked Roger in the head.

The big man let out a scream as the combined force of Swag's pull and the girl's kick ripped the ear from his head in a jagged bloody line that extended down to his jaw.

Roger dropped the gun, reflex or training twisting his fingers into a maiming move that glanced harmlessly off Swag's head as he fell back.

As Swag scrambled to his feet, the girl grabbed the gun

and held it on Roger, who was holding the side of his head with both hands. Blood poured from between his fingers.

"You motherfucker, you ripped my ear off," he said, moving his head back and forth against the pain.

"Shit happens," Swag answered and began to get up.

"Did you get the phone number at least?" the girl asked.

"Just barely," Jim Bob answered, slipping the .45 back into its holster. "His boss seems to be in Kandersteg. You know it."

"Oberland Bernes," she replied, slightly winded. "It's near Interlaken. Decent skiing."

Jim Bob nodded, then smiled. "You okay, darlin'?"

"I'm sorry, Jim Bob," the girl said. "He got away from me there."

"You did good, kid," came Jim Bob's answer. "He's a sneaky one. It only matters if it matters, right?" Then he walked to the overturned table, righted it, and set the phone down on it. He punched in ten digits, said, "Yeah, it's me," and repeated the number Catherwood had given him.

Roger had lifted himself to the couch, still holding the side of his head as blood ran down his arm.

Swag raised his hand up to discover he was still clutching Roger's severed ear. With his legs still shaky, he walked over to Roger and put the ear in his shirt pocket. "Here, this is yours," he said, and patted the bloody ear into place.

Roger stopped moving his head long enough to look down forlornly at the bloody spot at the front of his shirt, but didn't say anything.

Jim Bob hung up the phone then and walked back to where Roger sat on the couch. "Well, you have anything to add?"

"Yeah," Roger said, motioning to Catherwood's body, "he was an asshole. And you weren't going to do jackshit to us."

"You talkin' pretty big for a man with one ear," Jim Bob said. "Damn shame too, messes up that nice haircut."

"It's a look," the girl said, cocking her head to one side in an attitude of critical appraisal.

"What can you do to me?" Roger spat out, ignoring the girl. "Some bullshit conspiracy charge, maybe try for a RICO. Gimme a fuckin' break, huh."

"Don't be so sure," Jim Bob advised, motioning slightly with the .45. "Worst thing we could do is let you go. That little old software thing out in the Caymans could get you killed."

Roger managed to reach into his inside coat pocket then and brought out a handkerchief with two fingers, which he pressed tightly against the side of his head. "Prove it, asshole," he said challengingly. "They already know it was Catherwood. And he's dead. I was just doing like he told me. The man had expensive tastes."

"He had those all right, but he wasn't a thief," Jim Bob offered back. "And he wasn't an accountant either."

"*He's* an accountant?" Swag asked, his voice disbelieving as he motioned toward Roger.

"It's something to fall back on," Roger answered belligerently. "For my old age."

"You got a couple of numbered accounts out in the Virgin Islands," Jim Bob said. "That's where the stolen money from Euro-Zeitech was going."

"That sonofabitch, he set me up," Roger said. "It wasn't even for the money. He wanted me out."

"Appears that way, don't it?" Jim Bob answered easily. "I figure it'll be just about now that your bosses will be paying off some clerk for the name that goes with those numbers."

"Sonofabitch," Roger said. "He was cutting me out."

"Your Swiss banker, he got nervous and wanted out. Tried to cut a deal, leveraging information about the operation to get himself loose," Jim Bob said. "His wife Lorette was the bagman. She was to sell the information."

"And she was using the courier," Roger said. "I knew that. We took care of him. And her."

"Well, the courier peeked," Jim Bob said. "He didn't know what it was, but figured someone would buy. He called ol' Ziggy Lorette and tried to squeeze him. He didn't know what he had, but figured it was crooked. Ziggy hears that the courier peeked, and he panics. Suddenly he doesn't have exclusive rights."

"Ah, shit," Roger moaned. "It was the money network the courier saw, right? The daisy chain?"

"That's what it was," Jim Bob confirmed. "Ziggy backed out of the deal with us real fast, goes back to you boys and lays it on the line. And you pay him off."

"And we pay him off," Roger repeated.

"But the courier, well, he gets a little greedy or a little scared after the woman's killed. Maybe a little of both," Jim Bob continued. "He burned up the phone lines to the CIA, NSA, FBI, IRS, Department of Treasury, Defense Intelligence Agency, Army Intelligence, and the provosts. Now he's looking for more money and maybe a little protection from you boys."

Roger's eyes opened wide in disbelief. The utter stupidity of it was beyond comprehension.

"Anyway, seems that nobody believes him," Jim Bob said. "But me, I'm a sucker for a hard luck story. I get to feeling sorry for this poor little Swiss fella, so I pay off his hotel bill and give him pocket change."

"You still had nothing on us," Roger said. "No money was going through Zeitech. The operation had barely started."

"See, there, that's where you're wrong," Jim Bob said. "No money was going in, but there was money going out. You were using the same network to cover expenses. Medical bills from a Swiss clinic, a customized Mercedes limo, some real estate money for this apartment, some hush money for a certain Swiss courier, and a bunch of other stuff that just gets me curious."

"You got it all figured out, don't you?" Roger challenged.

"Just about," Jim Bob answered. "I'm counting on wrapping the thing up in the next week or two."

"I'll tell you something you can count on," Roger said. "Two, three years, max, and I come looking for you and that

Hawaiian-shirt-wearing asshole who took my ear off." He
was talking to Jim Bob, but pointing to Swag.

Jim Bob shrugged, as if being told he was two days over-
due on a library book.

"You hear that, pal?" Roger answered, still pointing the
finger as he turned to Swag. "You're a dead man, and
believe me, you'll never see it coming."

"Really," Swag said, tucking the Walther into his belt at
the front.

"Fuckin' really," Roger answered, still pointing.

That's when Swag walked over to where Roger was sitting on the couch. "Let me tell you something about this
town," he said. But before he could finish, Roger was grabbing for the Walther.

Swag caught his hand just as Roger came up off the
couch and the gun came out of the belt. By the time Roger
realized he'd been set up, it was already too late, Swag had
him by the forearm and was pushing him back toward a
blown-out window.

Roger tried to fire the Walther, but the safety was set.
Then Swag gave him a left cut to the stomach and another
sharp blow to the throat that sent him toppling out of the
broken window.

When Swag turned, he saw Jim Bob motioning to the
young woman not to fire the shiny .25.

A warm breeze blew in from the open windows as Swag
handed the gun over to Spurock.

"You know," Jim Bob said. "You could have gone all day
without doing that."

"You think he would have come after me?" Swag asked.

"Probably," Jim Bob answered.

"Now look at this," the girl said. She was on the other
side of the room, reaching into Catherwood's breast pocket,
pulling out the bloody envelope. "I can't send this back."

Swag turned to see the girl holding up the blood-soaked
envelope; the Bloomingdale's logo was still clearly visible.

"They'll send another," Jim Bob answered, tucking the

.45 into his overalls. "The way you empty their shelves, they'll send one out right quick."

"Where did you learn that?" the girl asked, turning now to Swag.

"Old cop trick," Swag answered. "Used to say they were search warrants, indictments. I just figured Jim Bob would have something to say."

"Whatever happened to good-cop, bad-cop?" the girl asked.

Swag thought a second and said, "It's kind of a variation, bad-cop, worse-cop."

Two men stood on the observation deck at LaGuardia Airport's international terminal. One was wearing a Hawaiian shirt, the other a light summer suit.

They looked out on the runway as two transport caskets, secured by wire binding, their tops laden with plastic-encased papers, moved up a conveyer belt. When both boxes vanished into the dark hold of the cargo plane, they turned from the window.

"About time this ol' boy had a vacation," the man in the suit said as he lifted a nylon carry-on.

"Where to, some ceiling-fan country?" the guy in the Hawaiian shirt asked.

"Norman," came the answer. "Norman, Oklahoma."

They were walking now, out past the small cafeteria, past the duty-free shop and into the main lobby.

"Know what bothers me?" Swag asked.

"Bunch of stuff, I imagine," Jim Bob said, looking straight ahead.

"How come a smart guy like Catherwood put in such a low-rent program to steal?"

Jim Bob stopped walking, then turned his head upward in thought, studying the ceiling. "Thieves fall out, now don't they?" he said. "Maybe they fall out a little faster with help."

Swag studied Jim Bob's face, but it gave away nothing. "You put it in, didn't you?"

"Now, I didn't say any such thing," Jim Bob replied slyly as he began to walk again. "No such thing at all."

"You could've done it, though," Swag said. "If you got that list of shell companies from the Swiss courier, over at the Carlyle."

"Now, which Swiss courier would that be?" Jim Bob asked. "This whole thing is just a mite confusing for this here country boy."

"The one that got a money transfer from a D.C. outfit," Swag said.

Jim Bob just smiled. "Well, you can't say it hasn't been fun," Jim Bob answered. "But you can say adios amigo."

They shook hands then, and Swag walked out through the automatic doors. He went out to the taxi stand and looked back through the doors, just in time to see Jim Bob, the light summer suit coat slung over one shoulder, head up the ramp marked International Departures.

The cab ride back to the city was uneventful. As they approached the midtown tunnel, the cabbie turned and said to his passenger, "So, where you from?"

"Here," Swag said, "I'm from the city."

"Huh," came the reply, "I thought you was a tourist. Must have been the shirt."

Here is an excerpt
from *Full Clip*—
Book 2 in the
remarkable new
Swag Town series by
L. S. Riker:

The place was called The Dead Banker Bar & Grill.
Wedged into the bottom floor of one of the unoccupied
buildings near Wall Street, it was at once shabby and anonymous, like a failing franchise. At one time it had aspired
to cater to an international crowd, so the faded sign out
front included French, German, Italian, and Japanese subtitles. And it was just dark enough to make drinking at
noon pleasant, but not too pleasant. Shaped like a shoebox,
The Dead Banker was a saloon where the downtown bottom-feeders did their small business deals over watered
drinks.

Swag was standing at the bar watching the barmaid
top off his beer under the spigot, then slide it over the
two or so feet so that it bumped against the cardboard
coaster advertising something called the Royale Deluxe
Escort Service. He took a long sip through the perfect
two-inch head and let it sit in his mouth for a brief
moment before swallowing. It was cold enough to make
his teeth ache.

Swag studied Kat Jones through the half-darkness of the

bar. When she was young, you would have called her pretty, perky even. Now that she was thirty-five, she was still good-looking, but in a better sort of way. The years had been good to Kat Jones.

"So, why'd you call me down?" Swag asked, then took another sip of beer.

There were a few suits lined up at the bar, talking in the low tones of conspiracy. Kat gave the suits a quick dismissive glance, then leaned over the bar toward Swag. "Remember E.C. Dullen?" she asked.

Swag shook his head.

"Yeah, you do," she insisted. "Everyone called him 'Easy.' Little guy, always on the hustle and always saying, 'Hey, I'm easy,' whenever he was negotiating."

"Vaguely," Swag answered, remembering a tiny dark-haired guy with bad skin who'd sell anything from Statue of Liberty pens to black-market jewelry.

"He was working over at the Vista hotel, bell-hopping," Kat said. "Flipped out a few weeks ago and they put him in Bellevue."

"Should I be interested in this?" Swag asked.

"Only if you want work," Kat answered, then pushed herself away from the bar to refill the suits' drinks.

"What's the deal on him?" Swag said when she returned.

"I'll lay it out for you like it was told to me," Kat answered, then paused to carefully gather the disparate threads of the story. "Easy's working at the Vista hauling Vuittons and hustling on the side. About a month ago he quits, raving to the bell captain and anyone else who would listen, that someone's out to get him."

"He probably burned someone," Swag said.

Kat made a small motion of annoyance for the interruption with her hand. "Yeah, but he goes into hiding," she said. "Locks himself in his room, SRO place near Canal Street. Doesn't come out for two weeks. When the manager breaks down the door, he flips out, jumps the guy, bites a piece of his nose off. And it takes six provosts to wrestle him down so they can throw him in Bellevue for observation."

Swag nodded to show he was paying attention.

"So, the docs at Bellevue diagnose an *acute paranoidal delusional state*, punch him full of psychotropes and toss him back out as *non-hazardous*."

"What about the nose-biting?" Swag asked.

"They chalked it up to malnutrition," Kat said. "He'd been in that room for a couple of weeks, ran out of food. Started drinking his own piss, if you want all the details. Anyway, they toss him back on the street, literally, 'cause he didn't want to leave. And a day later, someone pops him."

"Just because you're paranoid doesn't mean they're not after you, right?" Swag quipped and reached into the pocket of his Hawaiian shirt for a cigarette and held it between his lips while he searched his pockets for a match. Thai cigarettes were available that week. Next month it would be maybe Korean and hopefully not the MK Ultras, which were the government's own brand.

"Yeah, everyone's a little paranoid," she answered. "It's healthy, right?"

"Something like that," Swag said, still fumbling for a book of matches and not finding one.

Kat lit the cigarette with a deft movement from a disposable lighter, taking the opportunity to study Swag for the first time since he'd walked in. "Swag and his Hawaiian shirts," she sighed, pocketing the lighter. "They're like a trademark, right?"

"So, someone wants to know who killed Easy," Swag said, exhaling a lungful of smoke.

"They already know who killed him," Kat said as she retrieved a manila envelope from under the bar and slid it across to Swag. Inside were copies of the provost report, crime scene photos, and witness transcripts. Swag thumbed through them just enough to see the tops of the documents.

Swag ashed the cigarette and asked, "Who?"

"Some guy with a knife," Kat said without a trace of a smile. "What they want to know is the why."

Full Clip—an exciting
new book in the *Swag Town*
series—coming in November '92
from L. S. Riker and St. Martin's
Paperbacks!